D1796253

JOURNEY'S END

Recent Titles by Jean Saunders from Severn House

writing as Jean Saunders

GOLDEN DESTINY
JOURNEY'S END
THE KISSING TIME
PARTNERS IN LOVE
TO LOVE AND HONOUR
WITH THIS RING

writing as Rowena Summers

ANGEL OF THE EVENING
BARGAIN BRIDE
ELLIE'S ISLAND
FAMILY SHADOWS
HIDDEN CURRENTS
HIGHLAND HERITAGE
KILLIGREW CLAY
SAVAGE MOON
THE SWEET RED EARTH
VELVET DAWN
A WOMAN OF PROPERTY

JOURNEY'S END

Jean Saunders

This first world edition published in Great Britain 1996 by
SEVERN HOUSE PUBLISHERS LTD of
9–15 High Street, Sutton, Surrey SM1 1DF.
First published in the USA 1996 by
SEVERN HOUSE PUBLISHERS INC. of
595 Madison Avenue, New York, NY 10022.

British Library Cataloguing in Publication Data

Saunders, Jean, 1932–
    Journey's end
    1. English fiction – 20th century
    I. Title
823.9′14 [F]

    ISBN 0-7278-4935-2

Typeset by Palimpsest Book Production Limited,
Polmont, Stirlingshire, Scotland.
Printed and bound in Great Britain by
Hartnolls Ltd, Bodmin, Cornwall.

Chapter One

Los Angeles sweltered in the heat of an August afternoon. There was barely a breath of air to move the leaves on the trees in the outer non-fashionable suburbs, and the birds hovered motionless on their branches, as if carved out of stone. The Chevy had been parked in the shade outside the wood-framed apartment building, and Rose had found the bathroom and thankfully washed off the grime of travelling.

By the time she'd inspected every bit of Gracie and Merv's ground-floor apartment, ignored the gathering fluffs of dust and proclaimed it marvellous, she had begun to feel more human again. And finally she couldn't contain her excitement a minute longer. Her enormous eyes, that Mrs Pritchard had always likened to shiny bits of green glass when she got herself wound up, were nearer emerald now.

"Merv, were those advertisements I kept seeing all over the place really true?"

"What ads were those, honey?"

Here in his own home, feeling magnanimous and hospitable, her brother-in-law was prepared to be indulgent. Anyway, he liked the kid. He knew all about her background, of course. Gracie had recited it to him a thousand times already.

The little sister, named after the youngest of the English princesses, had been evacuated from London in 1939 at seven years old to some dreary Welsh backwater where

1

the houses crowded together so tightly you couldn't see the sun. And when you did, it was only to see it glinting on the treacherous black slag heaps from the coal pits.

It was a good thing they'd finally got her out of there. Merv easily overlooked the fact that he certainly hadn't wanted Rose here at the beginning of his marriage, and that it had taken him all these years to arrange it. It had suited him fine when the kid had pleaded to be sent to secretarial college in London once the war was over, and where she'd polished up her accent to keep up with the other girls. And now that she was here, he could see that she wasn't a kid any more. . . .

"What were the ads you saw, Rose honey?" her sister Gracie said lazily, completely Americanized in the years since she'd crossed the pond, as they called it, as a GI bride.

"Didn't you see them? I suppose it meant coach trips. You can take a trip to see the homes of the movie stars."

She almost tripped over the unfamiliar words. *Movie stars*! Goddesses of the silver screen, out of reach and unattainable . . . but apparently not *here*, where already to Rose everything seemed paved with gold. She was nearly eighteen years old and she knew she was reacting like a wide-eyed child on Christmas morning, and she didn't care.

This entire day was like a dream come true, and Hollywood and movie stars were part of the fantasy world. They had always been her make-believe family, when she'd had no one left of her own. Every time she went to the flicks, it was to remember that they originated in the part of the world where her sister Gracie now lived, and that one day she would be living there too. . . .

Rose blushed at her own wide-eyed clumsiness on hearing Merv's guffawing laugh. She still wasn't quite sure of Merv Hackett. Years ago, when he'd been slim

2

and glamorous like all the Yanks in their uniforms, she'd envied her sister Gracie so much. He'd been the knight in shining armour who'd finally whisked Gracie away on the boat from Southampton, while Rose was left behind, weeping in the unfeeling arms of Mrs Pritchard.

There were only the promises from Gracie and Merv that as soon as they could, they'd send for her. Well, so they had – eventually. And now Merv was thicker-set, the veins in his neck and arms purple and ropy. And Gracie, her lovely sister Gracie, was fatter, harder, unnaturally blonder, a blowsy stranger whose appearance had taken Rose completely by surprise.

She pushed down the small lingering feeling of resentment that it had taken them so long to send for her. It was all in the past, and she was here now.

"You won't need a coach trip, honey, whatever in the hell that is," Merv said.

"She means a bus," Gracie said.

He ignored his wife's correction, though his next words acknowledged that he'd noted it.

"You won't need a bus to see the homes of the stars, Rosie, because we'll take you in the Chevy."

Rose's mouth dropped open. *Catching flies*, Mrs Pritchard would have said severely. She knew she was being naïve, but so had Gracie been, once. Rose remembered very well, because she'd written it all down in her diary, in a young girl's poetic words, how Gracie had been so starry-eyed about her Yank. He hadn't had his fun and run, which was the current phrase among the young girls of the time, he'd come back and married her, despite Mam Pritchard saying caustically that it would never last.

It had all been so romantic . . . but Rose could still remember the feeling of shock when she'd finally realized that Gracie was going off to America with her Yank and they weren't taking her with them.

3

"You can't go without me," she'd sobbed, her tears wetting the front of Gracie's smart silk blouse and skirt that had taken all her clothing coupons for a month. "I've lost Mum and Dad, and now you. . . ."

"Love, it won't be for ever, I promise," Gracie had almost sobbed as well, except that she was the oldest in the family now, and everybody had to keep their ends up. They weren't the only family whose parents had been killed in the blitz.

"Listen, I'll be able to do far more for you once Merv and I are settled. I'll write often, and we'll pay the fees for that college you always wanted to go to. You won't have to stay with the Pritchards for ever!"

Rose knew it was a bribe, and had written it solemnly in her diary at the time. But it had lifted her spirits all the same, and softened the moments of parting, just a bit.

She just hadn't expected it to take so long for Gracie and Merv to get settled. Her college years had come and gone, leaving her feeling more rootless than ever. Going back to Wales for a short spell had underlined the fact that it still wasn't home. The house that had seemed small before, seemed to have shrunk to Lilliputian proportions now.

Then at last, after she'd written to Gracie in desperation, the ticket to freedom had finally arrived, and she would be eternally grateful to Merv for his generosity.

"Do movie stars really allow people to walk around their houses and meet them?" she said now, her head filled with excitement again.

So much so that her voice almost lapsed into the sing-song Welsh she hated and had always been determined to resist copying. The hell of it was that she had such a good ear for accents, as Mrs Pritchard had found to her cost, on the many times she'd caught young Rose Forster mimicking her ringing tones when she called her boyos home for supper.

She concentrated on her sister's similarly sharp tones. Funny how she'd never been struck by the similarity before. The accents were different, but the censure was the same.

"Of course they don't! Don't be so daft, our Rose," Gracie said, the glint in her eyes a mixture of impatience and amusement that immediately re-established their old roles. Older sister. Sibling rivalry. The one happy and fortunate. The other, lost and left behind.

Rose found the familiar phrases swirling round in her mind, and subdued them quickly. She'd only just arrived, for God's sake. She tried to remember that they were family, her *only* family, but the intervening years had made them strangers and it was a long way back to familiarity. They all had to step warily, to get to know each other again, and she knew it was pointless to start taking offence at Gracie's derision.

"The tours take you through the hills where the stars live, Rosie." Merv was more tolerant of her. "The guides show you Rodeo Drive and the avenues where your Monroes and Crawfords live. The buses aren't allowed to stop anywhere, but the guides point out the mansions and dish out whatever dirt they've got on the stars – and sometimes there's plenty. If it ain't genuine, they make it up. Some of the places are in sight of the road, but with others you can just about glimpse the roof behind the trees. Anyway, we'll take you if you wanna go there."

He was casual, fitting into his LA environment as if he was born to it, though Rose knew very well he'd been a trucker in the mid-West before he'd enlisted in the army. He'd been a tank-driver by the end of the war, stationed 'somewhere in England' as they termed it for security reasons.

At the time, Rose's Welsh foster mother had been caustic about the arrival of the Americans.

"Late as usual," she'd sniffed. "You can always rely

on these Yanks for that, *bach*. They were late in the First World War and late in this one. They'll be late at their own funerals, I shouldn't wonder."

However much Rose tried to stop them, these unwanted images of the past kept intruding into today, just when she didn't want them to. This was a new beginning, and the past was far behind them all. It didn't do to dwell on it too much. . . .

This wasn't exactly a home-coming, since she'd never set foot on American soil before, but she still felt that at last she was somewhere she could call home, with people she could call her own. And she didn't want Mrs Pritchard's narrow little philosophies to cloud her mind.

"Of course she'll wanna go and see the stars' homes," Gracie said dryly. "Our Rose was always star-struck."

The three of them sat out on the porch now. The ground-floor residence had the advantage of the rest of the apartments in the building, and away in front of them were woods that obscured any view of the city, but gave the area a certain privacy. Rose hadn't been here long enough yet to know it wasn't exactly the best neighbourhood to live in.

Merv sat back smugly in his cane chair. The fiercest heat of the day was lessening now, but LA still smouldered in a kind of indolent humidity that was tacky and unfamiliar to Rose, and the midges were beginning to bite. Almost the first thing she'd done was to get out of her smart travelling suit and stockings, and put on a checked lemon frock of cool cotton.

Gracie wore a shapeless cotton frock that was styled more for comfort than elegance, and Merv's long legs were encased in work trousers beneath a red vest. His hands were locked behind his head, and Rose tried not to look at the dark tufts of hair glistening in his armpits.

"I remember now," he grinned in answer to Gracie's comment. "I once called you Shirley Temple, and you

6

put on your plummiest English voice to tell me where to get off. I never did figure out what the hell it was that bugged you so much."

"I can't remember either. But I always hated my curly hair, because Mum spent such ages brushing out the tangles," Rose said, grimacing at the memory. "I dare say you calling me Shirley Temple just made me madder."

For a moment, an unreasonable resentment, as swift and sharp as a knife-edge at the brash GI's words to a sensitive child, swept over her.

"Well, I don't remember any of that," Gracie said, in the kind of voice that made Rose positive that she remembered it very well. "Anyway, your hair's not so curly now."

There it was again, a kind of smug satisfaction. Rose was always receptive to atmosphere, but she decided she was probably just imagining things today because she was so het-up. As if Gracie could have cared, even for an instant, in those far-off days, that Rose's hair was a mass of shiny baby curls, while hers hung straight as a pike-staff. Their appearances were more or less reversed now.

"I lost my natural curls long ago," Rose said. "This is a permanent wave. I had it done specially just before I left." She almost wanted to pat her own hair self-consciously, secretly loving the page-boy bob that was meant to make her look sleek and sophisticated. At least, that was what the progressive hairdresser in the small Welsh village had said, when she'd gone back for a final two weeks at the Pritchards'.

Mam Pritchard hadn't liked the new style, of course, but then, she'd generally been against everything Rose ever did . . . which made it all the more surprising when she'd broken down on Rose's shoulder at the moment of parting, and told her she'd always thought of her as the daughter she'd never had.

Rose had written those words in capital letters in her diary that night. They had been more important to her than she would have believed possible. *'I've been love-starved all these years,'* she wrote dramatically, *'but love was there all the time. It was just that Mam Pritchard didn't know how to show it.'*

"I reckon she looks more like Rita Hayworth now, don't you, babe?" Merv asked his wife.

Rose was aware that her brother-in-law was assessing her through narrowed eyes. She supposed he'd be comparing her with the last time he'd seen her, in dreary grey cardigan and skirt and school socks, weeping on the quay at Southampton. Waving her sister goodbye as Gracie too wept from the deck of the liner filled with GI brides, with or without their Yanks to comfort them. They all waved madly, to the tune of the ship's hooters blaring, and paper streamers fluttering everywhere, off to their golden future.

She'd been born too late, Rose had mourned then, just on the brink of adolescence. Too late to have a glamorous Yank boyfriend; too late to enjoy the war; too late to be anything but packed off as a boring evacuee with a cardboard label around her neck and a gas-mask over her shoulder, while Gracie and their parents remained in London.

Too late to be anything but permanently billeted with the Godfearing Pritchards in a dank coal-mining valley where life was ruled by the shifts at the pits all week, and the rigid call of Chapel on Sundays. To Rose, the only relief was the glorious singing of the local male voice choir that seemed to soar to the rafters of the chapel and slag heaps in equal measure, instilling both with greatness and glory.

Until the awful day when not even the soaring voices of a Welsh choir could minimize the pain and shock of a visit from an ashen-faced Gracie in her WRAC uniform to say there was no longer a house in London to go back to. A German bomb had seen to that. And both their parents had been blown to bits with it. The nightmares that those words had conjured up had haunted Rose's vivid imagination for years. . . .

When Gracie made no reply to Merv's comment that she looked more like Rita Hayworth than Shirley Temple, he shrugged his beefy shoulders.

"So what are we going to do with you now that you're here, Rose?" his lazy voice broke into her thoughts.

"Well, I shall look for a job as soon as I can, of course," she said quickly. "I don't intend being a drone, Merv. I mean to pay back every penny you've spent on me—"

"Did I ever ask you to pay me back?"

"No, you never did, but I'm going to all the same. My mother always said she was never beholden to anybody, and it was the only way to live and hold your head up high."

She didn't know why she'd said it, nor why the unexpected memory came into her head right then, but it was enough to make her throat thicken and the tears blind her eyes.

"Here you are, honey." Gracie was holding out a box of paper tissues. Rose took out a handful and blew her nose hard.

"You get through Kleenex at that rate and you'll be incurring the National Debt," Merv said mildly. "Now what say we all go out to eat this evening? We could take Rosie to Sea-Food Joe's, and show her off to the local jacks."

"What are they?" Rose said guardedly.

"Just the young guys who hang around the neighbourhood. They're gonna enjoy getting an eyeful of you, babe, and especially when you open your mouth."

He grinned at his wife as a new thought occurred to

9

him. "Hey, Grace, if we keep quiet about who she is, they might think we've hired an English maid!"

"Don't be stupid, Merv," Gracie snapped. "Where would people like us get the money to hire an English maid?"

Rose looked from one to the other. People like them? This place – it seemed pretty good to her, used to the small cramped Welsh house in the valley. Merv ran a big Chevrolet car and the furniture seemed comfortable enough, even if none of it was new or of the latest style.

In past years they'd sent just sufficient money to pay Rose's college fees and to give her a modest allowance. They'd paid her passage money to come over here, and she'd always assumed that Merv was one of the well-off Yanks that the war-torn English people assumed all of them to be.

A hideous thought occurred to her. Surely her expenses hadn't taken all Merv and Gracie had? The very last thing she wanted was to be indebted to them for an impossible amount. But she couldn't ask, at least not right now. It was something to remember for later.

"Is an English maid such a status symbol?" she said in the sudden prickly silence.

Merv hooted. "And I thought you went to the movies, Rose! Sure an English maid's a status symbol. Why? You wanna play that game with us?"

"Not particularly." She was cool, seeing that gleam in his eyes again, as if he was picturing her in some fancy maid's outfit the way the Hollywood movies portrayed them. Fluffy and long-legged, and an easy target for a lecherous boss. Merv suddenly made her nervous, and being nervous she spoke too fast.

"Actually, I did a bit of waitressing once, to make some extra pocket money when I was at college. It was all right, but I wouldn't want to do it all the time."

"*Actually*, you look far too classy for that, babe," Merv exaggerated her accent good-humouredly.

"Look, are we going out to eat or do I have to start making dinner?" Gracie said impatiently.

Rose jumped up. "I'll get changed—"

"We don't need to dress up for Sea-Food Joe's, honey. You look fine as you are," Merv drawled.

But surely *he* was going to change, Rose thought. He didn't mean to go out to dinner in that awful red vest and work trousers . . . she didn't want to feel so snobbish, but she wasn't used to the casual outlook of Americans yet – nor to eating regularly in restaurants. She might be almost adult, but she still felt like a gauche schoolgirl in many ways. And six years after the end of the war in Europe, food supplies at home still weren't plentiful enough for her to take American affluence for granted.

"You'd better smarten yourself up, Merv. Rose's got that Chapel look on her face again."

Before she could think how to answer, Merv laughed. "OK. I was going to put on a shirt anyway. That'll do, won't it? I don't want to stick out like a spare part at a wedding at Sea-Food Joe's, but I ain't dressing up like some fancy dude neither."

Rose went to her bedroom where there was actually a wash-basin in the corner, and swilled cold water around her face and neck to try and cool off. She'd forgotten that Merv could be so crude. She'd forgotten a great deal about him. And about Gracie too. Her own sister. She had still been seeing them through rose-coloured glasses, the way some of the boyos used to taunt her with a play on her name for her dreaming ways. She'd seen Gracie and Merv as the benefactors they undoubtedly were, and it hadn't mattered that Merv was hardly a Hollywood idol, or Gracie the devoted sister.

When they were children she and Gracie had constantly bickered. But the bickering had come to an end during the week before the war in Europe had been declared by Mr Chamberlain. That was when their parents had bundled Rose on the train bound for Wales with the rest of the bewildered crowds of little evacuees, some no more than babies.

She'd tried to be brave and not to cry. Her parents had been nearly crying too as they'd put her in the care of a teacher. But Gracie hadn't cried. She remembered that now, almost as if she saw it all being re-enacted on a moving screen. Gracie had dutifully hugged her small sister. She was ten years older than Rose and already envisaging joining up and wearing a uniform. From Rose's seven-year-old perspective, the last thing she saw as she pressed her tear-streaked face to the cold window glass of the slowly moving train was Gracie linking her arms through that of their mum and dad, as they all abandoned her.

"What in God's name is the matter with me?" she asked her reflection now, seeing the sudden pinched look around her mouth, and the huge eyes, made darker with the pain of remembering.

She used the blasphemous phrase Mam Pritchard despised so much, being so *Chapel*, and wondered for the first time in her life if Gracie had been so jealous of her smaller, prettier sister that she had actually welcomed the fact that Rose was being despatched to the country for the duration. It had never even occurred to her until this minute, and it was just about the stupidest time for it to happen.

She brushed out her dark hair until it framed her face in the sleek page-boy, suddenly finding no joy in the way it swung out from her head all in a piece to rest on her shoulders. This should be the happiest day of her life, and for no apparent reason the pleasure in it had all slipped sideways.

"You're an ungrateful pig," she muttered. "This is

the start of a new life, not a day for remembering the old."

Something she'd once read flashed into her mind.

'We're all what our past makes of us. What we've been, who we've met, where we've lived, all our past pleasures and pains, contribute to shape the people we are today. It's a fact that's inescapable, and so is the fact that these outside influences that affect our inner selves means that we're constantly changing. This is a healthy catalytic state. To remain static is to wither and die.'

It must have been some philosopher or other who said that, Rose thought. She couldn't even remember where she'd read it, except that it was almost certainly from one of the few learned tomes that Mam Pritchard kept in the house. Light reading was frowned upon, but the heavy stuff was much revered. Not that the two Pritchard boyos had ever so much as picked up a book, as far as she could recall.

"Are you going to be in there all day, honey?" Merv's voice bawled at her from outside her bedroom door.

She hastily composed her face before she unbolted the door and passed him in the narrow passageway, avoiding contact by drawing in her stomach muscles and trying not to breathe too deeply. It wasn't that he smelled rank, but there was a smell about him she hadn't readily defined until she realized it was petrol and engine oil. *Gas*, she reminded herself. She had to call petrol *gas* now. And Gracie had already commented that Merv spent half his spare time tinkering with what they both called the God-damned car, which probably accounted for his clothes and skin being impregnated with gas.

They all piled into the Chevy (apparently you didn't bother using long words when a shortened one would do) and drove the short distance to Sea-Food Joe's (apparently

13

you didn't walk when you could drive either). From the outside the place looked no more than a wooden shack with a neon sign outside. Inside it was warm and crowded and smoky with cigarette smoke and the seductive smells of seafood and hot vinegar and spices. Rose's mouth began to water, as Merv fought his way to a corner table for the three of them.

"I guess this is your first visit to an American food joint, honey," he shouted back at her above the noise.

"Yes," she said, wondering if it was always like this and not sure if she liked it or not. Jostling people, smiling faces, loud raucous laughter, and overall the easy cameraderie among friends and strangers alike that would never be tolerated at home. The little English snob in her was trying to come through again, Rose realized, and she quickly pushed the feeling away. As they all sat down at their table, she noticed that Gracie was grinning at her, her voice mellowed by the noise all around them.

"A bit like Joe Lyons', eh, Rosie?"

It was nothing like it at all, and yet without warning, Rose saw exactly what Gracie meant, and that this was a gesture of friendship that took no account of the years. It was almost like those lovely long-ago times when their parents had taken their girls into Joe Lyons' tea-shop in Charing Cross and treated them to afternoon tea, before old Hitler's histrionics came and ruined everything.

She smiled back across the table at Gracie, her eyes bright with remembering, and told her it was just like Joe Lyons'.

"Hey, who's your new gal, Merv? Have you moved into the starlet business now?"

The mood was broken, and Rose's head jerked up at the sound of the man's voice. It was a leering voice that she disliked at once, and all the more so when she saw how Merv immediately played up to him.

"Keep your distance, Chuck old buddy. This here's Gracie's sister, come over from England to stay with us, and she ain't planning on going into the movie business that I know of – or are you, honey?"

He paused momentarily before he directed his question to Rose, and she felt the warm flush rising from her neck at the undisguised scrutiny from her brother-in-law and the other man, both of them looking her over as if she was a kind of specimen.

Englishmen were never this blatant in their appraisal, she thought angrily, nor even Welshmen, except for some of the wilder pit-workers – and you could forgive them anything, living underground with danger every day of their lives as they hacked out the glittering coal from the rock.

"It wasn't my intention to do so, no," she said, her diction so correct and so beautifully modulated that the other man nearly fell off his chair in admiration. He whistled through his teeth, uncaring that he was in a public place. But nobody else cared either. Sea-Food Joe's was hardly the Ritz.

"Say, with that cut-glass accent you could really go places, couldn't she, Merv? And you never told us you had such a swell for a sister, Gracie. Where in hell have you been hiding her all these years?"

If the mood had been broken before, it was shattered now. Rose felt her sister's antagonism at once. Gracie wouldn't be at all pleased at the comparison this oaf was making between the two of them. Gracie had always preened herself as a glamour girl when the GIs came to town, and had had no trouble catching her Yank. While the wide-eyed little sister had been no more than a kid. . . .

Gracie snapped at the man. "You just keep your lecherous eyes off our Rose, Chuck. She'll be looking round for a good secretary's job, so don't start filling her head with any fancy ideas of being a starlet. We all know how they earn their money."

Any further discussion about the new arrival in town was curtailed by the arrival of the waitress. But the man turned back to his companions with a comment audible enough for Rose to hear.

"Oh yeah? And if Merv Hackett don't get around to exploiting that classy little gal, my name's not Chuck Bernstein. Who's taking a wager on it?"

Chapter Two

"I thought we were going to see the homes of the movie stars," Rose complained a week later. "All we've done so far is sit around the house."

She didn't mean to be so ungrateful, but it was all so boring, boring, boring. Gracie seemed content to do as little housework as possible, while Merv's days were erratic, to say the least. Some days he was out of the house by seven every morning and returned around six in the evening. Other times he'd laze around all morning, not moving himself until mid-afternoon, and then he was out until all hours.

"Where does he go?" Rose had asked.

"To work, of course. How d'you think he makes his money?"

"I haven't got the foggiest. He was a trucker or something before he enlisted, wasn't he?" Rose said, on the defensive at Gracie's surly tone.

She supposed she should already know what Merv did, but Gracie had never been forthcoming in her infrequent letters, and it hadn't seemed important enough at the time for Rose to ask.

"He does anything that's going. But it's valeting, mostly."

"He's a valet? A *servant*, you mean?"

To Rose, the word meant no more than that. The only valets she'd ever seen were the kind beloved by the Hollywood movie-makers, and they were always

stiff-necked Englishmen who had accents more aristocratic than royalty, and who seemed to spend all their
time carrying things on silver salvers, or brushing down
their masters' clothes every morning . . . and none of that
fitted Merv's brash image. . . .

"Heck, no! For pity's sake don't ever let Merv hear you
say such a thing, our Rose. He's a car valet. He puts folks'
cars away for them at one of the big hotels. You've heard
of The Pacific Grand, haven't you?"

"No. Should I have?"

Gracie looked at her impatiently. "Oh well, I don't
suppose there's any reason why you should. But it's only
one of the swankiest hotels on the West Coast, that's all.
Movie stars go there every night."

"And Merv puts their cars away?" Now she was
entranced.

Gracie looked at her sharply. "Movie stars aren't all
they're cracked up to be, Rose. You take a look at some
of the gossip columns and you'll find they're as human
as the next person. More so in most cases. Some of those
guys and gals have got to the top by pretty ruthless means,
and everybody knows about the casting couch system. I
guess it all depends on how much you want to be a star."
She said the word as if it was little short of damnation.

"I can't believe that," Rose said forcefully, not having
the faintest idea what was meant by the casting couch
system, but not daring to ask. "It must be wonderful to
be discovered serving coffee in a cafe, and be whisked
away to a film studio—"

"You've been reading too many movie magazines. It's
all publicity, Rose. How many movie stars do you really
think were picked up casually like that?"

"Well, I don't know—"

"Precious few, my girl! They fought tooth and claw to
get where they are, and don't you forget it. Merv could tell
you a thing or two about some of the so-called baby-faced

young stars who cuss in the spiciest gutter-language, and threaten to sue him if he puts one single mark on their precious cars."

"I don't believe it. You're making it up to put me off," Rose said flatly.

"Makes no difference to me. Just don't believe everything you read, that's all. This town's about as phoney as you'll ever see, Rose, and I'm just warning you not to let it get to you." She looked at her sister with sudden suspicion. "You aren't getting any daft ideas about trying for the flicks yourself, are you?"

"I might. Why not?"

It hadn't really occurred to her, not seriously. It was no more than one of those dreams that filled the hot sleepless nights with technicolour, but Gracie took her seriously.

"See here, now, our Rose, you'd better start looking in the paper for a decent secretary's job right away. That's what you've been trained for, so don't go getting any fancy ideas, just because you're living in LA. It's not all Hollywood, and we're not supporting you for ever while you go chasing rainbows."

"I know. I didn't mean it anyway. You just made me mad, that's all. And I am grateful, Gracie, honestly I am."

"You just be sure and show it then," her sister said, her feathers slightly less ruffled.

"Anyway, you still haven't said when we're going to see the homes of the movie stars." Rose reverted to her original grouse and tried not to sulk.

Gracie sighed impatiently. "OK, maybe we'll make it tomorrow. Merv's got nothing to do in the morning, so I'll get him to take us then. Does that suit you, star-eyes?"

"Oh yes! And it'll be something really exciting to write and tell Mam Pritchard!"

Gracie looked at her curiously. "Are you really gonna

19

keep writing to the old witch? It sounds as if you got quite fond of her in the end."

Rose's reply came smartly. "She was the only person I had in the end. Mum and Dad were dead, and you were in America, but Mam Pritchard was always there when I needed her. I never realized how much I depended on that. She told me all the things a mother should tell a daughter, and I owe her a lot. . . ." She stopped, surprised at her own defence of her foster mother.

"Good God. I can't imagine her explaining the birds and the bees," Gracie began to laugh, remembering Mam Pritchard's tight-pressed mouth whenever the talk was in danger of becoming too raucous.

"She didn't. I found that out for myself."

Gracie's mouth dropped open, and Rose just managed not to tell her she was catching flies. . . .

"Waddya mean, our Rose? You ain't been doing things you shouldn't, have you? We don't want that kind of trouble brought home here—"

"It's all right, I'm only teasing you – though the boyos showed plenty of curiosity at having a girl living in the house," she said, not wanting to remember too clearly those times when she'd wrestled silently with Dai and Evan. "I learned all I needed to know from the girls at college. One of them had a mother who was a nurse and explained it all clinically, and she told the rest of us."

"Oh, I see," Gracie broke into a laugh now. "Explained it all clinically, did she? Well, I hope the real thing won't be too much of a shock to you, little sister!"

Secretly, so did Rose. It wasn't fashionable to talk about intimate things as freely as Julia at college did, simply because her mother was a nurse. And she'd been screwed up with embarrassment as she and the other girls listened while Julia airily referred to the private parts of the body by their unfamiliar names, and the functions to which they were to be put when Mr Right came along. . . .

She'd still doubted whether it was totally true, and decided that Julia had made half of it up. It had sounded disgustingly unhygenic, and since the only married couples she knew were the Pritchards, and Gracie and her Yank, her imagination had simply shut off from then on.

The Pritchards surely *couldn't* unbend enough to do it, and at that time Gracie and Merv were still imbued in her mind with that starry-eyed transatlantic glamour, and she didn't want to imagine them doing anything so ugly. And boyfriends in the Welsh village had been few and fumbling, and quickly seen off by Mam Pritchard or the boyos.

She was still innocent, in the biblical sense that Mam thought so highly of . . . or had been, before she came here to LA, where the nights were so hot and sultry that bedroom windows had to be thrown open on the frequent occasions when the air-conditioning broke down. And the thrashing night-sounds that came from Gracie and Merv's room had definitely disillusioned her from any ideas of their being two gentle love-birds . . . so at least some of Julia's information had been true.

Rose shivered. She wasn't too sure about marriage if that was what it entailed. And yet, she did want it for herself, of course she did. Every girl did. It was natural to want a man of her own, to love and to cherish, and to keep from being alone . . . and she supposed she would submit to that other thing now and again, if she had to. . . .

"Don't tell me you're cold!" Gracie said, seeing the goose pimples on her arms. "You ain't coming down with a chill, are you, Rose?"

"No. But I don't know which is worse – the heat when the air-conditioning stops working, or the blast of cold air when it is," she said quickly, grateful for

21

the sudden rattle of the machinery to add weight to the comment.

"You'll get used to it. Now – d'you wanna come down to the grocery store with me and Mrs Olsen, or stay here?"

"I'll stay here, if you don't mind."

She'd already met Mrs Olsen from the apartment upstairs, a large and perspiring lady who thought cute little Rose was just darling, and continually screeched that she'd always meant to go over to England but her old man was just too mean to take her. Pity. She might have been able to look Rose up.

Rose thanked God for small mercies, quite sure she couldn't even stand a trip to the grocery store cramped up in Mrs Olsen's beat-up runabout, let alone have her arriving on her doorstep back home and gushing over li'l old England.

"OK, honey, make yourself at home, but don't do anything I wouldn't do," Gracie said breezily.

Once they'd gone, Rose let out her breath. She was hardly ever alone now, and she needed some space to call her own. It was ironic. For once she welcomed being alone, when there had been so many times when she'd compared being alone to heartbreak. But those were different days, of course.

And while she was eternally grateful to Gracie and Merv for bringing her here, they smothered her, the way Americans did.

Rose had already begun to realize that for the three of them to live together indefinitely just wasn't going to work. The ideal thing would be for her to find a job and get her own apartment. But a fat chance she'd ever have of affording one in LA, she thought. And she knew better than to say anything to Gracie about it yet.

She let herself dream for a moment, remembering

Gracie's probing question about wanting to go into the movies. It had never occurred to her before, and besides, she didn't know a thing about acting. Oh, she'd been in a few college productions, and even had the starring roles, mainly on account of her tall, willowy looks, she conceded. But according to the more scathing articles she'd read about some of the ambitious young starlets, who needed acting, anyway?

Rose shivered. If you had to submit to the sweaty pawings of some producer or director or other to make your mark in the movie world, then she'd rather sell flowers outside a London underground station.

For a moment she was hit with the most unexpected surge of nostalgia. It was just as though the hot blast of air from the underground when all the daily commuters emerged hit her nostrils . . . and it was only when she realized the damn air-conditioning had failed again and the room was getting humid that she told herself crossly not to be so pathetic. She'd achieved her goal in life, and it was a bit late in the day to start feeling a tug in her heart for old England.

She picked up the weekly newspaper that had all the job ads in it. It was quite true what Gracie said. She couldn't be dependent on her and Merv for ever, and it had never been her intention, anyway. All she had wanted was to be here.

Her eyes flicked down the columns of newsprint. There seemed to be plenty of secretarial jobs available, and a girl could rise to the top of the profession if she worked hard. She sighed, knowing that she just didn't want to be at some fat, cigar-smoking executive's beck and call.

But Gracie would be expecting her to try, and after circling several of the most promising ads, she picked up the phone that seemed to be almost an extension of Gracie's ear, and asked the nasal operator for the number of the Jefferson Printing Corporation.

"Say, are you British?" she heard the girl say curiously.

"Yes," Rose answered.

"Well, waddya know? Me and my room-mate were watching a British movie the other night, and you talk just like the woman in it, sort of plum in the mouth – you know what I mean? No offence meant, lady, o' course."

"None taken—"

"A British voice always sounds so swanky, don't it? What are you, a maid or somethin'?"

Rose stared in disbelief at the black bakelite phone. It was just like Merv and Gracie had joked about. Folk around here really did get impressed by the thought of having an English maid. . . . She pushed aside her amazement as she remembered the purpose of her call. It had taken enough nerve to try to speak to a receptionist at the Jefferson Printing Corporation, for goodness sake, without getting into a lengthy conversation with this quick-fire operator.

"Look, would you please connect me with the number I asked for?" she said, as authoritatively as she could.

"Sure thing," the girl said amiably. "It was nice talking with you, hon. Maybe we'll get to talk again."

There were a number of clicks in the background, and then an older female voice answered, announcing itself as the Jefferson Printing Corporation. Rose took a deep breath.

"You have a secretarial job advertised in the *Los Angeles Sentinel*," she said. "I wonder—"

"Do you have references?"

"I – well no. But I have typing and shorthand proficiency certificates from my secretarial college. I'm well qualified."

There was a brief silence at the other end.

"Are you a US citizen?"

"No. I'm English, but I'm living with my sister and

brother-in-law, who are US citizens," she said, wondering if her nationality was to be some kind of drawback for any job higher in status than maid or waitress after all.

"There may be some problem over that, but we can sort out a work permit and all the paperwork later if you prove suitable. Name, age, address and phone number, please."

Rose gave them quickly. The efficiency at the other end was starting to unnerve her. She could hear the tap of a typewriter in the background before the woman answered again.

"I can give you four-thirty on Friday afternoon, and be prepared to give a practical demonstration of your skills. My name is Mrs Hubbard, and you'll report to me here at reception."

The line went dead with a sharp click, and Rose felt the most ridiculous temptation to salute. Mrs Hubbard sounded a real battleaxe, and for two pins she'd simply not turn up for the interview. . . .

Then, without warning, her heart gave a joyous leap as she realized what she'd done. She'd got an interview with an important corporation, and whatever else happened, if she got the job, she'd be an LA secretary. The glamour of it superceded everything else.

She spent half an hour sorting through every single thing in her wardrobe, trying to decide what to wear. Nothing seemed remotely smart enough to compete with American secretaries, who would all surely resemble film stars waiting to be discovered. But by now, she refused to let such a thought depress her. She had a bit of money left, and there were still three days left to buy something new. Gracie would know the best stores to visit.

She was still preening herself when Gracie and Mrs Olsen returned, loaded with brown paper bags of groceries and complaining profusely about the heat.

"Put the kettle on, kid," Gracie said at once, flopping into one armchair, while Mrs Olsen flopped in the other.

"Don't you want to hear my news?" Rose said excitedly.

"What news? That old Welsh skinflint ain't actually called you from the *vath-ley*, has she?" Gracie exaggerated the Welsh accent as she flexed her feet.

Rose waved the newspaper in front of her.

"I've got an interview for a job at the Jefferson Printing Corporation on Friday afternoon, and I don't have anything good enough to wear. Can we go shopping to find something tomorrow, Gracie, *please*?"

She listened to herself, the young sister pleading with her superior to take her dress shopping, and just for a moment, she re-lived the hated memory of the young Rose begging her glamorous Gracie not to go away in the GI boat and leave her, but to take her with her. . . .

"The Jefferson Printing Corporation, huh?" Mrs Olsen said. "You're surely flying high, hon."

"Am I?" Rose said. "Is it something special then?"

"Only the biggest corporation in town, that's all. They employ hundreds of girls—"

"So nobody's likely to discover you for the flicks sitting behind a typewriter in the middle of that little lot, honey," Gracie added with a grin.

"I wasn't thinking anything of the sort," Rose said crossly. "Excuse me, I'll go and make that tea."

She went swiftly out to the kitchen, but not fast enough to miss Gracie telling Mrs Olsen how she'd always put on that frosty face when she wanted to clam up about something.

She caught sight of herself in the cracked mirror Gracie kept on the kitchen wall. *"Rose's frosty face is enough to freeze the balls off a brass monkey,"* she seemed to hear Dai Pritchard's taunting voice say.

And the devil of it was, he was right, and Gracie was right too. She *had* had a silly little fantasy of sitting behind a typewriter in the middle of a huge clattering typing pool, and finding an influential film director pausing at her desk and looking her over, and asking if she'd ever done any acting. . . .

"I ain't stopping for tea, Rose." She jumped as she suddenly heard Mrs Olsen's voice behind her. And then it lowered from its usual shriek. "Don't you take no notice of your Gracie, hon. She's jealous, that's all. You could knock spots off some of them starlets."

"Thanks, Mrs Olsen," Rose said, touched by the woman's shrewdness. She busied herself with the tea things, grateful for these moments alone. Gracie was still sprawled out when she took the tray back to the parlour, but she spoke casually.

"So what do you want to buy for this interview then?"

Rose thought. "Maybe a plain short jacket and skirt to match. And white gloves, of course. I've got a good pair of navy shoes that'll have to do, and a handbag—"

"It's called a purse," Gracie said absent-mindedly, already losing interest.

Rose bit back the retort that a purse was what she kept her small change in inside her handbag. But it wasn't worth the argument, and besides, she knew Gracie was right about something. She had to fall in with American ways now, and to try to remember the American words.

"So will you come with me?" she asked again. "You'll know the best places to go."

Gracie shrugged. "I don't know no fancy places—"

"I don't want fancy places. I don't have that much money to spend. Just somewhere I can buy something suitable."

"This is LA, honey. Everything comes pricey here, but at least we can look. We'll get Merv to drop us off after we've done our trip in the morning, and then get the bus back."

Rose looked blank for a moment, and then remembered.

She'd been so excited over the job interview that the tour around the homes of the movie stars had taken second place. But now it was all back in her head with a vengeance. And she could hardly wait. Nor could she dispel her special kind of dreams that night. They were all mixed up with seeing the palatial mansions in her imagination, and the glamour of being toasted as the brightest, newest English movie star to hit Hollywood. Picked up out of nowhere at some soda fountain, of course. . . .

She awoke to the depressing sound of rain hammering on the roof of the apartment building and dripping off the trees outside. It was a bad omen, and she rushed to her window to stare out at the mud pools in the yard that had been yesterday's heaps of sandy soil. She could hear the morning sounds from Merv and Gracie's bedroom and hurried along to the bathroom first.

"It's raining!" she stated dismally, when she went downstairs to where Gracie was making waffles and coffee.

"It won't last. It'll be gone in an hour and it won't stop us going out, unless you've changed your mind."

"Of course not. I just thought Merv might not want to take us in the rain—"

"Merv won't care. It's better for him than lying around all morning, which is what he usually does when he's on lates."

"Don't you mind him working such unsociable hours?" Rose asked curiously. She knew from the raucous noises of the Chevy that sometimes her brother-in-law didn't return home from work until two or three o'clock in the morning.

"It's a job," Gracie shrugged. "Besides, it gives me a bit of peace – know what I mean, kid?"

She winked, slapping down a pile of waffles on a

platter for Rose to help herself. Rose mumbled something under her breath. The second worst thing to hearing the thrashing sounds from Gracie's bedroom was hearing Gracie's innuendoes. She suddenly realized her sister was staring at her, her hands resting on her ample hips.

"You know, you'd better be careful, our Rose, or you'll be a sitting duck."

"What's that supposed to mean?"

Gracie gave a sideways grin. "You're still wet behind the ears when it comes to men, aren't you? Those randy boyos didn't teach you a damn thing, did they?"

"I told you, Julia's mother explained it all to her, and she told me—"

"Yeah, well, you just take it easy when any of these flash Corporation guys ask you out. They're all only after one thing, and you'll just be one more notch in their belts. A deep notch, too, with that cool English voice of yours."

Rose turned almost thankfully as Merv came into the room, belching noisily, and was just as instantly appalled to think she could welcome the appearance of this lout. Once she got her job, she thought desperately, she'd definitely be looking around for a flat of her own, no matter what they said. For some reason she remembered the nasal voice of the telephone operator, mentioning a room-mate. It sounded fun to share a place – if she ever got to know anybody that well.

"All ready for the trip, then, sweetie?" Merv asked.

"Ready as I'll ever be," she answered, resisting the urge to kick his shins, just so he'd take his hot eyes off her for a minute.

"We're going to the clothing store in Market Street afterwards, Merv," Gracie told him. "You can drop us there on your way downtown, can't you?"

"Guess so," he grunted.

Rose cheered up, remembering the purpose of the

shopping trip. Something smart but not too flashy, she thought, something really secretarial. . . .

Just as Gracie had said, the rain stopped as suddenly as it had begun, and the streets were soon steaming again under a hot sun. And a couple of hours later Rose couldn't think of anything but the tree-lined mansions they were cruising past in the Chevy.

She was dying to know who lived where, but it seemed that Merv wasn't exactly *au fait* with them all after all. He couldn't tell her where Marilyn lived, or Bing Crosby, and she felt a sliver of disappointment. But she should have known, of course. Merv's mouth had always been bigger than his brain.

But he took them right up to Bel-Air, and pointed out the homes of Dolores Montego and the Waverley brothers, and the new dark-haired star with the Italian-sounding name that she could never remember. It was a bitter disappointment that Rose could hardly see any of the mansions themselves. They were mostly set far back from the road, and well hidden behind high fences and thick evergreens, and Merv said that most of them were full of such intricate alarm systems that it would take a Houdini to break into one of them.

"Who would want to do that?" Rose said, awe-struck.

Merv laughed in amazement at her innocence. "Any guy wanting to fill his pockets with riches, angel-face! These places are crammed to the roofs with jewellery and paintings and art works that would make your British royalty look like paupers."

"Don't be daft," Rose said in annoyance. "Nobody could be that rich."

"Except the movie stars," Merv retorted. "Believe me, kid, I've been hired to do the occasional valeting up here for some of their bashes, and I've seen it all. Forget the President and all that Washington crowd.

Movie stars are the American royalty – or hadn't you noticed?"

"Merv knows what he's talking about, Rose," Gracie said from the back seat.

"Besides, you only have to be around on Academy Awards night to see the influence these movie guys and gals have," Merv went on. "You couldn't get anywhere near the RKO Pantages Theatre this year for traffic and fans, and farther out the rest of the city's always deserted because everybody's sitting by their radio sets so they don't miss hearing who gets what. In any case, it's safer that way. Two girls got crushed outside the Awards place one year, trying to get autographs."

Rose registered the horror of what he was saying, but it didn't make any difference, because it was all tempered by the growing excitement inside her, and the realization that this could be her life too. Any one of these beautiful Bel-Air homes could be her home.

If anyone could become President of the United States, then surely anyone could become a movie star. If it had been no more than the faintest foolish glimmer of an idea in her head before, it was far more than that now. It was leaping into a gigantic flame.

It could happen to anybody. . . . Anybody who ever read the gossip magazines about the stars knew that even the wonderful Joan Crawford had been a laundress, a waitress and a shopgirl before breaking into chorus lines and getting a Hollywood screen test. Rose drew in her breath, suddenly dazzled.

"You've gone very quiet, babe," Merv said. "You shouldn't let it upset you. It was their own fault. They practically threw themselves under the cars when the stars arrived—"

"It's all right," she said quickly.

But perhaps it was better to let him think she was upset by the thought of those poor stupid girls ending up so

31

tragically. Not for anything in the world would she let Gracie and Merv guess the way her thoughts were going now. They'd only think she was like some of those other British girls who'd set their sights on a wartime Yank, while secretly seeing the Hollywood streets shining with movie dust.

She might have arrived five years later than the last of the GI brides . . . but the feelings were just the same, and the ambition was just the same. She'd just never known it was there, that was all.

Chapter Three

"Did Merv say he'd actually worked in some of those homes?" Rose burst out, when he'd dropped her and Gracie off at the downtown clothing store in Market Street.

"Yeah. These folks are always giving parties, and reliable car valets get their names put on a register. Why?"

"Do you suppose he could get me a job there too? As a waitress or something – just for an evening?" The idea had shot into her mind so fast she could hardly think straight.

"I doubt it. Merv's not in the business of asking for favours. Besides, I thought you already had a job interview. I thought we were here to get you something suitable to wear to impress this Jefferson corporation guy?"

Gracie was getting tired of this whole excursion. The Chevy was playing up again, and the constant smell of gas while they drove around Bel-Air had made her nauseous. If Rose was changing her mind now, they might just as well have gone straight home. There was something else bothering her too. . . .

"Of course the interview's the most important," Rose said quickly. "I was just thinking I could do an occasional evening job as well."

"Well, you'll have to ask Merv about it," Gracie said irritably. "Look, I'm bushed, and the clothing store's over there. Unless you need me to come and hold your hand, I'm going to take a rest for five minutes, OK?"

She pointed to a small store that looked far too expensive for Rose's pocket, and sank down on one of the wooden benches on the sidewalk. She looked quite peaky, Rose realized with sudden alarm, but she knew of old that asking Gracie how she felt usually resulted in a snappy reply, so she resisted it.

"Of course I'll be all right," she said, and went inside the store by herself to browse through the items on the racks before she dared to enquire about any prices.

Ten minutes later she was outside again, stunned at the cost of everything. She realized that even so-called modest LA prices were way above her means, and she quickly revised her grand ideas about buying something new. It was only an interview, for God's sake, and her one good travelling suit would do very well, once she had given it a sponge and a press. It was neat and presentable, and it wasn't as if she was going to be swanning into some movie director's office for a screen test, all perfumed and glammed-up. . . .

"Well? Any luck?" Gracie's thick voice asked her.

"No – Gracie, what's wrong? Are you ill?" she asked in a panic, seeing the greyness in her sister's face now, and the beads of perspiration dotting her forehead.

"It's nothing. Let's just get the bus home. I'll be OK once I've had a lie down."

"You don't look OK—"

"God dammit, don't fuss me. It's only a grumbling appendix. I've had these twinges before, and they'll go away again in a while."

"Have you seen a doctor?"

"No, I bloody well haven't seen a doctor, and I ain't going to. Nobody's getting me into hospital to start cutting me up, thanks very much. Besides, doctors cost money."

Rose was shocked at the vehemence in her sister's voice. If you couldn't even afford to have a doctor look at you when you were ill, it seemed that maybe America wasn't so wonderful after all.

"How do you know it's your appendix if you haven't seen a doctor?" she asked nervously, as they made their way slowly around the corner to the bus depot.

"Mrs Olsen knows a thing or two about doctoring, and she gave me some stuff to take that eases the pain."

Thankfully, the bus was waiting, and they got onto it at once, and Gracie sat down heavily. There was a white line of pain around her mouth now, but Rose knew better than to start arguing that it seemed very foolish to take some of Mrs Olsen's medicine without knowing if it was the right thing to do. Mam Pritchard had told her so. She wouldn't even swallow an aspirin unless the doctor advised it, though that always seemed to Rose to be taking things too far.

It was an endless jolting bus ride home, and Gracie sat silently all the while, which only proved to Rose how bad she felt. But at last they got out, a hundred yards from the end of the road, and walked slowly towards the apartment building. Gracie acted like a very old woman, Rose thought in alarm, and the minute she got her sister indoors, she went racing upstairs to hammer on Mrs Olsen's door. Whatever Gracie said, she was sure she needed a doctor, and fast.

"Calm down, hon!" Mrs Olsen said. "She's had these attacks before, and no harm's been done. It looks worse than it is when you ain't seen it before. She'll be as bright as a silver dollar again in a little while. Has she taken some of that medicine I left for her?"

"Yes, but are you sure it's all right for her to take it? I'm sure we should send for a doctor—"

"She won't thank you for that, and even if one was agreeable to coming out here, she'd be better by the time he arrived, and it'd just be a waste of money," the woman said dryly. "Just see that she gets to bed and leave her be."

Rose gave in. Between the two of them she knew when she was beaten. It seemed a strange system when you didn't even know if a doctor was willing to come and visit a sick patient. It was all so different from dear old Doctor Rhys-Owen, who'd tended her childhood ailments in Pontyrowan and never charged Mam Pritchard a penny above the cost of a cup of tea laced with her medicinal brandy.

Waves of nostalgia suddenly swept over Rose, taking her so much by surprise that she almost stumbled back down the stairway to Gracie's apartment. She must be going real daft in the head, if she could get so soft-eyed over the old Welsh doctor with the bristly white whiskers who'd always managed to make a small scared evacuee laugh through her tears.

Here she was, where she had always wanted to be, yet her heart seemed to be constantly tugged back to that small Welsh valley and those impossible people.

But she knew she did them all an injustice by thinking of them like that. They'd been kind enough in their various ways, even if sometimes they'd seemed so strict and narrow, and fussy enough to make her want to scream.

Gracie had often mocked Mam Pritchard's fussy habits, like the lace covers with their beaded hems that she put over the jam pots, and the jugs for milk and water that she always kept separate for fear of germs entering one or the other. But Gracie had mocked everything about Rose's second family, and had made no bones about the fact that she was glad it was her sister who'd been sent away to Wales, and not herself.

"Rose, fetch me a glass of water, will you?" she heard Gracie's plaintive voice calling her from her bedroom, and she moved at once, wondering if it was really true that the grass was always greener on the other side of

36

the fence, until you actually stood on it. Much of LA's grass had to be constantly watered to keep it green, and it seemed ominously symbolic to Rose at that moment.

But the mood passed as quickly as Gracie's indisposition. By mid-afternoon, she had completely recovered, and Rose decided she'd been a fool to get so alarmed. Mrs Olsen obviously knew what was best for Gracie, and the doctor's bill had been avoided.

"Do you remember Doctor Rhys-Owen from Pontyrowan, Gracie?" she asked suddenly, as they were sitting out on the porch after their evening meal.

Her sister frowned. "Was he a squat little man who looked more like a garden gnome than a doctor?"

"He was very kind to me," Rose defended him.

"Well, that's what doctors are paid for, isn't it?" Gracie said.

Rose stared out into the dying daylight. No matter how much she tried, she couldn't get close to Gracie. There was still that distance between them that was as much in their personalities as in age and upbringing. The biggest part of her own childhood had been spent in Wales, and she suddenly mourned all those years of family closeness that had been lost because of the war. Because of bloody old Hitler, as Dai and Evan Pritchard had called him whenever their mother wasn't around. She grinned suddenly, remembering just how bold they could be – as long as they didn't have their mam's eagle eyes on them. She had even once imagined herself marrying Evan, with the starry-eyed devotion of a bewildered child finding a kinder heart in one brother than the other.

"Have I said something funny?" Gracie enquired.

"No. I was just thinking I'd go inside and write some letters. You don't mind, do you?"

Gracie shrugged. "Suit yourself. We don't have to live in one another's pockets, Rose."

Thank God. The words were in Rose's head before she

could stop them. She fetched the writing case that had been an unexpected parting gift from the Pritchards, and sat in the parlour composing letters until bed-time. She'd put off writing home until she had something positive to say, knowing how uneasy Mam had been about her making this journey at all.

But now she could write about the cost of things in LA, and the apartment, and Merv's job, and seeing the homes of the movie stars, and most of all, about the job interview. Mam would be pleased about that. *"A girl could get on in the business world as long as she could type and do shorthand,"* she almost heard Mam's strong Welsh voice telling her. *"A girl could do worse than get a good grounding in office work."*

And a girl could do a whole lot better, Rose thought now, her pen poised over the writing paper. But she wasn't going to think about that tonight, and nor was she going to mention Gracie's grumbling appendix to worry Mam. For all that her foster mother had never seemed to have much imagination, Rose knew that in her mind she'd be having Gracie dead and buried, and herself being left to the lecherous attentions of Gracie's Yank. Mam Pritchard had no time for Yanks, and had made it clear she thought Rose was going to the devil in even crossing the Atlantic.

For a moment, Rose felt a shiver run through her, as keen as a premonition. Without Gracie in the apartment, she knew she could never stay here. It wasn't that she mistrusted Merv exactly, it was more that she wouldn't want to put temptation in his way.

She felt more restless than usual that evening, still wondering what Merv would say if she asked him to get her an evening job at a movie star's home. From his often evasive replies, she suspected that he didn't really have that kind of influence at all, but it didn't hurt to dream. . . .

She jumped as she heard the ferocious yapping of two dogs fighting somewhere close by, and then the blasphemous hollering of the tenants above as windows were raised. Someone threw a bucket of cold water over the animals, and they went away howling. It put an effective end to dreaming, and Rose concentrated instead on her letters, and thinking about Friday's interview.

Mrs Hubbard was as frighteningly efficient as she had sounded on the phone. She was small and neatly packaged, with carefully waved grey hair, and she sported heavy-framed glasses that hung on a cord around her neck so that when she removed them to scrutinize Rose they sat on the shelf of her startlingly perky bosom.

"You will wait with the other applicants, please, Miss Forster. Mr Jefferson himself is sitting in on the interviews today, and he's running late," Mrs Hubbard said accusingly, as if was the applicants' faults.

Rose took her place beside three other girls, who all looked as frighteningly efficient as the receptionist, and were far slicker and more sophisticated than herself. They all stared straight ahead as if they were carved out of stone, unless the news that Mr Jefferson was sitting in on his own interviews that day had struck them all dumb.

Rose clasped her gloved hands together, and remembered not to cross her legs in a tight knot so that there wouldn't be red blotches on her legs when she unfolded them. She tried to remember all that Mr Phillips, the music teacher from Pontyrowan junior school, had told her about relaxing and breathing.

"Breathe deep from the abdomen, girl, not just through your nose. The nose is best kept for smelling the daisies, see?" he'd said, making them all laugh. "That's better. Now, sing, girl, *sing*, and let me hear the sounds come up from your boots!"

"My abdomen isn't in my boots," she remembered

saying in an aside to her best friend at the time. She'd got a cuff around the ear for her trouble. But she'd learned to sing, all the same, and how to relax. She breathed deeply now, all the way up from her abdomen, letting her shoulders hang looser, and hoping she looked calmer than she felt.

All the other girls went for their interviews before her. Mr Jefferson obviously didn't care how long he kept his applicants waiting. But why should he, when he was the head of a company that conducted its business in a huge glass building, with plush carpets on the floors and a magnificent oak desk for Mrs Hubbard, and Japanese design jardinières everywhere? There weren't just plants in them either . . . some of them actually held exotic, living trees that almost touched the ornate ceiling. And this was only the reception area.

By the time her name was called, Rose felt she had the decor imprinted on her memory for ever. But by now, much of her nervousness had gone, simply because she was resenting the great man's inconsideration for keeping her waiting so long. The normal business day was long over, but presumably Jefferson's staff were obliged to stay as long as necessary. Rose had learned long ago that anger was a good way of smothering any other emotion, and she was angry now.

She was shown into a vast room, where a Miss Simpson, similar in shape and style to Mrs Hubbard, greeted her and showed her to a desk at one end. She was instructed to take down dictation in shorthand, and then to type it out.

Rose quickly got the impression that in American business, efficiency was all. But since she was here for a job, she did as she was told, silently handing the finished product to Miss Simpson and awaiting her approval. The woman scanned it, and took it to the far end of the room, where Rose suddenly realized there was someone sitting in a hideously large red leather armchair. She couldn't see who it was. The back of the armchair was towards her, and the person was facing the ostentatiously large windows.

The entire scene suddenly seemed so farcical and so theatrical that Rose's remaining nerves vanished. She might have been on the set of some idiotic Hollywood movie: the little English *ingénue* faced with the all-powerful American entrepreneur. Well, nobody was getting the better of *this* particular English girl, she thought indignantly. She knew her worth as a secretary, and she lifted her chin as Miss Simpson returned to her, and then the list of questions began that the woman quickly ticked off or underlined on what was presumably a more personal application form.

Name, age, status, religion (what difference did that make, for heaven's sake!), education, commercial experience, hopes, ambitions. . . . Rose answered them all in her impeccably correct English voice, noting the carefully arched eyebrow of her inquisitor raise ever so slightly after each reply.

Suddenly she began to enjoy herself. She sensed that there was no way she was going to get this job, and the interview was merely a polite formality. The Jefferson Printing Corporation was obviously out of her league. It was a world away from applying for a little office job in a small Welsh town, where everybody knew everybody else. Here, any employee would be a tiny cog in a huge machine . . . so she might as well ham it up and get the hell out of there, she thought, as brash as Merv.

"So what special attributes do you think you could bring to the Jefferson Printing Corporation, Miss Forster?" she was asked by the frigid Miss Simpson, her pen poised.

"I consider myself to be a highly capable secretary, able to follow instructions, and with the ability to take charge of any office emergencies if necessary," she heard herself say grandly, in her best Joan Crawford style. "I would be a loyal employee, and always do my best for the company—"

As the words gathered momentum, to her horror she became aware of a slow handclap coming from the other side of that hideous red leather armchair. She stopped speaking at once, knowing she had made a complete fool of herself with her gushing reply, and wondering how soon she could decently edge towards the door.

The chair swivelled around, and Bradley Piers Jefferson the third rose out of it and began to cross the desert of the office towards her.

"That was quite a performance, Miss Forster," he said, in the sexiest voice she had heard outside of Pontyrowan's flea-pit cinema. "Which movie did you memorize it from?"

She went a fiery red. How dare he think she could be so devious? The guilty fact that she'd literally thought herself into a kind of play-acting to give her Dutch courage, had nothing to do with it. It was *his* performance that had started her off, anyway. This great ostentatious office, and the hidden figure behind the desk, supposedly putting the fear of God Almighty into her . . . it might have worked for those other applicants, but it hadn't worked on her. She refused to let herself be intimidated.

The sunlight streaming into the office through the vast window behind Jefferson prevented her from seeing him properly until he was within a few yards of her. When she did so, she couldn't help a start of surprise. She had somehow envisioned the boss of such an empire to be an elderly, cigar-smoking man with a pot-belly, grown fat and slug-sleek out of his business deals. But this man was surely straight out of a Hollywood movie, tall, lean and handsome, and looking her over now with amusement in his fathomless dark eyes.

She felt her mouth go dry, and she had to force herself to speak.

"I'm sorry. I didn't mean to sound so fatuous—"

"On the contrary, it was delivered with such taste that I could hardly disbelieve any of it. So tell me, Miss Forster, are you as wonderful a find as you sound?"

She looked up into his face, unsure how to answer that. He had a typical LA suntan, and a wide, generous mouth with typically even LA teeth. And she was becoming as cynical as Gracie . . . but dear God, here was star quality if she ever saw it, she found herself thinking faintly, as least as far as looks were concerned.

"I don't know how to answer that, sir," she said at last. "I'm just – well, myself, I suppose."

"And God forbid that they should ever change you," she thought she heard him say beneath his breath. But since she had no idea who *they* were, nor if she had heard him right, she didn't answer.

"So you want to work for me, do you? So I suggest that we both sit down and find out if we like one another well enough for that," Jefferson said now, motioning her to sit on one of the leather sofas at one side of the office, while he sat on another at right angles to it. She realized that Miss Simpson had retreated out of the office by now, and she hadn't even seen her leave.

But her heart leapt at his words, because perhaps she hadn't botched everything after all. The thought was borne out a few minutes later, when Miss Simpson returned with a tray of coffee that she put on the long occasional table between the sofas, and disappeared just as silently after being told by Jefferson to put all his calls on hold until tomorrow.

Presumably she had passed all the secretarial tests, and now it was down to personality and compatibility. It seemed a bit bizarre to go to all this trouble for just another secretary, which translated into English simply meant another typist . . . and now that she had seen the style of the place, she doubted that the underlings came into contact with Jefferson much at all.

"So tell me all about Miss Rose Forster," he said, handing Rose a cup of freshly-brewed coffee that smelled and tasted like nectar. She gave an embarrassed laugh.

"Don't you know that's just the kind of remark to make me forget everything immediately?" she said, and then thought how silly that sounded, when it was obvious that he wasn't asking her out of mere politeness, but needed to assess whether or not a prospective employee was going to come up to his high standards. "I'm sorry—"

"Don't be. You're refreshingly honest, Rose. And please stop saying sorry. You've nothing to be sorry for."

His use of her first name startled her. He didn't ask for the liberty, he just took it. She sensed that he was that kind of man. He simply took what he wanted. At the unexpectedly erotic implication of her own thoughts, her hands felt sticky inside her cotton gloves.

"I was brought up to be honest, sir," she murmured, not knowing how else to answer him, though she was secretly appalled to know how naïve she sounded. But this was her first major chance at a job, and she had no yardstick by which to measure whether or not she was behaving correctly.

"I like that. It's a rare commodity in this town."

"Is it?"

He had caught her attention now, and he gave a wry smile. Laughter lines at the corners of his eyes fanned out attractively whenever he smiled, and she was beginning to be overwhelmed by the fact that they were sitting here so cosily, drinking coffee, and that the time was going relentlessly on. A surreptitious glance at the clock on the wall showed that it was already well past six o'clock. Gracie would be wondering where she had got to. . . .

"How long have you been in LA, Rose?"

"Only a few weeks – and I dare say it shows." As she said it she laughed self-consciously.

"A little. So you won't have been here long enough to see all the corruption in our glittering town. I hope it never touches you."

"That's rather an odd thing to say, Mr Jefferson," Rose said without thinking. "Why should it touch me?"

"By its very nature, corruption has a habit of tainting everything young and fresh and pure," he said enigmatically, and Rose felt herself blush to the roots of her hair. She presumed it was meant to be a compliment, but dear Lord, it made her sound such a simpleton.

"I'm eighteen – almost," she said indignantly.

Jefferson laughed out loud, throwing his head back as if she had said something extraordinarily witty.

"Oh Rose, you do me a power of good. So you're eighteen – almost. But I'd bet every silver dollar in the Corporation's coffers that the rest of my words apply to you."

"I can't remember them," she lied.

"Yes you can. I called you young and fresh and pure. So you're not a babe in arms. How about the rest of it?"

Rose began to hear warning bells ringing in her head. What was that expression Gracie had used? The casting couch system? She'd said it in reference to getting into the movies, but it could apply just as well anywhere.

And here she was, alone in this vast office with a powerfully attractive man she'd never met before. He'd told his secretary to put all his calls on hold until tomorrow, and for all she knew the entire office building might be empty by now, except for the two of them sitting cosily together on matching leather sofas . . . and he was as good as asking her if she was still a virgin.

The almost-taboo word slid into her mind. And with

it came the insult of the question. Because of *course* she damn well was!

She replaced her cup on its saucer with a clatter, forgetting any etiquette she'd ever been taught. She spoke with quiet dignity.

"If there's nothing else you need to know about me, Mr Jefferson, I think I should be leaving."

He leaned back on the soft pungent leather of the sofa, his arms behind his head. His suit was perfectly-cut, and the exquisite material certainly hadn't come off Burton's ready-to-wear rack, Rose thought inconsequentially.

"I'd like to know everything there is to know about you, Rose Forster, and I'm loath to let you go, in case you take flight and I never see you again."

"Is this the way you always interview secretaries, sir?" she said stiffly. "I'm sorry. I know I'm unlikely to get the job now, and nor do I want it, but perhaps I could give you a bit of advice—"

She stopped, listening to herself in horror. What the Dickens was she doing, daring to speak to Bradley Piers Jefferson the third like that? But she was emboldened by the fact that once she walked out of here, she was never likely to come back.

"Go on," he said, full of amused indulgence.

"Well, I don't think you should make that kind of statement to anyone on such short acquaintance. Maybe the other girls who applied for the job aren't so – well, reserved as I am, and maybe I should take lessons from them, but it's going much too fast for my taste – and – and, well – well, *goodbye!*"

She suddenly took fright at the way he was just sitting perfectly still and saying nothing at all while she blathered on. She stood up quickly, but he was quicker. He caught hold of her wrists as she was about to head for the door, which suddenly seemed a million miles away.

"I'm the one who should be apologizing. And you don't

46

need to take lessons from anyone. As for your taste – you stand head and shoulders above anyone else who ever came into my office, gushing and fawning in the hope of earning a buck. The job's yours, if you want it – but on one condition."

"Oh? And what's that?" Rose said faintly.

"I want to make amends for treating you like a starlet instead of a lady, so let me take you out for dinner."

"I don't know. Is that ethical?" she said.

"What's not ethical about it?" he said, still amused, but with a hint of impatience. "I want you to have dinner with me so I can go on listening to that beautiful English voice of yours, and all you have to say is yes. So, what do you say?"

Nobody had ever called her voice beautiful before. After all, it was just a voice. . . .

"I say yes," she said huskily, before she could change her mind.

"I didn't think you meant right *now*!" Rose said in alarm. They were being whisked twenty-seven flights down to the ground floor in the silent elevator that operated right out of Jefferson's office, so that they didn't even need to see anyone else at all. She was almost surprised to see that it was still daylight, since she felt as though she'd travelled a hundred years since first meeting him.

"What's wrong with now? Aren't you hungry?" He leaned back against the padded wall of the elevator, dominating the space inside it, and she dare not let herself remember that she was literally trapped in here with him. Nor to think that there might be another meaning behind his words.

Hungry for what?

"It does seem a long time since I've eaten anything," she said as coolly as she could manage. "But I should let my sister know what's happening—"

"You're not a kid any more, Rose. You should learn to cut the apron strings and live a little," he said, in a softer voice that made her heart give a sudden lurch.

"It's just that I wouldn't want her to worry—"

Jefferson nodded. "OK. When we get to the restaurant I'll have Alberto call her and tell her you're out to dinner, and you'll be taken home later. Will that do?"

"Thank you," she said, having no idea who Alberto was.

She discovered his identity half an hour later when she walked into the dimly-lit restaurant high in the Hollywood hills on Jefferson's arm. By then, she was so tongue-tied she was sure she wouldn't be able to open her mouth to eat a thing. The elevator at the Jefferson building had taken them straight to the car parking area, and a sleek limousine had been brought round immediately by an efficient flunkey, reminding her of the work that Merv did.

Jefferson had driven them out of the city to the elegant restaurant where they sat now in a secluded alcove, and she had given Gracie's number to Alberto, the flamboyant owner of the restaurant, who promised to deliver the message personally. It didn't take much to know how important a customer he considered Jefferson, she noted.

"I should really have spoken to her myself," Rose said uneasily, wondering what reaction Alberto was going to get.

"When you've been in this town a little longer, Rose, you'll learn to do as little as possible for yourself, as long as there's somebody else to do it for you," Jefferson said.

She stared at him, and then stared at the other patrons of the restaurant. She felt so incongruous in her English travelling suit, when all around her there were elegant women in furs and jewels, even though it was so early in the evening – and more than one of them glanced at Jefferson in a way that could only be described as blatant. But his words sent the bubbling laughter to her lips.

"That's rich, isn't it, since I'm about to be hired to be at your beck and call – sir?" she said in a low voice.

He laughed back, seeing the irony in it, and as he did so, he put his hand over hers where it lay on the cream damask table cloth.

It was a brief, intimate contact, and despite the fact that she hadn't yet removed her gloves, it was enough to fill Rose with a sweet wild excitement she had never known before.

Chapter Four

It was nearly nine o'clock by the time Jefferson's limousine drew to a stop outside the Hacketts' apartment building. A superb dinner and sparkling conversation had held all Rose's attention, and the wine and the ambience had certainly gone to her head. So much so that she hardly even worried about Gracie's reaction to her late arrival home. After all, Alberto would have explained the situation.

She hadn't even felt unduly embarrassed at giving Jefferson directions, though she had seen his raised eyebrows when she gave him the address. By now she was well aware that it wasn't on the best side of town. But now that she was about to get out of the car, she felt gauche and tongue-tied.

"Thank you for a lovely evening," she said at last.

"It was my pleasure. And you'll be hearing from Miss Simpson officially in a day or two, and we'll get that work permit sorted out for you immediately."

"Oh – oh, of course. Yes. Thank you."

She couldn't seem to stop the staccato words tripping out. Business matters were in the foreground again, when for the last few hours she had regaled him with stories about her childhood and the Welsh valleys and Mam Pritchard, and he'd seemed to listen attentively enough. But she was hot with embarrassment now, wondering if he had thought her extremely stupid, or pathetically homesick.

Because suddenly they were two strangers again. He

was a man of some stature in this town, and she was the little *ingénue*, and he was telling her briskly that his secretary would be writing to her in a couple of days to offer her a job. . . .

She mumbled good-night and got out of the car quickly, closing the door behind her. It shut with a small click, instead of the noisy slams that Merv's Chevy needed. The limo moved off into the night with hardly a murmur, and Rose turned to go inside the building. Lights were going on all over LA by now, but the apartment was in semi-darkness. With any luck, Gracie was upstairs visiting with Mrs Olsen, Rose thought hopefully. The disreputable old Chevy wasn't parked outside, so thankfully Merv wasn't home yet. . . .

"Where the hell have you been until this hour?"

A screeching voice came at her out of the gloom of the parlour, and suddenly the room was full of noise as Gracie leapt up out of the chair where she'd been dozing.

Rose jumped, defensive at once. "You know where I've been. Didn't you get a message . . .?"

"Oh, sure I got a message, from some greaseball Eyetie or other, telling me Miss Forster was dining out and would be brought safely home. What was I supposed to make of that, when you told me you were going for a job interview at four-thirty this afternoon? So what the hell have you been doing all this time, you slut?"

Rose gasped, recoiling as if Gracie had hit her. Her face felt on fire, and all her pleasure in the evening vanished. She was suddenly a kid again, with her superior sister crowing over her and making her feel even smaller than she was. . . .

She was aware of the door of the Chevy doing its usual three slams, and then Merv came storming inside.

"So she's back, is she? Next time you want me to go chasing after her, make sure you know where the bloody restaurant is," he shouted at Gracie.

51

She rounded on him at once. "Don't start on at me, you bum! She's the one who's heading for trouble, not me!"

There was a sudden hammering on the ceiling from the apartment above. Several windows were flung open and abuse was being hurled down at the ground floor apartment.

Merv opened the parlour window and stuck his head out, yelling back.

"Up yours, buddy!"

He slammed the window shut again, and turned to glare at Rose. "Well? What do you have to say for yourself, kid?"

She shook so much she could hardly say anything. When she did, the words came out in a series of choking gasps.

"I think you're both pigs! You've spoiled everything. Mr Jefferson was very nice to me and took me out to dinner—"

"And any idiot knows what that means!" Merv yelled. "Next time he'll be in your knickers, and don't say I didn't warn you."

Rose clutched her handbag tightly to her chest. She had never loathed him more for spoiling her beautiful evening. And Gracie was no better, ready to think the worst of her without giving her a chance to explain. . . .

"I'm going to bed," she choked out. "And tomorrow I'll be looking for somewhere else to live."

She rushed from the room before giving either of them a chance to say anything more. She stripped off all her clothes and washed her face and hands in the wash-basin in the corner of her room, as if she could scrub away all the shaming things Gracie and Merv had said to her.

Then she crawled into bed, and closed her eyes tightly, shutting out the night and making her mind a blank. She wouldn't think of anything, then nothing could upset her. It was a little trick a lonely child in an unfamiliar Welsh terraced-house had learned, in the awful days when she hadn't known what was happening to her family in the London blitz.

"I've brought you a cup of tea, our Rose," she heard Gracie say. She opened her eyes a fraction to discover that it was morning. As her sister went on speaking, she registered that her voice was cautious and contrite.

"We were wrong to go on so at you last night, Rose, and we're sorry. But you don't know this town yet, and me and Merv were only looking out for you."

"Maybe you were," Rose said, sitting up slowly. "But you seem to forget that I'm not a baby any more, Gracie, and I'm not going to be treated like one. I'm a grown woman now, and I can make my own decisions."

"But you're not really thinking of finding your own place to live, are you, Rose? I'd think I'd failed you if you did that—"

"I didn't think you'd care," Rose muttered, suspicious of this new Gracie.

"Well, of course I do, and so does Merv." She smiled ingratiatingly and didn't notice Rose wince at the thought of Merv caring for her. "And if you get this job at Jefferson's and start making good money, well, maybe we can do up your room a bit more, and get some nice new chairs in the parlour so you won't be ashamed to bring anybody home. . . ."

It was suddenly all clear to Rose. They didn't really want her, but they wanted the little extras she could bring their way, once she was earning a good salary. It was transparent and pathetic. She slid her legs out of the bed and fiddled them into her slippers before heading out of the bedroom to the bathroom.

"I still think it will be best if I look for somewhere else," she said. "I may put an ad in the newspaper to see if anybody's wanting a room-mate."

The idea seemed to be ready-formed in her mind before she even said it. The telephone operator had begun it, and tracing down the hundreds of ads of all descriptions in the *Los Angeles Sentinel* had underlined it. It seemed that you could advertise for anything in LA, including room-mates. She heard Gracie's annoyed voice following her down the passage.

"You want to be careful about newspaper ads, honey. You never know where you're going to end up, if you don't know your way around. And in any case, we'd have the last word on it. You're a long way from being twenty-one yet, and we're responsible for you. What would your precious Mam Pritchard say if we threw you to the wolves?"

It was her trump card, and said with a kind of triumph. Which struck Rose as odd, since she more than suspected neither Gracie nor Merv had really wanted her here, otherwise they'd never have taken so long in sending for her. It was obvious that Gracie thought her the dumbest thing ever to cross the pond. She wondered for a moment if her sister had ever been this naïve when she first arrived here. But she'd have had her Yank by her side, of course, and she was already married. She had a status. While Rose did not.

She refused to worry her head about it any more. She had a job (almost), and a boss who put Clark Gable in the shade . . . she drew in her breath as she slammed the bolt of the bathroom door behind her. A fat lot of good it was going to do her if she started getting moony-eyed over Bradley Piers Jefferson the third! She'd do far better to remember what Gracie had said, and to accept that Gracie had been here far longer than she had, and knew these Yanks far better than she did. And maybe even a Bradley Piers Jefferson the third would be only after one thing too, and she would be no more than a deep English notch on his bedpost. . . .

She shivered, remembering for a moment when his hand had covered hers in the intimacy of the restaurant. Such a small touch, not even a caress, and yet the memory of it remained in her mind. She wasn't the type to be swept off her feet by a man, or she didn't think she was. But how could she know? It had never happened before. She had never been in this kind of town before, or in this kind of world, and if she was momentarily dazzled by it all, who could blame her?

"*Just you mind yourself, now, girl,*" Mam Pritchard had warned ambiguously before Rose left her to board the boat for America. "*You know what I mean, I dare say. You've got brains in that head of yours, I'll give you that, so use 'em wisely, and don't go getting into trouble, there's a good girl.*"

Rose waited in fever of suspense for the letter with the embossed crest in the corner of the envelope to arrive, choosing to ignore Merv's crass taunts that she'd be lucky to hear from the guy again now he'd seen the outside of the tumbledown apartment building.

They didn't have normal letter boxes as they did in England. There was a series of tin boxes stuck on posts at the end of the yard (you didn't say garden), each with the surname of the occupant painted on it, and the mailman merely stuffed the letters inside the appropriate one. No matter how often she watched and waited, and rushed down to the Hacketts' box, Rose was convinced that the letter must have gone astray, and that someone in another apartment had looked at her unfamiliar name, and simply dumped it as trash.

"You'll wear those boards out soon. You're worse than a cat on heat," Gracie snapped inelegantly on the third day, as she paced up and down on the porch around the time when the mailman was due.

Rose didn't deign to answer this. Gracie had never been

this coarse, or at least, she didn't remember her so. It was living with Merv that did it. Everything was reduced to basics as far as he was concerned.

Then she stopped caring about either of them as the mailman's van trundled up the hill and stopped at their yard. She flew down the path to meet him, and had to wait impatiently while he pushed some junk mail in Mrs Olsen's box, and a similar pile of circulars in the other tenants'.

"Is there anything for me today?" Rose said, trying not to sound breathless. The guy grinned at her, his eyes taking in her slim figure and her anxious blue eyes, and she was sure he was deliberately teasing her by keeping the Hacketts' box until last.

"Might be, girlie, but you know I ain't permitted to hand the mail over. It has to go inside the box, see?"

Infuriatingly, he seemed to take an age stuffing all the letters through, and then he whistled coolly as he got back in his van and drove away in a cloud of dust. Rose coughed, thinking incongruously that she would always know when she was in this particular part of LA by the dry, tainted smell of the dust.

But she had more important things on her mind, and she whipped out the letters quickly. Gracie and Merv rarely got letters now that Rose was living with them, and at first it seemed that there were only the usual circulars, and various offers to make yourself rich by subscribing to firms with dubious-sounding names. That was all, except one. One slim letter amongst all the others had the crest of the Jefferson Printing Corporation printed in gold lettering on the expensive-looking envelope, and Rose hugged it to her chest for a moment, as tenderly as if it was a lover.

"Ain't you going to open it then?" she heard Gracie call. "For Gawd's sake put us out of our misery, gel."

For a moment, the old East End accent was back in Gracie's voice, smothering the Yankee twang. It made

56

Rose think her sister was as keen for her to get on in the world, as people said, as she was herself. She grinned, waving the envelope as she rushed back to the porch where Gracie sprawled out on a canvas chair.

"I'm nearly afraid to look," she said.

Gracie snorted. "Don't be so damn feeble. After the way the toff splashed out on you the other night, he ain't going to let you go now!"

"I wish you wouldn't put it like that, Gracie," Rose said crossly, her fingers feeling all thumbs as she tore open the envelope and let the typed words dance in front of her eyes. Then she gasped.

"What is it? He ain't let you down, has he?" Gracie said sharply. "The bum! But didn't I tell you these flash guys are only out for what they can get . . .?"

"It's not that. It's a formal letter from Miss Simpson, his personal assistant. I'm being offered a temporary secretarial post, but then . . ." she gulped.

"What? *What*?"

"Miss Simpson says she's retiring at Christmas, and that if my secretarial work proves satisfactory, Mr Jefferson might add my name to the other applicants for the post."

"Good God. That means he definitely fancies you," Gracie said flatly. "I knew it."

Rose was more concerned with the churning in her stomach than her sister's snide comments.

"How could I possibly become personal assistant to the head of an international businessman! I don't have the experience – and what would all the other girls in the company think? They'll be at my throat!"

Gracie began to laugh. "Well, you'll just have to put on your best English voice, ducks, and tell them where to put their pencils!"

"You would say something like that. It's not funny, Gracie—"

"I should just say it's not," she said, suddenly angry. "You're being offered a plum job on a plate the minute you've stepped off the boat. Everybody wants to make money in this town, and here you are, having bloody cold feet about it. What the hell's wrong with you?"

Rose glared at her, knowing she didn't understand a damn thing about the way she felt. They were poles apart and always had been.

"You're not going to turn it down, are you?" Gracie persisted.

"Why? Are you worried about the chance of getting new chairs for the parlour disappearing?" she said, oozing unusual sarcasm.

"No," Gracie said. "I'm worried that you'll turn down the chance of a respectable job, despite this Jefferson's fancy for you, in favour of trying to get in the movies. Don't think I ain't seen the look in your eyes whenever Merv mentions anything about it."

"Would that be so awful?" Rose said, touched in spite of herself, at this apparently sincere concern.

To her surprise, Gracie leaned forward and smoothed the shining sleekness of her hair.

"Oh Rose, honey, you've got no idea how these gals can be exploited, and I don't want that to happen to you. I know I've been bloody neglectful in getting you to LA, but now that you're here, I do want to take care of you. It's what Mum and Dad would have expected."

It was hitting well below the belt, and both of them knew it, but Rose couldn't be bothered to argue any more. She'd got the precious letter, and she was starting work the very next week. As for the PA's job, well, she could consider it or not, she supposed. Miss Simpson wasn't retiring until Christmas, so that gave her more than four months to settle in and see how she liked working for Bradley Piers Jefferson the third, and for the other secretaries to get used to her. Her nerves began to settle into their normal grooves, and she gave a slow nod.

"Of course I'll be taking the job, and I'll be glad to be paying my way, Gracie. I owe you so much."

She looked down at the precious letter as she spoke, hoping that Gracie wouldn't detect the irony in her voice. But she couldn't help it. Gracie had always built up the glamour of her life in LA and the home she and Merv shared, and to Rose the reality of it was as ugly as the Welsh slag heaps that ravaged the unspoiled beauty of the valleys.

Merv wasn't working that night, and declared that they must go out and celebrate at Sea-Food Joe's, since it was one of Gracie's favourite eating-houses. Nobody asked Rose about her preference, despite the fact that it was her job they were celebrating. She might have resented it, if it had seemed worth the bother. But it didn't.

The salary the Jefferson Printing Corporation had quoted in their letter had been enough to make her eyes sparkle, and already she was dreaming of the amount she could put away each week towards better clothes and a share in an apartment. Nothing was going to deter her from her plans, but for now, she was quite prepared to indulge Gracie and Merv in their meagre ideas of celebrating, and the bawling greetings from their friends.

"So how's the little lady gettin' on?" she heard the one called Chuck Bernstein say. There were the same faces as before, and Rose wondered if they had shares in the place, or if they just permanently propped up the food counter.

"She's doin' just fine," Merv said, before she could say a word. "Landed herself a peachy job with no trouble at all, so you better just mind yourself when you talk to her from now on, Chuck."

"Is that so?" he said thoughtfully, swivelling around on his stool to inspect Rose more closely. "Well, that could be a pity. With her classy looks, I heard about summat she could've found real interesting, but mebbe she'd be too high and mighty for it now," he finished with a leering grin.

"Our Rose wouldn't be interested in any of your get-rich-quick schemes," Gracie told him sharply. "She's a respectable girl, so you just keep your ideas to yourself."

"Now then, woman, don't go off half-cocked. We could at least hear him out," Merv said tetchily, just as Rose half-suspected he would. "Come and sit with us, Chuck, and have a beer."

As the man slid off the bar stool and sauntered over, Rose hissed at Gracie.

"Why did he ask him over? I don't like him, and I'm not interested in anything he might have in mind."

"A good thing too," Gracie snapped. "But you know Merv. He won't let a thing go until he's heard it all. He's like a cat with a mouse in that respect."

Rose stared straight ahead as if the hawk-nosed Jew hadn't joined them, though from the waft of scent on his clothes, she was aware of the minute he sat down. Scent on a man was almost worse than the salty tang of Merv's body odours, she thought in some disgust. But she discovered she couldn't ignore either of them for long.

"I thought of your gal as soon as I saw the ads for a beauty pageant coming up in December," Chuck said importantly. "Miss Christmas Angel pageant it's called, and I reckon your gal here would win it hands down. There's also a prize of five hundred dollars, and maybe a movie test."

Rose's head seemed to move ever so slowly as she turned to stare at the weasly little man. She heard Gracie click her teeth in annoyance, and even Merv looked dubious, though his eyes narrowed speculatively.

"A beauty pageant, you say?"

"Sure, you know the kind of thing. The gals parade in front of an audience and a panel of judges until they choose the final five, and then the winner's crowned. Even if your Rose didn't win, it'd be good exposure, but I'd have no doubts about her chances—"

"What do you mean by exposure?" Gracie said sharply.

Rose looked from one to the other enquiringly, feeling totally detached, as if this conversation had nothing to do with her at all. They were crazy, the lot of them, and she certainly had no intention of parading in a beauty pageant. For a start, what the Dickens would Bradley Piers Jefferson the third have to say about such a thing! She had no idea why his name came into her head at that moment, nor why the disapproving faces of Mam Pritchard and her boyos should so quickly replace Jefferson's image in her mind.

"You know the score as well as I do, Gracie," Chuck Bernstein was saying. "You've seen the pictures of the winnin' lovelies in the newspapers—"

"Yes, and no sister of mine is going to strut about in a bathing suit for old leches like you to drool over!"

"Now, just hold on a God-damned minute, Gracie," Merv said, putting a large hand over her arm. "There ain't no harm in hearing what Chuck's got to say, and he's always got his nose nearer to money-making grindstones than you or me."

As if she had been holding her breath all this time while the three of them argued over her, Rose seemed to find her voice at that moment.

"Well, you can all forget it," she said, every bit as snooty as the young Princess Margaret Rose she was named after. "Nobody's getting me to parade around in a bathing suit in public, so there."

But although her voice was pure cut-glass snob, she

61

still felt as though she was symbolically sticking out her tongue at the lot of them.

"Ain't that what I've just been saying, our Rose?" Gracie snapped, glaring at her as if she was practically undressing there and then.

"You and me will get our heads together and talk later, Chuck," Merv said meaningfully, seeing how the womenfolk were ganging up on him.

"It won't make any difference," Rose began, suddenly nervous as his gaze raked her. She fancied she could see dollar signs flashing in those cold eyes, and felt a sudden chill, knowing he had the power to turn her out of his house if she didn't play by his rules.

Suddenly, she felt totally out of her depth in this town where money talked louder than decent feelings. She felt a ludicrous longing to be safe back home in the valley, listening to Mam Pritchard's voice intoning that it was as much of a sin to lust after money as to let the merest thought of the sins of the flesh enter a young girl's head.

"I'll look out for you in a coupla days then, Merv."

Chuck evidently realized he had outstayed his welcome at the corner table, and moved away. Slithered, more like, Rose thought, hating the very sight of the man. What was he, for heaven's sake? Was he simply a spiv, or even worse, was he one of those pimps, whose name she had only just discovered in one of the sleazy magazines Merv left lying around at the apartment?

"Take no notice, Rose, love," Gracie said, more kindly than before. "He don't mean any real harm, and I know you've got your head screwed on the right way."

Rose kept her head bent low as Sea-Food Joe brought the obscenely-heaped supper plates to their table. Such quantities would feed half of Pontyrowan Infants School, she thought inconsequentially.

But it served to hide her somewhat darker thoughts.

62

For what did Gracie know of her at all? she wondered. What did her sister know of the little thrill of excitement that had raced through, just for a moment, as she pictured herself being crowned as Miss Christmas Angel, with her picture in the *Los Angeles Sentinel* and various other newspapers? Maybe it would even appear in the movie magazines, where some casting director might just look at her image in her bathing suit and decide she was exactly the undiscovered star he was seeking for his next movie. . . .

"Good, ain't it?" she heard Merv say with relish as he attacked the enormous lobster on his plate.

"It's very good," she murmured, knowing that at least she could agree with that, as long as she tried not to notice the slobbery way Merv ate. She tried not to compare it all with the gentility of Alberto's Italian restaurant, but even being a snob was preferable to being a slob.

"What're you smiling at?" Merv asked now.

"You wouldn't be interested," Rose said airily. "I was sort of composing a little poem in my head."

Snob versus slob. . . .

"Gee, there's no end to the babe's talent, is there?" Merv said mockingly. "Don't forget to mention that you write poetry to the beauty pageant judges, hon. It'll go down a treat compared with some of the air-heads who'll be entering."

"I told you, I'm not *doing* it," Rose said, but she was talking to herself now, because Merv had already lost interest in all but tackling his food.

When she went to bed that evening, she decided to write to Evan Pritchard. She'd promised that she would, though she didn't really know why, nor why he'd wanted her to write to him, when he'd hear all her news from her letters to his Mam. They hadn't been specially close, but she'd always preferred him to his brother Dai. Evan was the more thoughtful and intelligent of the two, while Dai was a scatterbrain who could never keep anything to himself. If he heard any gossip or scandal, he crowed about it to anybody who would listen. He always liked to be cock of the heap. He was fun to be with, but it had always been to Evan that Rose had run with scratched knees or a horrible bout of homesickness.

For a moment she had a vision of herself, bewildered, no more than seven years old, being escorted from the train by the welfare lady to the tiny terraced-house in the row of identical linked houses in the Welsh valley, and seeing all the other scared evacuees taken to their appointed places of refuge, clutching cardboard suitcases or brown paper bags with all their belongings, each with their gas mask in its cardbox box slung over their shoulders.

How scared she had been, how alone and how frightened, and how big and dark the two boyos had seemed to her then. The welfare lady had told her firmly that she must think of them as her new *brothers*, and Rose hadn't missed Mam Pritchard's pursed lips at the familiarity. Even then, she'd sensed that she'd have to fight to win Mam's approval before she unbent enough to think of Rose as part of *her* family.

She reached for her writing case, already half-composing the letter to Evan in her mind. But how pathetic she was becoming, she thought angrily. Feeling a tug of longing for the likes of Evan Pritchard was the last thing she wanted to do. She was already over the brink of this dazzling new life, and who knew where it might lead? She dismissed the thought of the Miss Christmas Angel beauty pageant, but she couldn't dismiss the thought of Bradley Piers Jefferson the third, and the warmth in his dark eyes when he smiled at her.

"Damn them all," Rose said out loud. "They complicate the whole damn issue!"

"Who're you talking to in there, our Rose?" came Gracie's suspicious voice from the floor below.

The temptation to yell out that she had a dozen adoring men in her room was almost irresistible, but Gracie didn't have much sense of humour, and she wouldn't appreciate being made a fool of when she inevitably came to see for herself. But Rose waited too long before answering, and the next minute her door was flung open.

"Are you all right?" Gracie asked, her eyes taking in every corner of the room.

"Of course I am. Did you think I could sneak a bloke in here under Merv's eagle eyes? I wouldn't want to, anyway. In fact I was grumbling out loud about the whole damn lot of them, if you must know, and wondering why we had to have them around at all!"

Gracie stared at her as if she was cracked in the head, and then burst out laughing.

"My God, what's got into you tonight? A fat lot of good we'd be without men around, kid, and don't you forget it. They have plenty of other uses as well as bein' meal tickets, if you get my meanin'."

She gave a huge wink, and Rose squirmed at the innuendo.

"What's got your ass on fire, anyway?" Gracie went on. "Was it all that beauty pageant talk? Forget it, Rose. You wouldn't want to put yourself up against some of those professional gals who do the circuits of the pageants. You only have to look at the way they make up to the judges to know how they make most of their money."

"What do you mean?"

"Don't ask," Gracie said, bored with the conversation. "Just you have nothing to do with it, and you'll be OK."

She slouched out of the room, leaving Rose unsettled and full of a resentment she didn't quite understand. It was obvious that Gracie didn't want her entering any beauty pageant. Gracie wouldn't want to see the little sister fêted and showered with money and prizes, just for being beautiful. And it was perfectly obvious to Rose that sibling rivalry was still alive and well, and living in LA.

And then, as perversely as a child, the more she thought about Gracie's objections, the more insidiously Rose knew it was exactly what she was going to do.

Chapter Five

'Dear Evan,' she began.

'Well, I promised to write and tell you something about Los Angeles, so here I am. Evan, you wouldn't believe the difference between the rich and the poor here. Everybody's supposed to be equal, but you wouldn't really believe that if you were here. I know that nobody back home thinks anybody in America is poor, but even here in LA, there are the huge mansions of the movie stars and the men who grow fat on them, and then there's the rest, who live in squalor and scratch a living where they can.

In case I'm alarming you by saying that, I'd better qualify it quickly, or you'll be on the next boat to bring me home. Gracie and Merv don't live like movie stars, but they don't live in squalor either. Merv has a steady job and a big car, and although they don't own an entire house, the apartment is quite nice. The building's on the side of a hill, so we can look down and see the city from here. It's very pretty at night, with all the lights twinkling like stars.'

She didn't add that the hill was on the wrong side of town, or that the steady job and the big old car were nothing to brag about. She had too much pride to admit such things to Evan. She didn't tell him about the beauty pageant either. He'd be sure to disapprove. Nice girls didn't parade about in bathing suits for a line of men to ogle. . . .

'I've got a job now, Evan. I start on Monday, and by the time you get this letter I shall be quite used to it. It's a bit scary, as it's in a huge skyscraper building downtown. I'll be working on the 25th floor of the Jefferson Printing Corporation, and I'll just be a typist at first, though they call everybody a secretary here. But after Christmas, I might get a better job as personal assistant. Not bad, eh?

And don't laugh, but I do believe it was my plummy college accent that finally swung it. They really go for that over here. I know my shorthand and typing was OK, but I dare say the other girls up for interviews thought the same. And they all looked so much more sophisticated than me. I felt a real ugly duckling compared with some of those swans!'

It was a lie, and she didn't know why she wrote it. She hadn't felt ugly at all, just gauche and nervous. But she felt the need to put herself down a little, so that Evan wouldn't think she was getting swollen-headed over this marvellous new job and all the opportunities that were coming her way. She still needed the approval of her brother.

For a moment, she imagined him here, in this strange, exciting environment that she was slowly getting used to. She knew it would take someone like Evan far longer. She pictured him, twenty-two years old, large and broad-shouldered, and tall for a Welshman from the valleys, his dark hair always unruly no matter how much he tried to tame it, and dark eyes that were often unfathomable. Bradley Piers Jefferson the third had dark eyes too, but his were exciting eyes, while Evan's were simply kind.

Other than a certain comparison of colouring, however, she knew they were poles apart. But just thinking about Evan's kindness gave her a warm little glow. He'd had a way of soothing a bewildered kid from London's East End

68

that his po-faced Mam never mastered, and his brother Dai couldn't be bothered with, and preferred to mock Evan for being too soft with poor little Rosie-Posie.

But he wasn't soft. It took a strong man to ignore the jibes of a brother who was more popular with the local girls than himself, a brother who laughed and joked a lot, and preferred being the life and soul of the party to bothering with schoolwork. Rose felt a sharp and unexpected rush of affection for Evan, for if ever there was someone she could confide in, it was him.

She smiled ruefully. For God's sake, she'd had plenty of opportunity to confide in him before, and she hadn't taken it. Why think about such things now, when he was thousands of miles away? But she could still do so in her letters, and she could probably open up her heart more easily at a distance if the need arose. Evan had always been her prop, and still was, she decided. She bent her head and continued with her letter.

'You probably think I'm being daft, and you can tell me so, if you like. Just write anything at all. I want to hear about everything back home, and all about Dai's goings-on, since I know he'll never bother to write!

I'd better stop now, but just writing to my big brother gives me comfort.'

Rose stared at the last sentence, and immediately scratched it out. They were the words of a pathetic old woman, not an almost-eighteen-year-old beginning a wonderful new life in the city of her dreams. She wrote instead:

'I'd better stop now, so just you write soon, you hear? I miss my big brother.'

Dear Lord, that was just as bad. Rose screwed up the

entire letter and began again, leaving out anything that seemed the slightest bit sentimental. Her only concession was to scrawl a short row of kisses at the end. She sealed it quickly before she changed anything else, and took it down to the mailbox at the end of the yard.

"Where do you get entry forms for this beauty pageant, then?" she asked Merv casually over supper the next evening.

He spluttered over his mug of coffee – his favourite army issue mug that had never seen the inside of a barracks since Merv was demobbed, or whatever they called it here – and wiped his chin with his bare arm. Rose managed to resist showing her disgust, and waited for the uproar she knew was to come when Gracie brought the food to the table.

She didn't have to wait long. Even before Merv could answer, there was a screech from the kitchen, and the next minute Gracie had dumped the plates on the table and was glaring at her sister.

"You ain't falling for that caper, are you, our Rose? I've already told you, you'll just be asking for trouble—"

"Maybe our Rose's thinking she'll get noticed by one of the movie scouts who go to these pageants," Merv said slyly. "Is that it, hon?"

Rose shrugged, her heart hammering uncomfortably at the leer in his eyes, but knowing she had to see it through now.

"Maybe," she said, as if it didn't really matter a damn to her. "It just seems like a good way of getting some extra money, if I was to win, and I could put it towards moving into my own apartment someday."

"There's no need to worry about that," Gracie said, with a complete about-face.

"I'll tell you what," Merv said. "How about if I find out all I can about it, and if Rose feels she wants to enter

70

for it, then I'll act as her manager, and see that she comes to no harm. Whaddaya say?"

"And who the hell's going to be watching you?" Gracie snapped back. "And what the hell do you think your tight-arsed Mam Pritchard would have to say about you parading yourself in next to nothing like a tart?"

Rose flinched at her crudity. As far as she was concerned, any glamour in Gracie marrying her Yank had long disappeared, and there was nothing left but a rather seedy couple living on the wrong side of town. It was a pity she hadn't known the truth of it before she came out here. . . . She caught her thoughts up short, shocked at herself. Because it wasn't just her sister's good fortune that had made Rose long to be part of that life. It was the draw of LA itself, and the hopes and dreams that were played out in the movies, in the tinseltown of the rich and famous. . . .

Sometimes, she stood back a little, and looked at herself, and knew she was a fool for being so dazzled by it all. She knew it wasn't real, and that dreams were for children. But against all that, was the indisputable fact that movie stars had been discovered in all kinds of unlikely places, and fortunes could be made, if some producer had faith enough in you. She stared at Gracie coldly.

"Well, at least I shall never behave like a tart, and that's the most important thing, isn't it?"

In her haste and nervousness, she heard the occasional little Welsh lilt give a lift to her final words, and she bit her lip in annoyance.

"Well, I'll have nothing to do with it," Gracie said. "If you want to go ahead, I suppose I can't stop you—"

"And I'll be watching out for her," Merv said magnanimously. "I'll see about getting that entry form for you, Rose, and then you can just leave the details to me."

She wilted as Gracie began lashing out helpings of what she called her special chicken stew, which was really a mixture of last night's leftovers and a few more vegetables and stock added to it. Most of the chicken flavour had been boiled out of it by now, and it was dreary and unappetizing. A longing for one of Mam Pritchard's 'winter-warmers' of good old beef stew and dumplings, made Rose's mouth water, as she contemplated the dull fare at Gracie's table.

Monday came all too soon. By then, Rose was in a fine old tizzy, as Mam used to say. She found a run in her stockings at the last minute, and had to change them for another pair that had a few picks in them. Merv was taking her to the Jefferson Printing Company on this first day, simply because it coincided with some unusually early business of his own. But after today, she would be travelling by public bus. Until she had saved enough to buy her own car, Rose amended silently. Her own car, and her own place . . . they were still dreams, but dreams were worth nothing unless you had every hope of them coming true.

"Ready, hon?" Merv said appreciatively, not at all averse to taking this classy little gal downtown in his Chevy.

"Nearly," Rose said, knowing her face was paler than usual, and that she was as scared as All-Hallows at entering that vast building with all those other LA girls, who already knew all there was to know about being a Jefferson secretary.

"You'll be OK, our Rose," Grace said, with more insight for her feelings than Rose might have imagined. "Just keep your chin up, and think of England," she added with a chuckle and a sly grin at Merv.

"I'll see you later, then," Rose said, in what she hoped was a confident voice.

"Got your dinner money and some change for the drinks machine?" Gracie said, suddenly spoiling it all.

"Yes. And I've got a clean hanky, and I've been to the lav," she said, forgetting all her sophistication. She even forgot Mam Pritchard's tut-tutting at her East End roots, with Mam's own insistence on calling it the outdoor privvy, which always seemed just as bad to Rose.

"Well, there's no need to snap. I was only looking out for you," Gracie said, nettled.

"I know, and I'm sorry—"

"When you two have finished fussing, can we get going, for Christ's sake?" Merv bawled out. "I got somebody to see in less than an hour, and you know what the downtown traffic's like at this time of day."

Rose rushed out of the house in his wake. She sat stiffly beside him in the Chevy, praying that the unsavoury whiffs from its interior didn't hang around on her clothes, and keeping as far removed from Merv's beefy body as possible.

"Nervous, kid?" Merv said with a sideways glance, as the car juddered into action.

"A bit. It's only natural, isn't it?" she defended herself.

"Sure it is, but you don't need to worry. One look at those melting blue eyes of yours, and all the guys in the place will be falling for you."

"Thanks, but that's not what I'm there for," she said.

Merv laughed. He steered the car into the downtown flow of traffic and then squeezed her knee. She could feel the heat of his hand through her skirt and petticoat, and she wriggled away from him. He was never too clean, and if he had stained her beige linen skirt . . .

"You don't like me much, do you, Rosie?" he said, after a minute or two.

"I'm grateful to you, Merv, you know that," she said quickly, remembering that his money had brought her to LA, and she was living in his apartment, where he paid all the bills.

"How grateful is that, I wonder?"

She turned to look at him, seeing the fleshy mouth and the thick jowls, and the seediness of the Yank she had once thought so glamorous, and she shuddered.

"Just as grateful as Gracie would want me to be," she said, daring him to misunderstand.

He gave a grunt. "You catch on quick, Rose, I'll say that for you. You just mind out for yourself then. We don't want no trouble brought home to our door."

The nerve of him took Rose's breath away. One minute he was ogling her and hinting at her favours, and the next he was acting like a pompous goat.

"I'll try to remember," she said, poker-faced, thankful to see that the tall glass and concrete office buildings of the city were coming into view. And once he'd let her out of the car she breathed the comparatively fresh air of morning downtown, not yet polluted by the inrush of people from the suburbs, and the day's heat.

It was a different matter once she stepped over the threshold of the building, and was once more enveloped in the silent, carpeted splendour of the Jefferson building. She collected the pass with her name printed on it that was waiting for her with the uniformed desk clerk and went up in the silent elevator to the twenty-fifth floor, two below the palace she remembered as Jefferson's office.

The room where all the secretaries worked was one vast floor filled with a score of desks, each with its own typewriter and various other pieces of office equipment: some with telephones, some without; some with small adding machines, and most with little personal touches that established them as someone's territory. Rose's heart balked at the clatter of noise from girls who obviously knew one another well, and took no notice at all of the newcomer.

And then a woman with a superior air came towards her. She could have been forty years old or more, but she had such rigidly waved, fiercely-red hair, and a mask of make-up on her face, that it was hard to tell.

"Are you Rose Forster?" she asked, and without waiting for an answer, she waved at Rose to follow her, and continued speaking over her shoulder. "I'm Lacey Venables, head of department. If there's anything you're unsure about, you just ask. This is your desk. You'll be dealing with invoices for the time being. I take it you can use an adding machine?"

"Oh. Yes. Yes, of course. It was part of our training at secretarial college. . . ." Her voice trailed away as Lacey Venables turned to stare at her, and it was one of those odd moments when all conversation seemed to dry up, so that only Rose Forster's plummy English tones emerged loud and clear.

"All right then," the woman continued after a few silent seconds. "You'll get the stack of invoices delivered to you in twenty minutes. Meanwhile, acquaint yourself with your surroundings. Coffee's freely available, and the machine's at the end of the room."

"Thank you, Miss Venables—"

"The name's Lacey. We don't stand on ceremony here."

The way she said it seemed like a slight, as if Rose was setting herself up as a duchess, simply because of her accent. As Lacey swished away, the girl organizing her chaos of a desk alongside her gave her a sympathetic smile.

"Don't pay any attention, hon. It's Lacey's way of still hanging on to her youth. Once she starts having to answer to *Miss* Venables, she'll be looking for more grey hairs to dye than she's got already."

"Oh, I see," Rose said, relieved.

The girl smiled. "I'm Cindy Estrada. Do you want some coffee? It'll help to settle your nerves. I love the way you talk, by the way. It's real neat."

She went away to the coffee machine without waiting for an answer, and Rose wondered if everyone took assent for granted. They were all so full of self-confidence, she thought, and she found herself envying them so much, and wondering if she would ever get to be like them. It may not suit Mam Pritchard's code of behaviour, where a girl's modesty in speech, dress and thought, was to be valued above all things. But Mam Pritchard was half a world away now, and Rose had a life of her own to live.

By the time Cindy came back with two paper cups of coffee, several other girls had stopped by Rose's desk and introduced themselves. They were much friendlier than she had expected, and she gradually began to relax.

The pile of invoices was brought to her desk in precisely twenty minutes, and the procedure was explained to her. It wasn't that difficult. She merely had to use the adding machine to tot up the various items and transfer the amounts and totals onto the prepared invoices. It was something she had done a million times as exercise practise at college, and was routine office work that wouldn't tax anybody with half a brain. The main thing was to remember that the figures represented dollars and cents, and not pounds, shillings and pence.

At one o'clock the morning ended, and Cindy told her that most of the girls took their lunchbreak in the nearby park. Rose wasn't sure if this was an invitation to join them or not.

"Aren't you coming?" Cindy said, as she hung back. "If we're not back sharp at two, the red dragon will be after us."

So she spent her first lunchbreak in the park, where the grass had to be watered daily with sprinklers to keep it green. And although it wasn't quite as sweet and green as the valleys, and the temperature was climbing steadily, it was a welcome change to be outside after the air-conditioned perfection of the offices.

Half-way through the afternoon, Rose's heart gave a huge jolt. She was still getting used to the announcements than came over the intercom for any of the secretaries to report to whichever office required them. She certainly hadn't expected to hear her own name, thinking, and hoping, that she was far too small a cog in the huge Jefferson wheel to warrant such attention on her first day.

And then it happened. "Would Rose Forster please come to Mr Jefferson's office on the twenty-seventh floor?" she heard the nasal voice say.

For a moment, Rose felt as if all eyes in the room were looking at her. Her face flamed, wondering if she had done something terribly wrong. The completed invoices had been duly collected, and she was sure she had made no mistakes. Unless she had stupidly mistaken dollars for pounds. . . .

"Rose Forster." A moment later she heard Lacey Venables speak sharply at her side. "Please take the elevator at once and report to Mr Jefferson."

"I'm on my way," she said hastily. "Should I take anything with me?"

The woman looked at her as if she was crazy.

"Just yourself, I suspect," she said. "Since I understand you're to be included in the list of applicants as Miss Simpson's successor."

She didn't say it with undue sarcasm, but there was something in the flash of her eyes that told Rose instantly that Lacey wanted the job. And why shouldn't she? As the senior one here, and with the experience of working for Jefferson's for the Lord knew how long, it seemed only fair. . . . As Lacey swished away, Cindy spoke in a stage whisper.

"Take no notice. She'd never have got the job, anyway. She doesn't have the personality or the style, but anybody can see that you do, so go for it, Rose."

She gave Cindy a grateful smile, and walked down the length of the room with her chin high, remembering what Gracie had said. But she wasn't thinking of England. She was thinking of the last time she had seen Bradley Piers Jefferson the third, and the way his hand had closed over hers in that intimate way in Alberto's Italian restaurant.

Outside in the wide carpeted corridor, into which a dozen of Pontyrowan's terraced-houses would have fitted, she paused uncertainly, having no idea of the location of the elevator for the twenty-seventh floor. The corridor was deserted, and there was no one she could ask. All the doors looked the same, and she felt a moment's panic. And then she heard someone whistling, and she whirled round as a young delivery boy appeared from nowhere, his arms filled with sheaves of papers.

"Are you lost?" he said with a grin.

"I know it's silly, but can you tell me how I get to the twenty-seventh floor?" she said helplessly.

He stared so hard at her for a minute, that Rose wondered if she'd grown an extra head or something.

"Where you from, for God's sake? I ain't never heard a voice like that before!"

His attitude irritated her. She was already nervous at not knowing where to go, and here was this idiot, making her more dithery still.

"It's a perfectly ordinary English accent," she snapped. "It's only you people who have ruined it."

The minute she'd said it, she was appalled at herself for her rudeness. All the little East End evacuees in Pontyrowan had been mercilessly mocked for their accents, and in turn had ridiculed the very Welshness of their hosts, which frequently led to fist fights and bloody noses among boys and girls alike. Once she had outgrown it all, Rose had vowed never to mock anyone else's accent, and here she was now, doing exactly that.

"Well, pardon me for breathin', duchess!" the boy

retorted. "You want the elevator at the end of the corridor, but just remember who's the boss when you get up there."

Rose thanked him, and muttered an apology, but he was already swanning away from her, whistling unconcernedly. She sought out the elevator door marked Bradley Piers Jefferson the third, and with her mouth twisting a little at the sheer arrogance of it, she stepped inside and pressed the only button. Seconds later it had whisked her skywards and then stopped. A door at the far side slid silently open, and she stepped into Jefferson's outer office where Miss Simpson rose to greet her.

"Good-afternoon, Miss Forster," the woman said, with about as much welcome in her voice as a wet kipper. "Mr Jefferson has been expecting you."

Her voice implied that Rose was in disgrace for keeping the Great One waiting. And just as before, such deference to one man, no matter how successful, dissipated much of her nervousness.

"I lost my way," she said.

"Really?" Miss Simpson's eyebrows lifted a fraction, as if at a loss to imagine how anyone but a simpleton could lose their way between two floors. "Well, you're here now, so I'll buzz through to see if Mr Jefferson is ready for you."

"I thought he'd be pacing the floor by now, from the way everyone scuttles around him," she said without thinking.

She was treated to Miss Simpson's blank stare, and concluded that the woman had no sense of humour at all. Rose decided that she must be terribly efficient at her job to compensate.

She listened to the exchange of voices over the intercom, and heard Jefferson tell Miss Simpson to send her into his office. His voice was rich and warm, and full of an extra-special timbre that was even more obvious when he was physically absent. It wasn't sleazy, like Merv's, nor brash, like the young delivery boy's. . . .

"Well, go on. Don't stand there dreaming, girl. Mr Jefferson doesn't care to be kept waiting," Miss Simpson said crisply.

Rose tilted her chin and entered the luxurious vastness of the office she remembered from her interview. There was no sound as she moved inside the room, for the deep carpet muffled her footsteps, and only the click of the door behind her announced her presence.

Her gaze was drawn towards the window, not seeing Jefferson immediately. There was the huge, expensive desk and the hideous red leather chair by the window that could hide a man in its supple depths . . . and there were the matching sofas that were obviously designed to lull the Corporation clients and put them at their ease . . . or maybe where a sensual and powerful man might cajole an unsuspecting secretary into an hour or two of stolen pleasure. . . .

She jumped as she heard Jefferson's voice. He was standing by an open drinks cabinet in one of the office alcoves, and he was pouring two glasses of wine.

"Take no notice of Simmy," he said easily. "She's over-protective of me, but that's because she's been with the firm since my father's day, and knew me when I was in short pants. So, no matter who else scuttles about to do my bidding, I can assure you our Simmy doesn't."

"You were listening!" Rose said at once, annoyance replacing the astonishing fact of Miss Simpson even having a nickname, let alone one that was delivered in such an affectionate tone. Jefferson laughed.

"I didn't know the intercom was left on, but it does no harm to know what others think of you. Here you are."

He handed Rose a glass of wine, moving towards her with a lithe, animal grace for so large a man. He simply oozed self-confidence, together with a simmering sexuality that was all the more exciting because it was understated. Jefferson didn't need the brashness of lesser men. And Rose could see in a moment how any gullible little secretary might be swept off her feet and onto one of those soft, deep sofas . . . the casting couch. . . .

"I shouldn't be doing this," she stated flatly, stepping back a pace, and out of reach of the outstretched hand holding the crystal-stemmed glass.

"Doing what?" Jefferson asked, amused. "I'm merely inviting you to have a glass of wine in the afternoon in order to make you feel welcome in the company. It's a tradition that my father began."

"Oh," Rose said, feeling extremely foolish now, and accepting the wine with a murmur of thanks.

"Did you think I was about to seduce you?" Jefferson said. "Not that I find the idea unattractive, of course, but it's not my style."

"I'm sorry," she muttered, and took a heady gulp of her wine.

"Please don't start saying sorry again. It's not necessary. Come and sit down with me, Rose, and tell me how you've enjoyed your first day here."

He sat down easily on one of the sofas, and Rose sat on the other. Sighing, he got up and came to sit beside her.

"If there's one thing I dislike about success, it's how it divides people," he said. "Even the two sofas in this ridiculously large office seem to create an obstacle between us. Why are you afraid of me?"

"I'm not!"

"Good. You'll be no use here if you're going to burst into tears every time I snap at you – and I promise you, I *will* snap at you from time to time."

"I'm not in the habit of bursting into tears in public. There were plenty of times when I could have done so as a child, but I never showed them—" she stopped abruptly, wondering what had made her say such a thing.

81

"Poor little Rose," Jefferson said softly. "I can just imagine you being sent away to a place where they all spoke differently, and you were missing your parents and sister, and feeling betrayed."

Her head jerked up. He saw too much, far too much. She didn't want to be reminded of that sense of betrayal and vulnerability by anyone, least of all by him. And she had forgotten just how much she had told him of her early life when they had shared a meal at Alberto's Italian restaurant.

"I'm sure I exaggerated—"

"I'm sure you didn't," Jefferson said. "Drink your wine, and tell me how your day has been."

He changed as swiftly as a chameleon, she thought, and perhaps it was because he could see the vulnerability in her eyes that she still felt whenever she recalled that day when she had been put on the train for Wales. Paddington Station had been filled with small, breaking hearts that day, and hers had been one of them. She sipped her wine obediently.

"It's been an interesting day. I think I've done a good job without any mistakes—"

"You only think so? American secretaries would be bragging about how well they'd coped."

"But I'm not American, and we do things differently," she couldn't help saying.

She saw the way he was looking at her now, at her eyes and her mouth . . . especially her mouth . . . and she felt a sweet, strange sensation rush through her at that look. She drained her glass quickly, and asked if there was anything else. She prayed that it wasn't a leading question. She didn't want Jefferson to make a pass at her. She didn't want a silent tussle with him on the sofa. She didn't know what she wanted, or expected from him, but it certainly wasn't some quick, fumbling affair. She knew that much.

"There's nothing else for now then," he said quietly. "I'll let you go back to your desk, but if you and Jefferson's take to one another, we'll be making contact again about the possible PA's job. I take it you're interested?"

She'd be a fool not to know that while his voice said one thing, his eyes said another. Rose nodded slowly.

"I'm interested," she said huskily.

Chapter Six

"You never say much about this job of yours," Gracie complained. "You've been there nearly a month, and all I hear is about this Cindy."

If it hadn't been so unlikely to Rose, there might almost have been a note of jealousy in her sister's voice. She had quickly discovered that Gracie had few real friends among her acquaintances.

"What else do you want to know? I'm still doing invoices and the occasional letter, and I'm at everybody's beck and call!"

And the idea of being asked to be PA to Jefferson himself, seemed to be a dream that was just as unlikely to come true. Jefferson and Miss Simpson had gone east on a business trip, which meant New York. They'd gone in the company's private plane, she'd been told by Cindy, who obviously saw nothing flamboyant in the comment.

"Well, what's this Jefferson like? Old, young, fat, thin – or what?" Gracie said from her seat on the far side of the porch. "I've always said you can be as tight as a clam when you want to be, our Rose. He must have plenty of dough to be the head of a big corporation, that's for sure."

"Oh yes? Have you been checking the stocks and shares on the financial pages of the *Los Angeles Sentinel* then?" She caught her sister's glare and relented, but only a little way. "Well, you'd be impressed by the size of his portrait on his office wall," she told Gracie. "He's sitting in the red leather chair by his desk, and although the chair's pretty big, Mr Jefferson dominates it. He's as portly as a Toby Jug, and his hair's totally white, but he's still got a lot of it. He wears horn-rimmed glasses with thick lenses, but they can't hide the wicked twinkle in his eyes—"

Gracie had heard enough. She almost screeched out the words. "And you let an old lech like that take you to dinner the night he interviewed you for the job? Didn't I warn you about the guys in this town?"

Rose looked at her innocently, dimly remembering how she'd once believed Gracie must go out with a different Yank every night during the war, if the names her mother mentioned in her letters to the homesick Rose in Pontyrowan were anything to go by.

She laughed out loud now. "All right, I'll stop kidding! I'm talking about the portrait of the man who started the company! Bradley Piers Jefferson is his son. He's in his early thirties, I'd say, and he's always behaved like a perfect gentleman towards me."

And that first afternoon, when he'd asked her to his office to take a glass of wine with him, had turned out to be the normal courtesy he extended to all new employees. She'd felt an unreasonable tug of disappointment when Cindy had told her so, knowing it served her right for seeing anything more in it. Besides, she'd hardly seen him since. And now he'd gone east on business.

She realized Gracie wasn't looking amused, and wished for the umpteenth time that her sister had a sense of humour. She and Miss Simpson would make a good pair in that respect. Rose jumped up, offering to fetch some lemonade for them both. The day was still hot and humid, even for the end of September, and Gracie nodded, always ready to be waited on.

Rose was getting used to the way of things here now, and had accepted the shabbiness of the Hacketts' apartment building, and Gracie's careless attitude to housework. If the dust didn't move, there was no point in disturbing it, she'd heard her say a dozen times.

Rose enjoyed the routine office work, and continued to take her lunch in the park with Cindy and some of the other girls. There was plenty of speculation in the typing pool now, as to who would get the PA's job. Rose chose to say nothing about her own chances, keeping as close-lipped as the proverbial clam Gracie said she was. Anyway, she'd almost given up any thought of it by now, convinced it had just been a pleasantry and no more.

Merv came home while the two sisters were amicably sipping lemonade and eating pretzels. He was bursting with news, and waving a handful of leaflets.

"I've got the information about the beauty pageant, and your application form, Rose, and they're holding the event at the Plaza Hotel downtown."

Gracie sat up straight. "I thought you'd forgotten all that nonsense. Rose don't want to enter no beauty pageant—"

"Yes I do. It'll be fun, and I can't see any harm in it," she said quickly. "Let me see the application form, please, Merv."

She saw the little dart of triumph that passed from him to his wife. Their marriage frequently resembled a battleground, thought Rose, and each was never happier than when scoring over the other. She scanned the forms quickly. They needed to know an awful lot of information, including her height, colouring and measurements, and most importantly, her age. Girls under eighteen weren't allowed to enter for the Miss Christmas Angel beauty pageant.

"As long as you don't send in the form until after your birthday, you'll qualify all right, kid, and it's only a coupla weeks away now," Merv said, forestalling Gracie's objection. "And like I said, I'll be looking out for you."

"You don't think I'd let her enter something like this without me being there to keep an eye on her as well, do you?" Gracie said sharply.

"I keep telling you I'm not a baby, for goodness sake!" Rose snapped. "I can make my own decisions, and I don't need a chaperone."

"Most of the gals have one though," Merv informed her. "It keeps it all nice and proper, like."

"And some of those pageants aren't so nice, nor so proper," Gracie said meaningfully.

"Well, I'm entering this one, and that's that."

Rose looked through the information leaflet, and felt her heart plummet. There were dress requirements for a beauty pageant that she hadn't considered. She needed formal evening wear, and a bathing suit that was to be worn with high-heeled shoes, and an everyday outfit that was supposed to demonstrate to the judges what kind of personality she had.

"Maybe it's not such a good idea, after all. I don't have any formal evening wear," she said flatly, "and my bathing suit's only fit for the beach back home."

Merv brushed aside her objections. "You're earning decent money, aren't you? Buy yourself something special, and think of it as an investment. And me and Gracie will give you a few dollars for your birthday, so how's that?"

She didn't dare look at Gracie. Merv was taking over, moving too fast, not giving her time to think properly. And she already knew, from her trip to the Clothing Market, that even a modest formal evening gown was way out of her reach, and she said as much as she read out the dress requirements.

"We could always try the used clothing store," Gracie said, in one of her complete turnarounds. "Or take a look in a mail order catalogue. There's no shame in ordering from there, Rose, and paying on the never-never.

Everybody does it now. When you win the pageant, you can pay it all off in one go."

"*If* I win, you mean," Rose said slowly, but admitting that either of Gracie's ideas brought the chance of entering the contest within reach. She knew of old that the lines on Mam Pritchard's face would settle into black frowns the minute a used clothing store or a mail order catalogue was mentioned, but Mam Pritchard didn't have to know.

"What's all this?" Rose said, as pink as her name as she saw the vase of flowers on her desk on the morning of October the fourteenth. "Was this your idea, Cindy? It's sweet of you—"

"Not mine, hon. It's one of the things the Jefferson Corporation always does. You get a bunch of flowers on your desk on your birthday, and a bonus at Christmas."

"Oh. Is Mr Jefferson back from his business trip, then?" she said, trying not to sound too eager. Cindy hooted.

"Jeez, no. You don't think he goes out and buys the flowers himself, do you? Whenever anybody new is hired, the birthday date is registered with all the others at the florist's counter in the building, and they do the rest."

The swift pleasure Rose had felt at the gift quickly vanished. It was all so automated, so slick, like everything else here. And she was beginning to feel as much of an automaton as the rest of them.

"What are you doing to celebrate tonight?" Cindy said.

"I haven't planned anything—"

"*What*? But it's your eighteenth! You gotta do something to mark it. Splash out a bit, see the town!"

"I don't know about that. I'm trying to save my money for a special purpose at the moment." She avoided Cindy's eyes. She wasn't ashamed of entering for the Miss Christmas Angel beauty pageant, for pity's sake, but as yet, it wasn't something she had mentioned to anyone except her family.

"Hey, Gloria, Rose isn't doing anything for her birthday tonight. Whaddaya say?"

The black-haired girl called Gloria draped her elegant self over Rose's desk. "How about coming with us to the pizza parlour right after work, Rose?"

"Well, my sister will be expecting me—"

Gloria picked up Rose's phone and held it out to her.

"Then call her, why don't you? She won't be sending out search parties for you if you're a coupla hours late home, will she, hon?"

That was for sure. Nor was Gracie likely to have done anything special for her birthday. Such celebrations weren't Gracie's style. She asked the operator for the Hacketts' number before she could change her mind, and gave Gracie the message. Gracie didn't even seem concerned, Rose thought, and for some odd reason, she remembered the unexpected fuss Mam had made for her tenth birthday, baking her a cake and all. Of course, she hadn't known, then, that Mam had already heard the news about the blitz on the wireless, and was probably doing her best to make the little East Ender feel more at home, in case there was bad news to come.

And how Dai had sneaked up on her and waved a branch of a tree over her head and told her to pretend it was mistletoe, even though it wasn't anywhere near Christmas, just so she'd submit to his forceful kiss. And how Evan had pushed him aside and told him not to be so damn stupid, and kissed her properly, the way a brother should. He'd been her champion then all right, her hero. . . .

"All set, Rose? Nothing wrong, is there?" Cindy asked. "Your eyes have gone a bit funny. I can let you have some of the sparkly eye drops like the movie stars use, if you like."

"I'm all right," she said hastily, knowing that one of Cindy's desk drawers would do credit to a chemist's cosmetic and dispensing counters. "Just dreaming, that's all. So where is this pizza parlour where we're going?"

She didn't know if it was likely to be anything special or not. You couldn't always tell by the name or the outside of a place. Sea-Food Joe's was a good example of that.

"It's downtown," Cindy said casually.

"Is it anywhere near the Plaza Hotel?"

She heard Gloria snigger. "God, I should just say not! Who's been telling you about that dump, Rose? You be sure to keep well away from that side street. Plenty of sleaze-bags hang around there at night, and they're not looking for angels, neither."

At the ironic reference to angels, Rose flinched as though she'd been stung. The swish-sounding Plaza Hotel was where Merv was handing in her application form for the Miss Christmas Angel beauty pageant that very day. And according to Gloria, it sounded like nothing more than what some of the boyos had sniggeringly referred to behind their hands, as a knocking-shop. Rose hadn't known what it meant at the time, but she knew it now, and she felt her face flame, and bent over her desk to uncover her typewriter as the clatter of the machines began in earnest.

"What did your folks give you for your birthday, Rose?" Cindy said.

"I haven't had it yet, but they're going to give me some money," she mumbled, hoping it sounded a grander gift than she knew it would be.

"Great. Enjoy," Cindy said, already losing interest.

Rose knuckled down to work. There was a mass of invoices that day, but somehow the figures all became blurred, and she found it hard to concentrate properly. It was daft to feel so out of sorts on her birthday, when she should be feeling on top of the world . . . and she knew it had nothing to do with the fact that Gracie and Merv's monetary gift was slow in forthcoming. There was nothing new in that, anyway. It was because there had been nothing from Wales.

No letters, no cards, none of the usual little gifts; sensible ones from Mam, humorous or self-made ones from the boyos. . . . It was doubly daft to fret, because the post was notoriously slow in getting from there to here, despite the air mail service, and it would be more of a miracle than anything else for mail to arrive exactly on the day.

All the same, she knew she was missing the contact with her make-believe family, and the fine tea Mam would have prepared around a roaring fire. It would be banked high with slack from the pit where Dai worked now, scorching their faces tomato-red by the time they'd worked their way through Mam's fat, cream-filled scones, and the hot, thick-sliced ham and Welsh cakes.

She hadn't eaten pizza before. She wasn't even sure what it was, nor if she would like it. One thing she did know: the portions would be huge, disgustingly so, and she was still remembering how Mam had scrimped and saved their coupons every time one of the birthdays came around, to give them their own special treat, with no discrimination towards their evacuee.

"Damn!" she said out loud, though she wasn't sure whether the exclamation was due more to the fact that she'd just ruined an invoice by carelessly converting dollars into pounds, or by her annoyance with her own stupid thoughts.

Cindy threw across a typewriter rubber, and Rose scratched out the offending mistake. It looked worse now, and, angry at herself, she felt her eyes begin to smart.

"I'll get you another invoice form," she heard Cindy say sympathetically. "Don't worry so much, Rose. It happens to all of us, and you won't get fired for one mistake."

But it wasn't the only one she made that day. Her fingers seemed to be all thumbs, and by the end of the afternoon, she had such a headache that she decided to cry off the birthday celebration. The others went without her, and she took the bus home, thoroughly miserable. It didn't help when Gracie told her there was nothing to eat. She hadn't been expecting her back, and she was just doing herself a fry-up, since Merv was working on lates.

"A fry-up will be fine for me too," Rose said. "I don't want any fuss, Gracie. I just want a couple of aspirins, that's all."

"You do look a bit peaky," Gracie said, as if only just noticing. "What a shame, on your birthday."

"What did you do on yours?" Rose said.

"My what?"

"Your eighteenth birthday. Was it special?"

As she spoke, Rose felt unexpected pangs of jealousy, remembering that at eighteen, Gracie would still have been in London, living at home with their mum and dad, and going out to meet one of her Yanks. The house in the East End was still intact then. Hitler hadn't yet blown it to smithereens, along with the two people she'd loved most in all the world.

Gracie had had all that, while she had been packed off to an alien place, to a terraced-house in a narrow, winding valley from which the sun was often blotted out by the black heaps of glittering coal slack that flanked it.

All the nostalgia she'd been feeling for her Welsh family vanished in a trice, in the resentment she'd thought had been buried for ever. But it was still there, still simmering. And all the old promises to see her safe, to take the place of their mum and dad, and to bring her to America, had been too long being fulfilled.

"Good God, I can't remember now," Gracie said irritably, standing back a pace as she put more slices of bacon into the spitting, blackened pan. "We didn't have much to eat, I know that. While you were living it up in your Welsh valley, we had to make do with scraps, and looking out for Hitler's buzz bombs every night. You had the best of it, kid, and don't you forget it."

"But you had home, and Mum and Dad."

Gracie put her hands on her ample hips. Her hair was even more frizzed out than usual tonight, Rose thought, and it didn't look as if it had seen a comb all day.

"It's no use looking back, Rose. What's past is over and done with, and you've got to look to the future now. Anyway, you got what you wanted, didn't you? You came to LA."

Rose bit back the retort that it had taken Gracie long enough to remember that she even had a sister. Instead, she reminded herself that Merv had paid her secretarial college fees, whether or not it had salved his conscience over having his wife's kid sister living with him. Like Gracie said, she was here now, and she'd got what she wanted.

"I'm being a pig," she muttered. "I'm sorry. It's probably my headache making me grumpy—"

"Keep an eye on this pan while I fetch you those aspirins, then," Gracie said, not caring to listen to any hint of sentiment.

Rose did as she was told. The smell was making her feel slightly nauseous, but somebody had told her the best cure for a headache was to eat something, and so she would. She heard the phone ring while she was turning the bacon over, and then Gracie's voice as she answered it. Next minute, she'd come back to the kitchen.

"It's a call for you, Rose. He didn't give his name, but I think—"

"*He?*" Rose echoed. But she didn't know anybody. Unless it was Jefferson, calling her from New York to wish her a happy birthday . . . the wild thought was in her head, even though she knew it was absurd. She went out into the hallway and grabbed the receiver that Gracie had left dangling.

"Hello," she said quickly, and there was a delay from the other end, so that she wondered if anybody was there at all. And then, despite the intermittent crackling over the wire, she heard an accent that was warm and familiar, the voice as close as if its owner was standing in the room.

"Is that you, Rose? It's Evan here. Evan Pritchard. I wanted to wish you a happy birthday, and this seemed the quickest way to do it, even if it's costing a small fortune, and it's the middle of the night."

Rose stared at a grease-spot on the strip of hall carpet while her mind was working overtime. She certainly hadn't expected this. Evan had bothered to call her all the way from Wales to wish her a happy birthday. . . . Her swift disappointment that it hadn't been Bradley Piers Jefferson the third calling from New York, was quickly tempered by a rush of gratitude and jubilation.

"Evan, it's *you*!" she said stupidly.

She heard him laugh. She had never spoken to him on the phone before, and she was as much attuned to his disembodied voice as she had been to that of Jefferson's. His Welshness was not so much emphasized as refined, but of course, he was working for a firm of solicitors now, and had smoothed off his rough edges, unlike his brother.

"Is that all you've got to say to me? Thanks for your letter, by the way. I'll be answering it soon. We've all sent cards, but we didn't know if you'd get them in time or not. Have they arrived?"

"Not yet. But this is better. Oh, Evan, this is so much better!"

"Well, don't cry, *cariad*, or I'll be thinking you're homesick, and it didn't sound that way in your letter. Is everything all right?"

"Everything's fine," Rose said brightly. "And you *will* write back to me, won't you?"

"I said I would. But Mam wants a word with you now."

Suddenly she wanted to say: *"Don't go. Stay with me. Talk to me, and let me feel part of a real family once more, instead of feeling so much on the edge of this one."* But the moment was gone, and after a bit more crackling down the line, she heard the stern tones of Mam Pritchard's voice.

"Now then, girl, have you had a good day?"

Rose knew this was her way of wishing her a happy birthday. She felt a lump in her throat, recognizing the briskness as a way of hiding emotions Mam didn't care to show.

"A very good day, Mam," she said huskily. "I'm not doing anything special, mind, and Gracie and me are just having a fry-up for tea."

She heard the snort of disapproval down the wire, and felt her mouth curving into a grin.

"And how's the new life then? Still enjoying it, are you? Not wanting to come home again yet?"

"Did you think I would?" Rose said with a little laugh.

"I thought you might," Mam said, to her surprise. "Things don't always turn out the way you expect them to, but well, as long as you're all right, then."

"I'm fine, honestly."

The momentary silence was longer than the transatlantic delay between every sentence they uttered.

"Well then," Mam said finally, giving up the awkward attempt at being sociable over so many miles. "I'll hand you back to Evan. You mind yourself, now."

"And you, Mam . . ." but she found she was talking to thin air until Evan came back on the line again.

"You'll have to excuse her, Rose. She's not happy talking to the telephone."

"I thought she was talking to me!"

"You know what I mean. Anyway, I shouldn't keep you any longer, *cariad*—"

"Don't go yet! I want to know what you're doing, and how you all are!" She bit her lip, for hadn't he said that this call was costing a small fortune? And here she was, talking of trivialities. "I'm sorry, Evan. I'm wasting your time—"

"Don't be so daft. When did I ever say it was a waste of time talking to my lovely girl?"

"You never did, and in case I forgot to tell you, you're the best brother I ever had," Rose said sincerely.

The crackling on the line was stronger now, and the delay more prolonged. She couldn't hear what he replied, but it seemed an awfully long time before she heard his voice properly again, and then he had to shout.

"This line's terrible, but I'll call you again sometime, Rose. Meantime, look out for your birthday cards and my letter, all right?"

"I will. Goodbye then, Evan. Oh – and give my love to everyone in Pontyrowan."

She hung up the phone slowly, standing perfectly still a moment longer while she savoured the closeness they had shared for those few precious minutes. The glow of past days enveloped her, and it was only broken when she heard Gracie yelling at her to come and eat this fry-up before the bacon disappeared in a puff of smoke. She blinked, finding that her eyes were moist. How daft, and how odd, to be getting all sentimental over a phone call from Evan Pritchard!

"So what did he say, your Welshman?" Gracie said, when Rose sat down to stare at the shrivelled pieces of bacon swimming in fat on her plate.

"He's hardly my *Welshman*! I always thought of him as my brother—"

"He never was, though, was he? And I bet he don't think of you as his sister, neither. Not now you're

96

all grown-up, anyway, like you keep telling me you are."

"Yes, he does! He's still my brother and my best friend," Rose said in some heat, hardly knowing why she was bothering to get upset over such a trifling bit of bickering from Gracie.

"Oh yes," Gracie said sarcastically, "and I'm Hitler's fancy piece. Eat your fry-up before it gets cold."

By now the food was so revolting it was all Rose could do to get any of it down. She wasn't hungry, anyway. In the end she said she'd rather have an apple and some bread and cheese, and Gracie frowned in annoyance.

"You're not going to start this slimming craze, are you, Rose? I'd have thought after all that food rationing you'd want plenty of good solid food that sticks to your ribs, and not all that faddy stuff."

Referring to what was on her plate as good solid food was so ludicrous that Rose laughed out loud.

"I like apples and bread and cheese," she said stubbornly. "It's all I want right now. I'm not slimming madly, either, though I've no intention of getting fat."

She almost said 'like you', and stopped herself in time. But Gracie's eyes flashed all the same.

"Thinking of the way you'll look in that bathing suit for the beauty pageant, I suppose," she sneered. "What did your Welshman and his mam have to say about that?"

"Nothing," Rose said. *Because I didn't tell them. . . .* It irked her how Gracie seemed to have caught on to the stupid tag of 'her Welshman' now. She'd forgotten how bitchy Gracie could be at times, or maybe she'd never known her well enough in her growing-up years to notice it.

"Look, kid," Gracie said, after a minute or two when neither of them had said anything, and the silence stretched into awkwardness. "It's still your birthday. Why don't we do something together?"

"Like what? Where is there to go?"

"Good God, Rose, this is LA, not some tin-pot little village in the Welsh valleys. There are a thousand places to go! We could go star-spotting, if you like."

Rose looked at her suspiciously. "Are you talking about movie stars, or stars in the sky?"

Gracie grinned. "The only time I spent outdoors gazing up at the sky, I wasn't looking at stars, if you know what I mean," she said coarsely.

"I don't feel like going out," Rose said, suddenly depressed. If there couldn't be a proper birthday celebration, she didn't want to make do with her sister's crude comments, or a trail around some of the hotels where they just might see a movie star or two, but were far more likely not to.

"Suit yourself then. If you don't want my company, I'm going up to visit with Mrs Olsen for an hour, OK?"

"That's OK, Gracie." It was more than OK. It relieved them both of having to make conversation when the tension between them had suddenly become scratchy. She let out a sigh of relief when her sister had gone up to Mrs Olsen's apartment, and revelled in the rarity of having the apartment to herself.

In a burst of energy, she decided to tackle the washing-up, and to clean away some of the accumulated grease on Gracie's pots and pans. It was hardly the way to celebrate an eighteenth birthday, she thought with a wry smile, but at least it got rid of some of her aggression.

And Mam would be proud of her, she thought later, surveying the shining row of pots hanging on the hooks now. Mam's kitchen had been a testament to cleanliness and elbow grease. No speck of dust was allowed to remain in the house for very long, and woe betide a fly that dared to land within inches of any foodstuff.

Rose imagined she could hear the swish of Mam's fly-swatter right now, and Dai's laughing remark that if his Mam had ever got old Hitler in her sights, the old bugger wouldn't last another day. At which outrage, that sullied the saintly walls of the Pritchard house, Mam would round on her youngest, and swat him about the ears as well. It was almost a comic ritual between them, and it never failed to have the young Rose in fits of laughter as Dai yelped and danced, with his mam chasing him around the furniture.

She was caught up in the sweet, childhood memory of it all. She gazed unseeingly through the window, looking into a forgotten world and listening to the solitary sound of her own laughter in the cluttered kitchen of the Hacketts' apartment. And suddenly, without any warning, the laughter turned to tears, and she couldn't have said why.

Chapter Seven

Merv came home in the early hours of the morning, evidently too bushed to undress and climb into bed with Gracie. Rose found them arguing when she went downstairs for breakfast, the evidence of beer bottles strewn all around Merv's chair where he'd spent what was left of the night, and the smell of stale clothes very evident. Rose tried not to show her disgust, and the minute Merv saw her, he perked up.

"I been waiting to talk to you, Rose," he said. "Then I'll do what her highness wants, and get to bed."

"I don't want you sleeping in the daytime, you bum," Gracie yelled.

"Why not? It won't exactly disturb you from doing the cleaning, will it?" he sneered. "That'll be the day, my ass."

Rose thought desperately that she had to get away from here soon. They were impossible, the pair of them. They deserved each other, but she didn't deserve either of them. Between them, they trod on her dreams and shattered them.

"I got a job for you, Rosie," Merv said importantly.

"I've already got a job," she said.

He chuckled. "Not so fast, little lady, and get that stuffy Princess Margaret Rose look off your face. I thought you was interested in seein' how the movie stars live."

He'd got her attention now, and she managed to reorganize her face into showing some interest.

"That's better," he drawled. "The job's for next Saturday night. I'm on loan from The Pacific Grand for the evening, and I'll be valeting at the home of Joanna Del Mar. I heard they was short of a cocktail waitress for this shindig they're giving for her husband's seventieth birthday, and I managed to put in a word for you with their snooty butler. I said you'd got plenty of experience, and that you not only looked like a British princess, but talked like one too."

Rose gasped, but the thought of actually going inside a movie star's home was completely overshadowed by his sheer bloody nerve. "You must be mad! I know nothing about being a cocktail waitress—"

"What's there to know, for Christ's sake? You take the loaded trays of drinks from the bar and walk around the guests with it until it's empty. Then you start all over again. Any fool could do that!"

He was sharp as a tack that she didn't jump with joy at his arrangements. But it certainly didn't sound like the kind of glamorous occasion she might have hoped for. Joanna Del Mar was a name from the past, well past her prime, and living on past silent movie credits. If her husband was almost seventy, Joanna Del Mar herself couldn't be many years behind, and was more well known nowadays for having the tight-drawn expression of the star with too many face-lifts.

As she thought it, Rose knew guiltily that she was being as uncharitable and bitchy as the dreaded Lacey Venables at the office. To her surprise, Gracie suddenly added her encouragement to Merv's scowling face.

"Merv's right, Rose, and you shouldn't be so ungrateful when he's done this for you. Go and enjoy yourself, and see how the other half lives. It's what you always wanted, isn't it?" she added slyly.

"Perhaps. But not as a cocktail waitress," she muttered, and Merv hooted derisively.

"More than one starlet's been discovered in such places, hon, so don't give up hope yet."

"What am I supposed to wear, anyway?" Rose wailed next, ignoring the remark, and thinking that something like a sensible Joe Lyons outfit wouldn't be nearly swanky enough for the home of a Hollywood star.

"You'll be given your uniform when you arrive," Merv told her. "We have to get there an hour before the party's due to start, and you'll get all your instructions then."

She realized he was avoiding her eyes at that moment, and a great suspicion surged into her mind, wondering just what instructions were to be included, along with the handing round of drinks. But it was pointless to speculate, and in any case, a thrill of excitement was starting to rush through her veins. She was actually going to see the inside of one of those fabulous homes, and she was an ungrateful pig for not showing more enthusiasm.

Her eyes suddenly sparkled, and she managed not to wince as she hugged Merv's arm for a brief moment.

"I am grateful for the chance, Merv! And I know it's going to be wonderful—"

"Don't go thinking it's going to open doors for you, kid, that's all," Gracie warned, backtracking at once. "Just put it all down to experience. And you be sure to keep an eye on her, Merv."

She frowned meaningfully at her husband, but whatever the unspoken words were meant to convey, their meaning was lost on Rose. All she could think of now, was Saturday night, and rubbing shoulders with all the celebrities and stars who'd naturally be invited to the party.

By then, she was a nervous wreck. She'd said nothing to the girls at the office about her extra job, not sure what they'd think about it. They called it moonlighting back home, taking on more than one job at a time, and it was generally frowned on, probably due to the fact that there were still not enough jobs to go around for all the boys and girls who'd been demobbed from the services. She didn't know how they viewed it here, but in any case, she was too steeped in English – and Welsh – ways, to care to admit that she was going to be a cocktail waitress for an evening.

"OK?" Merv asked, as he parked the Chevy at the rear of the mansion. He'd had to speak into some electrical device and announce himself before some remote control opened the great iron gates at the end of the driveway, and as they approached the house, lights went on every few yards.

This wasn't just to guide their way, Merv told her. It was to let the remote cameras inside the house see who was approaching. Rose's mouth was dry at the thought of being watched, of having so much power and money, and most of all, of the need for such security.

"I'm as OK as I'll ever be," she mouthed, realizing they were parked at the back entrance now, and thankful for it. If they'd had to swan in at the front of that imposing mansion, she'd have just died, she thought, in best movie star jargon . . . though even the rear of the place was ablaze with lights, and like nothing she had ever seen before.

"You'll be fine. Just be yourself. That's what they'll be wanting."

"Will they? I can't imagine that Joanna Del Mar and her husband will even be aware of me," she said.

"I wasn't meaning them. There'll be plenty of others there, Rose, and you just be nice to them, you hear?"

"Well, of course I will!"

She heard Merv give a sigh at her indignant words. Sometimes she didn't understand him at all, she thought. But she let him lead the way to the door and ring the bell, and the next minute it was opened by a pale-haired girl in a skimpy maid's uniform, of the kind most generally seen in a movie where all waitresses were portrayed as dumb, wisecracking blondes. But the girl herself was beautiful, with wide-set eyes, and when she spoke, it was in a strong Scandinavian accent.

"Good-evening, Mr Hackett. So this will be Rose, then. I am Ilsa, and I will take you at once to Bovington."

"What's Bovington?" Rose whispered, as the girl whisked away from her on heels that looked more like stilts.

"He's the butler. Just follow Ilsa, Rose, and I'll see you later."

"Oh, but—"

But Merv was gone, and it dawned on her that if he was valeting for the evening, it was hardly likely that he'd keep an eye on her as Gracie had fondly hoped. But, for pity's sake, she was eighteen years old, not a baby, and she didn't need looking after. She followed Ilsa to a room along a corridor, where the carpet was so deep-piled it made no sound at all beneath her feet, and the costly-looking jardinières and framed paintings certainly hadn't come from Woolworth's.

"Here is Bovington," Ilsa said quaintly, and a middle-aged man looked Rose over from head to toe and grunted.

"I'm told you're English, and that had better be right. We needed one to make up the set."

"I beg your pardon?" Rose said, gaping.

Bovington shrugged. "If that's a genuine accent, you'll do nicely. No tricks, mind."

"I'm afraid I still don't have the faintest idea what you're talking about."

Bovington obviously wasn't a man to waste words, and he spoke crisply. "It's a theme evening. All the waitresses dress alike, but they all have different nationalities. We were short of a Britisher. Some of the guests will be wearing little flags in their lapels to indicate their choice, and each waitress will serve those from her own background."

"I see."

But she didn't. It sounded silly and theatrical, and besides, what was the point of choosing a special waitress, if all she had to do was to hand round drinks?

"I give Rose the uniform now?" Ilsa said.

"Please do, and report to the ante-room with the other girls in fifteen minutes."

He was gone, as stiff as any English butler, Rose thought, though the only ones she had ever seen or heard had been on the cinema screen. But he unnerved her thoroughly, and she breathed a sigh of relief when he'd gone. Ilsa smiled sympathetically.

"I guess, your first time?"

"Oh yes. I'm actually a secretary in a large company downtown. . . ."

But she was talking to herself. Ilsa was sliding open a door, behind which there was a rack of maids' uniforms, similar to her own. She quickly sized Rose up and selected the short flared black satin skirt and sleeveless top, with the frilled white apron and cap to go with it. There were also sheer black nylons and high-heeled shoes similar to Ilsa's, all at her disposal in various sizes.

It was all a crazy game, Rose decided. These people couldn't be real, to provide such things for a single evening. And hiring staff in various nationalities too, with herself as the token Englishwoman. . . . Suddenly she was finding the whole situation hilarious, and she decided to enjoy herself. Maybe she could even throw in a bit of a Welsh lilt from time to time too, to confuse the customers. . . .

Fifteen minutes later she was lining up with eleven other girls, dressed exactly the same as herself, and with Bovington inspecting them all and asking for the same set phrase from each of them. It was all so bizarre, as she listened to the German and the Dutch, the French and the Spanish, the Swedish, the Mexican, and all the others, and finally herself.

"Good-evening, sir. My name is Rose," she heard herself say. "If I can be of any special service to you, please don't hesitate to ask."

She smothered an urge to giggle. It was so ludicrously formal to speak this way, just to be offering cocktails from a tray. . . .

"When the gentleman accepts, you will find your allocated rooms on the first floor. Each nationality has its flag outside the door, so go and take careful note of it now, and be sure not to interrupt anyone else's pleasure," Bovington said.

Rose felt her eyes glaze and burn. Her heart thumped, and her breath was tight in her chest, because he surely couldn't be saying what she thought he was saying. . . . She wasn't naïve, but she couldn't believe that in this sophisticated mansion, with the type of people worth millions, such sordid things could go on. She looked around wildly, but the other girls were dispersing now, chattering among themselves and heading for the back stairs to the first floor, to find their allocated rooms. She caught at Ilsa's arm.

"What does he mean? What special services do gentlemen require? I was only hired to serve drinks," She said hoarsely.

"Honey," Ilsa said, emphasizing the first syllable heavily, "we're all here to serve drinks, but we all have other jobs too. If you want to call yours being a secretary, that's all right."

"So what's your other job?"

Ilsa shrugged her slender shoulders. "Like the rest of them, of course. I answer the telephone and make appointments with gentlemen, and then I give them pleasure."

Rose backed away. "That's it then! I'm not staying here. I'm getting out right now——"

"You can't. The door will be locked against intruders," Ilsa said, clearly puzzled. "But you may give as much or as little service as is required, Rose. Most gentlemen will understand if you're new to the game."

The game . . . dear God! Rose dimly remembered one of their old East End neighbours scathingly referring to the girls who hung around Piccadilly and King's Cross as being on "*the game . . . prostitutes and tarts, the lot of them, and heading straight for the devil's evil clutches*," the old harridan would say, even in little Rose's hearing.

And here was little Rose now, dressed up like a tart, and expected to be at any gentleman's pleasure. . . .

"I can't do this, Ilsa," she said, still in that hoarse voice. "I've never done it——"

"No?" Ilsa said, her eyes showing new interest. "Perhaps I should introduce you to one of my special gentlemen, then, who will be gentle."

"You don't understand!" Rose said, still backing away. "I've no intention of selling myself to anybody. I'm no prostitute! It's all a terrible mistake!"

And she hated Merv even more now, for getting her into this situation, whether or not he realized it. She couldn't believe he knew the full extent of what went on here, but he must have known some of it. She was aware that Ilsa's eyes were flashing angrily now.

"I am no prostitute, either. I am a high-class call girl, with some very important clients. You insult me by calling me that name, Rose."

Dear God, it went from bad to worse. Ilsa was insulted by being called a prostitute, but she spoke proudly of being a high-class call girl, answering the telephone to make appointments with gentlemen and giving them pleasure . . . but since Ilsa was her only ally, Rose knew it would be madness to alienate her.

"I'm sorry," she said. "I didn't understand. So what must I do to put them off?"

Ilsa stared at her for a moment and then shrugged. "Some gentlemen just like to talk about their lives. If you find one like that, you'll have no problems. If one insists on laying you, and you can't bear the thought of it, lift your knee hard and flatten his balls."

Rose swallowed.

"You really are a baby, aren't you?" Ilsa said, seeing the swift colour rush to Rose's face. "I'll tell you something else. You can always say you're fully engaged for the evening. They will accept this, though you won't get paid as much if you don't give full service."

"I don't care about that!" Rose said, almost weeping with gratitude at this last instruction. She would most certainly tell any so-called gentleman who approached her that she was engaged for the evening! Anything, rather than have a stranger pawing her and taking her innocence. . . .

"Come then," Ilsa said, more kindly. "I must show you your room, or it will be frowned upon."

But she would never use it, Rose vowed, when she saw the Union flag proudly in its holder outside a bedroom door. It shamed the flag to be used in such a manner, and while she might not be the world's most patriotic person, she couldn't bear it to be used in such a way. But there was nothing she could do about it, and once this long evening was over, she would tell Merv Hackett in no uncertain terms that she wanted no more of his sleazy jobs.

Half-way through the evening, Rose's ruffled feelings were lulled. The party was full of over-bright, mainly elderly people who were obviously Joanna Del Mar's

108

contemporaries, and there were few celebrity faces Rose recognized. Probably due to the face-lifts and eye tucks, she thought cynically.

The gentlemen all wore immaculate tuxedos with their chosen flags in their lapels. The ladies were mostly in glittering gowns, each clearly trying to outdo the next one. The array of diamonds and sapphires and every other gemstone in the ballroom would have done justice to the crown jewels, Rose thought, and there must be a fortune in baubles here. No wonder the security arrangements were so strict, including the discreet cameras that Ilsa had pointed out to her hidden in various nooks around the house.

There were some couples who had arrived together, but Rose kept a wary eye out for the many single gentlemen, keeping Ilsa's instructions in mind. She knew her accent attracted more than one of them, and she felt herself tremble when she was finally asked to show one of the gentlemen the flag of her country.

"I'm sorry," she said through stiff lips. "But I'm afraid I'm fully engaged for the evening."

"Say, that's a real shame," the blue-rinsed guy with the gold cuff links said, still looking her over. "Another time then, maybe."

"Maybe," Rose murmured, wanting to flee, but wild with relief that her reply wasn't questioned.

It happened half a dozen more times, and each time the guy went away regretfully, without any argument. There was a strange code of honour here, she thought, if you could call it honour. . . .

"Will you show me the flag of your country?" said a new voice behind her. She closed her eyes for a moment, praying that it wasn't the voice she knew, and desperate for the floor to open up and swallow her, as a character would say in all the best movies. . . .

109

"I said, will you please show me the flag of your country?" the voice said, more sharply.

Rose turned slowly, the few remaining cocktail glasses on her tray wobbling alarmingly. She kept her eyes down, refusing to meet the man's gaze.

"I'm sorry, but I'm afraid I'm fully engaged for the evening," she said, her voice barely audible.

"Don't give me that crap," said Bradley Piers Jefferson the third. "Unless you want me to make a scene, put that bloody tray down before you drop it, and lead the way to your room. And try to look as if you're enjoying it."

Rose's head jerked up then, and she looked straight into the hard, accusing face of her employer. Her heart hammered so fast she could hardly breathe. What must he think of her, posing in this terrible maid's outfit . . .? And on the coat-tails of that thought came another one. What the hell was he doing here, anyway, at the kind of Hollywood party where it was clearly the usual thing for a man to invite a girl to a room for one purpose only?

Her embarrassment turned to anger, and she stalked away from him on her impossibly high heels, praying that they wouldn't catch in the carpet and send her sprawling. She felt lower than she had ever done in her life before, and she couldn't imagine what Jefferson was trying to do to her. Ilsa's words came back to haunt her at that moment.

"If one insists on laying you, and you can't bear the thought of it, lift your knee hard and flatten his balls."

Could she do that to Jefferson? She had long forgotten how attracted she had first been to him, but she was still aware of his magnetism and his power, and in an intimate situation, who knew how she might respond . . .? And it had never yet been put to the test.

As she mounted the stairs ahead of Jefferson, the distaste she had felt at the thought of some stranger pawing her was becoming overtaken by a force that

110

was much stronger. However unwelcome, the erotic excitement of being taken by someone like him, who could surely have any woman he wanted, was suddenly an aphrodisiac as heady as wine.

She opened the door with the Union flag outside, and went inside. She hadn't looked into the room before, but now she saw that it was a bedroom, and that the shutters were closed. The several lamps around the room were lit, throwing a rosy, intimate glow around the room and the satin furnishings, and she turned to Jefferson with a trembling expectation in her soul.

If she had to lose her virginity to someone, then she supposed she could be thankful it was someone like him . . . but even as the outrageous thought swam wickedly through her senses, Rose realized the thought was only there because she had sipped one glass of champagne too many, each time she returned to the bar for more supplies.

She tipped up her face to Jefferson, her eyes closing, half-expecting that he would sweep her into his arms and into the bed without giving her time to refuse . . . wasn't that the way they did it in the movies . . .?

"What the hell do you think you're doing here?" Jefferson snapped. "I thought you were different. I never expected to find you with these sleaze-balls, nor to see you dressed like a whore!"

Rose's eyes jerked open with shock as the taboo word struck her with the force of a physical blow. She saw the disgust in Jefferson's face, and was hot with shame, immediately wanting to cover her satin-clad body and her exposed length of legs from that disapproving stare. And just as suddenly, she was aware of a raging anger.

"How *dare* you!" she spluttered. "You sanctimonious prig! What the hell are *you* doing here, may I ask, if it's not for one purpose only? It's more a case of the pot calling the kettle black, isn't it – *sir*? *And* getting it all wrong, too," she snapped, uncaring that she was insulting her boss, and assuredly in line for being sacked on the spot.

Jefferson folded his arms. In this room, despite her slim height and the high heels, he still stood head and shoulders above her, towering over her like some Colossus, she raged, as if he thought he could intimidate her by his sheer size and personality. Well, it may work with some people, but not for her. Not any more.

"And just how have I got it all wrong, may I ask?" he snapped back. "I see what my eyes tell me—"

"Well, they tell you wrong," Rose said, suddenly calm. "And if you think I won't scream rape if you touch me, you've got that wrong, too."

He said nothing for a minute, and then his eyes narrowed.

"So what are you after? Money? Is that the game you're playing, my too-sweet innocent English Rose?"

Afterwards, she couldn't have said how it happened. One minute she was standing in front of Jefferson, blazing at the insult that she might be resorting to some kind of blackmail. The next, she had swung her arm upwards with all her strength, and cracked him full in the face. Caught off-balance, he reeled slightly, and then grabbed her shoulders to steady himself. His fingers dug into her bare flesh and she had a job not to cry out with the pain of it.

"You little bitch," he said hoarsely. "Nobody strikes a Jefferson and gets away with it. So maybe this is what you wanted all along."

He pulled her towards him with a savagery that shocked her. She was pressed so hard against his chest that it all but winded her, and then she couldn't breathe at all as his mouth fastened cruelly over hers, forcing it open until she could taste blood. At first she fought against him, struggling to get free, and when she knew it was hopeless, she simply stayed completely motionless in his arms.

The kiss, if such oral rape could be called a kiss, finally ended, and Jefferson put her slowly away from him. He stared long and deep into her eyes, while she tried to remain unflinching, fighting back the threatening tears.

"You really didn't want that, did you?" he said slowly.

"No," said Rose, almost inaudibly. Her head drooped, and although she knew she must resemble a naughty schoolgirl, caught in some despicable act, she couldn't help it. Her spirit, as well as her head, was wilting, and all the fire of resistance had gone out of her. She felt exactly what she was: a naïve eighteen-year-old, way out of her depth in a situation she just didn't know how to handle.

"Then I apologize, Rose," Jefferson said. "I begin to suspect that you didn't know what you were getting yourself into, in coming here."

"Of course I didn't," she said swiftly. "Do you think I'm the kind of girl who sells herself cheap?"

He rubbed at his sore cheek, where the dull redness was a reminder of her desperate attack.

"I know that you're not," he said, with a wry smile. "And I'm sorry for hurting you too."

She saw that he was looking at her shoulders, where the scratches in her skin showed evidence of where his nails had dug into her. What a mess, she thought, both scarred as if they had been engaged in battle, instead of what everyone would naturally believe of two people who had gone to one of the upstairs rooms. . . .

"You seem to find something funny," Jefferson said, seeing the look in her eyes now.

"I was just wondering how I could decently get out of here," she said honestly. "I really don't think I could stand another couple of hours of walking around with a tray of cocktails in my hands. Besides which, these damn movie star heels are killing me."

He laughed. "Let's both get out of here. My car's outside, and if you can get changed out of that salacious outfit, we'll go to a quiet hamburger bar and have some coffee to calm down. What do you say?"

"No strings?" Rose said, hardly daring to believe that she was questioning her boss in such a way.

"I think you know that," Jefferson said dryly. "Besides, I wouldn't dare. But tell me, how did you get here in the first place? I wasn't aware that Joanna was advertising for staff."

"My brother-in-law," she said. "He's valeting for the evening, and he'll be waiting to take me home later."

"Let him wait. Anyone who gets you into this situation doesn't deserve a second thought."

She looked at him gratefully. And then she thought of something else too.

"But why are you here?" she said, the little niggle of suspicion not yet leaving her. For all that any attraction she had felt towards him was now stone dead, she didn't like to think he was the kind of man who frequented parties just to take girls upstairs . . . he surely didn't need that. . . .

"Joanna's my great-aunt," he said. "LA folk have some strange claims to fame, honey, and this is my particular albatross. She likes to parade her successful business relative in public, so I show up at her parties, but I never stay long, and tonight I reckon I've done more than my duty."

Rose felt suitably impressed and subdued at the same time. She'd never thought of family relationships being the reason for him being here. Somehow LA didn't seem like a town that nurtured the kind of close family relationships she'd known back home, but she was probably being churlish in thinking that way. Anyway, she wouldn't care to have the grotesque Joanna Del Mar as any relation of hers!

They went down the back stairs, feeling like two conspirators, and once Rose had changed out of the satin outfit into her own clothes, she began to feel human again.

"I still think I should tell my brother-in-law I'm leaving," she said doubtfully, but it was another valet in a green waistcoat and matching trousers who leapt to bring Jefferson's car to the front of the mansion, and Merv was nowhere to be seen.

She decided against leaving a message with the other car valet, and for the second time since arriving in LA, Rose found herself sitting beside Bradley Piers Jefferson the third in his sleek black limousine. They drove silently out of the lighted driveway of the Del Mar mansion, and down through the tree-lined avenues of Bel-Air, where the twinkling lights of the city of angels lay spread out before them like fairyland.

"Beautiful, isn't it?" Jefferson said, after the silence between them had begun to lengthen uncomfortably. "It makes you wonder how something so beautiful can hide such corruption."

"It can't all be corrupt," Rose said swiftly. "There's some good in everyone."

"And bad too. We all have a good side and a bad side, Rose, and for some people it's a constant battle as to which side wins. Others don't even try."

She didn't dare ask which comment applied to himself. In any case, it was none of her business.

"Now I'm embarrassing you. Perhaps we'd better forego the coffee after all, and I'll just take you home."

"I think I'd prefer that," she murmured.

And she couldn't bear to sit in a crowded hamburger bar, making small talk with a man wearing a five-hundred dollar suit and expensive jewellery, with his swish limousine parked outside. A hamburger bar wasn't his rightful place, and slumming with him wasn't hers. Sometimes, for all that she tried so hard to be a Californian girl, she knew she was still little Rose Forster from the valleys. . . . *No*, from the *East End of London*, she corrected herself swiftly.

Chapter Eight

The apartment building was all in darkness by the time the limousine slid to a stop outside. Rose felt stiff with embarrassment, not knowing what to say to Jefferson now, but he said it for her.

"Put this evening down to experience, Rose, and then forget it," he said quietly, using almost the same words as Gracie had done. "As far as I'm concerned it never happened, all right?"

"All right," she murmured. "And thank you."

"No. Thank you, honey, for reminding me that there's still some goodness to be found in this rotten town."

Before she knew what he was going to do, he had leaned towards her. She could smell the faint hint of cologne on his skin, but it was a clean, fresh scent, not a cloying aroma like that of a Chuck Bernstein. Seconds before Jefferson's mouth touched hers for the second time that evening, she closed her eyes, wondering if she was to be assaulted after all. But there was no more than a featherlight touch on her lips that wasn't meant to stir her senses at all. It was more the kind of kiss a brother might give to a sister in passing.

"Good-night, Rose," Jefferson said, reaching across her to open the door, without any attempt to take advantage of the situation. "No doubt you'll be at the office bright and early on Monday morning."

"I'm not fired then?" she couldn't help asking.

"Why should you be? Because of something that never happened? I told you, tonight's forgotten."

She got out of the car gratefully, and let herself into the apartment without looking back. She leaned against the door for long moments, trying to get her breath back. She felt as though she had been running a long way, after travelling a long journey. And whether or not she would eventually be able to forget all that had occurred that evening, she knew it wasn't going to happen in a hurry.

She crept into her room and undressed quickly, glad of the thin nightgown to cover her burning skin. The humiliation of the situation Merv had put her in, was still too vivid in her mind to forget, and without warning, she suddenly felt as if all her limbs had turned to water.

She crawled into bed, shivering all over, wanting to hide beneath the bedclothes in a way she hadn't done since she was a child and less afraid of the dark than of old Hitler's bombs. And just as the tears had flowed then, they flowed now. She couldn't help it. She felt as weak and vulnerable as a kitten, wishing herself a thousand miles away from this town where you didn't need to go looking for corruption. It simply reached out and touched you. So much for Hollywood's bright, glamorous image, she thought bitterly. So much for dreams.

She was half-asleep from sheer tiredness when she heard Merv come home. Everybody in the apartment building must have heard him too. The Chevy door banged shut, followed by the front door of the apartment, and the next minute he was hollering out her name. She sat up in a fright, pulling the bedcovers up tight to her chin as her bedroom door burst open and the light was snapped on.

"What bloody game do you think you're playing?" he snarled as Rose's eyes rebelled against the glare of the electric light. Even from across the room, she could smell the drink on him.

"I don't know what you mean—" she said hoarsely.

"No? I didn't expect to make a fortune out of you tonight, but when I told you to be nice to folk, I didn't expect you to give every damn one of them that old chestnut of being fully engaged for the evening."

Rose registered several things at once. Merv had set her up. He had clearly expected to get a few backhanders for the *gentlemen* she had entertained in her room. And someone had been annoyed enough to split on her. Her disgust for him boiled over. She grabbed for her dressing gown and slid out of the bed, quickly tying the garment around herself. She felt less vulnerable out of the bed with this oaf leering at her.

"Was it Ilsa who told you?" she raged. "It was her idea, anyway, and I thank God that it was. What kind of a girl do you think I am?"

His eyes narrowed. "I ain't too sure, babe," he sneered. "You ain't the same type as your sister, that's for sure. Gracie wouldn't have balked at a bit of fun, nor put on the frightened virgin act the minute a guy looked at her."

"Well I'm not Gracie, and not all of us thought the sun shone out of every GI's backside, thank you very much," she whipped back, hating him more than she had ever hated anyone at that moment. And even more so for making her so mad that she retorted in words that brought her down to his level.

To her surprise he started to laugh. "You've got spunk, kid, I'll give you that much. I'll bet there were times, though, when you wished you were old enough to do what your Gracie did."

His voice had grown sly and mocking, and Rose was suddenly afraid of him. The whole apartment building was sleeping, and hopefully Gracie would be out for the count after taking a couple of her Dexies, if she'd remembered to take them. And Merv Hackett was taking a great interest in the way her nightdress and dressing gown were clinging

119

to her body, and how her nipples were prominent against them. He moved towards her, and she took a quick pace backwards. But there was nowhere to go, and the door was beyond him on the other side of the room.

"Well, if you couldn't be nice to the guys who were willing to pay for it, how about giving your old brother-in-law a kiss for free?" he taunted. "Maybe it's a bit of rough that you fancy, same as Gracie. Is that it, babe?"

He lunged towards her, pinning her against the wall. She couldn't move. She was fanned by his breath, stale with drink and tobacco, and she twisted her head sharply, feeling her neck crick. But he was too quick for her, and his huge hand reached up and twisted her face back towards him.

"I'll scream if you touch me," she croaked. "I'll let everybody know—"

To her horror, his hand slid down to encircle her throat. She could feel the pressure of it, and the blood pounded in her veins.

"I could snap this pretty neck of yours as easy as cracking a nut," he said smoothly. "I was in a tough unit during the war, so if you want to try me out, just go ahead and scream, sweet pie."

Rose stood dumbly, her legs threatening to fold up beneath her. But if they did, the pressure on her neck would surely increase, and then where would she be? She closed her eyes, trying not to notice when the fleshy mouth pressed itself to hers, and then she felt his other hand reaching for her breast, fondling and circling and squeezing. Her nipples reacted involuntarily to the erotic touch, and against all her instincts, she felt a quickening, explosive sensation in her groin, and her breathing became more laboured.

Then she was aware of something else. By now, Merv had an enormous erection, and it was pressing hard against her. Thankfully, the shameful, mechanical response to the sort of caresses she hadn't experienced before, vanished as quickly as it came, and she pushed against him with all her might. He was caught off-balance and went crashing backwards into the dressing-table, sending it rocking.

"You bloody little tart!" he yelled, and the next minute the door burst open, Gracie had snapped on the light, and was staring owlishly at the pair of them.

If the situation hadn't been so awful, Rose might have laughed out loud at the bizarre sight of her once-glamorous sister. Her hair was a mass of curlers, her feet pushed into mules that had seen better days, and she had dragged Merv's old tartan dressing gown over her nightgown as she came to see what all the noise was about. She'd obviously forgotten to take her nightly Dexedrine tablets after all, Rose thought incongruously.

"It's this one," Merv shouted, the complete turncoat. "Playing fast and loose with some of the old guys at Joanna Del Mar's mansion, she was, and I doubt that she'll be asked to do service up there again."

His eyes dared Rose to argue with him, and while she was still trying to find enough breath to hurl abuse back at him, Gracie rounded on her.

"Is this true, our Rose?"

Merv didn't give her a chance to answer. "'Course it's true. I'm telling you, ain't I? Look at the marks on her neck if you don't believe me. If they ain't love bites, I don't know what are."

"Of course they're not love bites!" Rose yelled back, without a clue what love bites were. "You should know what they are, you pig!"

She felt the sting of Gracie's slap on her face then, and wondered if she was going to be black and blue by morning. What with Jefferson's fingernails digging into her shoulders, and Merv's cruel pressure on her neck, and now this. . . .

"Don't you speak to Merv like that, Miss," Gracie snapped. "This is his house, and you just apologize to him, you hear?"

"I will not!"

Without warning, she was seven years old again, standing defiantly in front of her parents and a sniggering older sister, and being told that she was going to be sent away for the duration. She didn't even know what the duration meant. She only knew that her dad was angrily telling her to apologize to her mum, for something she didn't know she'd done. Whatever it was, it was clearly something terrible for her to be sent away like that, while Gracie, the oldest and the favoured one, was staying behind with them.

It had been many months before the feeling even started to go away. And now it had come hurtling back. Rose swallowed dryly. Whatever Merv was, and whatever Gracie had become, they either moved closer together at that moment, or else it was an illusion. Whatever it was, to Rose's eyes they became a united front, and she knew it was useless to blurt out Merv's pathetic attempt at seduction, because Gracie simply wouldn't believe it.

"Well, Miss?" Gracie persisted sharply. "Do we have to stand here all night, or are you going to apologize?"

"I've done nothing to apologize for."

"You've disrupted my night's sleep, for a start."

"Didn't you take your tablets? I'll get them for you, if you like."

Oh God, now she was starting to sound like an eager schoolkid, desperate for a word of praise from her superior.

"I'll get 'em," Merv said. "Then, for Pete's sake, let's all just get to bed and sleep on it until the morning."

"That suits me fine," Rose muttered.

For a minute, she thought Gracie was going to continue the argument. For the life of her, she couldn't move away from Gracie's penetrating stare. Gracie stood perfectly still, as if she could see right through Rose, and knew everything that had gone on. But if she knew that, she'd know about Merv, and from the way she suddenly linked her arm in his, Rose knew it couldn't be the case.

"Put the lights out and get to bed, Rose," she ordered, and the two of them disappeared out of the room, leaving Rose wilting. She felt as if a kind of battle had been fought, but she wasn't sure which side had won, or if anything at all had been resolved. But she was suddenly so exhausted that she was past caring, anyway.

"I'm not going to say any more about last night, Rose," Gracie announced over a late Sunday breakfast.

Merv hadn't shown his face yet, and wouldn't before noon, for which Rose was thankful. But although Gracie probably meant what she said, she couldn't quite let it rest there.

"Maybe you'll be more careful in future, and see that this town isn't all the glitter and gold you people think it is," she went on severely.

"Who do mean by 'you people'"? Rose said, full of resentment.

"I mean crazy kids with stars in their eyes, thinking they're coming out to Hollywood to make it big in the movies. Being discovered drinking sodas by some wandering talent scout, and all that garbage. It don't work, Rose."

"Isn't that how you saw it when you came out here with your – Merv?" She had very nearly said 'your Yank'.

"I was already married," Gracie said, with a little note of triumph in her voice. "I wasn't one of those hopefuls who came over on a wish and a promise. I already had a ring on my finger, and I wasn't looking for anything but a new life with my husband."

"Well, I'm certainly not thinking of going into the

123

movies," Rose said vigorously. "I don't have the talent for it, nor the stomach, either, after the things I've heard."

Gracie grinned. "Oh well, maybe last night did you some good then. Anyway, you did Merv a favour in insisting that he brought you home early," she said. Rose tried to keep a straight face at this blatant lie, while wondering how many others Merv had told his wife to keep her sweet and unsuspecting.

"Why do you say that?" she couldn't resist asking.

"These old dames have a special way of ending their parties, hon. Merv says most of them have their own projection room in their houses. Party guests don't have to sing for their supper. They just have to sit through some boring old silent movie, with the old dame thinking she looks the same now as she did when she was your age. Pathetic, isn't it? But it also means the car valets sometimes have to be there until the early hours of the morning."

Rose agreed that it was pathetic, though not in the same sarcastic way that Gracie meant it. It truly was pathetic, to be living so much in the past that you couldn't appreciate today or enjoy the thought of tomorrow . . . and just for a minute, she wondered if she was thinking more about herself than about Joanna Del Mar right then.

She went into the Jefferson building on Monday morning, thankful that she'd said nothing to any of the other girls about her moonlighting job. What they didn't know about, they couldn't ask about. Though it was ironic that the only person in this huge glass and concrete building who knew of her embarrassment, was Bradley Piers Jefferson himself.

Her heart leapt when her name was called over the office intercom. Any thought that Jefferson might give her a chance at the PA job was slipping away so fast now, she didn't even consider it as the reason he wanted to speak to her.

"Would Rose Forster report to Mr Jefferson's office at four o'clock this afternoon?" came Miss Simpson's stiffly nasal tones over the intercom.

While Rose's heart jumped, she saw several of the girls eyeing her with interest. And then Lacey Venables strode through the office and stopped at Rose's desk.

"What have you been doing to curry favour, you bitch?" she hissed, under cover of bending down to retrieve some papers she'd dropped, accidentally-on-purpose.

Rose flinched. The antagonism emanating from the older woman was potentially evil, and she stammered in response.

"I don't know what you mean. I've done nothing—"

"You've been here long enough to know that at four o'clock in the afternoon, Jefferson never sees anyone but interviewees, or important clients he intends to entertain to dinner. That's what I mean. So either you're up for my job, or you've been playing out of school, bitch."

The insinuation was obvious. And the reference to *her* job was clearly the post of PA she was wild to get when Miss Simpson retired.

"You've got it all wrong," Rose began, but before she could get any further, Cindy spoke loudly enough for everyone around them to hear.

"Why don't you leave the kid alone, Lacey? You may not have what it takes to hook a big fish any more, but if Rose has, good luck to her."

Rose gasped, furious now at the way they were talking about her as if she wasn't there, and putting all the wrong ideas into everyone else's heads. She was aware of a pause in the clatter of the typewriters, and she heard one girl hiss into her phone, "I'll call you back", before she slammed down the receiver, and concentrated on the more interesting goings-on in the office.

"I assure you I've no intentions of hooking a big fish, as you call it," she snapped, in her best English voice. "Nor do I have the faintest idea what Mr Jefferson might want to see me about. If it happens to be anything that could remotely interest you, Miss Venables, I'll be sure and report back to you. All right?"

Her use of Lacey's full name brought the predictable flash to the woman's eyes.

"Don't give me that," she sneered. "We all know about you Britishers, and how they sucked up to the GIs for their chocolates and nylons. Didn't your own sister marry a GI for the cushy life?"

It was so near, and yet so far, from the truth that Rose could do nothing but burst out laughing.

"I was too young at the time to be interested in a GI or anybody else," she said, ignoring Lacey's insult about Gracie. "In any case, I've got a boyfriend back home who's worth ten of anybody I've met here so far."

"Oh yes. And I suppose you connect by telepathy," Lacey delivered the final jibe before she swished back to her own little office, slapping the pile of papers onto Rose's desk. "Sort these into proper order, and be quick about it."

As she stared gloomily at the mass of disorganized work in front of her, Cindy gave her an encouraging smile.

"Take no notice, Rose. She's just jealous. She always wanted to travel to Europe, but she's never made it. Your accent rubs her up the wrong way, as well as everything else."

"What do you call everything else?"

Cindy laughed. "Are you kidding? With your looks and colouring, and the way you walk? I tell you, hon, you could star in a dozen movies any day of the week. But you've never said anything about this boyfriend. Are

126

you going to give us the low-down? Is he a Britisher, like yourself?"

Rose stared blankly, aware that Gloria had leaned forward from her desk as well. Boyfriend? What boyfriend? Whatever she had said had been said in the heat of the moment, and she could hardly remember it now. But these two Californian girls were waiting all agog to know who she'd been talking about, and the only image that came into her mind right then was Evan Pritchard.

"I wish you wouldn't call me a Britisher," she said in a small fit of pique. "I'm English, and Evan's Welsh."

"So, what's Welsh?" Gloria said.

"For Pete's sake, Gloria," Cindy put irritably. "Welsh is the language they speak in Wales. Isn't that right, Rose?"

"Well, not many of them do, actually. The old Celtic language is still used a lot in north Wales, but in the south they all speak English." And a damn sight better than you do, she added silently.

"So who's this Evan, then? And when's he coming over?" Gloria asked next.

"Coming over?"

"Well, isn't he? There's no future in carrying on a relationship with somebody when you're thousands of miles apart," Cindy said.

"Plenty of servicemen and their girlfriends had to do just that during the war," Rose said, not liking their logic at all, and wishing she'd never mentioned Evan's name. If only Lacey Venables hadn't goaded her into it. . . .

"Well, we're not at war now, so tell us about him while Lacey's out of the office," Gloria said, seeing that Rose was getting that sniffy look on her face that she reckoned could freeze a guy at ten paces.

Rose shrugged, as a swift image came into her mind. What harm would it do to indulge them, anyway? "All

127

right then, if you insist. Evan's tall and dark and quite good-looking, and he's got a lovely voice—"

"Singing, you mean? Didn't I hear somewhere that all Welshmen burst into song every five minutes?" Cindy grinned.

"He's got a lovely speaking voice," Rose said, ignoring the daftness of such a remark, and suddenly remembering instead the warm, dark, intimate timbre of Evan's voice when he'd called her on the phone to wish her a happy birthday. In fact, the richness of it was so vivid in her head at that moment, she almost felt as if she could turn around and he'd be there. . . .

"Has he asked you to do it yet?" Gloria said.

"What?" Rose said blankly.

Gloria laughed out loud.

"Jeez, Rose, how can somebody with your looks be so naïve? Has he screwed you yet?"

Rose felt her face burn. Then, as another voice bellowed down the length of the room, she thought she'd never been more thankful to hear Lacey Venables' raucous tones ordering them to get back to work before she reported the lot of them. Reluctantly, Gloria slid off Rose's desk and sauntered back to her own.

Rose bent industriously over the sheaf of papers she was still sorting, annoyed to find that her hands were shaking. Naïve she might be, compared with Cindy and Gloria's LA brand of sophistication, but she knew what Gloria had meant right enough. And now she wished desperately that she hadn't brought up Evan's name, and had him shamed like that. It wasn't right, and she'd done a damn stupid thing in calling him her boyfriend, when he'd been as dear to her as a brother, and always would be.

She paused over the muddled papers for a moment, as a wild, unexpected picture swept into her mind. Evan Pritchard wasn't her brother, any more than Dai or Merv, or Jefferson was. He was no longer a boy, either. In the last few years he'd grown in stature, broadened and toughened into a man. And Rose had been so busy growing up herself, and spending all her spare time brooding over her frustrated longing to go to America, that she'd never really looked at him as a man, only as her make-believe brother and champion.

But she was looking at the fantasy of it now. Turning over the curious thought in her mind that Evan Pritchard was a man who was ripe and ready for the right girl to fall in love with . . . a girl who was on hand to catch his eye, and not thousands of miles across oceans and continents . . . and if she had ever had any notions of him falling for her, she'd well and truly blitzed her chances by leaving him to all those fresh-faced valley girls who'd be hungry for his touch.

She was breathing so shallowly that Cindy looked at her in sudden concern.

"Say, are you OK, Rose? You're not going to hyper-ventilate or anything, are you? You don't want to take any notice of Gloria's crap. She was always partial to a bit of gutter-talk."

"I'm OK," Rose muttered, taking a few deep breaths, and refusing to take notice of Gloria's knowing eyes.

It was just as if she sensed how the stirring in Rose's loins was making her squirm right then, just by thinking about Evan Pritchard. She'd only known this odd feeling a couple of times before, and never so vibrantly as when Merv pressed himself against her after the Joanna Del Mar fiasco. It had revolted her then, but with the image of Evan so strong in her head, it wasn't revolting her now. And it should. As long as she still thought of him as a kind of brother. . . .

At four o'clock exactly, she presented herself at Jefferson's office. Lacey Venables' taunts still rang in her ears, and she couldn't forget the last time she had faced her boss. He'd been so furious with her . . . but then she remembered the way his voice had gentled, and that sweet kiss he had given her. He understood. . . .

One look at the hardness in his eyes, and all her finer feelings vanished. He told her curtly to sit down, not on one of the plush sofas, but on one of the leather business chairs on the other side of his vast desk. It separated them more that anything else could have done, and Rose's hands felt clammy, despite the horrendously cold air-conditioning.

"You won't need any of that," Jefferson said, seeing the way she clutched her notebook and pencil.

"I assumed you wanted me to take some dictation," she began nervously.

"And why would you assume that? Do you think I don't have a hundred girls at my disposal to take down dictation, or anything else I may require?"

Rose gasped. This was another side of him, and she no longer knew him. He sat back in his horrible red leather chair, his back to the huge office window, and yet he seemed to tower over her. Or maybe it was just the effect he had on her, that made her feel as if she was shrinking back from him.

She ran her tongue around her dry lips. "What is it you want of me then – sir?" she remembered to add huskily.

He flung a tabloid newspaper at her. She recognized it at once as the kind of downmarket rag that Gracie devoured. Its reporters delighted in detailing who was who at the stars' parties, and more importantly, who was on the A list, who was relegated to the B list, and who was simply no longer invited to any of them. Merv had once told her that once you had ambitions to be a celebrity, this was a killer town. As long as you were in favour, you did all right, but once you were out, you might as well pack your bags and go

130

back to where you came from. Rose was prepared to believe it.

She looked up at Jefferson, not knowing what she was supposed to say, but from the way her heart was beating so fast, she knew she wasn't in for any soft-soaping.

"Turn to the centre pages, my sweet innocent," he said impatiently.

Rose did so with shaking fingers. She had already guessed that there would be photos of the Saturday night party, and so there were. She recognized the various overblown stars and the skinny starlets with enormous hairstyles and glossy lips who pouted out at her, together with the leering, cigar-smoking figures of bloated businessmen.

And there were a couple of waitresses in full view. There was Ilsa, clearly laughing up into some lech's face. And there was Rose. She was in the background of the photo, but there was some oaf's hand creeping up her backside, and she had a smile on her face as she half-turned towards him.

She remembered the incident instantly. The smile had only lasted a second before she realized what was happening, and she had squirmed away from him as fast as she could. But whoever had taken the picture hadn't bothered to record that. In any case, his camera had been pointing at the movie star in the foreground, and the waitresses were just incidental in the background.

Except, it appeared now, to Jefferson.

"You don't think I was enjoying that, I hope?" she said in a choked voice. "I can assure you it lasted no more than a second—"

He was around the desk very quickly for such a big man, and he had yanked her to her feet before she had any idea what he was about.

"What I think is that all this innocence is no more than a pose," he snapped. "I've seen hundreds of girls come to this town, playing the same kind of game, but I admit you had me fooled, honey. You really fooled me, especially after your performance when I took you home. You're a much better actress than I gave you credit for."

"*No* – you're completely *wrong* – and you're hurting me," she gasped, as his grip tightened around her wrists.

He gave a harsh laugh, and there was nothing but derision in his handsome dark eyes.

"And I suppose you're going to tell me you had no idea that most of the girls who are employed at the house-parties are call girls? Your friend Ilsa, for instance, who seemed to be doing a bloody good job in instructing you. . . ."

Rose couldn't speak. She was so breathless that the restriction in her chest became tight and painful. Her face flooded with colour and then Jefferson pulled her unceremoniously into his arms.

"Nobody's that naïve, so maybe this is what you wanted after all," he said brutally.

The next minute she was being propelled back to one of the plush sofas and pushed down onto it. All the breath was knocked out of her, and she struggled to break free from his heavy weight as he pressed savage kisses on her mouth, forcing it open with his own until she could taste blood on her teeth. She could feel his hand crawling up her skirt, and she clamped her legs tightly together. Dear God, this couldn't be happening . . .

With some semblance of sanity, she resorted to something she'd once seen in a movie, and dissolved into undignified weeping. Her whole body shook, and she went limp and unresisting in his arms. And there was one last thing she would do if she had to. . . . the *very, very last* totally demoralizing thing that she had once heard about . . . she would simply pee all over him if he got anywhere near her. . . .

Jefferson suddenly stood up, staring down at her with

narrowed eyes as she frantically pulled her skirt down and sat up stiff and straight.

"My God, you're either up for an Oscar, or you should get the hell back to Wales where you belong," he said, turning on his heel and striding away from her. "Get out of my sight and go home."

"Am I fired?" Rose said.

She couldn't believe she was lowering herself to ask such a question, but if she lost this job, there would be an almighty inquisition from Gracie and Merv, and she couldn't bear that. At least now, Jefferson would surely leave her alone. He laughed.

"No, you're not fired, honey, as long as you don't expect to get any farther in this company. Do your work and collect your pay. Apart from that, I won't know you exist."

Chapter Nine

Rose *knew* she should put it all down to experience, but it wasn't the kind of experience she'd anticipated when she came to LA. All her dreams were shattered, and people here were rotten. And if common sense told her it couldn't apply to everybody, it seemed as if the ones she had encountered so far fell very easily into that category.

It wasn't something she could tell Gracie about, either. She'd be far too humiliated, and she just prayed that Gracie wouldn't see the newspaper with Rose's photo in it. Or Merv . . . or he might get the idea that she'd gone along with the lech all along. And that would give him every excuse to try his own luck, Gracie or no Gracie.

She had to think seriously about moving out of their place and getting something of her own. Or maybe sharing with another girl. It was awful to finally realize that while she didn't care for Merv, even her own sister was far from being the person she had once known. They had all changed, Rose thought. Nobody stayed the same after all these years.

She had been a kid with stars in her eyes when Gracie went to America with her Yank, but she wasn't a kid any more, and the stars were fast beginning to fade. . . .

The one bright spot was that from then on Jefferson left her strictly alone. There were no more calls to his office, and he rarely made an appearance in the general typing pool. And she could put up with the snide remarks from Lacey Venables that she must have fallen out of favour fast. She just got on with her work and collected her salary, which was what she was paid to do.

Sea-Food Joe's was still the social highlight of the Hacketts' week, and at any other time when Gracie felt disinclined to make dinner, which was pretty often. And Chuck Bernstein was becoming even more adamant about getting her a movie test.

"That little gal of yours has blossomed since coming here, Merv," he said admiringly, and loudly enough so the whole place could hear. He leaned forward and tickled Rose beneath the chin.

Rose fumed at his touch. It was the way elderly uncles treated five year olds, only in this case, Chuck's leering eyes were anything but fond, and the touch was anything but innocent. She flinched back, just managing to resist the urge to scrub at her skin where his fingers had caressed it.

"Whaddaya say, doll? Do you want old Chuck to get you a screen test? I got a bit of influence with the studios, and they're always ready to snap up an English actress with class."

"Well, that's where I'd be no good at all," Rose said, as cut-glass British as she could manage. "I can't act for toffee, and they'd see through me in a minute."

"Aw, come on, anybody can act—"

"Do you think so? Well, why don't you get Gracie to do it then?" Rose said, hating the attention this conversation was getting from the other diners. "I'm sure she hasn't forgotten *all* her vowel sounds yet."

"Don't bring me into it, hon," Gracie said lazily, too disinterested to take offence. "I ain't never had any leanings towards the movies."

"Well, neither have I!" Rose said, knowing it was only half the truth.

135

"Gee, you hear that, guys?" Chuck said, turning to several diners close by. "The way she says n*eye*ther – it's real sweet, ain't it? Baby, you'd get by on your looks and accent alone. Who the hell needs acting with what you've got?"

The more he went on, the more upset Rose became. It wasn't real flattery. It was coarse and humiliating. She felt like a piece of meat on a butcher's slab, inspected and prodded by anybody who took a fancy to her. She remembered instantly that they were Mam Pritchard's words, from way back when a local bathing beauty contest had been held in Cardiff, and all the newspapers had photographed the line-up of girls for everybody to see.

"Shaming, that's what it is," Mam had sniffed. "Showing off their legs and bosoms like that. I've no doubt they're no better than they should be."

Which was a remark that had completely mystified the small Rose Forster at the time, and she'd gone to Evan to ask him what it meant. He'd laughed, swinging her round in his strong arms from his lofty height.

"You don't want to take no notice of Mam, Rose. She's living in the past, and there's nothing wrong with respectable bathing beauty contests. Anyway, you'd win it hands down, girl, even a tiddler like you."

Which hadn't explained anything, but it had given her a warm glow at the time. Evan wasn't a fast talker, but when he gave a compliment, he meant it.

She blinked now, as she realized Chuck Bernstein was still leaning towards her. He didn't give up easily, and he'd seen the sudden dreamy look in the kid's eyes. Maybe there was some ambition there after all, and it only needed a bit of tactful persuasion to bring it out. And managing this one's affairs would be the kind of meal ticket Chuck had often dreamed about himself.

"Well, whaddaya think about the Miss Christmas Angel pageant then, babe? You ain't forgotten about that, have you? You win that, and you'll be on your way, and you don't need no acting talent to mince about on the stage in your bathing duds and high heels."

He ran his tongue around his lips as he finished, already seeing Rose Forster in his imagination, those luscious curves busting out of a bathing top, and those long, long legs that seemed to stretch right up to her armpits. . . .

His comments were so near, and yet so far, from Rose's own thoughts about Mam and Evan, that she felt her face burn with colour. Because there was all the difference in the world between Evan's reassurance to a young child, and this sleaze-ball's innuendoes.

"I'm not interested," she snapped. "All I'm interested in is eating my dinner if the waitress ever gets around to bringing it."

She turned her back on him, sitting ramrod straight in her chair, and seeing the small grin play around Gracie's mouth. Gracie didn't like Chuck Bernstein, but Rose had learned by now that Gracie didn't like many people. Gracie had an inborn suspicion of folk, and even though it was depressing, Rose was starting to realize it wasn't such a bad thing to have.

"Well done, kid," Gracie said. "You don't want to get mixed up with any of that acting and modelling crap."

"Why the hell not?" Merv said. "She could make big bucks, and pay us back some of the dough we've poured into her over the years."

Rose gasped. For all his brashness, he'd never put it in so many words before. And in public too. The guys who knew Merv Hackett for a tightwad looked on with renewed interest, and Rose could just guess what they were thinking. Merv didn't do anything for nothing. And if he'd brought this sweet little gal over from England to live with him and his sourpuss Gracie, it could only be for one thing.

The waitress brought their food, and Rose leaned over

it at once. For the first time she could see what this place was doing to her. LA was fast-moving, glittering and glamorous as far as Hollywood and the movie stars went – but that was all that ordinary folk ever really got to hear about it.

And underneath . . . underneath, there was so much corruption, and she was only just beginning to see the tip of the iceberg. Even Bradley Piers Jefferson the third, that so-respectable businessman, considered any girl fair game. And she didn't need to look very far to know that there were plenty who'd be willing to do anything he asked. Everybody had their price.

"Well?" Merv persisted. "Cat got your tongue, kid?"

"Can we just get on with our dinner?" she said in a choked voice. "I didn't come here to have an argument, especially one that's going nowhere."

"Rose is right," Gracie said. "You just keep your mouth buttoned, Chuck Bernstein, and leave Rose alone. If she wants to go in for the Miss Christmas Angel pageant, she'll decide for herself when she's good and ready."

Rose viciously attacked the broiled rib on her plate. Gracie had become very good at appearing to say one thing, while meaning another. There was no doubt in Rose's mind that Gracie, as well as Merv, could see the big bucks sign loud and clear over Rose's head. Well, they could just whistle for them. She wasn't parading herself in a cattle market for anybody.

"You'd win it hands down, girl, even a tiddler like you. . . ."

Gradually, Gracie seemed to get the message that Rose had reached the limit of her patience regarding the beauty contest. Over the next few weeks, she simply refused to speak about it. If Merv brought up the subject, Rose either changed the conversation, or stared stubbornly into space. It always infuriated him, but it also had the desired effect of seeing him stump outside to work on the troublesome Chevy, usually starting with a savage kick at the tyres to get rid of some of his aggression.

"You know you wind him up, Rose," Gracie said, with a mixture of annoyance and satisfaction.

"Why? Because I won't do everything he says? Anyway, I don't see you being a dutiful little wifey, our Gracie," she added, to soften the slight.

"Not likely," Gracie retorted. "You gotta keep a man in his place, kid, and that's one thing you'll learn when you find a guy of your own. Nobody on the horizon yet, I suppose?"

Rose blushed. Gracie liked to make arch remarks about Rose finding a man to marry. Rich, of course. He'd have to be rich, and capable of providing for Rose's entire family, which would mean that Merv could retire from the car valeting. . . .

"No," she snapped. "And I wish you'd stop asking me. There's nobody at the office I'm remotely interested in, and I don't know anybody else."

"OK, OK!" Gracie said, pretending to back off. "So what about the boss? You're not being stupid enough to give him the cold shoulder, are you?"

Rose hadn't told her sister a thing about the various encounters she'd had with Jefferson. Gracie would tell Merv, and she wouldn't put it past Merv to do something stupid, like going all moral on Rose's behalf, and demanding money from Jefferson if he didn't want his reputation revealed to the gutter press.

Maybe she was letting her imagination run away with her, but by now she wouldn't put anything past Merv.

"I don't fancy him, that's all," she said distantly. "And there are too many beautiful girls working for the Jefferson Printing Corporation for him to single me out."

"Don't underestimate yourself, Rose. Besides, you've got what they ain't."

She knew she shouldn't ask. But as usual, from long habit, she took Gracie's bait.

"And what's that?"

"Your *Englishness*, dummy!"

"*Dieu*, and here's me thinking I was no more than a litle ninny from the *vall*eys," Rose said, in her heaviest Welsh accent that would do credit to a Swansea docker.

Gracie didn't see the joke.

"You'll be sorry when you don't bag a rich husband, our Rose, and have to settle for what you can get. You're too damn picky by half, and that sharp tongue of yours will get the better of you one of these days."

God, that was rich, coming from her! But Rose let the irony of it pass, as Gracie suddenly clutched at her side, and her face broke out in the ugly bluish sweat Rose had seen on it before.

"What's wrong?" she said quickly.

"Nothing. Just a twinge. Don't make a fuss. Just get me some tranqus."

But those short, gasping sentences alerted Rose to the fact that there was something very wrong. Gracie had slumped on her chair now, bent double, and Rose was pretty sure that tranquillizers weren't going to do her any good. She twisted on her heel and ran out of the apartment, shouting for Merv to come inside.

"Whaddaya want?" he said irritably, without lifting his head from beneath the hood of the car.

"It's Gracie. She needs a doctor—"

"Oh yeah? And she'll see pigs fly before she agrees to that!" he said, without moving.

"I don't care what she says," she shouted. "She needs a doctor, I tell you. There's something seriously wrong, and if you won't do anything about it, I will!"

She'd got his attention now. He stood up quickly, cursing loudly as he hit his head on the hood of the car, and wiping his hands on an oily rag.

"This had better be on the level," he snarled, as he followed her into the apartment. "We ain't got money to pay for unnecessary doctor's bills, and I'll decide whether or not she needs to see anybody. You got that?"

She wasn't listening to him any more. She could hear the groaning from inside the apartment, and when she rushed inside, she saw that Gracie had slid to the floor. She was barely conscious, and her eyes were glazed.

"*Jesus Christ!*" Merv said. "Go ask Mrs Olsen to come down and take a look at her, while I send for an ambulance. She needs more'n a doctor, by the looks of her. We'll be lucky if we don't need the coroner."

Rose felt murderous towards him at that moment, but there was no time for hate right now. Gracie looked so ill, and however callously Merv had put it, there was a dreadful fear in Rose's gut that he might just be right.

She hammered on the door of the upstairs apartment, thankful to have something to do. She needed direction. She needed Mam. And Evan. And even Dai . . . the valleymen were so used to dealing with disasters.

When the pit siren sounded, warning of escaping gas in a mine, or a fire, or a collapse of pit props that could bury the men under tons of choking rubble, the valleymen, and their women, proved their strength of character a thousandfold.

They were always calm under unbelievable stress and dangers, while she . . . who'd really believed she had assimilated some of that calmness, was very much in danger of going to pieces when the first crisis struck.

"What the hell's going on?"

Mrs Olsen flung open the door of her apartment, sending out an overpowering whiff of frying onions and garlic. The combined scents mingled with Mrs Olsen's cheap perfume, and almost made Rose gag.

"Gracie's ill, and it looks bad. Merv's sending for

an ambulance. Please come down and tell us what you think," she gasped out.

"Christ A'mighty, didn't I always say this was going to happen one of these days? I been tellin' her for weeks to get herself seen to. Just give me a second to turn off me gas before the whole place blows up, and I'll be down directly."

Rose didn't wait for her. She tore back down the stairs again, ignoring the interested residents whose doors were opening now, to see what all the commotion was about.

She was consumed with an almighty feeling of guilt. If Mrs Olsen had been telling Gracie for weeks to get herself seen to, why hadn't *she* noticed anything wrong?

Or had she just got so used to Gracie's whinings, and too wrapped up in her own affairs that she'd just closed her mind to it? Her own sister . . .

She smothered a sob as she rushed back into the apartment where Merv was hollering into the phone.

"God dammit, I'm telling you we need an ambulance here right now. My wife's in a bad way, and if you don't get a bloody move on, she'll probably croak before you get here, and if that happens I'll have you in court so fast your feet won't touch the ground."

Rose rushed to where Gracie lay on the floor. She was as white as a sheet now, her lips totally bloodless, and she was shivering badly. Rose ran into her bedroom and pulled the comforter off the bed to place gently over her sister. She didn't know what else to do, and then she heard Mrs Olsen's gasp as the woman heaved herself into the room.

"Jeez, this looks bad all right," she muttered. "Has she had a stroke?"

"I don't know!" Rose said, shivering almost as badly as Gracie now.

Merv had stopped shouting for a minute while he listened to the speaker at the other end. Then he exploded.

"All right, then I'll take her myself, and I hope you buggers rot in hell," he yelled, slamming the phone down in a blind rage.

"Won't they come?" Rose said, tears streaming down her cheeks now at this unbelievable situation.

"There's been a pile-up on the freeway out of LA and every available ambulance is out on call," he snapped. "So God help anybody else who needs attention right now."

"But just look at her! If she doesn't get help, she might *die*!"

Now she'd said the word, and, like Mam always preached, she said a swift prayer, in case God thought she was inviting the worst by just saying it. . . .

"We're taking her to the hospital ourselves," Merv said. "They can't refuse to take her in when they see the state she's in—"

"They can, if you ain't got medical insurance," Mrs Olsen said keenly. "You do have it, don't you, Merv?"

Rose saw his face darken. Dear God, what kind of a country was this, where they could refuse to treat a sick woman if you didn't have the means to pay the hospital bills?

"Look, whatever it costs, I'll help out," she heard herself stutter wildly. "I'm earning a fair salary now, and I dare say my boss would advance me the money if Gracie had anything serious. Besides, it may not be anything at all. We don't *know* for sure, do we?"

They all knew that it was a fair bet that it was. But Merv hooked on to her words like a sinking man grasping at straws.

"You're right, kid. You just say that you're a personal friend of the Jefferson guy, and work for the Jefferson Printing Corporation, and they won't refuse us."

Rose didn't dare say that looking the way Merv did, his vest filthy and his hands still ingrained with engine oil, he hardly looked like a man with the means to pay for hospital treatment of any kind.

"Let's get her to the hospital then," Mrs Olsen said briskly. "You sit in the front with Merv, Rose, and I'll hold on to Gracie in the back seat."

"Maybe it would be best if you sat in the front, Mrs Olsen," Rose said swiftly. The woman's short laugh shook all the ample folds of her body.

"OK, I get your meaning, hon. There wouldn't be much space for her to stretch out with me taking up most of the room, would there?"

"Can we cut the cackle and get her out of here?" Merv said, with sudden urgency.

He couldn't deal with illness, and Gracie was starting to look bloody awful, and nothing like the flash tart he'd met and married in such an all-fired hurry back in England. She looked *old*, and her pinched white face made her look even older when she was alongside the fresh-faced kid sister.

They carried Gracie out to the Chevy and put her in the back seat without too much ceremony. It didn't seem to matter any more. She was out cold, and only the shallow breathing and the involuntary moaning confirmed that she was still in the land of the living, Merv thought grimly.

He drove as fast as he could through the back streets, avoiding the main streets where traffic lights would hold them up. If they headed for one of the three hospitals in the district, they needn't go anywhere near the freeway where the pile-up had occurred. For the first time, Merv wondered uneasily if there would be a bed for Gracie. . . .

The first and second hospitals turned them away, saying they were too full of casualties from the freeway accident, and they headed for the Cedars of Hope.

By now, Merv was in a towering rage, and fearful that Gracie was going to die right then and there in the back seat of the Chevy. He'd never be able to drive it again without the thought of having to haul out her body. . . . He shuddered, trying not to be so bloody morbid. But it was difficult, with Mrs Olsen screeching abuse at any driver who got in their way, and the kid snivelling behind him.

A couple of male hospital attendants who looked no older than college kids, hurried out of the emergency entrance with a stretcher on a trolley when they saw Merv's battered car pull up, and the three of them tried to get Gracie out of the back seat. Rose frowned as Merv leaned towards the women.

"I'll do the talking," he said.

"You'd better leave the patient to us, sir," one of the college kids said accusingly. "We're experienced in handling accident victims, and you should have waited for an ambulance."

Rose saw instantly that they assumed that Gracie had been in the freeway pile-up, which wasn't surprising, considering the state of the Chevy . . . but Merv surely wasn't going to let them go on thinking it. . . .

"We didn't dare wait," he said. "My wife looked so bad, we thought we should get her here right away."

"OK, sir."

They lifted Gracie onto the trolley, and removed the comforter. There was a split-second of silence, and then the first one spoke more sharply. Apart from the fact that Gracie looked like death, there were no visible signs of injury.

"You *were* in the traffic accident, were you, sir? This hospital is only dealing with freeway victims at this time—"

"God dammit, man, look at the woman! Can't you see she's near to snuffin' it?"

Right on cue, Gracie gave an involuntary scream of pain. Her legs suddenly bent upwards towards her chest and she twisted on the trolley in apparent agony.

145

"Please don't refuse to take her in," Rose gasped. "You must see how ill she is, and we just don't know what's wrong with her."

The attendants gaped at this vision with the impeccable English accent. The tears streaking down her face did nothing to take away the impact of her glorious green eyes. And since she was accompanied by the slob in the filthy red vest and the fat woman smelling of garlic, they were completely taken aback for a moment. Recklessly, uncaring what lies she told any more, Rose pressed home the advantage.

"I work for the Jefferson Printing Corporation, and I'm a personal friend and colleague of Mr Jefferson," she said quietly. "I'm sure he would be willing to give the hospital a handsome donation if I tell him how considerate you were in attending to my sister."

They didn't hesitate. In seconds they had pushed the trolley quickly through the swing doors of the hospital into the antiseptic interior. Just before they followed, Merv clutched at Rose's hand and squeezed it.

"Now don't tell me you weren't born to be an actress, babe. That was some swell performance you just gave."

She shook off his hand. "It wasn't a performance," she snapped. "I did it for Gracie, that's all."

And the likelihood of Bradley Piers Jefferson the third giving a handsome donation to the Cedars of Hope on account of Rose Forster's sister, was as likely as flying to Mars. . . .

The way in was blocked by a reception desk, behind which a well-starched, steely-eyed nurse, looked them over while the attendants explained the situation as far as they knew it.

"Name and address of the patient," the nurse said. She punched it out on a typewriter, delaying the need for urgent treatment which Gracie obviously needed.

146

"Will you please hurry," Rose pleaded. "My sister is in such pain. . . ."

The nurse looked at her coldly, clearly unimpressed by the accent.

"We see a lot of pain here, Miss. Does she have medical insurance?"

"No, she doesn't have bloody medical insurance," Merv yelled. "But you needn't worry about her medical bills, you slag. My sister-in-law here has got the means to pay, and I don't know where the hell you've been living if you don't recognize an aristocratic English accent when you hear one. . . ."

Dear God, what was he *saying*! Rose felt so humiliated that she wished the floor would open up and swallow her. Did he really think this nurse was going to believe one word of it? Out of the corner of her eye she saw a white-coated doctor approach. He'd obviously overheard all that had gone on, and even though he'd had a muttered conversation with the attendants Rose guessed they'd soon be out on their ears.

She wondered if Merv would simply refuse to budge. The whole situation was getting to be more like a farce, she thought hysterically, or it would be, if it wasn't so God-damned awful. . . . The doctor spoke sharply to Merv.

"I'll thank you not to abuse my nurses, sir."

His glance flicked over Rose, and she held her breath. If only she'd thought to wear her tiara, she found herself thinking wildly . . . then he looked at the attendants and gave a brief nod.

"Take the patient into cubicle three, and I'll take a quick look at her. You people please wait here."

Rose couldn't believe it. She had no idea what had swayed them all, but there was no doubt in Merv's mind. Nor in Mrs Olsen's.

"Remind me to take you with me when I come up

147

against trouble, hon," the woman said admiringly. "You got such a sweet way of talking I reckon you could get away with murder."

"Sweet talking's not going to pay the medical bills, though," Rose muttered.

"Don't you believe it," Merv said, with a leering wink now they'd got over the first hurdle. "Sweet talking's paid more'n one little lady's bills. And I've got to hand it to you, saying your boss would make a donation to the hospital. Smart girl."

Rose stared stonily ahead, trying to concentrate all her energies on what was going on behind the cubicle curtains to find out what was wrong with Gracie. If she died . . . for the first time, she realized what that would imply. Apart from her own feelings for her sister, she would be entirely dependent on Merv Hackett's generosity in keeping a roof over her head . . . and she couldn't bear to think about that.

It underlined her resolve to move out as soon as she could. Once she had a place of her own, then whatever happened, she wouldn't be in his clutches. She'd managed to save a bit of money since working at Jefferson's, and she could surely manage the rent of a small apartment, especially if she found somebody to share. . . .

She went over and over the idea she'd thought about so many times already, but with a definite resolve in her mind now. She *had* to get out of the Hacketts' apartment. . . . She concentrated all her thoughts on the prospect, if only to stop her thinking too deeply of why they were sitting here in this sterile atmosphere, like the three witches in Macbeth. . . .

The doctor came out of the cubicle, his face grave, and Rose's heart lurched sickeningly. He spoke to her, rather than Merv.

"Your sister has a burst appendix, Miss . . .?"

"Forster," she said.

"Miss Forster. She needs immediate surgery, and I can't imagine how she's been putting up with the pain without seeing a doctor."

"She don't hold with 'em," Merv put in. "So what's going to happen to her now, Doc?"

The doctor looked at him icily. "My nurse will give you the forms to sign, and we'll be taking her up to the theatre right away."

"She won't like being cut about," Merv said at once.

"My dear sir," the doctor said, giving insulting weight to the word. "If she doesn't have the surgery right now, she will die. I can't put it any plainer than that."

"He'll sign the forms, Doctor," Rose stuttered, since Merv seemed to have temporarily lost the capacity for speech. "Can I see my sister for a minute?"

He shrugged. "There's no point. She's heavily sedated. I suggest you all go home and call later this evening. There won't be any news for some hours until she's in the recovery room. Now, if you'll excuse me. . . ."

He turned quickly, and Merv folded his arms stubbornly as a nurse approached him with a sheaf of forms, showing clear disapproval at the sight of him.

"I ain't leaving here until I know Gracie's OK," he snapped.

"We usually advise relatives to go home, take a bath and relax before you come visit your wife later," the nurse said pointedly.

The words were bland enough, but Rose followed her meaning exactly. Merv let the place down, and so did Mrs Olsen, for all her good nature. If it wasn't for herself . . . she wasn't a snob, but even Rose could see that she was the only one of the three who looked half decent.

"We'll do as you say," she said, taking charge. "Sign the forms, Merv, and let's go. Gracie's in good hands here."

Expensive hands . . . but she wasn't going to think

about that. Nor how long the operation and recovery might take. You didn't measure a sister's life in dollars and cents.

She waited for Merv to scrawl his name on the forms that allowed the doctors to do whatever was required for Gracie, then followed him out into the sunlight, feeling as though she'd aged a hundred years in a couple of hours.

Chapter Ten

To Rose's relief, Merv eventually decided that a bath was a good idea. He needed to wash off the grime of the Chevy, since he had no more stomach for working on it today. Rose declined to take a bath right after him. Guiltily, she knew she never really fancied using the Hacketts' tub at all, and she always scrubbed it with a wire brush and cleaning powder before she ever stepped into it. She also covered the bath mat with her own towel before she put her bare feet on it.

She wondered if she was becoming paranoid, or simply over-fussy. She pushed it to the back of her mind as she drank more cups of coffee with Mrs Olsen, who had insisted on making it for them all when they got back to the apartment building. They stayed in Gracie and Merv's apartment, just in case the telephone rang . . . but Rose didn't dare allow herself to think about that, since it could only be the worst of news regarding Gracie. . . . While Merv was occupied in the bathroom, she forced herself to try and relax.

"I never knew much about your Gracie's background," Mrs Olsen said conversationally. "I only came here to live here a coupla years ago, and they was here before that. She never talked much about the old days."

"Please don't talk about her as if she's dead," Rose said quickly.

Mrs Olsen looked genuinely upset. "Hey, hon, I never meant no such thing. It's just that the two of you are so different. Nobody would take you for sisters, and I was just curious, that's all, and I thought you might want to talk to take your mind off things. Take no notice of me."

"I'm sorry," Rose said. "I know you only mean to help. And you're right. We're not alike at all, really. Chalk and cheese, Evan used to say."

"Who's Evan?" Mrs Olsen said, perking up.

"Evan's one of the boys at the house in Wales where I was evacuated during the war."

"Jeez, it must have been terrible for you and Gracie to be sent away from your folks," she said sympathetically.

Rose didn't speak for a minute, but without warning, all the bitter resentment was back in full force. It might be shameful to feel it at such a time, but she could never completely forget what was so deeply ingrained.

"Gracie wasn't evacuated," she said curtly. "Gracie was older than me, so she stayed in London with my parents, then we were bombed out, and my parents were killed. Gracie came down to Wales to tell me."

She stopped abruptly as the pain of that day over-whelmed her, as real and as sharp as if it was happening all over again. Gracie's guarded, wary voice was in her head, and if she'd been old enough to recognize it then, she'd have known that Gracie certainly didn't want the encumbrance of a kid sister hanging around while she was having a whale of a time with the Yanks in London.

"Look, you'll be all right, our Rose. The Pritchards will take good care of you, and you won't have to worry about money or nothing, because I'll send you some when I can. You're far better off here than back in the smoke with old Hitler's bombs falling everywhere. . . ."

Rose had thrown herself into Gracie's arms then, sobbing her heart out, because Gracie was the only one she had left now.

"But I want to be with you. I want to go home. Why can't I go home?"

Gracie had clumsily unfastened the clinging little arms from around her smart WRAC uniform.

"*Because you can't, that's why. Now don't you go and make a fuss when these nice folks have taken you in, Rose. I got my work to do, and I can't take care of you, see? Besides, I've met somebody.*"

"*Who?*" Rose sobbed.

"*He's a Yank, and he's very nice. And you never know, I might even marry him and go to America after the war. If I do, you can come and live with us,*" she said recklessly, without ever considering how a small child would cling on to those words like a lifeline.

"Are you all right, hon?"

Mrs Olsen's voice penetrated the remembered sense of betrayal Rose had felt during all those years when Gracie never sent for her, fobbing her off with excuses: she was still saving the money for her fare; they didn't yet have a good enough place to live; Merv didn't have a decent job, or a hundred and one other expenses had come up unexpectedly to delay the day. . . .

"I'm fine," Rose said.

"So what was this place in Wales like, then?" Mrs Olsen persisted, seeing as how she wasn't going to get any more information about Gracie. "A mansion, was it?"

Rose stared at her. "What?"

"Well, from the way you talk so nice, I dare say you lived with nice country folk with a bit of money. . . ."

Rose heard herself laugh. It was the very opposite to the way she'd describe the Pritchards' two up and two down, fronting right on to the street . . . though the other bit was right enough. They were nice folk. They were the best.

"It wasn't anything like that, Mrs Olsen. It was a small house in a Welsh valley, and most of the men worked in the coal mines. They weren't posh, or rich, and I hated being abandoned there at first. Then I grew to love them," she said, almost to her own surprise, and she went on quickly

153

before she got maudlin. "I can give you a sample of my best Welsh accent, if you like."

She launched into the sing-song patois of the valleys, as she spoke about Evan and Dai, and the strait-laced Chapel-going Mam Pritchard, while Mrs Olsen sat wide-eyed, hearing about people and places beyond her comprehension.

"You've got a real gift for takin' off other folks, hon," she declared at last. "I reckon you could talk just like your Queen Elizabeth if you put your mind to it."

"Oh yes, of course one could. Can't anyone?" Rose said with airy dignity, and they both convulsed with laughter, quite forgetting why they'd been sitting here drinking endless cups of coffee from late afternoon into early evening.

When the telephone shrilled out, Rose flinched visibly. The laughter dissolved in an instant, and all the fears for Gracie came surging back. Merv was still in the bathroom, so she had no choice but to pick up the receiver herself. She almost fainted when she recognized the caller.

"Hello there, little lady," came Chuck Bernstein's oily voice. "You're just the one I want to talk to. It's about this here beauty pageant—"

"I can't talk about that now," Rose said in a choked voice. "I've already told you I'm not interested, and besides, we've got trouble here."

"Trouble? What kind of trouble? Merv ain't been gettin' all hot under the collar over you, has he, babe?" he said, with a lecherous chuckle. "You know you only to have to say the word and old Chuck will come and sort him out—"

And who would come and sort old Chuck out . . .?

"Gracie's been taken into hospital with a burst appendix," she said jerkily. "We have to keep this line clear in case there's any news, so I'm hanging up right now."

She slammed down the receiver, her hands shaking,

154

knowing she was going to be a nervous wreck if she went on like this. And before Mrs Olsen could try to persuade her to take some of her tranquillizers to calm her down, she took some deep breaths and closed her eyes for a few moments.

"It wasn't the hospital then?" Mrs Olsen said, clearly having heard every word.

"It was Chuck Bernstein," Rose muttered. "He's a pain in the – in the—"

"In the butt, kid, for want of usin' a stronger word. But I reckoned you handled him OK. Whatever it was, you just keep saying no, and eventually he'll get tired. His sort always do."

Rose wasn't so sure. He was more persistent than she'd expected. But however much he pestered her, she had a mind and a will of her own, and nobody was going to force her into doing anything she didn't want to do. They'd forced her to go to Wales when she was a frightened, bewildered kid, but she wasn't a kid any more . . . and damn Mrs Olsen for bringing it all so vividly to her mind again.

"If you've got anything to do, I'll be perfectly all right," she said awkwardly. She didn't want to appear ungrateful, but the events of the last hours had exhausted her, and if she had to breathe in much more of Mrs Olsen's mingled aromas, she was sure she was going to puke.

She swallowed, realizing how she was picking up Merv's favourite expressions as easily as she'd picked up the Welsh. And the one thing she was never going to do, whatever happened, was to lose her Englishness. It made her what she was. . . .

"I ain't got nothing else to do, hon," Mrs Olsen said comfortably. "Besides, you and Merv don't exactly make the best of bedfellows, do you?"

She could have put that differently, Rose thought, but

she had to admit that she and Merv didn't get on, and probably never would. She shrugged.

"We're all right," she muttered.

"Yes, well, you're family, so that counts for summat, I dare say."

Before she could make some indignant remark about Merv not being her real family, he came lumbering back to the sitting-room, a mite fresher and cleaner than before, still rubbing his damp hair with a towel and leaving it in unruly spikes all over his head without bothering to comb it.

"Who was that on the phone?" he asked. "Was it somebody with a job for me?"

Rose looked at him with active dislike.

"It *could* have been the hospital," she said sharply. "It *might* have been bad news about Gracie—"

"Nah. You'd have come hammering on the bathroom door if it had been anything like that," he said carelessly. "So who was it?"

Mrs Olsen spoke up when Rose appeared to be struck dumb at his insensitivity.

"It was that buddy of yours. That Chuck Bernstein, wanting to talk to Rose."

"Oh yeah? What did he want, Rose?"

"I don't want to talk about it," she snapped. "I've got more important things on my mind right now than listening to his stupid beauty pageant ideas."

"You wouldn't say that if you was the winner," Merv snapped back. "Nor if it meant getting a screen test out of it. Ain't that what you English gals always dream about when you come over here?"

She didn't miss the sneer in his voice, and her own was shrill with anger when she answered.

"It wasn't what Gracie dreamed about. All she wanted was to marry somebody she loved and live in a nice place – and look what she got!"

His face darkened, and for a second she thought he was going to hit her. Mrs Olsen evidently thought so too, because she was on her feet with great alacrity for such a big woman, standing between the two of them.

"Why don't the two of you cool down?" she said quickly. "And Rose, you got no call to speak to Merv like that, when he took you in."

"For pity's sake, I'm not a refugee, Mrs Olsen! And it was a long time ago that I was evacuated too. It was my choice to come here. It's natural that I'd want to see my sister after all these years."

But not the oaf she married. . . .

"I can see I ain't doing neither of you any good now," the woman declared. "So I'll get back upstairs, and you just call if you need me for anythin'. And you be sure and let me know when you get any news from the hospital, you hear?"

"Yeah, yeah," Merv said.

When Mrs Olsen left the apartment in an obvious huff, Rose realized how hungry she was. It was a long time since they'd had any food, and the tension that had been building up all this time was adding to the gnawing inside her.

"Do you want something to eat?" she said abruptly to Merv, when the silence between them became embarrassing.

"Sure. Why not?" he said, in the irritating way he had of answering a question with a question. "Bacon, two eggs over-easy, mushrooms and tomatoes. You'll find it all in the refrigerator."

As if he didn't have a care in the world, he sprawled out in an armchair, took the top off a bottle of beer and swigged half of it down before he turned on the television. Rose didn't move for a minute. He turned and looked at her, dragging his eyes away from the antics of the cartoon characters on the screen.

"Well, go on. Get us summat to eat, can't you?"

"Don't you care at all about Gracie?" Rose burst out.

"What the hell's that supposed to mean? She's my wife, ain't she?"

Rose stared at him, remembering what he was, so smart and handsome in his GI uniform, and seeing what he had become. But the sarcastic retort stuck in her throat, as one of Mam Pritchard's sayings soared into her head.

"We're all as God made us, girl, and if some of us let things slide a bit, well, I'm sure God won't mind when the Great Day comes."

It wasn't the Forster parents' way to talk so freely about God, and Gracie never mentioned Him at all. And while Rose squirmed with embarrassment at Mam's apparent conversations with the Almighty, Dai always tried his best not to snigger at her red face, for fear of getting a clip around the ear from his Mam, and Evan had usually managed to squeeze Rose's hand sympathetically.

"Well?" Merv snapped. "Are you sayin' I ain't done right by Gracie all these years? If so, you can clear out of here with your snooty ideas. I ain't heard no complaints from Gracie, and I sure as hell ain't standing for any criticism from a chit like you."

"I never thought anything of the sort," Rose muttered, hoping God wouldn't strike her down dead for such a blatant lie. "I just mean that you don't seem too concerned about her being taken into hospital, that's all."

"I'm more concerned with how we're going to pay the bills if she has to stay in for any length of time, and you can pick the bones out of that as much as you like. But moping all over the place still won't pay for doctors and nurses and hospital beds."

Just for one moment his forehead creased into a deep frown and he ran his beefy hands through his already tangled hair. And Rose grudgingly forgave him, because what he said was exactly right. She knew by now that they lived from day to day, and as far as ambition went, Merv was never going to amount to much. But if Gracie loved him, then she was being a narrow-minded bitch for criticizing them both.

"I'm sorry. But even though I was too young to know what it was all about, I know my parents always saved money for emergencies, and Mam Pritchard always insisted the boys put some of their coal money aside in case anything bad happened to them, like it did to their daddy. I just thought Gracie would have done the same," Rose finished lamely.

"Maybe she would have done, kid, if we hadn't had so many other expenses over the years," Merv said neatly.

Rose reddened, knowing he referred to her education and general living expenses in England, and the fare to bring her here. But he was right, damn him. Now that she saw how they lived, it couldn't have been all that easy.

"Whatever bills there are, Merv, I'll help out," she said, just as quickly. "I owe you both a lot, and I don't forget that. So if it relieves your mind a little—"

Before she could guess what he was about to do, he'd got out of his chair and pulled her into his arms in a bear-hug. And despite his recent bath, the LA humidity was already making him start to sweat, and the familiar odour wafted up between them.

She struggled to break free, but his grip tightened, and her breasts were squashed against him.

"Aw, come on, honey, don't be standoffish. You can spare your old Merv a coupla kisses, can't you?"

"Get off me, you pig!" she shrieked. "Remember your wife's in the hospital and probably having an operation right this minute. Have you got no feelings at all?"

She shoved him away, and he staggered a little. He hadn't been drinking heavily, but she knew that would be the next step, and suddenly, Rose was very afraid. If Gracie was going to be in hospital for any length of

159

time, then she would be alone in the apartment with Merv Hackett. And she was no longer under any illusions about him.

"'Course I've got feelings, you silly little bitch," he snarled, his mood changing quickly. "And nobody can say any different. I brought you here on account of Gracie, didn't I? She kept on about it for long enough."

His words stopped Rose in mid-thought. She rubbed at her shoulders where Merv had gripped them, and spoke haltingly.

"She really did want me here, then?"

"Hell, you're family, ain'tcha? 'Course she wanted you, and she plagued the life outa me until I forked out the money to send for you."

"I thought it was no more than an obligation," Rose muttered. "I didn't realize—"

"You don't realize a lotta things, babe, but one thing you and me have got to get straight between us. You're Gracie's kin, and that means you're welcome here, but you gotta play by our rules, savvy?"

"I pull my weight. I help with the housework and the cooking when Gracie doesn't feel like it – and I thought you said something about wanting bacon and eggs?"

She prayed that mentioning food would stop the gleam in his eyes when he'd said Rose had to play by their rules. Whatever rules Merv had in mind, it wasn't going to include playing around with Gracie's kid sister, she thought, with a violence she didn't know she possessed.

"OK, kid. Get the food," Merv said, suddenly bored with the whole argument, and turned back to the TV set. "I want to watch the game, anyway."

"And then we should call the hospital for news," Rose reminded him.

"Yeah, yeah," he said absent-mindedly as the baseball teams marched out onto the pitch to the roars from the crowd and the flouncing of the cheerleaders in their short skirts and pouting breasts.

Rose went into the kitchen, her stomach tied up in knots. This had been a hell of a day so far, and that lout didn't give a tuppenny toss about what was happening to Gracie. Her eyes stung with sudden tears. If Gracie died . . . dear God, if Gracie died . . . for the first time she let her imagination soar.

If that happened, she wouldn't stay here. She'd go anywhere, rather than be dependent on Merv Hackett. She'd go home, where she belonged. Home to Mam Pritchard and the boyos. . . . She bit her lip, springing into action as Merv gave a shout from the living-room, and she knew his team must be winning. That was all he really cared about.

"I *hate* him," she said viciously, knowing he'd be too intent to hear, even if she shouted it from the rooftops. "I really hate him."

She put the bacon into the sizzling fat and broke the eggs into a bowl. She felt more like hurling them at the wall than making them the way Merv liked them, over-easy with the yolks all runny and the whites just set. He'd pig it out with everything she put in front of him, but she knew she couldn't eat a thing. . . .

But even as she thought it, the treacherous saliva began to gather in her mouth as the smell of the bacon teased her nostrils, and she told herself to be sensible and eat. Starving herself wasn't going to do Gracie any good.

An hour or so later, Merv was still entranced with his ball game, so she called the hospital herself. Her hands twisted the cord anxiously as she waited to be put through to Dr Leandra's office.

"This is Dr Leandra's nurse. How may I help you?" The starchy voice of the woman they had seen earlier, sounded as welcoming as before. Clearly, patients were a nuisance

161

to her. Well, tough luck, Rose thought savagely. If you didn't have patients, you'd be out of a job. . . .

"I'm enquiring about my sister. Mrs Gracie Hackett. She was having an emergency operation for a burst appendix this afternoon."

There was a long pause at the other end, and Rose's heart began to beat painfully fast. Why couldn't the stupid woman tell her right away that Gracie was fine and in the recovery room, and could receive visitors tomorrow . . .?

"If you'll wait a moment, I'll put you through to Dr Leandra. I believe he wants a word with you, Miss Hackett—"

"I'm not Miss Hackett," Rose said unnecessarily. "I'm Rose Forster. . . ."

She heard the clicks at the other end, and realized she was talking to herself, and it seemed a long while before the doctor's voice came on the line. While she waited, she had tried to detect anything in the nurse's voice to alarm her, but it had been as bland as ever. These people had to be specially chosen for their so-called professional manners, which just meant their lousy dealings with patients, Rose thought.

"You're calling about Mrs Gracie Hackett, I understand," she finally heard the doctor's voice. "She's had the surgery, and she's in the recovery room. . . ."

So why the hell couldn't Miss starch-face have told her that . . .?

"Since you're calling on behalf of Mr Hackett, will you pass on the message that I'd like to see him as soon as possible, please?"

"What's wrong?" Rose gasped. "I'm her sister, and you can tell me—"

"The husband is required to get signed consent and undertaking to pay for any further treatment that may be required," he said impatiently.

162

"What further treatment? Did you find something else that you're not telling me?"

"I don't discuss my patients over the phone," Dr Leandra said coldly. "If you and Mr Hackett come to my office in the morning we may have a clearer picture. You're fortunate that I'm on duty this weekend, so I can follow this patient through."

Was she supposed to bow and scrape to this? Rose wondered. In a fury of frustration, she hung up the phone before she could say any more. Bad manners or not, she couldn't listen to one more word from this pompous God-Almighty surgeon.

She smothered a sob, and went back to the living-room. Without asking, she turned off the TV set, and got the expected howl of rage from Merv.

"I've called the hospital, and we both have to go there in the morning to speak with the doctor. He has to have your consent for any further treatment Gracie might need."

"What bloody further treatment? If he's taken out her appendix, then that's the end of it," Merv snarled. "I ain't paying for Gracie to be cut about when it ain't necessary."

"He didn't say that," Rose said, though her own self-confidence was slipping badly now. "And there's no point in worrying about it until we hear what he's got to say."

Merv glowered at her and then shrugged his shoulders and turned on the TV set again.

"You're right. There's no point in worrying, and I'll soon sort the bugger out in the morning. Fetch me some beer, will you, doll?"

Several hours later Rose lay sleepless on top of her bed-clothes. The year was entering its last quarter, but the air in LA was still stifling. It was enough to make sleeping with the windows closed highly uncomfortable. But however small a crack you left open, the bugs were sure to get in.

163

Rose was so tired she'd thought she'd be able to fall asleep right away, and be able to close her mind to all that had happened that day. But sleep wouldn't come, and all she could think about was Gracie, and the fact that she'd nagged at Merv for so long to bring her over here.

And if there was anything guaranteed to make her feel guilty for the way she'd sneered at the way they lived, or allowing the old feelings of sibling rivalry to come to the fore in her mind, that was it. Gracie had been the one to want her here after all, and Merv hadn't. But he wanted her now.

She gave a shudder. He seemed to have a compulsion to try and touch her whenever he got the chance, and he never failed to make some sexual innuendo, whether or not Gracie was around. Rose had made sure she locked her door when she came to bed, but in any case she didn't think Merv would be bothering her tonight.

He'd asked for beer, and she'd kept him so well supplied with bottles from the refrigerator that she guessed he'd be out on his feet as soon as he went to bed. She'd heard him bumbling about an hour ago, cursing as he stubbed his toes, and by now his heavy snoring was vibrating rhythmically through the bedroom walls.

Normally, she hated this disgusting evidence of his presence, and found herself matching her own breathing to lessen the impact of the noise. But tonight, she was thankful for it, sure that nothing short of an earthquake was going to waken him from his drunken stupor.

The phone rang out in the middle of the night, and Rose leapt out of bed, her heart in her mouth. It had to be bad news. It had to be about Gracie. She'd had a relapse. Or the operation had failed after all. Or she was – she was . . .

She flew to the phone. She didn't want to know what the message was, but she couldn't bear not to know either. Her brain didn't seem to be functioning properly, and she grabbed at the receiver with sweaty hands. Merv was obviously out cold if he hadn't even heard the phone. She croaked into it.

"Who's that?" she heard Evan Pritchard's beautiful, melodious, gloriously Welsh voice say. "I'm not sure if I've got the right number—"

"Yes, you have, Evan!" Rose managed to say after taking an enormous gasp to force some breath down into her lungs. "It's me, and I'm so *glad* to hear your voice."

"Thank God. You sounded so strange."

After the briefest pause while Rose gathered up her thoughts to try to tell him the news, he went on.

"So what's wrong? Mam had this feeling, Rose, and you know what she's like when she gets that sixth sense of hers that something's wrong. She wouldn't let it rest until I spoke to you to settle her worries, despite the hour."

"Mam was right. It's Gracie," Rose said huskily. "She's in hospital with a burst appendix. She's had an operation and the doctor says she may need more treatment, but I'm so afraid, Evan. I'm really afraid. . . ."

The words dwindled away in a choking sound, and she realized the tears were streaming down her cheeks. He seemed so near, and yet she was never more conscious that he was thousands of miles away. So far, when she wanted nothing more than to feel his arms around her, comforting her like the big brother he'd always been. Cherishing her. Loving her.

"*Dieu*, but I wish I could be there with you," she heard him say. "But the doctors know what they're doing, *cariad*, and I'm sure your sister's in good hands. Is the husband taking care of you?"

Oh yes. And he'd take even greater care of me if I'd let him. . . .

For a minute she wondered if she'd said the words aloud, and just how shocked Evan would be if she'd done so. But before she could answer she heard another

165

voice muttering to him, and then a woman's voice came on the line.

"Rose, Evan's just told me your news," Mam Pritchard said, as awkward and stilted as ever on the phone. "Now you're not to worry unduly. I seen it in the cards that there was trouble, but they tell me that nothing worse will come of it. And I'll pray for Gracie at chapel."

Her voice ended on the upward lilt that Rose remembered so well. She swallowed, finding such a diversity in Mam's attachment to the tarot cards, that some said were the instruments of the devil, and her strong Chapel links.

"Thank you, Mam. That's a comfort to me."

"Yes well, you go back to bed now. Evan tells me it's the middle of the night, so I'm sorry if we disturbed you."

She was gone, and then Evan was back again, the champion of her childhood.

"I'm sorry too, my Rose—"

"I'm not," Rose said, her throat suddenly full. "I'm never sorry to hear your voice, Evan. It brings you so near, and I – I miss you so much."

There. She had said it now. But it was a natural enough thing for a sister to say to a brother, wasn't it?

"God knows I miss you too. I'll call you again in a couple of days to find out how Gracie is. Good-night, *cariad*."

She whispered good-night, and hung up the phone, her head filled with the sweet sound of that lovely Welsh word in his deep, caring voice. *Cariad* . . . darling . . . and she found herself wishing she'd had the nerve to say it back to him.

Chapter Eleven

Gracie developed a high temperature, and there was fear of peritonitis. By the time Monday came, Rose was in a state of nerves. They phoned the hospital early, but there had been no change overnight, and Gracie was being kept sedated, so there was no point in visiting. Merv had already left for an early morning job of picking people up from the airport.

Rose wanted to stay home by the phone, but the no-nonsense Mrs Olsen said there was nothing she could do, and besides, the people at the hospital would contact her at the Jefferson Printing Corporation if there was any significant change, so she went in to work.

Lacey Venables took one look at her and asked if she was sick, her voice implying that it was a crime.

"You'll be no good to me here if you are, and I don't want to risk infection spreading around the rest of the office. Take the day off if you can't cope."

Rose took a deep breath.

"I'm not sick," she said. "My sister's in hospital, and I've had a hell of a weekend, that's all. Don't worry. I won't let you down."

"What's wrong with your sister, Rose?" Cindy said, concerned at once.

"A burst appendix, and now she's got some kind of a fever," Rose said in a choked voice. "She should have gone to the doctor ages ago, but she wouldn't."

"Couldn't pay the bills, I dare say," Lacey said as a parting shot before swishing away.

167

"Take no notice of that cow, Rose," Cindy said. "But you do look awful. Will you last out the day?"

"I need to work. I need the money."

She hadn't meant to say it, but it was out now. The future loomed ahead of her, working her tail off to pay Gracie's medical bills, but she had too much pride to state it quite as bluntly.

"Your brother-in-law will have medical insurance. It'll be OK, Rose. You'll see."

She didn't comment. There was no point. And she didn't want to air all their dirty linen in public. It wasn't the British way. Her mouth twisted, and then her nerves jangled as her phone shrilled out. But it was only somebody in despatch asking if she had some invoices ready, and her hands were shaking uncontrollably as she replaced the receiver.

She had to hold herself together. The phones would be ringing all day, including hers, and if she went to pieces every time, thinking it was bad news about Gracie, she'd end up in a shrink's office.

She listened to herself, thinking in sharp, brash LA jargon, and could have wept. This wasn't what she wanted when she came here. She was turning into one of them – one of the Lacey Venables types – and even if she hadn't been so stupid as to think she could change the world by her Englishness, at least she hadn't wanted to abandon it.

She concentrated hard on her work. There were no messages from the hospital. She phoned twice during the day and was told again that she'd be informed of any change in her sister's condition. She could hear the starched disapproval in the disembodied voice. She wouldn't phone again. But she'd damn well go down there straight after work and see for herself.

By four o'clock she could hardly see straight. She'd had little sleep over the weekend, and the figures on the invoices were starting to dance in front of her eyes. She was making mistakes, and she knew it. She could hear Lacey's strident voice at her side, thrusting a pile of papers back at her, and belittling her. She turned to scream at her, but before she could get the words out, the woman's image became hazy and disjointed, and Rose simply buckled over and slid to the floor.

There was a strong, pungent smell under her nose, and she jerked her head away from it. The smell of ammonia was making her gag, and she coughed, trying to force the feeling down.

"She's coming round. What a time for it to happen. She'll be so embarrassed."

Was that Cindy's voice?

"Oh yes, a very fine time. Unless it was calculated. You can't trust these innocent English bitches."

No prizes for guessing whose voice *that* was.

Rose opened her eyes a fraction. She was lying on a couch in the women's rest room, and Cindy was crouching beside her. Lacey Venables' eyes were spitting acid as they glared down at her, and the corporation nurse was replacing the stopper on the bottle of sal-volatile.

"She should rest awhile," the nurse said. "She's obviously been under a strain this weekend from what you've told me."

"She can't rest. Mr Jefferson wants to see her," Lacey snapped.

The nurse looked at her with active dislike.

"Miss Venables, for the moment Rose is my patient, and I say she needs at least ten minutes' rest before she sees Mr Jefferson."

"What does he want to see me about?" Rose said huskily. Though she could guess. It was probably to give her the sack. She was more trouble than she was worth. And it was all she wanted. Right now, when she needed to keep this job so desperately. She struggled to sit up.

"I'm feeling better, now. Really."

"Ten minutes," the nurse said firmly. "Whatever he wants, it will keep. And I'm staying with you until the time is up."

"You know best," Lacey said, stiff and sarcastic. "But you won't need the rest of us."

Rose watched her and Cindy leave the rest room, and she looked gratefully at the nurse.

"Thanks. But what happened?"

"You passed out, that's all, and you hit your head on the corner of the desk as you went down. Nothing serious, but you'll have a shiner by the morning."

Until that moment Rose hadn't been aware of the throbbing pain around her temple and her eye, but now she touched it gingerly, and winced.

"I've put witch hazel on it, which will help, but you should take it easy for twenty-four hours, Rose, and don't come into the office tomorrow."

She didn't bother to answer. There would probably be no job for her to come in to, anyway. She was glad when the ten minutes were up, and the nurse helped her to sit up. She still felt decidedly groggy, and she still had to face Jefferson.

She was ushered into his office by Miss Simpson, who gave no indication of what the meeting was to be about, even if she knew. Jefferson walked towards her, taking her hand, and sitting down beside her on one of the plush casting couches. For the life of her, Rose couldn't get the words out of her head, but dear God, this wasn't the time. This *definitely* wasn't the time, when she was as vulnerable as a kitten.

"Poor Rose," Jefferson said softly. "You've had one hell of a time, haven't you?"

Her eyes filled with tears, and she angrily tried to dash them away. But it hurt her head. . . .

"They've told you about Gracie then?" she muttered.

"I heard," he said briefly. "But I've phoned the hospital myself to find out the exact details."

Rose looked at him in amazement. Why on earth would he bother to do that? Unless he didn't even believe her story! But of course, the hospital dragons would have been only too ready to give the important Bradley Piers Jefferson the third every detail he wanted to know.

"You know I was telling the truth then."

"Good God, nobody would ever doubt that of you. I just wanted to know the situation, that's all. And I understand that you've given my name as surety for the medical bills."

Rose closed her eyes in shame and humiliation. She should never have done that, but at the time it had seemed the only way to guarantee that Gracie got the best of care.

"I'm sorry," she mumbled.

"Don't be," he said, his hand closing over hers. She almost snatched it away.

"Well, don't think I'm going to cash in on your good nature. I intend to pay all the bills myself, even if I have to work all the hours God sends—"

"For Christ's sake, Rose, calm down. Have you any idea how much hospital bills cost in this town?"

She didn't, and from the tone of his voice she didn't want to know.

"I'll offer to pay on instalments. They'll accept that, won't they? As long as I've still got my job, so they know the money's secure."

He stared at her for a long time. She had once thought him so charismatic, and she still did. But there was a ruthless side to him that she didn't trust. She had once thought he would be so easy to fall in love with. Now she knew that she never could.

"You're too bloody independent for your own good,

171

honey, but have it your way. Just let me know if you get in real trouble, and I'll help out. We do have an emergency fund for employees' needs, you know. Jefferson's is all heart."

She bit her lip, hearing his sarcasm, but if what he said was true, then maybe she wouldn't have to work herself to death after all. She didn't imagine she'd get much help from Merv. He spent everything as soon as he earned it. As if he was reading her thoughts, Jefferson spoke again.

"What about the husband? Doesn't he have a bean? Your sister's his responsibility – and why in God's name did he take her to the most expensive hospital in that part of town?"

"We had no choice. There was a pile-up on the freeway, and all the other hospitals were full."

And she couldn't bear to sit here one minute longer, exposing the disaster of her sister's marriage and making small talk. Her head throbbed, and she needed to see for herself that Gracie was all right. She moved away from him on the vast sofa.

"Can I go now, sir? I want to go to the hospital."

"I intended to take you myself—"

"Oh no! Really, it's not necessary."

"Yes, it is. If only to prove to those hospital ghouls that you really do work for me, and I've got your best interests at heart."

They'd see that all right. And she could see that once the Jefferson limo drew up outside the Cedars of Hope, she'd be marked down as something more special than just a little typist. But right now, she didn't give a damn.

"All right, and thank you. I'm very grateful."

He put one finger on her cheek, caressing its softness, and she gritted her teeth. Please God, not this again, she thought. This wasn't the payment for his concern, was it? She heard him give a short laugh.

"You're also very transparent, Rose. Let's go."

* * *

172

As expected, the arrival of the Jefferson limo created its own atmosphere. He made a point of stepping out of it with Rose, and escorting her to the nurses' station. She had already entreated him not to stay, saying she'd return home with Merv that evening – when he deigned to show up, she added silently.

But the presence of Jefferson meant that Rose had star treatment. And once she was directed to Gracie's room, she saw that her sister was getting the same. There was a nurse in twenty-four hour attendance, and Gracie was wired up to a battery of instruments and equipment. There was a drip in her arm. Rose moved forward, her heart in her mouth.

Gracie was sleeping now, but she looked so ill, and so *old*. Rose had never realized that illness, however sudden, could ravage a person's features so.

"She'll be OK, hon," the nurse said.

"She looks terrible," Rose whispered. "What do all these wires and things mean?"

"It means Dr Leandra's providing the best possible treatment," the nurse said crisply. "This equipment is the very latest. Any trouble, and we're bleeped at once."

The very latest, and the very best, and very expensive. . . . Rose couldn't stop the thought screaming through her head, even while she hated herself for it. She didn't know what to say to the nurse, and then Gracie opened her eyes and gave a weak smile. The nurse moistened her mouth with a damp tissue, and motioned Rose to sit beside her.

"How are you, Gracie?" she asked inanely.

"Oh, just great, kid!" she croaked. "But I'll be a damn sight better when I get outa here. Tell you what. You go down to Sea-Food Joe's and order me a steak, rare and bloody, OK?"

Rose's eyes filled.

"Oh, Gracie!"

"For God's sake, don't start blubbing. I ain't dead yet. And don't try to make me laugh. It hurts when I laugh and when I cough and when I fart."

The nurse evidently didn't think that was funny, and turned away to fiddle with the bleeper equipment. But once Gracie started talking, she couldn't be stopped.

"Are you in much pain now, Gracie?" Rose asked.

Gracie snorted, and winced as she did so.

"What do you think? But never mind all that. How are you managing at home – and what the hell's that lump on your forehead? Merv ain't been knocking you about, has he?"

"Of course not. I fainted at the office and hit my head, that's all. I'm all right, Gracie, it was just due to lack of sleep."

"Well, you get the nurses here to take a look at it. God knows we're paying 'em enough for all this fancy equipment."

That was rich, thought Rose, since she was paying none of it. But even as she tried to think of an answer she could see that Gracie had had enough talking after all, and her eyes were drooping.

"It's the effects of the drugs we're giving her," the nurse said. "She'll sleep for a while now. Do you want to get some coffee? There's a machine down the corridor. You can come back and sit awhile if you want to."

"All right. I want to wait until my brother-in-law arrives, anyway."

He was a long time coming, but when he did, Gracie hadn't woken again, and looked set to be out for the night. Nurses and doctors came and went, and it all began to pass in a mist over Rose's head. Finally, Merv said it was nine o'clock and they might as well go home.

Rose saw with a shock that he was right, and the darkening city was already starting its chameleon-like transformation, with its fluorescent street lighting turning

174

even the seedier parts of town into a fairyland. Merv insisted that they stop off at a fast food place. Rose didn't think she could eat a thing, but the smell of the food started her stomach gnawing, reminding her how long it was since she'd eaten, and she was glad of a meal. Once they were on the road again, Merv glanced at her.

"Just you and me now then, kid."

Something in his voice, bland though it was, made Rose's temper spill over in the darkness of the Chevy.

"You can just forget any daft ideas you might have about that, you hear?" she snapped. "If you dare come near my room, or try to put one finger on me while Gracie's in hospital, I'll scream rape so loud you'll wonder what hit you."

There was real astonishment in his voice now.

"Christ, what's got into you?"

"*Nothing*, and it's going to stay that way," she said meaningfully, knowing he'd understand perfectly well what she meant. "I mean what I say, Merv."

"OK, OK! I get the message!" he snapped back. "And you needn't worry. I got better things to do with my time than mess about with kids."

Well, that was a surprise to her, but she wasn't going to prolong the conversation, and he was quiet for the rest of the drive back to the apartment. He'd been surprised too. He hadn't expected such a vicious reaction to an innocent remark, but in a strange way, he admired her for it. Rose was no longer the wimpish, wide-eyed little sister he'd taken her for. She had guts. He admired her for that too. In fact, with hindsight, he realized just what it must have taken to stand up to him and the leches at Joanna Del Mar's party, to say nothing of that high-powered boss of hers. Yes, little Rose was growing up all right.

Whatever she had said, Rose realized Merv was taking her at her word, and treating her with rather more respect than

175

previously. All the same, she firmly bolted her bedroom door that night, and was thankful when the phone didn't ring until morning, when the dawn light was spreading an ethereal pink and golden light across the city. At such a time Rose always thought it really lived up to its name, the city of angels.

But she had no such thoughts now as she flew to answer the phone, sure that Merv would still be dead to the world.

"I thought this was the better time to call, *cariad*," she heard Evan say. "Less worrying for you than in the middle of your night."

"Much better, Evan," she said chokily, for all kinds of reasons.

"So how is she?"

She stared at the wall opposite in the tiny hallway, with the hideous pictures Gracie had nailed to the wallpaper, and dragged her thoughts back to why Evan was calling at all. The joyousness of hearing his voice had blotted out everything else for the moment.

"They say she's improving, but she looks pretty bad. She's got these wires and things. . . ." She started to choke up again, and tried to swallow.

"Take it slowly, love, I've got plenty of time."

"No, you haven't. These calls must be costing a fortune—"

"Don't be so daft. If I can't spend time talking to my best girl, it's a poor job. So how long do they expect her to be in hospital?"

"I don't know," Rose said, glowing at hearing him call her his best girl. She'd felt sure there would be another one in his life by now. A *real* girl, one for him to love and kiss and hold. . . .

"What's the position then?"

She couldn't think what he meant. She was too wrapped up in the sudden misery of imagining Evan with a girl in his arms, and knowing the girl wasn't her. It was crazy, because why on earth would he ever want to hold *her* in that way, anyway?

"I mean about money, Rose," Evan went on, when she didn't answer. "You have to pay for hospital care over there, don't you? I know a bit about the legal side of things, remember."

"It's all right. I'm taking care of it," she said quickly – too quickly.

"You? You're not telling me they don't have medical insurance, are you?" His voice was suddenly sharp and disbelieving. And, illogically, Rose felt as if was a personal slight against herself.

"Please don't go on at me, Evan. They do things differently here—"

"I know that, love! That's why I'm asking about the medical insurance."

She had forgotten how persistent he could be. He may not be as chirpy as his brother Dai, but he had a relentless way of finding out what he wanted to know. And right now, he wanted to know who was paying Gracie's medical bills. It was sweet and dear of him, but it shouldn't concern him.

"I'm not sure," she hedged. "But please don't worry about it, Evan. We'll manage."

She heard him give a low oath.

"I've always worried about you, Rose. I thought you knew that."

"Well, that was all right when we were children, but I don't need it now. I'm fine, Evan, really I am."

The habitual pause over the wire became suddenly strained.

"Would you prefer that I no longer worried over you, then? Or are you trying to tell me you're forgetting all about us already?"

"Don't be daft." She was angry now. "How could I

ever forget you, or want to? I miss you, Evan. I miss you all."

"No more than I miss you, *cariad*," he said. "But if you're sure Gracie's going on all right for the time being, then I'll pass on the news to Mam."

"All right. And Evan – as soon as she's on the mend, I'll call you to let you know."

"You watch out for yourself, mind. Gracie's got a husband to take care of her, so don't go thinking you can take the whole world on your shoulders."

It was something he used to say to her when she was so prickly about being so small and female in a household of boys, and tried to be as good as they were in everything. Now she knew that she could never be the same, because they weren't the same and never could be.

"Goodbye, *cariad*," Evan said softly.

"Goodbye," she replied.

She turned quickly, and went into the tiny kitchen to make herself some tea and toast. It was far too early for breakfast, but she knew she'd never be able to sleep if she went back to bed. She turned the radio on quietly, and listened to some early morning music while she half-dozed in a chair, waiting for the kettle to boil. And thought of Evan.

In particular she thought of a remark somebody had once made at the office. About how crazy she was to leave a man like him behind. But it wasn't as if he'd been her *lover*. The emotive word rippled through Rose's mind. She savoured the taste of it on her tongue. Her lover. Such a thing was an unknown quantity to her, and there was no reason on earth why she should equate it with regard to Evan Pritchard.

All the same . . . there was something in the way he said that sweet Welsh word . . . *cariad* . . . that made her toes tingle. He'd said it often enough before when she was a small child, and it had meant nothing. It was just a

178

comforting word for a frightened little evacuee, so why should it mean anything more now? Was it just that she had never heard it for what it was before? Had she never really been listening?

She shivered as the piercing whistle of the kettle shattered her thoughts, and she ran to switch it off before it disturbed Merv. But it wasn't the first time she had found these bewildering emotions about Evan replacing the sisterly affection she'd always felt for him.

And it was all too late. It was all too frustratingly late if she was to discover that what she really felt for him was far from sisterly.

"Was that the kettle? What Goddamned time is it?" she heard Merv growl, and she jumped as he appeared in the kitchen, unshaven and swaying revoltingly.

"I'm sorry if it woke you. I'm just making some tea," she said quickly. "I got up to answer the phone – and before you ask, it wasn't the hospital. It was Evan."

"Good God, don't they ever sleep in that Welsh hole?"

"He was concerned over Gracie," she said. "And besides, it's two o'clock in the afternoon at home."

At home. She bit her lip, but she knew it was going to be a long time before she could really accept that this apartment was home. The thought of moving out was still in her mind, but if there were large medical bills to pay, the prospect of it was receding more every day.

"How long do you think they'll keep Gracie in hospital?" she said, when they were both eating a frugal breakfast.

"How the hell do I know? I ain't no doctor. But no longer than necessary, I hope. We ain't made of money."

"You do have some then?" Rose said at once.

179

His eyes narrowed. "Oh yeah. Last week's pay, and the rent money on the apartment, if you want to see us thrown out on the streets. In any case you said you were going to see to it. I reckon it's the least you can do, to pay us back a bit."

"I said I would, and so I will," she said coldly, wondering if he had any pride at all.

"What was this I heard about gettin' a private nurse in for Gracie when she comes home?"

Rose felt alarmed. They surely couldn't afford such a service, but if Gracie needed it . . . she ran her tongue around her dry lips.

"Let's hear what the doctor says about that, though I'm sure it won't be necessary. I could always ask for advance holiday time off from the office and look after her myself. And if you're home most daytimes, we could manage it between us, couldn't we?"

Not that she could see Merv as a nursemaid, but he was Gracie's husband, and she stared him out unflinchingly.

"Oh, I dare say," he said ungraciously. "And Mrs Olsen will always give an eye to her. She's a nosey enough old bag when she's not wanted."

"I'm going to use the bathroom and then I'm getting dressed," Rose said, despite the early hour, and unable to listen to a minute more of this.

"Suit yourself. I'm going back to bed," Merv said.

Gracie was in the hospital for two weeks, and at the end of it, Rose got the itemized bill for medical and surgical expenses. It was staggering, and she couldn't possibly afford to pay it outright. But by now, she'd rather die than approach Jefferson for a hand-out, even from his so-called emergency corporation fund. Whether or not it was foolish to feel that way, to Rose it smacked too much of going on welfare.

She was forced to humble herself in asking the hospital almoner if it would be all right to pay on instalments.

"I wouldn't trouble you in this way, but you know that the money's guaranteed through my job at the Jefferson Printing Corporation," she threw in for extra measure. "I don't want to embarrass Mr Jefferson by asking for the money all in one go, especially when he might well be prepared to make a donation to the hospital at some future date."

She knew she was taking a great risk in saying such things, for she had never mentioned it to Jefferson, and she also knew that she never would. It was just her own brand of insurance to get her over this particular hurdle. And it worked. She was granted permission to pay the bill in instalments, even though it would eat an enormous hole out of her salary every week.

The letter from Evan came a few days after Gracie came home. She was still weak, playing for attention, and nagging Rose to get that time off to stay with her.

Rose tore open the envelope with the familiar writing on it, and stared in disbelief as she saw a banker's order for a substantial amount of money enclosed inside the letter.

'Rose, love,' she read,
    'This is to help you out with Gracie's expenses, since I'm sure the bulk of it is going to fall on you. I can imagine how you're feeling right now at seeing the amount I've sent, but I suspect it's still just a drop in the ocean. So get that angry, proud look off your face and just take it in the spirit of love and friendship in which it's given. I don't want gratitude. I just don't want you to be exploited, or to feel that you're out of your depth.'
    It was signed, 'Your loving Evan.'

And it had the effect of sending the tears streaming down

her face. She couldn't take this – and yet, how could she refuse? She needed it so much, and it would be throwing Evan's generosity back in his face if she were to send it back.

He was right, too. It still left the debt far short of what was needed. And it finally made up her mind for her. If she could only win the Miss Christmas Angel pageant, she would have five hundred dollars to put towards the hospital bills.

And she certainly couldn't speak to Evan on the phone right now, nor tell him what she intended to do. He'd hate the very idea of her parading herself. And if she were to hear his caring voice when she tried to thank him, she knew she'd only end up weeping, and that would be awful. So she wrote back immediately, trying to be as unemotional as possible in the circumstances, while she thanked him with all her heart.

Chapter Twelve

On the night of the Miss Christmas Angel beauty pageant, Rose lined up with the rest of the girls at the downtown Plaza Hotel, trying to keep herself as detached as possible from all that was happening. The row of thirty girls in bathing suits and high-heeled shoes were required to parade individually at first, and to twirl around in front of the audience and the five male judges seated in the front row of the darkened hotel, while the girls themselves were in the glare of the spotlights.

At least it meant that they couldn't see the faces of the judges too clearly, Rose thought thankfully, though when the line-up had been whittled down to seven finalists, and the contestants were to be individually interviewed, the lights in the hotel went up. It wasn't hard to see, then, that the judges were less interested in each girl's background and ambitions, than in the size of her bust and the length of her legs. And at the sea of faces beyond the judges, including Gracie's pale face, and Merv and Chuck's leering ones, she felt more like turning tail and running out of there.

But she couldn't do that. Not with the five hundred dollars at stake that she badly needed. And at least she was one of the finalists. She had come this far. And even if her face and figure weren't going to make her fortune, she had one ace up her sleeve that the other girls didn't have. She had her English voice.

"Number five, step forward please," she heard herself being called. "Tell us something about yourself, girlie."

She drew a deep breath. "My name is Rose Forster, and I'm eighteen years old. I come from London, England, although I live here in Los Angeles now with my sister and brother-in-law. I think I'm already fulfilling one of my dearest ambitions, which was always to come to America."

She knew that would go down well, knowing the arrogance of some of these guys who thought the sun shone out of American skies and nowhere else . . . and she carefully avoided saying that she worked for the Jefferson Printing Corporation. There were reporters taking down every bit of information for the entertainment rags, and she didn't think Jefferson would be too pleased at having his name associated with this dump. Rose pushed down the unease she felt about the whole affair, and thought instead of the money.

"Thank you, now can number fourteen step forward, please," the voice said, and she gaped. Was that all? She had hardly had a chance to say anything. But she found herself being nudged to the back of the stage and the next contestant was moving forward. By now, she was a bundle of nerves, wondering how any girl could go on the circuit regularly, and do this kind of thing for a pastime. Yet she knew many of them did. Some of the girls here did so, and one had bothered to advise her on her make-up, and told her how to rub vaseline into her lips to keep her smile more easily fixed. It worked too, she discovered.

After what seemed an age while the judges deliberated, and a crooner belted out a slushy romantic song, at last the time came for the final results to be announced. Rose's heart beat so fast she thought she was going to faint, but she kept her hands rigidly by her sides and tried to keep that smile fixed. She wasn't one of the four lesser prize-winners, who all got bottles of champagne

184

tied up with pink ribbons, to the accompaniment of wild applause.

"Now we come to the final three," the organizer said with a leer. "One of these three lovelies will be crowned Miss Christmas Angel here tonight."

He turned round to encompass all three of them, to a fanfare of music from the so-called musical duo, and the catcalls and whistles, and obscene remarks from the back of the audience that made Rose's face burn.

"Ignore it, kid. You'll get used to it," one of the other finalists said out of the side of her mouth, and Rose marvelled how she could say the words while her smile never moved. And then she heard the girl's name called, and the smile still didn't waver, even though she had only come third, officially called the second runner-up, with a prize of champagne and chocolates and a fifty dollar cheque.

So it was between Rose and the tall blonde-haired girl called Elena something-or-other who looked like a Swedish model. . . . Rose could hardly breathe now, and whatever happened, she found herself vowing never, *never*, to go through this embarrassment again.

"The first runner-up to Miss Christmas Angel is Miss Rose Forster, who also wins a prize of champagne and chocolates, and a cheque for fifty dollars."

The searing disappointment was too much. She *needed* that five hundred dollars, and all she'd got was fifty. She stammered out her thanks, and accepted the organizer's damp kiss, trying hard not to fall apart and shame herself. She left that to the Swedish-looking Elena, who was preparing to burst into ready tears of delight at her award, while being careful not to disturb her mascara.

Rose couldn't wait to get off the stage and into the dressing-room to change into her ordinary clothes. Some of the other girls congratulated her, others commiserated on her near-miss, and a few of the professional pageant contestants were openly annoyed that she had got that far at her first attempt. She didn't care. All she wanted was to get out of there, and forget it had ever happened.

"Is Rose Forster here?" a male voice called out, coming straight into the dressing-room after a brief knock. The youth looked all around the room, eyeing up everything in sight, and one of the girls pushed him right out again. His response was indignant. "Hey, slag, get your hands off me. It's Rose Forster who's wanted out front. Theo Klinkski wants to talk to her."

Rose's head jerked up. She didn't know any Theo Klinkski, but Elena did. He was one of the judges.

"Go for it, Rose. If he's offering you a modelling job, you'll make bigger bucks than anything you could have earned here tonight."

"Who is he, then?"

"Jeez, have you just got off the boat? He owns the Klinkski modelling agency on the east side of town, and he can put plenty of work your way."

Rose felt a new excitement run through her veins. A modelling agency – and this Theo Klinkski was asking to see *her*, and nobody else from the line-up of girls. She finished dressing quickly, and lifted her head up high as she swept out of the communal dressing-room.

The youth was lounging against the wall outside. "Mr Klinkski's in the boss's office," he said in a bored voice. "I'll show you the way."

"Will you please let my people know I'm having an interview and to wait for me?" she said quickly. "They're on Chuck Bernstein's table."

"Sure thing," he said, obviously well aware of who Chuck Bernstein was.

Rose didn't give any of them a second thought as she was shown into the hotel manager's office, to be greeted by the cigar-smoking man she remembered seeing among the judges.

"Sit down, little lady," he said affably in a strong, nasal New York accent. "I was very impressed by you tonight."

"Were you?" Rose said. "I thought it was only the winner of the pageant who'd be interviewed."

"Yeah, well, that's left to the newsguys. This is something else."

Rose ran her tongue around her dry lips as he looked her over with eyes that seemed to see right through her dress to the flesh beneath. But he'd have seen plenty of that already, she thought quickly, so she shouldn't let it bother her. Bathing suits didn't leave much to the imagination.

"I think I could do something for you, Rose," he went on. "You interested in making money?"

"Isn't everybody?" she hedged.

Klinkski laughed, showing teeth with gold fillings. "That's a good answer, babe. So how'd you like to do some part-time modelling for me? Say, one day a week, on Saturdays, maybe, until we see how we like each other? Nothing sleazy, of course, just tasteful shots, maybe some in a bathing suit, like you did here tonight."

"I don't know," Rose said slowly.

"Aw, come on, what have you got to lose? You can make real dough from doing calendar shots, and once you sign up with me, it's all legal and above-board. And I'll tell you what. Once we've struck a deal, I'll pay you something upfront as a gesture of goodwill. A coupla hundred dollars wouldn't go amiss, would it, babe?"

She swallowed. It certainly wouldn't. It would help out with the medical bills that still stretched endlessly ahead. Gracie was under a doctor's care now. And whereas before, she'd rejected any thought of seeing doctors, now she was pathetically finding everything wrong with her that she could, and taking every medication under the sun. All of which had to be paid for.

"I'd need to see what I'm signing before I agreed."

"Of course you would, and I've got the contract right here. It's all legal, like I said. There's nothing shady about the Klinkski Agency."

He beamed at her like a Dutch uncle, and Rose skimmed through the contract, though she couldn't make sense of half of it. She knew she should get someone to check it, but it ended with several impressive signatures, including a company auditor and solicitor. It had to be all right. In the end, she signed where Klinkski indicated, and he folded up the contract and put it back in his pocket.

"Don't I keep that?" Rose asked in some alarm.

"This goes in my files, Rose, but I'll have a copy ready for you in a week or two. So we have a deal, and I'll see you around ten on Saturday morning. I'll give you my card, and you'll have no trouble finding the place. You don't need to bring your own bathing suit. We've got plenty of selections at the studio, and you'll need to make changes anyway. And it's not all bathing suit work, of course. I know it's going to be a pleasure working with you."

He shook her hand, and Rose walked out of there in a daze, wondering what she had let herself in for. But it was going to be so exciting, and many girls would give their eyeteeth for such a chance. Fancy getting into modelling without even trying!

Gracie screamed at her when she told her the news.

"Are you completely mad? Before you know it, you'll find pictures of yourself in some low-life girlie mag, and what will your precious Jefferson have to say about that?"

"I doubt that Mr Jefferson ever sees such things," Rose snapped, but taken aback at this violent reaction. "In any case, it's for calendar work. I signed a contract to that effect, and I trust Mr Klinkski."

Gracie's face suddenly softened. "Oh Rose, honey, you don't know this town yet. You only see the surface of it, and not the corruption underneath. You can't trust anybody, and you're still dazzled by the movies—"

"No, I'm not. I don't want to be a movie star. I'm no actress, and I accept that."

"You're no slick operator, either, but I bet this Klinkski is. How much is he paying you?"

"I don't know yet—"

"*What*?"

"But I'm getting two hundred dollars upfront before I do a thing. That shows he's got faith in me, doesn't it?"

Gracie shook her head in disbelief. "Well, I just hope you know what you're doing, that's all. And the minute he asks you to do something you're uncomfortable with, you get out of there fast, you hear? God knows what Mum would have said if she knew what I'm letting you get into."

It was so rare for Gracie to mention their mother that Rose ran to her at once and put her arms around her.

"Gracie, I'm not a baby any more. I keep telling you that. I can take care of myself, and whatever I choose to do with my life, well, it's still my life."

Merv thought it was a great chance. He knew nothing about any modelling agency, but the fact that the guy had sought Rose out from all the contestants, must mean he thought she had potential, and he offered to drive her to do the studio on Saturday morning.

"You mean you'll get out of bed just for my benefit?"

He grinned, and she could almost see the words forming in his brain.

"I'd rather get into it for your benefit, babe. . . ."

But she stared him out, daring him to say it, and the words remained unsaid.

She didn't mention any of it at the office. None of them knew she'd entered for the pageant, and it wasn't reported in any but the lesser entertainment magazines that none of the girls here would touch with a bargepole. And she certainly didn't mention anything about her moonlighting with the Klinkski modelling agency. Not until she became famous, Rose thought half-dreamily.

Well, why not? It could happen!

Merv deposited her at the studio on Saturday morning, and said he'd come back for her when she called to say she was ready to leave. His Saturdays were usually spent sprawled out in front of the TV set, or fiddling under the hood of the Chevy, anyway. And maybe he'd give Gracie a ride later that day, to take her mind off her latest imaginary ailment, he thought, scowling. She'd turned completely since that scare with her appendix. Now she thought she suffered from every Goddamned thing, and it was costing a fortune in medical bills.

"Go on, then," Merv said, as Rose seemed reluctant to get out of the car. "They ain't going to eat you, kid."

She got out and rang the bell on the wooden door with its peeling paint and the equally shabby sign above that pronounced it the Klinkski Modelling Agency. It didn't exactly look like a classy place, Rose thought uneasily, but the next minute a girl dressed in a sweater and skirt opened the door to her and gave her a cheerful smile.

"Hi. You must be Rose. I'm Dolly. I work for Theo as receptionist cum secretary. It's nice to meet you, and I've been hearing a lot about you. English, aren't you?"

She was chatty enough to put Rose instantly at her ease. Dolly gave her coffee at once, and then she was shown into a little cubicle where a selection of bathing suits and evening wear hung all around the walls, and she breathed easier still.

"This will be your space for now," Dolly said. "Theo

190

likes to give the girls plenty of elbow-room, but you're the only one here today. Theo thinks that first-timers need to relax before they meet the rest of the crew. So there'll only be you, me and Theo, and the photographer."

"Oh – he doesn't take the photos himself then?"

"Sometimes. But we have a really great photographer for the special shots. You'll like him. His name's Gleeson. I'll take you through to the studio now, and he and Theo will tell you what they want you to do today."

The nerves were back, but there was no turning back now. And she wasn't a wimp, for God's sake. This was a new experience, a new job, and something to tell Evan about . . . as the thought slipped into her mind, she wondered immediately if she would tell him. He definitely wouldn't approve, and she had always needed his approval in everything.

The studio was large and bright, with the kind of photographic equipment Rose had only ever seen in the movies or in magazine articles. It all looked terribly professional, and as Dolly had said, she quite liked Gleeson. He was as Bohemian a figure as Theo, and obviously took his art seriously. There was nothing to be alarmed about.

"You can choose any of the outfits in your cubicle you like, Rose," Theo said. "We'll do some prelim shots in the clothes of your choice, just to see how you shape up and to put you at your ease. After lunch we'll do some bathing suit pics, if it's OK with you."

"That's fine," she said, relieved that she wasn't expected to strip off right away.

The morning passed quickly, and Gleeson was very patient with her, getting her to pose exactly as he wanted her, and in a very professional way. Rose was impressed with his attention to detail.

They took a sandwich and coffee lunch in the yard at the back of the studio, and Rose was glad that Dolly was also staying all day. Then came the afternoon session.

There was a selection of satin bathing suits to choose from, some with extremely high-cut legs, which looked terribly daring, and unlikely to be seen on any beach.

"Don't worry about the skimpiness of them, Rose," Theo said when she looked at them dubiously. "A normal bathing suit looks all wrong on a calendar, and what the punters want to see is plenty of cleavage and plenty of leg. But you don't need to think about that. Just think of it as a job, and you'll be OK."

She chose a bright sapphire blue one, and felt horribly exposed when she put it on. The plunging neckline went right down to her navel, and she'd dearly liked to have tugged it around her if it hadn't seemed so ridiculous. But it was one thing to stand beside thirty other girls in a beauty pageant. That was bad enough. To be the only one half-dressed in a modelling studio made her feel less than comfortable. She smothered her inhibitions, remembering the two hundred dollars she was picking up today, and went out of the cubicle.

Theo whistled when he saw her.

"Great. You've got an eye for colour, babe. Now I want you to look at these pics, and try out some similar poses for Gleeson. He'll direct you, but this is the kind of thing we want."

Rose looked at the portfolio of beautiful girls in undeniably sexy poses, with pouting mouths, and come-hither eyes, some half-turning, so that their backsides jutted out towards the camera. Others had the girls leaning forward, so that their breasts all but popped out of the bathing suits.

"I'm not sure about this," she said uneasily.

"There's nothing to it, kid," Gleeson said. "You just ignore me and pretend you're at the beach making out with some guy that you're mad about. Look into the camera as if you're really lusting over him, OK?"

Rose stared at him. She had never lusted over anybody

in her life, and couldn't think of anybody she cared to fantasize about, which was what he seemed to want. Certainly not Jefferson, or any of the guys she'd met at Joanna Del Mar's. There was only Evan. Without warning, a dreamy look filled her eyes, and her tongue ran around her soft mouth again, and Gleeson immediately latched on to it.

"Hey, that's the look, babe. Whoever the guy is, keep him in mind, or wherever else you want him."

She didn't answer. The posing was long and tedious enough, and she tried hard to emulate the postures in the portfolio that Theo was holding up to her from time to time. She didn't really care for what she was doing it, and the only way she could forget herself was to do as Gleeson said, and imagine she was looking straight into her lover's eyes, instead of the impersonal eye of the camera.

"OK. That's enough for today," Theo said, when she'd changed bathing suits several times. "That was a good session, and you've earned your money, Rose."

"Thank you," she said, relieved that it was over, and that he was honouring his word. "Can I call my brother-in-law to come and collect me?"

"Oh sure," Theo said. "You can wait in reception with Dolly until he arrives, and I'll see you again next week, same time, OK?"

She dressed quickly, feeling more respectable by the minute, and starting to wonder why she'd been so anxious. Dolly was friendly, and Merv seemed to arrive in double-quick time, so that by four o'clock she was relating all that had happened to Gracie, prone on the sofa in the apartment.

"And the guy didn't try anything on?" Gracie said for the third time.

"I've told you, no! It was all very proper, so stop worrying. It's good money, and next week I dare say I'll see the pics Gleeson took today."

It was an exciting concept. She'd never thought of herself as a pin-up girl before, not like those pics of Betty Grable that supposedly decorated so many GIs' locker rooms during the war. But Rose realized they were exactly the kind the poses she'd done today, and it hadn't been so bad.

She felt more cheerful during the next week. The pageant was behind her, and nobody at the office seemed to have heard about it, to her relief. And when Saturday came around again, she didn't bother Merv, but took the bus that she discovered stopped less than a block away from the studio. Dolly let her in again, and showed her straight through to the studio where Theo and Gleeson were waiting for her.

"Here's my little lady," Theo said at once. "Ready to see your glamour shots from last week?"

He opened a portfolio marked Rose Forster, and she gasped at the beautiful photographs Gleeson had taken of her. He had made a subtle use of lighting, and she looked both sexy and innocent. She had never thought she could look like that. It was her, and yet it wasn't her. . . .

"Like them?" Gleeson said with a smile.

"Of course I do," she said. "Even if they do make me look much better than I do in real life."

"Of course they don't. Most girls don't realize their potential until they have a skilled photographer bringing out the best in them. And you have it all, babe," Gleeson said approvingly.

"We want to do something different today, Rose," Theo said smoothly. "It all goes to make up the portfolio we need to show around to the calendar people and magazine editors."

Warning bells sounded in Rose's head at the mention of magazines, even more so than the mention of calendars.

"What sort of something different?" she said.

"Now don't get alarmed. Everything's done with good

taste here," Theo went on, clearly the spokesman now. "You'll need these to begin with."

He reached for a pile of different-coloured chiffon scarves that had been lying on the posing sofa. Rose looked at them stupidly.

"You've no objection to nudity, have you, Rose?" Gleeson said casually. "Some of the greatest statues of all time have been nudes—"

"But I'm not a statue, and if you think I'm going to take all my clothes off—"

"Now calm down!" Theo said. "Gleeson and myself are professionals. We've seen hundreds of naked girls, and there's nothing you've got that we haven't seen before, honey."

"Well, I'm not going to do it, and that's flat," she said, close to tears. "And if that's what you expect from me from now on, you can keep your rotten job!"

She may be close to tears, but she wouldn't let them see it. All her dreams were falling apart, and this studio, that she had thought so fine, was nothing but a front for dirty photographs. She had no doubt of that now, however tasteful Theo protested the shots would be.

"You signed a contract, honey," he said in that nasal New York twang.

"I didn't sign to say I'd pose nude, and you can't force me to do it."

"You signed to do anything that was required of you, babe, and it's all legal and binding. You wanna take another look at the contract?"

Rose shook her head blindly. This couldn't be happening. But they still couldn't force her to do it. She held on to that fact, and although the stricken look on her face was starting to bug him, Theo's hard face relaxed.

"Look, I'll make a deal with you. We'll forget the nude shots and try something else instead. With that accent, you'll add a bit of class to the movies we're shooting."

"Movies?" Rose said, her attention caught at once.

"Sure. After lunch today we're shooting a short movie. You wanna be in it?"

She knew she was weakening. "What kind of a movie?"

"The best. Don't worry, there'll be three other girls beside yourself and one guy. They'll see you through."

"But I won't know what to do. Is there a script?"

She heard Gleeson give a strangled laugh, and Theo glared at him.

"Just play it by ear, honey, like the rest of the cast. Call it a kind of silent movie, if you like. Dolly's taking part today, so you'll be OK."

It relieved Rose to know it. She liked Dolly, though she couldn't get a thing out of her when she asked what the movie was about. Everybody was so vague. Maybe this was the way it was on low-budget movies, she thought, but when Theo mentioned the fee he'd be paying, she forgot her qualms and said all right. Anything would be better than having to do nude shots.

When the other actors arrived she felt slightly better. The girls looked so normal, and the guy was what they called typical Californian beefcake. He grinned at her, and said he thought they'd get along just fine, and if she wanted to whisper sweet nothings in his ear while they were filming, he'd have no objections. Rose didn't like him at all.

She discovered the studio had been cleared of the regular photographic equipment while she and Dolly ate lunch. It was subtly lit now, with the sofa replaced by a large heart-shaped bed, draped in black satin sheets and with mirrors all around the room.

Rose's mouth suddenly dried. She wasn't born yesterday, despite what these people might think, and the kind of movie it was to be shrieked out at her. It would be pornographic, one of those things that odious old men watched in the seedy little red-light establishments like the ones in Soho. While the thoughts were still whirling around in her head, she saw the guy – Bruce – strip off his clothes, until he was only wearing a G-string. He might as well have been completely naked already, and Rose felt her face flame with hot colour.

By now, the other girls were also taking off all their clothes and chatting naturally all the while. But why worry about nudity, when a camera was about to close in on them and reveal their most intimate actions? And mirrored a dozen times from every angle so that nothing was left to the imagination at all. It was the worst humiliation Rose had ever experienced. Dolly looked at her uneasily.

"Come on, kid. Theo doesn't like to be kept waiting, and nor does Bruce," she ended with a giggle.

"I can't do this," she said furiously. "I *won't* do it. I'm getting out of here—"

She suddenly felt Theo's hand grab her around her wrist. She hadn't been aware that he was anywhere near, but now he snapped at her, his face a hard mask.

"You'll do it, lady, or I'll sue you for breach of contract so hard you'll be paying off the debt for the next twenty years."

Rose had no idea whether or not he was bluffing, but she wasn't staying around to find out. With an almighty shove, she sent him staggering back against one of the mirrors. It shattered at once, and Theo howled with rage and pain as he was struck by slivers of glass.

"Get out of here, bitch, but don't think I've done with you yet. Nobody crosses Theo Klinkski and gets away with it!"

Sobbing wildly, Rose fled out of the studio and she didn't stop running until she was two blocks away from where she had to catch her bus. It didn't matter. She couldn't face people anyway. She had never felt so dirty and ashamed, knowing how she had let herself be taken in by that man. Thank God she had got out of there when she did.

Otherwise . . . she shuddered. The thought of anybody knowing that she had been in a porn movie . . . or worse still, that anybody should have actually *seen* her in it . . . was so degrading she would rather have killed herself than face the shame of it.

"Are you all right, Miss?" she heard a man's voice say as she ran, wild-eyed and hardly knowing where she was going.

He touched her arm, and she screamed. He immediately backed away, shouting angrily that he was only trying to help, and that Goddamned bitches like her should keep off the streets. It was the end. Out of the corner of her eye she saw a cruising taxi, and she waved madly for it, falling into its stuffy interior and gasping out the address of the Hacketts' apartment.

Chapter Thirteen

Gracie was resting as usual when the taxi drew up outside the Hacketts' apartment building, but Merv roused himself enough from his TV programme to see her get out of the cab, and to glare at her the minute she came indoors.

"Swanking a bit, ain't we, doll? Splashing out on taxi fares ain't going to help pay the bills—"

"Don't you dare criticize me," Rose screamed out in a fury. "I've had about all I can take for today, and when you start paying the bills yourself, you can have a say in how I spend my money. Until then, keep your damn mouth shut."

She tore past him and into her bedroom, ignoring the comically-startled look on his face at this outburst. She crashed the bedroom door shut behind her and slammed the bolt tight. She didn't care if the whole neighbourhood heard her screaming at Merv. It was only what he deserved.

But she'd overlooked any reaction from Gracie. The next minute she was hammering on Rose's door and demanding to know what the hell was going on. And Rose knew her well enough to know that she'd stand there hammering all day if she had to. She got up from the bed on which she'd flung herself, and opened the door a crack. Gracie pushed it wide open and marched inside.

"You'll have everybody in the bloody apartment building craning their necks out of their windows if you carry on creating at Merv like that, our Rose! Have you completely lost your marbles, or what?"

"No, I haven't," Rose snapped. "I feel ill and I'm hot and tired, and I'm going to take a bath, *if* it's not too much to ask to use some of your precious hot water."

Instead of retaliating as usual, Gracie looked at her silently. This wasn't the Rose she was used to. This was a girl on the edge. Her entire attitude shrieked of shock and brittle sarcasm, and Gracie had no idea what had caused it. She knew where Rose had been all day though.

"Has there been any trouble at that agency place?" she said suspiciously.

Rose gave a short laugh. "Nothing that I couldn't handle. But I'm never going back, and that's *all* I'm going to say about it. Except that you'd better cut down your doctor's visits in future, if you expect me to keep on paying the bills out of my salary at Jefferson's. Anyway, you don't need any more treatment. You're in a damn sight better shape than I am right now."

She grabbed her washing bag and towel and pushed past her sister before she could ask any more questions. She bolted the bathroom door shut and filled the tub with hot steamy water, and then she stripped off all her clothes and sank into it, scrubbing every inch of her body as if to scrub away every bit of the corruption she had discovered today. And when she was tingling and sore from the relentless assault on her skin, she lay back in the bath and sobbed her heart out.

By Monday, a different kind of reaction had set in. She had been aggressively tight-lipped all weekend, and neither Gracie nor Merv could get anything out of her, no matter how hard they tried. But the very thought of Klinkski suing her, taking her to court for breach of contract and exposing her stupidity, was enough to terrify her.

She didn't question whether or not it would be in his

interests to do such a thing, or whether he'd risk bringing himself and his operations into the open by doing so. All she knew was that she couldn't let it happen, but she had no idea how to stop it.

There was only one person who could advise her, though it went against all her instincts to go to him. It certainly wouldn't be her brother-in-law, or Chuck Bernstein, and she had no other reliable male confidantes. She would never go to Gracie, and she couldn't risk asking the girls at the office for advice. But Jefferson knew this town like the back of his hand. In the end, she knew he was the only one she could go to, even if it meant throwing herself on his mercy.

She went to Lacey Venables' office and asked if she could arrange an appointment with Jefferson that afternoon. Lacey wanted to know at once what she was up to.

"It's a personal matter," Rose said.

She was white and strained, and she looked the way anyone would look if they were in shock. All the girls had commented on her appearance, and Lacey's eyes narrowed now as they raked up and down her figure.

"You aren't trying anything on, are you?" she hissed. "Better girls than you have tried it, and got nowhere."

"I don't know what you mean—"

"No? I'm talking about extortion, honey. Well, a clinical test will soon sort you out, if that's your game. But OK, I'll fix your appointment, and then I'll sit back and see how far it gets you."

So at four o'clock Rose was once again in Jefferson's office. He took one look at her and his expression changed.

"Good God, what's happened? Is it your sister . . .?"

"No. It's not Gracie. It's – it's—"

To her horror she burst into tears, but there was no going back now. He handed her a box of tissues and a glass of brandy, and when she'd calmed down enough, he made her tell him everything in the finest detail. All about the

201

Miss Christmas Angel pageant and the Klinkski modelling agency, and the nude shots, and the porn movie.

"You bloody little idiot," Jefferson said savagely. "And that bastard of a brother-in-law of yours set you up for this, did he?"

"I'm not blaming Merv," Rose said, awash with misery. "At least, not entirely. He wanted me to enter the beauty pageant, but it was all my fault for believing what Klinkski said and letting my head be turned by the thought of the money. And the fame too, I suppose."

"And what kind of fame do you think that would be?" he snapped. "Let me show you the kind of magazine your pictures would have been in if you'd gone through with it."

He strode across to a desk drawer and pulled out a pile of magazines. He threw them at her, and she opened one or two of them gingerly. Horrified, Rose thought the photographs of naked girls were totally disgusting, and she had never thought such things could be on the market without somebody being prosecuted.

The fact that Jefferson had them so readily to hand never crossed her mind right then. All she could see was the shame of having her own body exposed like this, for Gracie and Merv to see, and all the Chuck Bernstein types to lust over . . . and other men too, who might leer over such filth wherever men gathered together. She'd heard of such places . . . and dear God, what would the Pritchard boys have thought of her, if they'd ever seen her like this!

She threw the magazines down, her hands shaking.

"I don't want to see any more," she croaked. "I want your advice on what to *do*. Will he sue me, do you think?"

He looked at her steadily, seeing the pinched face and trembling mouth. Seeing how young and vulnerable she really was, and how totally out of her depth.

"He won't sue. I can promise you that."

"How can you be so sure?" she said perversely now at the arrogance in his voice. "Are you God or something?"

"Or something," Jefferson said grimly.

Rose was often up first in the apartment. She liked the feeling of being on her own, without Gracie's whining, or having Merv breathing down her neck. And two days after the interview with Jefferson she picked up a hand-delivered packet from the mat inside the front door. It had obviously been delivered at some Godforsaken hour of the morning.

Rose had a horrible premonition as soon as she saw it. She took it to the bathroom, unaccountably sick to her stomach. She was quite sure it would be a summons from Klinkski's lawyers about her breach of contract. He wasn't the type to let some little innocent get the better of him. But instead, there were several newspaper cuttings, heavily ringed in black, and she read them with a feeling of growing horror.

'A downtown, so-called modelling agency was burned to the ground last night. The owner and photographer, and several out-of-work actors suspected of working on a porn movie, were thought to be inside. Because of the highly inflammable photographic equipment, there was no hope of rescue. The studio and the entire building went up like an inferno, and everyone inside it perished within minutes.

The agency, owned by second-generation Russian immigrant, Theo Klinkski, has long been under surveillance for pornographic activities, and for harbouring undercover Communist sympathizers. It was well known that Klinkski had many enemies, and an investigation is already under way.

Preliminary indications point to arson, but it's likely that the truth will never be known about the cause of the blaze. All available documents were totally destroyed, and the building is now a pile of rubble and charred remains.'

Rose felt herself shivering as if she suffered from a fatal disease. It was poetic justice, she thought frantically. Klinkski was an evil man, dealing in evil goods . . . but that didn't mean he deserved such a horrible fate. And there was someone else who was just as evil. Because she knew in her soul that this fire was no accident. She knew it as surely as she breathed.

She also knew exactly who had done this, and why she had been sent the cuttings even before the newspapers hit the streets that morning. It had all the hallmarks of someone who wielded a lot of power in this town. Someone who had said he wasn't God, but something just as powerful.

Rose knew without any doubt that Jefferson had been responsible. He had dealt with her little problem in his own ruthless way, and if she had feared him before, she feared him even more now. Any romantic feelings she had ever had for him vanished as quickly as putting snow on a furnace.

"Rose, are you staying in there all day?" Merv hollered out, banging on the bathroom door. "Are you sick or something?"

"I'll be out in a minute," she croaked, desperately trying to calm her wildly-beating heart, and praying she wasn't going to burst into hysterical tears and blurt out everything. But she daren't let anybody know, since it would immediately involve her. Jefferson knew that, she thought instantly. In sending her the cuttings, he had made her a virtual accessory to his crime. He'd know that too. He always knew exactly what he was doing.

"If you're sick, you better stay home today, Rose," Gracie called out next.

"I think I will. I'll go back to bed for an hour or so," she gasped out, for the last thing she could do today was to go into the office. She couldn't face anybody.

She bundled the cuttings into her washing bag and escaped from the bathroom and slid back into bed, still shivering from head to foot.

"Do you want a doctor?" Gracie said a couple of hours later, once she had properly surfaced.

"*No*. I just want to sleep and to be left alone. I'll be all right. Don't fuss." *Just go away.* . . .

For once, Gracie did as she was asked without any more probing. In any case, there was such a commotion out front as Merv came roaring back in the Chevy that she had to go see what was happening.

"It's that bloody modelling agency where Rose has been working," he spluttered out, waving his favourite scandal-rag under her nose. "It was burned to the ground last night with people still in it. They all ended up like cinders—"

"*What*?" Gracie grabbed the newspaper out of his hands and scanned the report quickly. Her face went white.

"That could have been our Rose in there," she said in a scratchy voice. "It could have been *Rose*, Merv. She coulda *died* because of me."

"Whaddya mean, because of you?"

Gracie was suddenly hitting out at him, beating her hands against his chest.

"You know bloody well she was trying to make extra money from this Goddamned modelling place to pay my bills, you bum!" she screeched. "It shoulda been up to you, but you've always been too Goddamned lazy to think of anybody but yourself—"

"Oh yeah? And that's why I married you and took you away from that tin-pot little life you were living in

London, is it? So who paid for your kid sister's college fees—"

"You only did that because it meant you could put off the day when we brought her here. You're a prize bastard, Merv Hackett, and I wish to God I'd never set eyes on you."

"You didn't bloody well say that when you latched on to my GI uniform and the nylons and chocolates, like all the rest of you Limey chicks who thought you were on to a good thing, did you?" he snarled.

"Well, I just hope the rest of them got a better deal than I did!" Gracie screamed.

They both jumped as Rose's voice suddenly shrilled out above the wrangling.

"Will you both stop it! I can't bear it any more. I just can't bear it!" She put her hands over her ears, swaying on her feet, and with tears running down her cheeks until she could taste them salty in her mouth.

"*Now* see what you've done," Gracie lashed out at Merv, before putting her arms around her sister.

"Rose, honey, you don't want to take no notice of us. If me and Merv go on at each other sometimes, it just clears the air, that's all. It's the way we are, and it don't mean nothing," she said, alarmed at the wild look in Rose's eyes.

Rose couldn't answer. She'd been dozing fitfully when she'd heard the raised voices, and she knew well enough that what was said in anger was often truer than anything else. Merv hadn't wanted her here at all. But Gracie had. She drew a little crumb of comfort from that.

"What was it all about, anyway?" she muttered, not really caring, but knowing she'd better say something. She felt utterly drained, with no will of her own any more. She had been manipulated from the moment she set foot in LA, and she was only just beginning to realize it.

"It's that modelling agency," Merv said brutally, not

bothering to dress it up. "You can thank your lucky stars you weren't there last night, kid, because they all got burned to a crisp. Serves the bastards right for being Commie sympathizers if you ask me."

Rose looked at him numbly, and he thrust the newspaper at her as if she was an imbecile, unable to take in what he was saying. She forced herself to glance at the words she already knew by heart, her lips shaking uncontrollably.

"You shouldn't have come out with it just like that, Merv," Gracie snapped. "Look at the shock you've given her. She looks real bad now. Rose, honey, you go back to bed and I'll make you a hot drink and put one of my Dexies in it. And then I'm going to call Jefferson's and say you ain't coming in for the rest of the week."

Like a leaf in the wind, Rose allowed herself to be directed, and to do as she was told. Even to taking the sleeping pill. Anything would be better than the waking nightmare of knowing she had caused the death of all those people . . . she hadn't torched the studio, but in her own mind she was just as guilty as those who had.

In this town, Gracie told her the following Saturday, the incident of a slummy studio burning down would be no more than a five-minute wonder. They'd never catch who did it, and they wouldn't care, such was the deep mistrust of any Communist sympathizers. You only had to be labelled as such, and you ran the risk of your days being numbered. And that dumb Klinkski would have done better to change his name. . . .

"That's terrible," Rose said, wondering at such a twisted sense of justice. She assumed that Communist ideals must mean something to those who believed in them, but she was growing wise enough not to say so.

"Yeah well, that's America for you," Gracie said. She looked at Rose cautiously. "Listen, honey. Me and Merv are going down to Sea-Food Joe's tonight. You coming with us?"

Rose shook her head. She hadn't left the house since she'd had the confrontation with Jefferson, and she wasn't ready yet. But Gracie seemed quite ready to be out on the town now, and to spend money on eating out, when the medical bills still hadn't been fully settled.

Rose's weekly salary had come through the mail that morning, and she'd hardly been able to open it, praying that there wouldn't be some little note from Jefferson inside. There wasn't, of course, and she'd been crazy to even think that there would be. It wasn't his style, and she knew that nothing would ever be mentioned about their collusion.

"I'll stay in," she said now. "I want to write to Evan, anyway."

"You write to him a lot, don't you, Rose?" Gracie remarked. "Is there anything I should know about?"

Rose flushed. "How could there be, with him so far away and me stuck over here?"

She stared at a stain on the worn carpet, hardly able to believe she'd said such a thing. As if she was in some kind of prison now . . . as if all she longed for was the freedom of the fragrant hillsides above the treacherous coal tips, and to be with Evan again.

"We did try to do right by you, Rose," Gracie said, affronted.

"I know," she whispered. "And I'm grateful, really I am. It's just—"

"It's just not all that you thought it would be, is it? I tried to tell you that, but you wouldn't listen."

"Well, I'm here now and I'm going to make the best of it," Rose said, taking a deep breath. "And I'm going back to work on Monday."

Because she knew well enough that at the vast office complex there was little chance of ever seeing Jefferson unless she was sent for. And somehow Rose didn't think that was likely to happen.

It was a relief for her to be on her own again, and not to have Gracie and Merv hovering over her as if she was in danger of falling apart. She had thought so herself for a few days, but with the bitter realization of how nearly she had been duped, she was discovering a strength she didn't know she had. And in the long, sleepless hours of the nights when she'd refused to take Gracie's Dexies, she had resolved not to let this town, or anyone in it, break her.

She fully intended to write to Evan that night. Whenever she wrote to him, it was as if he was there beside her for a while. She could hear his voice in her head, answering her questions, and teasing her, and it was just as clear as when he spoke to her on the telephone.

But somehow, after all, she couldn't put the words on paper. What news did she have to tell him, except for the torment she'd been in for the past week, and all that had led up to it? And she had already vowed never to tell him any of it. It was too shaming, and he would think badly of her. And that was something else she couldn't bear.

She knew that tonight a letter was too one-sided, despite the feeling of being close to him while she wrote. It wasn't the same as hearing his voice . . . and finally, the temptation to do just that became too strong to resist. She asked the operator for the long distance number and waited to be connected, praying that he'd be there. God knew what time it was in Pontyrowan, but she didn't care. It would be early morning at any rate.

"Hello. Evan Pritchard speaking."

But just like before, at the sound of his voice, so warm and so near, Rose couldn't speak. What a fool she was, calling somebody on the telephone, and then going completely tongue-tied. She took a deep breath as she heard Evan's voice grow impatient.

"Look, whoever you are, would you get off this line unless it's urgent, please. I'm expecting a call from the hospital."

It was enough to break her silence. "The hospital! Evan, what's wrong?"

"*Dieu*, Rosie, is that you? You must be psychic or something. I was going to call you this evening."

She brushed his words aside. "You said you're keeping the line clear for a call from the hospital. What's happened, Evan? Is it Mam?"

It had to be, of course. Unless . . . the memories of the terrible pit accidents, and the black-clad women gathering on the hillside to find out which of their men had been trapped underground, or gassed, or suffocated, or brought out at last on a blanket-covered stretcher, was so very real in Rose's mind. She had been there, and seen it all. And Dai still worked down the pit. . . .

He spoke quickly. "Mam's been unwell, but she's going to be all right, Rose. It was just that I thought it might be some kids messing around on the phone. We've had a bit of that nonsense around here lately."

"Tell me about Mam, then. Is she really in hospital?"

And if she isn't, how *dare* you frighten me like that! she thought, suddenly furious with him.

"Yes, she is, but it's no more than a bad attack of bronchitis," he said, underplaying the seriousness of the attack. "Everybody in the valley is prone to chest ailments, and Mam's chest has been playing her up for years. You know that well enough."

"I know it's never been bad enough to put her in hospital before," Rose said.

"She's getting old, and the doctor thought it wiser this time. I'd have told you if it was anything to get really alarmed about."

"Well, if it wasn't, why did you say you were going to

210

call me tonight?" She was accusing now, contrary, and ready to argue with anything he said.

"Are you all right, Rose? You don't sound yourself."

"I'm fine." *Give or take a little incident where my boss burned down an entire photographic studio and the people in it to save me from a scandal.* . . . "So tell me why you were going to call me tonight."

"I wanted to hear how Gracie was going on, that's all. And I wanted to hear your voice. Is that so very strange?"

Rose stared into the wall, her eyes filling with tears. She was being so very aggressive, and Evan was being so very dear. Without being in the least priggish, he was such a decent man – and just a little time ago she had been in grave danger of being so corrupted . . . she didn't deserve his concern, or his love.

"I'm sorry," she said in a small voice. "I've had a bad week, that's all. I had a few days off work and I'm still feeling a bit groggy."

"And Gracie's not doing much to help, I'll bet," he said shrewdly.

"She's coping better now," Rose defended her.

"And you're still paying. Do you need any more money, *cariad*?"

"*No*. Please, Evan, it's all right. Everything's under control now, really." She crossed her fingers as she spoke.

"All right. Well, you just get in touch if you do. And take care of yourself. You're precious to me, you know."

"Am I?" she whispered.

"Well, if you don't know that by now," he finished with a short laugh, and she couldn't tell if he was serious or not. In any case, there was something else she still had to say, and the cost of this call was starting to mount up.

"Will you let me know as soon as Mam's out of hospital – so I know she's all right? Please. I shall only worry until I know for sure."

"Of course I will. But you can stop worrying right now. She's in good hands, and the doctor's pleased with her progress. You just get on with enjoying life out there."

Rose bit her lips hard. Even if she'd wanted to confide in him, she couldn't do it now, because for all his fine words, she recognized the worry in his voice about Mam. She had always been able to pick up every nuance in that rich Welsh voice of his. And long after they had said goodbye, Rose couldn't rid herself of a deep anxiety.

By the time Gracie and Merv came home, Rose was sitting on the porch in the half-light, watching the twinkling lights of the city far below. The two of them had had plenty to drink by the sound of them, and were obviously in great spirits for a change. Rose found their unpredictable mood swings hard to take. One minute they were screeching and hurling abuse at one another, and the next, they were canoodling and smooching enough to make her sick.

"So what's new, Rose?" Gracie said gaily.

"Mam Pritchard's in hospital with bronchitis—"

"Has that Evan guy called you again?" she said with an indulgent grin. "I reckon it must be love, our Rose. Or lust," she added slyly.

"He didn't call me. I called him," Rose said, becoming more irritated with every stupid thing Gracie said.

"*What*?" Gracie yelled, her face changing at once. "You want to think twice before you go acting so daft. You let him call you, and leave him to do all the running. Do you know how much these damn long distance calls cost?"

It wasn't only Gracie who could change moods like a chameleon. Rose saw red so fast she leapt up from the wicker chair on the porch, knocking it over and marching indoors, with her sister following. She snatched up her purse with her untouched week's salary in it, and flung the envelope at her.

"Here. Take it. Take everything. It's all you want out

of me, isn't it?" she shouted. "You don't want me here, except for what you can get out of me."

Gracie looked at her with genuine astonishment. "That's not true, Rose. For God's sake, you know it's not true! I couldn't help getting sick, any more than your old Mam Pritchard could help it. These things happen, and we just have to stick together when they do. You know I'd always stand by you if you got in trouble."

Gracie was clearly doing her best to defuse the situation, and trying to stay calm. Rose knew it would make sense if she did likewise, and she tried to talk more slowly.

"All right, maybe I do. But I'm honestly starting to wonder if I made a big mistake in coming here at all. It hasn't exactly been all wine and roses, has it?"

"Maybe not, but you know what they say. You can't ever go back. Nothing stays the same, and even your old Welsh valley wouldn't be the same any more."

"Don't be daft. It's not that long since I left it. . . ." But then she paused.

It had only been a few months in real time, and yet it seemed like years. And she still didn't dare let herself admit out loud what she really felt. But deep down she knew it only too well. Her heart was still back there in that little Welsh valley, where everyone knew everyone else. And where the Pritchards had taken in a lonely, bewildered child from the London back streets and made her their own.

No. She wasn't ready to admit that yet. She'd come here to make a new life, and she had to give it a chance. But surely those words that Gracie had just said . . . *you can't ever go back* . . . surely they were the saddest words in the English language.

Merv poked his head in at the front door now, waving an oily rag like a flag of truce in front of him.

"Is it OK to come in yet, or am I going to get caught in the crossfire?"

"Come on in, you dope," Gracie said with a leer. "Fetch Rose and me a coupla bottles of beer and we'll drink it on the porch while it's still warm enough. All right, hon?"

"All right," she said huskily. After all, she had nothing else to do with her time.

"You know, we'll have to be thinking about Christmas soon," Gracie went on a bit later, just as if there had been no animosity between them at all.

"Gracie likes to invite the neighbours in for a few drinks," Merv said, grinning. "Makes her think she's one of them gracious English country-set broads she's seen in a magazine."

Gracie dug him in the ribs, making him grunt.

"So what if I do? And you just better start looking for some extra jobs to pay for it, Merv. We ain't relying on our Rose to do all that as well."

Rose stared ahead into the beautiful soft night, to where a full moon was rising now against a backdrop of stars. It was the perfect setting to a city of angels that hid more devils in its midst than she had ever dreamed existed.

She listened to Gracie and Merv wrangling and arguing and playfully cuffing one another, without really hearing them at all. Instead, she simply let her mind wander and absorb the ambience of the night, together with the muted sound of a distant, out of tune, guitar from one of the upstairs apartments. And longing to know if Evan would be looking at the same moon and stars, and thinking of her, when night fell over Pontyrowan.

Chapter Fourteen

The following Monday, Rose learned that unexpected corporation business had taken Jefferson east again for several weeks. Whether it was contrived or official, the news gave her such a boost that she felt almost happy for the first time in ages. Just knowing that he wasn't around gave her a breathing space to recover from her feeling of inadequacy, and her bruised self-confidence.

And when Cindy and Gloria asked if she wanted to go out to a movie, she didn't give them her usual refusal. Instead, she took them by surprise and said yes.

"Hey, that's great," Cindy said, delighted. "We began to think you were going to hibernate for the winter."

"I thought so, too," Rose said.

"OK. Well, what we normally do is go to a pizza house straight after work, then take a drive down to the beach and see what's around, if you see what I mean, and go on to the movie later, OK? You can call your sister to let her know."

"You mean tonight?"

"Sure, tonight. What's wrong with tonight?"

"Nothing." It was time she stopped being cautious and needing two weeks' notice before she did anything. And it would do Gracie good to know Rose didn't intend to be always at her beck and call.

"Great," Gloria said. "We've decided to take you in hand, Rose. And isn't it about time you thought about leaving that apartment you share with your folks? You'd have far more freedom living in a place of your own, or sharing."

"I know, and I'll probably do it sometime," she hedged, knowing she'd have to save up for the initial down payment deposit on an apartment all over again, even a shared one. "I'm in no hurry, though. My sister's still not completely over the complications from her operation."

"Well, just as long as she's not playing on your good nature," Cindy said, with more perception than Rose gave her credit for.

She didn't answer that, but she called Gracie and told her she'd be home late that evening, so not to bother about her evening meal, knowing Gracie wouldn't be in the least bothered about it. Gloria had a little runabout car and said she'd drop her off at the apartment after the movie, but Rose knew that when the time came she'd protest that it was out of her way and take a cab. Anything was better than letting these smart city girls see the shabby place where she lived.

Later, she wondered why she'd never gone out with them before. They were fun, and the places they took her to were fun. They were too classy to go to any low dives or doubtful nightclubs, and for that, Rose was thankful. The pizza house was full of young people like themselves, just intent on having a good time and talking nineteen to the dozen.

It was just the way she'd always pictured LA, Rose thought, bright and noisy and brash and straight out of a movie set. They drove down to the beach, and cruised along the ocean road where the sight of the surfing rollers made her feel ridiculously nostalgic for the muddy Thames, and even the grey waters of the Bristol Channel.

And when it came to the movie, it wasn't even in a cinema, as she had expected. It was a drive-in movie, where all the cars and their occupants were lined up in the open air, facing an enormous outdoor screen. Rose almost began to feel as if *she* was taking part in a movie, since the first time she had gaped at anything like this was on the screen at the Pontyrowan flea-pit. She had wondered, then, if such things really existed.

Now she knew that they did, and it felt strange and exhilarating to be in the company of all these other people in cars watching the flickering pictures on the huge outdoor screen beneath the stars. Excitement was bubbling up inside her. It wasn't as if she'd never been out on the town before, back home. But it was the first time she'd really let herself go in such a way since she'd come here, and now she simply couldn't understand why it had taken her so long.

She relaxed for the first time since the shattering experience at Klinkski's. And except for their accents, Cindy and Gloria were no different from the girls she'd known at college. The things girls talked about here were the same everywhere. Boys, hair-styles, make-up, hopes and dreams and ambitions. . . . As the night grew darker, Rose felt more in tune with the place and the people than at any time since crossing the pond. She smiled into the darkness, thinking how deliciously American that made her sound. . . .

"We'd better call it a day," Cindy said, yawning. "Lacey will be on our tails if we're sleeping on the job tomorrow, and it's well past midnight already."

Rose gasped. "Gracie will kill me—"

"No, she won't. Act your age, Rose!" Gloria said impatiently. "Anyway, I'll drive you home first."

"I can get a cab—"

"Are you crazy? Any girl who gets in a cab at this time of night takes a risk."

Rose didn't ask what she meant. Besides, Gloria was already starting up the car and weaving it in and out of those who looked as if they were parked for the night.

From the look of some of the steamed-up windows, not all of them were interested in movies, either. Rose felt a sweet envy for those couples whose shadows seemed to merge into one inside the intimate privacy of their cars.

She gave directions to the apartment building, and as if it was an afterthought she asked Gloria to drop her off at the corner of her street.

"I don't want to wake the neighbours with the sound of a car so late at night," she said, and hoped the others didn't realize how incongruous that sounded when the regular sounds of police sirens screamed through these streets, and this particular neighbourhood looked as if it was well used to being disturbed at night.

"OK. If that's what you want," Gloria said carelessly. "See you tomorrow, hon."

Rose opened the car door thankfully. From this moonlit distance, the apartment building didn't look so bad, she thought thankfully. And yes, she was a snob.

To her relief the Hacketts' apartment was all in darkness. The Chevy wasn't parked outside, so Merv must be out on a job, and Gracie had evidently gone to bed with a Dexy. Rose didn't put on any lights, feeling her way cautiously to her bedroom. Once there, she let out her breath with a rueful smile, knowing that for all her enjoyment that evening she still felt very much the little sister when it came to facing Gracie's mercurial moods.

But she found herself humming silently as she undressed and got into bed, feeling for the first time that she belonged here. She had friends, and for a little while, in the anonymity of the drive-in movie, she had felt as if she was part of LA. Her heart lifted. It just took time to get acclimatized, that was all, and it was being naïve of her to expect everything to happen yesterday . . . or even tomorrow. She drifted off to sleep with that thought uppermost in her mind.

*   *   *

She awoke as early as she usually did and went into the kitchen to make some coffee. And then she saw the note Gracie had left for her, propped up against the cookie jar.

'The Pritchard boy called. Said he'd call again tomorrow. No message.'

Rose's heart lurched, the high spirits of last night plummeting at once. Evan had phoned her and she wasn't here to take the call. It had to be bad news. She rushed into Gracie's bedroom, knowing from the rhythmic sound of his snoring that Merv would be dead to the world for hours yet. Gracie jumped up with an angry yell when Rose shook her.

"What the hell's going on? Is there a fire or summat? Whaddya want, Rose?"

"Evan called," Rose said, stuttering. "What did he say? Was it about Mam?"

Gracie tried to get her morning thoughts together to answer this maniac who'd interrupted her sleep.

"I don't bloody know," she snarled. "Christ, I said there was no message, didn't I? He wouldn't tell me anything, just said he wanted to talk to you and he'd call again. I told him you were out painting the town red."

Rose stared at her. The way she said it, God knows what Evan must have made of that remark. The one night . . . the *one night* she had gone to a late movie, and she'd missed his call. She could have wept.

"If Mam had got worse, he'd have told you, wouldn't he?" she almost begged Gracie to confirm.

Her sister was already snuggling down into the bed-clothes again, and throwing a fleshy arm around Merv's back. He grunted in his sleep, while the snores never abated, and Rose couldn't bear to watch them.

"Aw, you'll find out when he calls again tonight. Now let me go back to sleep, for God's sake," Gracie said.

Rose left them to it, glancing quickly at the clock. It was six-thirty in the morning in LA, which meant it was two-thirty in the afternoon now in Pontyrowan. So Evan must have called her in their morning, and that must surely mean something was wrong. The thoughts in her head worked themselves through in jerky, logical sentences. And she knew she couldn't wait. She picked up the phone and asked for the number with fear in her voice.

In what seemed an interminable time, she heard Dai Pritchard's voice at the other end.

"Dai, it's me, Rose. Rose Forster," she gasped.

"Rosie!" he said, after the usual infuriating pause while the transatlantic line delayed the voice impulses over land and under sea. "What a surprise. You're lucky you caught me in for once. How are you, *cariad?*"

Don't call me that. I don't want to hear that word from your lips. . . .

"I'm fine. Is Evan there?" Her words were clipped.

"No, love. He's gone out for the afternoon, and I've only just got in myself."

"Then how's Mam?" Rose almost shrieked into the phone, maddened by all these inanities.

"Mam? She's all right," he said, ending with that upward lilt in his voice as if he was questioning her sanity in asking such a question. "Gone to bed for a nap and sleeping the sleep of the just by now, I dare say. Why?"

Rose stared at the phone stupidly, full of rage that she'd been so scared, and seemingly all for nothing.

"I just wanted to know," she snapped. "Tell Evan I called, will you?"

"All right, but look, don't go so fast—"

She couldn't listen to any more of his boyish enthusiasm. She slammed down the phone before Gracie came storming out to ask what the hell she thought she was doing, calling somebody up at this hour of the day. She was shaking all over and she made the coffee quickly, took it back to her bedroom and drank it black and unsweetened, and never noticed.

220

She sat down abruptly on her bed. What a fool she was to get so upset over nothing. She was angry with herself for not taking things more calmly. She was angry with Gracie for frightening her with such a curt message. She was angry with Dai for his damn cheerfulness. And she was angry with Evan for not being there when she needed him so much. And then she swallowed slowly, feeling her face go painfully hot, as she finally faced the truth.

It wasn't just that she missed Pontyrowan and was having a hard job getting used to this city, despite the euphoria of last night at the drive-in movie. It wasn't just that she missed the supporting shoulder of her big brother. She didn't just miss him. She loved him. And the love she felt for him wasn't remotely like the love a sister had for a brother.

"You're being a crazy fool," she muttered, giving herself a lecture. "You're just fantasizing about something you can't have. If he was here right now, you'd realize he was the same Evan he's always been, but you're not the same any more. You've moved on. You're doing what you always wanted to do, and you're where you always wanted to be."

But if that was so, why did the earth move whenever she heard his voice? And if that wasn't a corny old line from a movie, she didn't know what was, she thought cynically. But it was true. She only had to hear his voice . . . his beautiful, warm, melodiously rich voice that could make her melt. . . .

She rolled over on her stomach, letting loose all the emotions inside her that had been too long under control. Clutching her pillow as if she clutched Evan to her heart, and wanting him . . . wanting him so much, with a need that made her gasp with the surge of sweet sensations running through her. She wanted him everywhere. She wanted him to hold her and kiss her and touch every part of her. She wanted the feel of his

221

hands and his mouth and his arms. She wanted all of him. . . .

"Oh Evan, am I fooling myself?" she whispered into the pillow. "Is it just because you're so far away and I can't have you that I want you so much? And even if you were here with me now, would you want me this way? Would you love me, the way I want you to love me?"

The next minute somebody was thumping on her door and Gracie came into the room, and she released the stranglehold on her pillow.

"Who were you talking to? You ain't been using that phone again, have you?"

"I was talking to myself," Rose snapped, hating her for interrupting her lovely waking dream.

"Yeah, well you know what they say about that. I thought you were up, anyway. Make me some coffee, will you, kid? You've woken me up good and proper now."

Rose almost leapt out of bed, upset and disturbed. Now that the dreaming was over and the cold light of an LA morning was making her shiver, she knew it was true what Gracie had once said. You couldn't ever go back, and she'd chosen to come here so she had to make the best of it.

She was glad when the time came to go to the office, but she found it hard to concentrate. Evan had phoned her for a reason last night, and she still didn't know what it was. By the time the day was out she'd been hauled over the coals a dozen times by Lacey Venables for making stupid mistakes, and had to put up with plenty of jibes about the unlikelihood of her ever getting the PA job when Miss Simpson retired.

If Rose went on the way she did, Lacey said triumphantly, there'd be no chance in Hades of her ever getting it . . . but despite the rise in salary and the kudos that went with it in the corporation, Rose wasn't sure that she wanted it now. Not if it meant working

222

closely with Jefferson and accompanying him on various business trips.

"I don't blame you," Cindy said, when they were alone in the women's room. "I wouldn't want to be at his beck and call if all the rumours are true."

Rose was alerted at once. "What rumours?"

"Oh, it's nothing, and I'm just talking out of line. Take no notice of me, Rose."

"But I do take notice of you, and I don't think you'd repeat something unless you were pretty sure about it. So what rumours, Cindy? Please. I've got to know, in case I really do stand any chance of getting the PA job."

Cindy shrugged. "Oh well, I suppose you do at that. It's just that plenty of girls here have caught his eye and done him a few favours, if you know what I mean."

"Not really—"

"Come on, Rose, you're not that naïve. They say he's into all kinds of stuff, dressing up in women's clothes and a bit of sado-masochism thrown in—"

"*What*?"

"Do you mean what is it, or what, my *God*?"

"I know what it is. It's when somebody likes being whipped and humiliated."

"Yeah. Well, Jefferson goes in for all that stuff, or so the rumours go," Cindy said. "And all the girls who got involved with him left the corporation soon afterwards, and we never heard what happened to them."

Rose's eyes were huge now, and Cindy gave a short uneasy laugh as she dried her hands on a paper towel.

"Look, I don't mean that they disappeared or were disposed of, or anything like that. I just mean they quietly left the corporation, probably with a big pay-off to keep their mouths shut. But you're too nice a person for me to want anything like that to happen to you."

"And you took long enough to warn me," Rose said, when she was able to speak.

All those times she'd been alone with Jefferson. . . . She thought instantly of the incident when he'd shown her the dirty magazines in his office, so readily available in his desk drawer, and it seemed to support all that Cindy was saying. And the fact of him being responsible for burning down Klinkski's modelling agency was no longer an impossible horror. He'd been so furious about the way she was being exploited by the guys at Joanna Del Mar's, and by the thought of her being lured into porn movies . . . she couldn't understand it, unless he was just playing with her, like a cat with a mouse, waiting to pounce. . . .

"We'd better get back," Cindy said. "Are you OK, Rose? I haven't shocked you too much, have I? I'm sure nothing bad will happen to you, but just be on your guard, that's all."

"I'm OK. And thanks."

But for the rest of the day she couldn't stop thinking about the double standards of people she'd believed in. Jefferson had seemed such a champion, a knight in shining armour, and instead of that, he was tarred with the same rotten brush as the Klinkski set-up. Worse, in fact, because he hid his rottenness beneath a cloak of such high-powered respectability.

She began to wonder if she could really trust anyone any more. Nobody was what they seemed. Except, ironically, her brother-in-law Merv, Rose thought with the growing cynicism that branded an LA girl. There was never any pretence about what Merv wanted.

By the time Evan called her that night, she was aware of a new bitterness in herself. And somehow all the loving feelings she'd felt towards him that morning seemed to have vanished like will-o'-the-wisp. She was unable to relax with him, and when she heard his voice she asked him quickly why he'd called last night and got her into such a tizzy by not leaving any message.

"I just wanted to check on Gracie and let you know Mam was out of the wood," he said, but he was too quick to notice the curtness in her responses to waste time with apologies. "What's wrong, Rose?"

"Wrong? Nothing's wrong? You scared me, that's all, and so did Gracie, just leaving me a note to say you'd called and nothing else. I had all day today to worry about it, and Dai was no help."

God, she was making such a hash of this, but for the life of her she couldn't stop the accusing note in her voice.

"Oh yes, he said you'd called back, and I'm sorry I was out."

"Yes, well, I don't expect you to be sitting indoors all the time waiting for a call from me, do I?"

"No more do I expect you to be sitting home, either. Did you have a good night out?"

It was awful. They were both mentally accusing one another, and she felt suddenly reckless.

"It was great. I went to a drive-in movie with some people from the office. And where were you?"

"Out for a walk."

"Oh," Rose said.

She could imagine him out walking with a girl, kissing her and holding hands. The scene was so vivid in her mind that tears blurred her eyes.

"So you're sure Mam's all right now?" she said blindly.

"For the time being," Evan said. "As long as she takes care, the doctor says she could go on for years yet."

Or she might not, he thought, crossing his fingers behind his back as he remembered the doctor's words. But there was no sense in worrying Rose when she was so far away.

"I'd better let you go then," she said inanely. "Give Mam my love, and tell her I'll write to her soon."

"I will."

She couldn't say any more, nor listen to lengthy good-byes. She put down the phone quickly, and wondered if everyone in love went through such pain. Or if it was only those who had to contend with a one-sided love.

She was snappy with Gracie for the rest of the night, and stared at the television screen unseeingly. At least it was a kind of panacea that she didn't need to focus on too much. It left her free to concentrate on the pangs of jealousy that were sharper than she'd ever known before, even though she knew it was madness to feel jealous of some unknown girl.

When Gracie switched the television programme over to a romantic wartime movie, it was more than she could bear.

"I'm going for a walk," she said.

Gracie looked at her in amazement. "What the hell for? Nobody walks in LA and the nights are getting cold now. Besides, where do you think you're going, for God's sake? This ain't the best of neighbourhoods, and you'll risk getting picked up, Rose. Look, if you wanna do something else, we'll play cards or something."

She knew that everything Gracie said was right. Nobody walked around at night in this part of LA without heading for trouble. And she'd already had enough of that.

"How about if I cook us a proper meal instead?" Rose said. "I know Merv won't be back until the small hours, and I don't know about you, but I'm starving." Gracie had been satisfied with a sandwich, and expected Rose to find that enough too, after a day's work.

"If you like. There's food in the refrigerator. I'll eat anything."

It was surprising how quickly she'd got over her initial picky eating habits after her operation, Rose thought savagely. As long as somebody was prepared to wait on her, Gracie would eat anything that was put in front of her, which was why she was getting so grossly fat. But at

226

the sight of some large steaks in the refrigerator and some wilting tomatoes and mushrooms, Rose's mouth began to water. It was a world away from the kind of homely fare Mam Pritchard put on her table, but Rose wasn't in Pontyrowan now, and the days of scrappy meat portions and ration books were long gone. Recklessly, she put two of the largest steaks in a pan and watched them sizzle with an onion garnish.

"By God, Rose, that was good," Gracie said later, when they were both stuffed full and she had drunk a couple of beers to Rose's one, to wash it all down. "You wouldn't like to take on a full-time job of chief cook and bottle-washer, would you, hon?"

"Sure. As long as you pay me the going rate that I'm getting at Jefferson's," Rose said smartly.

Gracie eyed her up and down. "You know, you've changed, our Rose. You ain't such a little innocent as when you first came here, and sometimes your tongue's so sharp you'll cut yourself on it if you're not careful."

"Did you expect me to stay the same then? You were the one who said you can't ever go back, and that means in every way, doesn't it? We all have to look to the future and not the past, and that's just what I'm doing."

"Yeah, well, you don't want to let 'em change you too much, kid."

"Who?"

Gracie snorted, already fed up with giving advice and ready to fall asleep in front of the television after that big blow-out meal.

"Everybody. Jefferson. Those friends of yours at the office. That Klinski guy, not that he'll be bothering you any more, poor bugger. Hell, I don't know. LA in general! What I'm trying to say is don't ever lose sight of yourself, Rose, that's all. And I ain't saying no more on the subject. You're old enough to look out for yourself."

"Well, I'm glad you think so at last," Rose said lightly,

but oddly touched that Gracie had actually put it all into words.

The next minute she knew that in some ways, Gracie herself certainly hadn't changed.

"Christmas will be here soon, and Merv told you we always like to have folks in for drinks and bits and pieces, didn't he?"

"Yes," said Rose, waiting.

"I don't want to put on you, Rose, and God knows you've done more'n enough in picking up my medical bills, but if you could see your way clear to helping out with the expenses, just a bit, mind—"

"No, I can't. All my spare money is going to finish paying the bills, Gracie, and you know that," she said flatly. "What I will do, though, is prepare all the food for you—"

"Hell, we don't do it ourselves. We hire a catering place to send it all up—"

"Well, it will be much cheaper, and much better, if I do it myself," Rose insisted. "Mam Pritchard taught me how to turn my hand to most things in the kitchen, and that's my last and only offer. You and Merv see to getting in the supplies, and paying for them, and I'll do the baking and preparing."

She stared her sister out, thinking that there never was a woman less aptly named than Gracie Hackett née Forster. There was nothing gracious about her at all, but for once she seemed to know when she was beaten, and she scowled as she backed down.

"All right, you win, though I know Merv was banking on you helpin' out—"

"And I will be. But not with money."

Christmas was almost on them now, and coming round faster than Rose had expected. Things at the office had cooled down, and Jefferson never sent for her again. In fact, she hadn't seen anything of him since the day she had gone to him about Klinkski, but she was told he always put in an appearance at the office party.

Cards had begun arriving at the Hacketts' apartment, including three from Pontyrowan, and Rose had almost wept over the one signed in Mam's shaky hand, a surprisingly ugly thing sent to faraway friends, with the crib and baby Jesus edged in silver glitter that came away on her fingers. There was one from Dai with a cheeky reindeer on the front, and one with a Christmas scene that was simply signed 'with love, Evan'.

A week before Christmas, Merv had hauled in a great tree that took up most of the living-room, but since it had been a free gift, it wasn't in his nature to refuse it.

"It's ridiculous," Rose said. "It takes all the light from the window, and there'll hardly be room to swing a cat. How many people are coming, anyway?"

"About ten or so, usually," Gracie said vaguely. "Unless they bring any more folks with them, of course."

And they all had to cram in this room with all the windows shut tight because snow was threatening, and with the heating turned up full the way Gracie liked it the minute the weather turned colder.

"It would be useful to know exactly, so I know how many sausage rolls and mince pies to bake," Rose complained.

Just saying the words made her think of the long-ago days in the steamy Pontyrowan kitchen, with a red-faced Mam fussing over numbers and slapping the wrists of the three young 'uns for picking at the Christmas supplies. Days when the Christmas fare had been made with powdered eggs and honey instead of sugar, and carefully hoarded bits of dried fruit that had been collected in a tin for months whenever they came in to the local grocery store.

"Well, make sure you do more than you think we'll

229

need. What we don't eat, we'll throw to the birds," Merv said.

"You wouldn't say things like that if you'd lived through wartime rationing," Rose snapped. "It's wicked to be so wasteful."

"Yeah, well, that's your British mentality, kid, but you gotta remember you're in the land of plenty now," he said, with such smug satisfaction that Rose could have hit him.

"Take no notice, Rose," Gracie said, standing up for her. "We all know the GIs had the best of both worlds. They had the pick of our girls, and all the food supplies they needed. It was only us poor buggers who had to scratch around to put food in our bellies."

"Well, you've sure made up for it since, babe," Merv said with a grin, and a playful dig at her ample shape.

As Gracie screamed with laughter, Rose gave up on the pair of them. But as long as Merv was paying for the food supplies, she told them she'd make all the goodies they wanted while he took Gracie out to buy the booze at a cheap liquor place downtown. She suddenly longed to have the place to herself, knowing it would be far more enjoyable to be here on her own, doing what she'd done so many times before. It would be almost like a breath of home.

Chapter Fifteen

Over the next weeks, office work was becoming incidental to the excitement over the forthcoming lavish Christmas party that Jefferson's always gave for the staff. It was held at a downtown hotel, and Cindy told Rose there was always a huge buffet meal and gifts for everyone, and the drink flowed freely. As a final bit of showmanship, Jefferson always put as many corporation cars and buses at the disposal of the staff as were required to take them home afterwards, and gave the drivers a handsome bonus for their trouble.

"I'm not sure I want to go. I'm not much for office parties," Rose said.

"Are you crazy? Of course you'll go! It's the highlight of the year, and all the warehouse and despatch guys will be there, as well as the senior male office staff who manage to let their hair down," Gloria said with a wink. "We always have a great time."

"I've got nothing suitable to wear for a start. . . ."

Cindy gave a heavy sigh. "Rose, honey, stop making excuses and finding objections. Didn't you ever hear of clothing stores? We'll all go downtown on Saturday afternoon and buy ourselves something wild and glittery that will knock the guys' eyes out. OK?"

"Oh, OK," Rose said after a minute, starting to laugh. And hadn't she spent enough on other people? Maybe it was time to spend something on herself. "I suppose it's only money, after all."

"Now you're talking!" Gloria said approvingly.

And if she splashed out an entire month's salary on one super dress that she might never wear again, so what? Rose thought recklessly. This was definitely the LA mentality coming out, she decided, and knew she was still smarting inside from Merv's sneering reference to her British mentality that counted every penny. Well, serve him right if she had nothing left to contribute towards his folksy drinks party at the apartment. She hadn't intended doing so anyway.

On Saturday she caught the bus downtown, having arranged to meet Cindy and Gloria at a drugstore where they were already on their third cup of coffee. It was getting colder by the day now, and a light drift of snow had fallen overnight, sparkling the streets and dusting the distant hills into a magical scene, straight out of a movie set.

Rose had snuggled into her nylon fur-collared winter coat and boots, and the others were similarly warmly attired. But one thing you could be sure of, Rose thought keenly, the stores would have abandoned their air-conditioning now, and turned up their heating until they were Mediterranean hot, and the streets would seem even colder afterwards.

"We'll try Askey's first. They've usually got some end of season bargains," Cindy said. "If we don't find anything we like there, we'll go to Holt's Emporium."

"Holt's is very expensive, isn't it?" Rose said, remembering the mail order catalogues that came through the post for Gracie. She was endlessly sending for catalogues, but she never ordered anything, and Rose could never understand why the companies didn't simply stop supplying them.

"Sure it is, but they also have a used clothes department, where you can pick up marvellous bargains at greatly reduced prices."

"You mean people actually take clothes back when they've been worn?" Rose said, not liking the sound of it.

"Get that sniffy look off your face, hon," Gloria said amicably. "When you see the kind of stuff that's returned, you won't turn up your nose so fast. People who go to these swish Hollywood parties won't be seen dead in the same dress twice, so they trade them in for cleaning and re-selling in upmarket emporiums like Holt's. It's done all the time around here."

"I see," Rose said.

And she remembered instantly the fabulous clothes on the women at Joanna Del Mar's party in the Hollywood hills. There must have been a fortune there that night, in gowns and jewellery alone. But since Cindy and Gloria were unaware that she'd ever been inside one of those film star homes, and worse still, the circumstances of her being there, she knew better than to say anything about it.

Instead, she let herself sound reconciled to the fact of wearing second-hand clothes if need be. Second-hand Rose, the thought whirled around in her head. . . .

In the end, it was to Holt's Emporium that they went. Askey's was a far smaller store, and had nothing that any of them liked. But the used clothes department in Holt's basement drew them like a magnet, as it seemingly drew every other woman in town who was looking for a Christmas outfit.

Cindy and Gloria knew exactly what they wanted. It had to be slinky and sexy with as much glitter as possible, and in this town that wasn't hard to find. They each tried on a dozen dresses and took ages making up their minds. Rose was just as bad. For her, it came down to a choice of two, and she finally tried on a dress in soft red chiffon that was floaty and full-skirted. It had a low-necked, tight-fitting bodice with a subtle hint of glitter in it that emphasized her shape with every movement she made. She looked at herself from every angle in the changing-room mirror, and wondered if it was really herself looking back at her. She looked sensual and classy at the same time. Even she could see that. . . .

"Wow!" Cindy said, when she came out of the changing-room and paraded in it. "You've just gotta have that one, Rose. It's perfect."

The price tag was astronomical, even at a reduced rate, but Rose felt suddenly reckless. Ever since she'd arrived in LA, she'd either been scrimping and saving, or splashing out all her salary on Gracie's medical bills. She'd bought very little for herself, except for the essential office wear. This time, it was her turn.

"Why don't you try this with it, Rose?" Gloria said, draping a silvery stole around her shoulders. "Yep, that does it. All you need now is a string of pearls and pearl earrings, and you'll look like a million dollars. Let's settle up here and go find the jewellery counter."

"I haven't exactly made up my mind to buy this little lot yet," Rose protested.

"But you will," Cindy said, and Rose laughed.

"Yes, I will," she agreed.

Gracie gaped when she saw Rose carrying the exclusive Holt's Emporium packages.

"Have you taken leave of your senses, shopping there? Those prices are way out of our league, Rose."

"I needed something special for the office party, and they had just what I wanted, so I splashed out for once. It's my money, remember?" she answered smartly.

"OK, OK. Let's see it then," Gracie said, eyes narrowed at this new and defiant Rose. "Go put it on, and then tell me what it cost, if you dare."

"I'll put it on, but the price tag is between Holt's and me," Rose said lightly. "You don't need to know, Gracie."

And she wasn't going to know. She'd only start screaming, and it was none of her business. Rose deliberately tore the receipt into tiny pieces and flushed them down the toilet. Holt's never took back third-hand clothes, so there was no point in keeping the receipt. It scared her to look at it, anyway.

In her bedroom she changed out of her winter clothes and put the beautiful dress on again, loving the sensual feel of the tight-fitting bodice against her skin, and the flowing, romantic skirt. Gloria was right. Anyone who wore it would feel like a million dollars, especially when it was complemented by the silvery stole and the pearl accessories.

She wished that Evan could see her in it. He had never seen her in anything so beautiful. God, how she wished he was here right now, seeing her in the dress. . . . She closed her eyes and tried to imagine his reaction, making-believe she was one of those glamorous movie stars sweeping down a curving staircase into the arms of her lover, and seeing all the love in the world in his eyes. . . .

"Come on, our Rose! I'm waiting to see what you've spent all your money on," came Gracie's impatient voice.

Rose turned quickly and went back to the living-room, twirling round slowly for her sister, so she would get the full effect.

Gracie looked at her silently, as if she was seeing her for the first time. Or as if she was seeing the ghost of the girl she herself had once been in this vision in front of her. She had once been as slim as this. And as glowingly young and desirable as this. Merv hadn't been slow to tell her so then, and he had never been able to keep his hands off her, in the halcyon, dangerous wartime days when she'd got her Yank, and fallen madly in love with the man and the uniform.

"*Well?*" Rose said. "What do you think? Isn't it just gorgeous?"

Of course it was gorgeous, but it wasn't just the dress, Gracie thought. Any man who saw Rose in it would be dazzled by her. It didn't take a genius to know that.

"It sure is," she said generously. "But you just be careful, Rose. You know what office parties are like. People always have too much to drink and go wild, and more girls have got themselves pregnant as a result of office parties than at any other time of the year."

"Yes, well, that's not going to happen to me," Rose said, wondering why Gracie always had to spoil things. One minute she was openly admiring the dress, and looking almost envious and wistful. And the next, she was bringing everything ugly into the conversation.

"I don't mean to spoil things for you," Gracie said, almost as if she had read Rose's thoughts. "I just want you to be careful, that's all."

"I know," she said, recognizing the genuine words. Sometimes, just sometimes, Gracie's concern was so real that it could reach out and touch her. And it happened so rarely that it always took her by surprise.

Merv came blustering indoors, stamping his feet from the cold, while she was still parading in the party outfit. He stopped in his tracks and whistled noisily when he saw her.

"Jeez, you're a sight for sore eyes, kid. Going somewhere?"

"I'm just showing it off for Gracie's benefit. It's for the office party."

"Lucky bums," Merv grinned, and she didn't need to ask what he meant. She gave him an icy stare and said she was going to hang it up in her closet now.

"Bit extravagant for one party, ain't it?" Merv's voice followed her.

"Probably," she called back. "So what?"

"That little lady's got a will of her own, Gracie," she heard him grumble. "She never used to be so outspoken."

"She's not a kid any more, Merv—"

"She sure ain't. I could see that."

Rose didn't want to hear any more, and she closed her bedroom door behind her before she had to listen to any lewd remarks about her figure. She shut the door on the pair of them and shut them out of her mind. Instead, she studied herself in the mirror again, and liked what she saw. She imagined floating around the room in somebody's arms, dancing to a band that played slow, romantic tunes, and the only arms she imagined herself in were Evan's.

As she changed out of the dress, and put on her warmer clothes again, the mood of elation she'd known ever since buying the dreamy dress unexpectedly began to evaporate. Because of course Evan would never see her in it. Evan would never hold her close this Christmas, or kiss her beneath the mistletoe and tell her she was beautiful.

She thought about what Evan would be doing to celebrate Christmas in Pontyrowan. Evan would dance with someone at the local village hop. She couldn't blame him for that, even though she knew it was the place she'd rather be. She'd change places in an instant with that unknown girl. . . . But what was the use of holding a torch for a man who was thousands of miles away, who she could only contact by letter or phone?

She forgot her fine sentiments about the way thousands of couples had had to endure such partings during the war. She could only see the futility of loving someone who was getting on with his life without her, the way she should be getting on with hers without him. It was just her bad luck that she'd discovered too late how much he meant to her.

The office party was held two days before Christmas, when the office would be closing down for a week for the holidays. Rose declined Merv's offer to drive her there, preferring to call a taxi instead. He was due out on a job anyway. His valeting services were very much in demand at this time of year, and he often came home with the perks from the well-heeled homes, whether in the form of monetary tips or food from the kitchens. He and Gracie didn't do so badly, Rose was beginning to realize. And she had also realized long ago that the pair of them were takers, not givers.

But she wasn't going to think of that tonight. Tonight she felt like Cinderella going to the ball, and she even wondered if Cinderella would find her prince. He wouldn't be Evan, but she had faced the truth of her situation. Evan wasn't here, and he was never going to be here, and she still had a life to live.

In the splendid foyer of the hotel that could have housed the whole ground floor of the Hacketts' apartment building, she had her name checked off on the list that ensured there were no gate-crashers. The downtown hotel was ablaze with lights, and festooned with balloons and Christmas baubles. As Rose went to deposit her winter coat in the cloakroom, she glimpsed an enormous, decorated Christmas tree that shimmered in one corner of the main ballroom.

She looked around uncertainly to where people were gathering and chattering in groups before making their entrance. It was far more sophisticated an occasion than she had expected, and she wished desperately that she hadn't arrived alone. Everyone looked so different out of their everyday working clothes. Most of the men wore suits, some even wore tuxedos, and the women had put on every ounce of glamour and glitter they could find. Thank God she'd bought the dress, but even so, she knew it paled in comparison with some of the others.

"So here you are," she heard Cindy say, and she turned with huge relief to see her and Gloria bearing down on her. They already had two escorts in tow that Rose recognized from despatch. "Come into the ballroom and be greeted," she said with a grin, "and then we can do what we like."

238

"What do you mean, be greeted?"

Gloria laughed. "Jefferson always does things right, honey. You'll see."

"Can't you tell me?" But by now she was being swept along by the crowd coming in behind her, and being almost pushed into the ballroom. The batteries of lights hurt her eyes, and music blared out from a band already on stage. Then she realized that some of the flashing lights were from the photographers taking pictures of everyone on their arrival. Rose had bad memories of photographers, and it made her nervous, but she held up her chin and told herself not to be so stupid.

"Go ahead. Give him your name," Cindy whispered.

Rose gaped. They had all shuffled forward now, and there was a large, red-coated figure in front of her, wearing a heavy gold chain of office around his neck. He virtually barred her way, as if to keep out undesirables. Whether he was supposed to be the Master of Ceremonies or a proper Toastmaster, Rose had never seen his like before, and she felt her mouth drying in awe. But Gloria was right. Jefferson did things in some style.

"Rose Forster," she stuttered.

"Rose Forster," the Toastmaster boomed out, and stood back to let her pass. Waiting to greet his guests was Bradley Piers Jefferson the third. He was immaculate in a white tuxedo jacket and bow tie, with slim black pants and the glimpse of a dark red cummerbund around his waist. He looked marvellous, Rose thought, and wondered how anyone with such charismatic charm could hide such a satanic nature.

"Rose. You look simply stunning, and you must save a dance for me later on," Jefferson said.

He had taken her hand between both of his, and she didn't miss the extra squeeze he gave her as his eyes looked her over. She felt a little shiver. Despite the way she'd assumed he'd washed his hands of her, it was a look that said that he wasn't done with her yet.

"I'm sure you're far too important to dance with me," she murmured.

"We'll see," he said, smiling, and let her go as he turned to greet Cindy and Gloria, close behind her.

Automatically, Rose took a glass of wine from the girl holding a drinks tray alongside Jefferson, and remembered how she had done the very same thing, in what seemed a lifetime ago at Joanna Del Mar's party.

"Come on, let's go and let our hair down," Gloria said, once the formalities were over. "What did he say to you, Rose? He didn't even pass the time of day with me."

"He just asked me to save a dance for him later," she muttered.

"Good grief, girl, you've got it made," she said admiringly. "And it's gotta be more than the dress, if you see what I mean. It's everything about you that's different from every other gal here."

"I don't want to be different," Rose said.

Gloria's escort spoke with practised smoothness. "You shouldn't even try, babe. It's your cool English look that makes you such a dish."

Rose looked at him, telling herself she shouldn't dislike anybody on sight. Gloria seemed besotted by him, but he certainly wasn't Rose's type. He was blond and tanned, and so good-looking he could surely be in the movies. But she gave another shiver, knowing just why she mentally backed away from him. He reminded her too much of the guy at Klinkski's, the one who was going to take part in the porn movie. And she was never going to trust men with movie star looks again. . . .

The next couple of hours were spent in eating, drinking and dancing. Lacey Venables put in a haughty appearance and quickly disappeared again, and Miss Simpson only stayed long enough to be presented with a gift on her retirement on behalf of Jefferson and the management. This obviously wasn't her kind of party.

"Rose, this is Lucky. He wants to dance with you," Cindy said, urging a freckle-faced guy forward in Rose's direction. He looked harmless enough, and anything was better than having to listen to the gush coming from the smoothie's lips. Gloria was now attached to him tighter than a leech, and Cindy was obviously playing the field. Rose smiled at the newcomer and let herself be led out into the middle of the ballroom.

"I've seen you before," Lucky said eventually, as if he'd been gathering up courage for the last five minutes to say something intelligent. It hadn't bothered Rose, since any conversation was hardly possible above the noise of the music.

"Well, that's very likely, since we both work at Jefferson's. Which department are you in?"

"I've just been made up to warehouse loading under-supervisor," he said, making it sound as impressive as if he was a military general.

"Oh. Well, congratulations."

"Say, would you like to go out sometime? On a date, I mean?" he said next, clearly taking her reaction as encouragement.

"I don't think so, but thank you for asking," Rose said carefully. "I take care of my sister, you see, and she hasn't been at all well lately. . . ."

She listened to herself, telling the most appalling lies, and seeing the crestfallen look come over Lucky's face.

"It's OK," he said at once. "It's no more than I expected."

Rose felt awash with embarrassment then. "Why do you say that? And why do they call you Lucky, anyway?" she said curiously. At his reply, she could have bitten out her tongue.

"It's a joke really. I'm about the *un*luckiest guy alive. Unlucky in cards and unlucky in love. But just this once, I was hoping my bet would have come off."

"What bet?" Rose said, knowing she shouldn't ask, but unable to stop herself.

"It's nothing," Lucky shrugged.

"All right, if you don't want to tell me," she said, hoping now that he wouldn't.

But once he got started, he was obviously the kind who couldn't let things rest.

"The guys bet me I wouldn't ask you for a date," he blurted out.

"Well, you asked me, so you've won your bet, haven't you?" Rose said.

His face lightened. He really wasn't very bright, she thought. And he was the last person in the world she would want touching her in any way. Almost. But at least in this kind of dancing you could keep well apart.

As if all the fates were against her at that moment, the music abruptly changed, the lights went down to a mere glow, and the bandleader announced that all the guys and gals could close up together for a *smooch*. . . .

Before she could utter a word, Rose felt herself snatched into Lucky's sweating arms. He fastened her against him so tightly she could hardly breathe, and she was angry and annoyed with herself for feeling so panicky.

"This will do nearly as well," she heard him say hoarsely against her cheek. "The guys will be sure to notice us, Rose."

At that, she didn't know whether to be furious or sorry for him. If this was the only way he could get his kicks, it probably wasn't doing any harm, but she was more than glad when the tune ended and the lights went up once more. Then, to her horror, Lucky fastened his mouth on hers and a great cheer went up all around them.

Rose twisted out of his grasp and pushed him away,

but she couldn't forget his red, grinning face as his mates cheered him to the bar. He melted into the crowd and Rose struggled through to the other side of the room and the buffet bar to look for Cindy while the rock and roll music belted out once more. She needed a breather after that close encounter, and at last she located her friend.

"Don't bring any more guys like that one anywhere near me, you hear?" she hissed, when she finally found her. "I'm not going to be anybody's prize for the evening."

"How about being mine for the next dance?" Jefferson's voice said alongside her.

She turned around, feeling as if the world was suddenly moving in slow motion, as the strains of the next slow dance replaced the hectic rock and roll music.

You couldn't refuse your boss, Rose thought desperately, even though she would dearly love to. But you couldn't snub him in front of everybody, particularly those girls who were looking at her enviously now, and some that were openly hostile. She forced a smile to her lips, and moved into his arms.

It was very different from the way Lucky had danced with her. For all the way he had grabbed her to him, there had been no feeling of sensuality about it, the way there was now, when Jefferson held her as close as if he wanted to share her skin, one hand behind her head and softly caressing her hair, before it moved sensuously downwards, over the tight-fitting bodice of her dress, to the curve of her buttocks.

Rose could hardly breathe, but not for the same reason as when Lucky held her. It was outrageous, she thought. It was practically rape on the dance floor, and even though the lights were lowered again, she was perfectly sure there were plenty of eyes watching them, and marking her down for Jefferson's next victim. She wished she hadn't thought of the word, but once she had, it wouldn't go out of her head. She lifted her face to look at him and mumbled into his shoulder.

"I don't think you should be doing this – sir."

"Don't you? Are you going to continue acting the little prude with me, Rose? When I saw the way you looked tonight in that hot little number, I hoped we could break through that silly pretence."

"What pretence?"

He pressed her closer to him, and she knew exactly the effect she was having on him. She could feel it in every sinew of his body.

"You're not that naïve, honey, and you must have known what you were in for at that certain establishment we both know about. I reckon you were all primed up to go ahead with the porn movie until you got cold feet. . . ."

She looked at him, shocked and upset.

"I certainly was not, and how dare you accuse me—"

"It would be only your word against an anonymous tip-off if anything came out about the activities of the place, and their prospective new star, wouldn't it?"

Rose felt as if the ground beneath her feet was slipping away from her. She felt suddenly boneless, and without Jefferson's supporting arms, she was quite sure she would have slid to the floor in a quivering heap.

"You wouldn't," she whispered. "I can't believe that even someone like you would do such a despicable thing."

He gave a short laugh. "Thanks for the vote of confidence, honey, even if it was a back-handed compliment. But I'm sure we can come to some arrangement where you needn't feel threatened by any exposure."

She licked her dry lips, not wanting to ask what he meant. Not wanting to know. But he told her anyway, whispering in her ear under cover of nuzzling the nape of her neck.

"Maybe a few private photos for my eyes only? I have

a very discreet friend who'll take them. The two of us together would be fun, wouldn't it?"

Somehow Rose pushed him away from her, and he went staggering into the smooching couples nearby. It was only automatic quick thinking that stopped him going headlong, and it would have been an appalling sight for the head of the company to have gone sprawling. Rose didn't care. She was too humiliated to look at him any more, and she rushed out of the ballroom and into the women's rest room, shutting herself inside one of the toilet cubicles. She sank onto the seat, feeling as if her legs wouldn't hold her up a minute longer, and shook from head to foot.

"Rose, was that you? Honey, are you all right? You looked like a whirling dervish, rushing in there," she heard Gloria's giggling voice say from outside the door.

She hadn't seen Gloria in ages, but she had no doubt Gloria had been having a great time with her smoothie, and was in here now to patch up the make-up and straighten her nylons.

"Rose. *Rose*, answer me, for God's sake. You're scaring me, hon." The voice got sharper, and the next minute Rose saw her peering through the gap at the side of the cubicle, and she glared back, hating these American toilets that gave you so little privacy, even in a good hotel.

"I'm all right," she snapped, feeling very far from all right. "I'll be out in a minute."

"Well, I'm not leaving here until you do," Gloria said. "You look real strange to me."

So would you if you'd just been propositioned to make dirty pictures by a sleazy boss. . . .

After a minute she pressed the flush and came out of the cubicle. Gloria gasped at once.

"Oh, look at your lovely dress! How did that happen?"

Rose looked down stupidly, seeing the long rip in the chiffon skirt where the hem was hanging down now. She had no idea how it happened, and she didn't care. If she ever felt like wearing it again, it would mend, which was more than her sense of decency would right now. Jefferson had made her feel so dirty, and a torn dress was the least of her worries.

"It doesn't matter," she muttered.

"Of course it does. Sit still and I'll get it fixed for you," Gloria insisted, pushing her onto one of the pink, plush-covered chairs scattered around the rest room. "The attendant will have a needle and thread, and it'll stop it tearing any further. You can't go out there again looking like that. No wonder you looked so upset."

Rose listened to her, blaming everything on a stupid torn bit of chiffon, and she sat rigidly while the woman attendant did a quick repair job. She gave her the obligatory tip afterwards. Nobody did anything for nothing in this town, she thought cynically. Everything had its price. She was learning that more and more with every day she lived here. It was well past midnight, and just like Cinderella, her bubble had burst. . . .

Chapter Sixteen

On Christmas Eve the Hacketts were going to entertain. Rose spent the entire day, and the day before that, in baking and preparing food, thankful to have Gracie out of the way upstairs with Mrs Olsen, preferring to get out from under Rose's feet, as she put it. Translated, that meant she was quite happy to let Rose get on with the work.

Rose rolled pastry and slapped sausage meat into neat little pastry cases, and filled the metal baking trays with mince pies, trying to be completely occupied with what she was doing, and clearing her mind of anything else. Even the memory of Mam Pritchard's warm and wonderful kitchen smells over Christmas, with her innovative ways of stretching the meagre rations. And one thing Rose certainly wasn't going to concern herself with, was the reaction she'd get from Jefferson when she went back to work after New Year.

If she had her notice in her wage packet, that would settle it once and for all. But there was still the thought of the PA job that would be assigned right after they all returned to work. If by some remote chance it was offered to her now, she wondered if she would even have the nerve to take it, regardless of the money. But there was a little devil inside her that had to know if Jefferson had the cheek to offer it to her, after the way she had publicly humiliated him. It would be just like him, baiting her with the job he knew she needed, and then watching her squirm while she tussled with her conscience over taking it.

Cindy and Gloria had finally wormed out of her what had actually happened on the night of the office party.

"You mean you practically sent him flying in the middle of the ballroom?" Cindy said with a mixture of disbelief and admiration. "That took some nerve, Rose. And I missed it! Where the hell was I when it happened?"

"Probably elsewhere engaged," Gloria said slyly. "But never mind all that. What we want to know, Rose, is what he actually said to you to make you lose your cool."

She was instantly cautious. Gloria could be a prize gossip when she wanted to be, and if she started praising Rose's indiscretion, the repercussions would surely come back to her. Whatever she did with her own life from now on, Rose knew these girls had a future at Jefferson's, and the less they knew about any involvement she had ever had with him, the better. She forced a shamefaced smile.

"Well, in retrospect I know I probably over-reacted, and it was nothing much really. He was just making suggestive remarks, like most of the other guys after they'd had too much to drink. I panicked, that's all. You should know me by now," she finished lamely.

They were disappointed not to hear any more, but Cindy gave her an unexpected hug. "You're a nice kid, Rose, and you did right to react like you did. It was time somebody gave Jefferson his comeuppance, and a lot of other girls would wish they had your nerve."

Merv suggested she should wear the red dress for their own party, but Rose flatly refused, saying she'd have to get it cleaned before she wore it again, and wondering in her heart if she would ever do so. She felt tainted by the very thought of it now. Instead, she wore a flouncy black dress with a net underskirt that had been a bargain buy in one of the local malls. Gracie had made an effort with her hair and her clothes, and looked half decent in a flowered blouse, and bulging out of a tight-fitting white skirt, and Merv had managed to put on a proper shirt for once, and was washed and shaved before people began arriving.

All in all, it wasn't a bad evening, Rose reflected afterwards. Mrs Olsen took up half the room, and Chuck Bernstein proved how much garlic he'd eaten with his supper whenever he was near her, but the rest of the neighbours were all in high spirits and ready to sing carols at the tops of their voices. People all around the world would be doing the same at this time of year, Rose thought, with a sudden catch in her throat. It made one great family of them all.

"I suppose your Mam Pritchard will be at Chapel on Christmas Day, singing her heart out," Merv said, just as if he knew where her thoughts were straying.

"I expect so," Rose said. "And Christmas Eve as well. There's always a concert on, with the local male voice choir."

"It sounds real nice, this little place of yours, Rose," Mrs Olsen said. "Sort of sweet and olde worlde—"

"Behind the times, you mean," Merv grinned. "God, when I remember the one time I took Gracie down there to visit Rose, I thought I'd gone back in time. They don't live down there. They just go through the motions."

Rose couldn't let that go. "Don't be mean, Merv. They were some of the best people I ever met in my life, or am ever likely to meet," she snapped. "They were my family when I didn't have anybody else."

"Yeah, well, who's fault was that?" Merv went on. "After your folks were killed, you couldn't expect Gracie to go take care of a kid. She was busy doing war work, in case you hadn't noticed."

Busy setting her sights on any available Yank, more like. . . .

"We're not going to talk about the war tonight, or any other time," Gracie said testily. "It's over and done with, and I'm sure Rose don't want to be reminded of it, any more than we do."

"OK, I get the message," Merv was agreeable enough, already expansive with beer. "Though some of us didn't have such a bad war, did we, babe?"

He gave her a nudge that had her screeching with laughter, and Rose turned away from the pair of them to hand round more sausage rolls and sandwiches and mince pies, and little fishy things on sticks. It didn't bother her to act as unpaid waitress while Gracie held court. It stopped her from thinking how very different this Christmas was going to be from the last one, when she'd gone down to Wales and been instantly welcomed back into the Pritchard family as if she'd never been away. Their Christmas dinner was always modest, a large chicken with all the usual trimmings, and a bottle of wine to toast the King.

Tomorrow, Gracie would be cooking an obscenely large turkey and sweet potatoes, with parsnips and brussels sprouts and spoon-standing gravy, which they would eat around three o'clock in the afternoon, and Rose didn't need three guesses to know that Merv would be stupefied with liquor by the time he slept it all off for the rest of the day.

He was booked on a valeting job for the late evening and didn't expect to be back until God knew when on Boxing Day morning. Gracie never seemed to mind his odd working hours, but to Rose it was a strange kind of life, when most families and friends wanted to spend time together at Christmas.

"How's about a kiss under the mistletoe, little lady?" she heard Chuck Bernstein say when the party began to show signs of breaking up.

"We don't have any," she said thankfully, twisting her head to the side as his breath wafted towards her.

"Oh yes we do!" he said triumphantly, and produced

a limp-looking bunch of greenery and berries from his hip pocket. "I been saving this all night for the right moment, so come here and give your old Uncle Chuck a smackeroo, babe."

Some of the neighbours cheered, and Merv grinned at the look on Rose's face.

"Come on, kid, show a bit of transatlantic friendship. Nobody refuses a few kisses at Christmas. I bet there's plenty of your Welsh boyos making hay with the village girlies tonight."

Rose hated him for that remark. He didn't have to mention them at all, nor in that sneering manner. But that was Merv. What he didn't really understand, he mocked. And never in a million years could he understand the qualities of men like Evan and Dai and the miners who risked their lives every day for the coal beneath the ground.

But she couldn't escape Chuck's grabbing hands, nor the way people seemed to be pushing her towards him while somebody held the mistletoe over her head. She suffered the kiss he planted on her lips, and jerked back in disgust as she felt the tip of his tongue trying to prise open her mouth.

"That's all you get," she said, trying to sound normal and to smile, even while he revolted her as much as ever. "I'm used to rationing, remember, and that goes for kisses too."

They all seemed to think this was very witty, and although she would dearly love to scrub away the taste of the garlic kiss from her lips, she was obliged to put up with kisses from every other male in the room, including her brother-in-law.

"I been waiting five months for this, babe," he said gleefully, reminding her that she had been here for nearly half a year already, and she felt no more used to the place than the day she arrived. Then she was grabbed in Merv's powerful arms and held tight while he kissed her soundly.

"Hey, that's enough," she heard Gracie protest with a laugh. "He's my GI, remember?"

"You'd better have him, then," Rose laughed back, but she didn't miss the glint in Gracie's eyes as she pushed Merv towards her. Just as if she wanted any more of this treatment, she thought. Just as if she'd give a brass farthing to be Merv Hackett's girl. . . .

The phone call from Pontyrowan came just before they were getting ready to sit down for their Christmas dinner. Rose wiped her hands on a drying-up cloth and took the phone out of Gracie's hands.

"We just wanted to wish you all a happy Christmas, Rose," Evan said, "and to hope that the new year brings you everything you want."

She stared into the phone. All that she wanted was right there at the end of the line, she thought stupidly. But a new year resolution had already begun to form in her mind. There was no use crying over spilt milk, as Mam used to say. She'd made her choice, and she had to make the best of it. She made her voice as bright as she could.

"If it brings me the PA job at Jefferson's, I'll be on the right track," she said. "I'll know as soon as the holidays are over if I've got it or not."

"That's great, love," Evan said. "I always knew you'd make a success of whatever you did."

Even acting in a porn movie?

"What's it like in Pontyrowan? Has it snowed there today?"

They didn't always have snow at Christmas. It often came later, turning the slag heaps into a wonderland. Farther up the valley, deep into mid-Wales, the winters could be harsh and bitter, but Pontyrowan and the surrounding areas were sheltered from the worst of it.

"Just a sprinkling. How about you? Do you have snow?"

252

"Yes. And it's cold."

She thought how inane this conversation was. It was the prattle of two people who had nothing much to say to one another, so they resorted to talking about the weather.

"How's Mam keeping? I hope she didn't over do it," she said quickly.

"She's all right. Me and Dai did our bit, and we had a girl from the village come in to help her. You remember Rhiannon Williams, I dare say?

"Rose?" he said, when the pause between sentences seemed longer than usual.

"I remember," she said.

"Yes, well, she's been very good to Mam lately, so she had Christmas dinner with us. Anyway, Mam wants a word with you, and I've got to go out, *cariad*, so I'll say goodbye."

"Goodbye, Evan."

And where are you going? To meet pretty little Rhiannon Williams from up the valley, with her dark flashing eyes and bubbly laugh?

"Hello Rose, love," she heard Mam's voice, and she didn't miss the wheeziness of it. "I can't talk for long. The winter doesn't suit this cough of mine, but you'd want a Christmas message from home, I'm sure. And you're all right, are you?"

"Yes, I am. Mam, you take care of yourself, you hear? Take your medicine and do as the doctor tells you—"

She heard the snort at the other end, and hid a rueful smile, knowing that Mam didn't hold with too much doctoring.

"Still ordering me about, are you, love? You're a good girl, Rose, and you have a merry Christmas with your sister."

She hung up, never one for prolonged goodbyes, and Rose's eyes were damp as she slowly followed suit.

"Is the old girl about ready to snuff it?" Gracie said. "You shouldn't let it worry you, Rose. There's nothing you can do about it, so you might just as well let those sons of hers do the worrying."

"I still care about her," Rose said. "She was good to me and I'll never forget that."

She turned away so that Gracie wouldn't see the stinging tears in her eyes. For it seemed obvious to her now where Evan would be going that evening in Pontyrowan. He'd go meet pretty Rhiannon Williams. She'd had Christmas dinner with them, and in Pontyrowan's terms that was good as an engagement.

Gracie eyed Rose thoughtfully as Merv began carving the enormous turkey that had browned to a succulent and glistening colour in the oven. Mrs Olsen had joined them for dinner since she was on her own, and if Rose had once thought her gross and fat, she knew now that her good nature far outweighed her size.

"Well, suit yourself," Gracie said. "But it seems to me you've still got one foot in that Welsh camp, and it's time you made up your mind where you really want to be."

"I made up my mind about that a long time ago, far sooner than you did. And until your medical bills are finally settled, there's no chance of anything changing, is there?"

Gracie's face flushed even redder than it was already from the heat of the oven.

"All right, I asked for that. But I don't want to fight with you, Rose, especially not on Christmas Day."

"I don't want to fight with you at all," Rose said, as she handed over her plate to have the thick slices of turkey and a dollop of stuffing slapped onto it.

The Christmas holidays were never a lazy time for Merv.

There was plenty of work going, with all the Christmas and New Year parties. It meant extra cash in his hand to splash out on extra beers and extravagant meals out at Sea-Food Joe's, when they could very well eat at home without turning out in the bitter weather. Finally, Rose could stand his stupid extravagance no longer, and reminded him sharply that it was time he put something into the kitty for the bills.

"Getting above yourself, ain't you, kid?" he said. "You do what you want with your dough, and I'll do what I want with mine. Remember you're the guest here, and nobody tells me what to do in my own place."

"So what if my contributions to Gracie's bills dry up?" she said.

"But they won't, will they? Not if you get this wonderful new job you're always bleating about."

He had no pride, she thought. He didn't give a damn that she was holding this household together every bit as much as he was himself. And she still hadn't made up her mind about whether or not to take the PA job if it was offered. Miss Simpson wasn't coming back after the holidays, so the Christmas party had also been her farewell, together with a handsome bonus from the corporation.

The day before the office opened again after an extended holiday period, Merv came bursting into the house waving a copy of the *Los Angeles Sentinel* at her. Rose's heart leapt painfully, thinking that Jefferson surely hadn't done his worst and exposed her association with Klinkski's after all. If he had, she couldn't bear it. . . .

"Seems like your boss has got himself all set up with an heiress, Rose. They say money attracts money, and he ain't done at all bad for himself, getting tied up with one of the rich Halliday girls from Philadelphia. No wonder he goes east on so many trips."

"What do you mean?" she asked.

"It's all here. Take a look."

He thrust the newspaper at her, and Jefferson's handsome, smiling face looked out at her. At his side was a beautiful blonde girl, slim and elegant. Her left arm was linked through Jefferson's, and on the third finger of her hand there was an enormous diamond ring. Rose read the caption underneath the photograph.

"'Millionaire businessman Bradley Piers Jefferson the third, to wed Philadelphia socialite Miss Amanda Halliday.'"

The report went on to detail the engagement of Bradley Piers Jefferson the third, to the younger daughter of a shipping magnate, while on holiday with Miss Halliday's family in their Philadelphia mansion this Christmas. The wedding would take place sometime later in the summer, and the honeymoon would be spent in Bermuda.

It was all cut and dried, and the news was a total surprise to Rose. She was quite sure no one else at the office had known anything about it either. Jefferson must have flown out as soon as the place closed down for the holidays, and had probably had this planned the whole time.

And if his imminent engagement hadn't stopped him flirting with everything in skirts, Rose thought, there was something like relief in her veins now. Because presumably, Jefferson would be spending more time out east, with his fiancée. Maybe he'd even open up another branch of the corporation there, she thought hopefully, and she'd hardly have to see him again at all. The possibilities winged ahead in her mind in leaps and bounds.

"Well, there goes your chance of catching a millionaire, Rose," she heard Gracie say nastily, scanning the newspaper over her shoulder. "Slipped up, didn't you? We could all have been living the life of Riley by now if you'd given him a bit more encouragement."

After the way Gracie had gone on at her about being exploited on that first day when Jefferson took her out to dinner, the sheer gall of it took Rose's breath away. She couldn't even answer such a stupid remark.

But giving Jefferson any sort of encouragement was the last thing she would have done, she thought savagely. And from all the things Cindy had told her about his unsavoury activities, and what she already knew about his ruthlessness, his fiancée was more than welcome to him.

Naturally, the engagement was the talk of the office when the holidays were over, and Lacey Venables was already organizing an office whip-round to buy the couple a suitable engagement present.

"What the hell do you buy two people who will want for nothing?" Gloria said after she had dropped her contribution into Lacey's rattling tin. "Anyway, you can bet your bottom dollar Venables is only doing this to curry favour for the PA's job. It still hasn't been allocated yet, but she's living in hopes of being called up to Jefferson's office this afternoon."

Rose felt a shiver run down her spine at the thought. The PA job carried such a substantial rise in salary, but all the same. . . . But nobody was called up to the hierarchy for several days, and the atmosphere in the typing pool had begun to get very scratchy. Rumours were flying, and girls were eyeing one another up, some of them wondering who had done enough favours for Jefferson to be on his list of likelies.

Then the speculation switched. Surely he didn't plan to bring in somebody from outside? A little nobody, who wouldn't know the ropes?

"It depends what you mean by knowing the ropes," Gloria said sourly. "Office skills are the least important to Jefferson. Are you still interested in getting the job, Rose?"

"Only for the extra salary," she said, staying cool. "Though I suppose that's hardly the right attitude when you're applying for a new job."

"Did you actually apply for it?" Cindy asked.

"Well, I didn't fill in any forms, if that's what you mean, but he told me a while ago I could be in line for it with my qualifications. And I mean my office skills," she added deliberately.

Cindy whistled. "And Lacey will know you didn't even fill in an application form, so she'll be pig sick if you get it over her, when she's made all the running for years."

"There's just one difference, though," Gloria couldn't resist saying. "Jefferson's never had any interest in getting into Lacey's knickers."

Rose didn't rise to the bait. In any case Lacey was bearing down on them, and they each bent over their typewriters and got on with their work as she stalked her way through the rows of girls. But if they only knew, Rose was thinking. They all thought Jefferson was pretty rotten, but it was still all speculation, and they didn't know the half of it. They didn't know he had arranged for Klinkski's modelling agency to be burned to the ground with all the people in it. She didn't know it either, except in her heart. But they didn't know he was a murderer – and she could never tell.

Lacey had almost reached Rose's desk now, and she was steeling herself up to deal with the battering of verbal abuse she was getting used to. It had shocked and hurt her at first. Now it just washed over her, and she put it down to the viciousness of a frustrated woman. And then, just before Lacey reached her, the announcement came over the tannoy system.

"Would Mary-Lou Templar please come to Mr Jefferson's office at four o'clock this afternoon."

All eyes turned to the fluffy, blonde-haired girl with pouting lips who modelled herself on Marilyn Monroe. Mary-Lou smiled brightly around at them all, crossing her long, slim legs in their high-heeled shoes, and then lowering her china-blue eyes as she got on with her two-finger typing.

"I'll never know how she got that job," Cindy said, shaking her head. "She's useless and totally brainless, and probably only good for decoration."

"You've answered your own question, haven't you?" Gloria said. "That's all Jefferson wanted when he hired her."

Rose always felt uneasy when they talked so openly about Jefferson. He was the boss, after all. He paid their salaries, and there was such a thing as loyalty, however undeserved. In business, he was an undisputed wizard and she knew he had raised this corporation to new heights since taking over from his father. Rose couldn't fault him for that, and as long as it didn't involve her, his private life was his own.

A few minutes before four o'clock they all watched Mary-Lou Templar swish through the main office and turn to smile at everybody before taking the elevator up to Jefferson's office. It was an exit that was pure Hollywood. She hadn't returned by the time the rest of them went home, and the next morning they discovered that her desk had been cleared of all her belongings. There was a prominent memo on every notice-board to the effect that Mary-Lou Templar had been appointed as Mr Jefferson's new PA.

"So now we know," Gloria said. "You see what you have to do to get ahead in business, Rose?"

She shut up quickly, catching Lacey's eye. Lacey was at her most venomous, and snapping at everyone in sight.

"A fat lot of good your high-class accent did you," she jeered at Rose. "Maybe you should have started wearing your tiara to work to impress him—"

"And maybe you should go boil your head in milk to counteract some of that acid," Rose snapped back.

The minute she'd said it, her mouth dropped open,

unable to believe she'd reacted that way. It was so unlike Rose Forster from the valleys. . . . Lacey looked at her with furious disbelief, and whatever she was going to say was drowned out by the sound of loud applause from every girl in the typing pool. Without another word, Lacey turned on her heel and slammed back into her own office, her face scarlet with rage.

"Hey, Rose, that was some performance," Cindy said. "I didn't know you had it in you."

Rose was shaking inside now. "Neither did I. Will she report me, do you think?"

"What the hell if she does? Jefferson knows her well enough by now, and he's pleased with your work, so don't worry about it."

"But not pleased enough to give me the PA's job."

"Did you really want it?"

Rose thought. She certainly hadn't wanted to be in close contact with Jefferson. She had only wanted the extra money, but now that there was no chance of her getting it, she felt freer than she had felt for a long time. And if it meant taking a bit longer to clear Gracie's bill, it was a small price to pay for not being in Jefferson's clutches.

"I can manage without," she said with a smile.

She realized she had become the heroine of the typing pool. Few of the girls ever stood up to Lacey's venom, and most of them had known the sting of it in their time. Suddenly Rose was very much in favour, and if her spirit was bruised by the thought that Evan Pritchard and Rhiannon Williams might be more than friends, she knew she had a new life here, and she'd be a fool to let something she couldn't change overshadow her entire future.

Right after the holiday, when the new year had established itself as 1951, the photos from the office party were pinned up on notice-boards for the employees to purchase.

"Rose, you look gorgeous in that dress," Cindy said. "You've got to buy a couple of them. You could send one back to that guy of yours in Wales."

"I don't think so," Rose said, looking at the vision in the photo and wondering if Evan would even recognize her smart American look. Everyone had been photographed on arrival before they got a glass in their hands and got pie-eyed, as Gracie would call it. Rose looked stunning in the red dress. Even she could see that. And she had so wanted Evan to see her in it. Now, she didn't know what she wanted. But she let Cindy nag her into ordering two copies, anyway. And when they were ready, in a mood of defiance, she sent one of them off to Mam. They would all see that she was making the most of life here.

As the weeks passed, Rose made sure her new year's resolve became a fact. She started going out a lot more. She went to the movies and ate out in the evenings with the girls from the office. She went to concerts and the zoo, and felt that she was fitting in properly for the first time since arriving in LA. She spent as much of her salary as she chose, and put just enough towards Gracie's medical bills to keep the instalments going. She had her hair cut into a new and sophisticated style and told herself that the ties of the past were loosening at last.

And whatever was going on in that faraway Welsh village didn't concern her. At least, not as far as Evan and Dai were concerned. She still worried over Mam's health, and the letters to and fro were as regular as ever. And if Rhiannon Williams' name was occasionally mentioned in one of the letters from Pontyrowan, Rose told herself that musn't concern her either, and she tried to wish Evan well.

Mary-Lou Templar was evidently doing everything required of her in her new role as PA to Jefferson. He was often out of town on business, and Mary-Lou accompanied him far more than the older Miss Simpson had ever done.

"Speaks for itself, doesn't it?" Cindy said. They were taking a lunch break in the canteen at the end of February, when it was far too cold to be outdoors. "He's got his fiancée safely tucked away in Philly with all her daddy's money, and he's having it away with his little bit on the side."

"You don't know that," Rose said.

"Oh, Rose, grow up! You're not living in that old Welsh backwater any more. This is California, hon, where anything goes," Cindy said.

Rose could still feel annoyed at the implication that Pontyrowan was so far behind the times. Maybe it was, compared with what went on here, in the exciting world of the movies, and the high-powered business deals. And all the sleaze that went with it, that she'd never dreamed existed until she got here. This wasn't what her dreams were made of. . . .

"You don't know anything about what life was like in Pontyrowan," she said coolly, "so don't sneer at it."

"I know you've changed since coming here," Cindy said, without taking offence. "You're smarter and slicker, and you fit in. On the surface you're a real California girl now, Rose, but you still can't seem to let go of that other place."

And she thought she was doing that quite well. . . .

"Well, it was a pretty important part of my life," she said defensively. "And what do you mean – I can't let go?"

Cindy shrugged. "I wonder if you even know how often you refer to it? And especially to that guy who calls you up every now and then. Kind of a brother, I think you called him. Brother, my eye."

"I won't talk about it any more then," Rose said. "If it bores you so much, be sure to stop me any time."

"Now I've upset you, and I didn't mean to—"

"You haven't upset me. You've just reminded me that I should be looking forward, not back."

Chapter Seventeen

Evan promised he'd phone once a month to keep her up to date about Mam's health. He told her how pleased they were to see the photo she'd sent, and to see how well and happy she looked. She could hear the restraint in his voice, and it nearly broke her heart.

"Mam's put the photo in a frame, and she shows it to everybody who comes to the house," he said.

"Does she?" she said, feeling oddly touched by this. "I didn't expect anything like that."

"Why not? You were always her special girl, Rose."

And yours?

"And she's really all right, is she?" she said instead. "I do worry about her a lot."

"She's fine. I told you. You just get on with enjoying your life and stop worrying about us. We're all fine."

He had never sounded so stilted before. She couldn't seem to reach him any more, and she wondered if he was trying to avoid telling her any more than he intended. Did he really want her to stop worrying about them all, as if she could cut them out of her life as if they had never existed? Was that what he was really saying? That he wanted her to stop clinging on to her surrogate family like the frightened little evacuee she'd once been, and let them get on with their own lives?

Or was it simply the impact of the photo, she thought all in a rush – that so-glamorous photo of a sophisticated girl in a red dress, that didn't look anything like the girl who'd said goodbye to them all. She had never considered it until that moment.

"I still miss you all, Evan," she burst out, unable to bear this. "I still think of you a lot—"

"And we miss you too, *cariad*," he said with a short laugh. "But from your letters you seem to be having a wonderful time with your new friends now, and that's only right. And from all you've told us about your boss, he seems to have taken a real shine to you too."

"Oh sure, I'm having a great time," Rose said, with all the brittle brightness of the California girl. "And at the end of the month Cindy and Gloria and me are going downtown to get a glimpse of the movie stars arriving at the theatre for the Academy Awards."

"Wow!" Evan said, in a tone that was far from being impressed. "That'll be something to see. You were always mad on the film stars, I remember."

"Yes, well, I'll write and tell Mam all about it. I know she'll be interested." Even if you're not, she added silently.

In the small pause that followed, Rose bit her lip. Whenever they spoke on the phone now, they never said the things she wanted to say or to hear him say. Like: *You never mention Rhiannon Williams any more, and I don't know why. Is she out of your life, or so much in it that you don't want to talk about her to me?*

"Rose, I'm sorry, but I've got to go now. I'll call you again in a month."

"Evan —" but he had already gone, and she would never know if she'd have had the nerve to ask him what she was burning to know.

"We're meeting some guys downtown," Cindy announced on the night of the Academy Awards at the end of March. "Gloria won't want to drive in all that traffic, and the guys have got a big car that will take us all, OK?"

"OK, just as long as you don't try pairing me off again," Rose said.

"Would I ever?" Cindy said innocently.

It wasn't that she was averse to going out with a guy as long as he didn't try anything. She was eighteen and she was perfectly normal in that respect, but she hadn't met anybody in LA yet who came remotely near what she was looking for. Nor was she looking for anyone in particular. There was plenty of time for that. But she knew by now that if California girls didn't have a date on a Saturday night, they were dead. Which meant that she was well and truly dead, Rose thought with a grin, unless you counted a phone call from thousands of miles away with the only man she cared about.

She pushed the thought out of her mind, and agreed to let the others pick her up on the corner of her street. It was better than letting Gracie see her go. Gracie was fed up because Merv refused pointblank to take her downtown to watch the comings and goings of the movie stars. He'd be too busy ferrying about the cars of important folk to spend time with his wife, and Gracie had to content herself with listening to all the excitement on the wireless instead.

"Pity there ain't room for me in your car, Rose," she had said hopefully. "Couldn't you ask your friends to squeeze in another one?"

"You know I can't. It's not my car, and I don't even know the people we're going with." And she tried not to sound too relieved as she said it.

The end of March wasn't the best time for hanging about outside the glittering RKO Pantages Theatre, where the Awards were being made that year. It was cold and blustery, and Rose began to wonder if it was all worthwhile, because they couldn't see very much. Tom's car had broken down on the way and he'd taken ages to get it going again, so that by the time they had parked some distance away and walked to the theatre, the crush of people in front of them was enormous.

"This is a good waste of time," Cindy grumbled. "Your sister had the right idea after all, Rose."

"I'll be sure and tell her," Rose said, shivering, and wondering just why she had ever thought this occasion had sounded so wonderful.

But it was, of course, as long as you were seated inside the theatre in the midst of all the glamour and glitter. All the wireless announcers told you so, and the gushing interviews with the stars had always made her envious that she couldn't actually be there to watch. But out here, glimpsing the occasional recognizable face and hearing a cheer go up from those in front of you, was little more than boring.

"Isn't that Jefferson?" Gloria said suddenly. "And, my God, he's got Mary-Lou with him!"

Rose craned her neck, and saw that Gloria was right. Jefferson looked handsome enough to rival any movie star tonight. He wore a black tuxedo, a dazzling white shirt and a scarlet bow tie. On his arm, Mary-Lou looked like an angel, in a white, clinging gown, with a white fur stole draped around her shoulders. They paused for effect, and for the waiting photographers to snap them in a blaze of flashbulbs. Together, the contrast between them was stunning, and Rose could hear the vague whispers in the crowd.

"They're trying to decide if it's Marilyn Monroe," she said in a choked voice. "What a nerve she's got!"

"What a nerve Jefferson's got, more like," Cindy said. "Still, his fiancée's far enough away, and what would he care, anyway? To someone of his sort, a PA is a very useful tag to put on a girlfriend. He'll get away with anything."

It didn't matter to Rose what Jefferson did. In fact, if he was interested in somebody other than her, so much the better. The only galling thought in her mind, and one that she knew wasn't worthy of her, was that if she hadn't been such an innocent herself, she could have been going to the Academy Awards on Jefferson's arm, and having a ringside seat.

Once all the celebrities had gone inside the theatre, the crowds began to thin out, though many of them would hang around to hear the results relayed on giant loudspeakers outside. It was the tenth anniversary of the Oscar ceremonies, and it was widely tipped that Jose Ferrer would win Best Actor for *Cyrano*. Contesting for Best Actress were Gloria Swanson for *Sunset Boulevard* and Rose's favourite, Judy Holliday for *Born Yesterday*.

Long before the nominations and speeches reached that part of the proceedings, Rose's friends had got bored with hanging around while the endless speeches went on. By now, Tom and the other two guys had got into a huddle, and were trying to persuade the girls to go down to the beach at Malibu.

"On a cold night like this?" Rose said.

Tom grinned. "There's more things to do at the beach than swim in the sea, babe. My brother's out of town, and his beach house is at our disposal for as long as we like. We'll have a few drinks, maybe watch a movie, and then do whatever comes naturally. We've got all night at our disposal."

"Not me," she said at once. "I have to get back. I thought you knew that. My sister—"

"Rose, you don't have to get back. And that sister of yours is just an excuse," Gloria snapped at once.

Rose felt her temper flare up. Maybe she was going to ruin the party for the rest of them, but she'd be damned if she was going to spend the night necking with a guy she didn't even like very much, just to keep the numbers even.

"Well, I'm sorry if you feel like that, but I've no

intention of going to any beach house, and that's flat. I'm going home."

"Aw, come on, hon, don't be like that," Tom said persuasively. "I'll show you a good time—"

She wrenched away from him. "I don't want a good time. I told you. I'm going home, and you can all do what the hell you like."

She twisted her way through the crowd. She was miles away from the apartment, and she was prepared to walk all the way if she had to. But there were cruising taxis in the vicinity now, having deposited their important clients earlier and with little to do until the Awards ceremony was over and people began to disperse. A taxi drew up beside her almost at once, and she fell inside.

"Seen all you want to, girlie?" the driver said amicably. "I don't blame you. My old lady keeps well away from these places. She always says movie stars look a hundred per cent better on the screen than in the flesh, anyway, and those make-up artists can work wonders with any old lump of flesh. Where do you wanna go?"

"Your wife's probably right," Rose said, as he paused for breath, and she gave the address quickly.

"Say, are you British?" he said, with sudden interest.

Rose didn't feel in the least like making conversation, but once you got inside an LA cab, it seemed almost obligatory.

"That's right," she said.

"I was over there for a coupla months in '43 before we were shipped out. It was in a little place in Devonshire near Slapton Sands. Do you know it?" he said, as if England itself was a village where everybody knew everybody else.

"No," she said. "I come from London, but I spent the war years in Wales."

"Say, is that right? Were you one of those evacuee kids? That must have been rough."

269

In the driving mirror, she could see his eyes, glancing at her. He was about Merv's age, and from what he said, she knew he must have been a GI too.

"It was all right," she said huskily. "I lived with a very kind family."

"Well, that's nice."

He prattled on about his time in England, and the good folk in the Slapton Sands area, and the talk all washed over Rose's head. When he pulled up, she realized with a start that they had reached the apartment building without her even noticing the route they'd taken. As she got out, she fumbled in her purse for her fare, and the driver leaned across and put his hand over hers.

"You have this trip on me, hon, as a kind of thank you for the hospitality shown to me over there. They were good times, and I count myself lucky to have come back safely. Some of my buddies didn't."

He drove off before she could answer, but her eyes stung at this unexpected generosity. She hadn't had much of it since coming to LA.

She hurried indoors, to where Gracie and Mrs Olsen now were sitting as close to the wireless as they could get, and obviously not interested in any explanation on Rose's early appearance.

"Back already? Don't talk then," Gracie said. "We're getting to the best of it now."

Rose slipped her arms out of her coat and draped it over the back of a chair. She knew better than to talk when Gracie had her ear glued to the wireless. Besides, she was just as interested herself, and she had to admit, it was easier to listen to it here than with all the chattering crowds outside the theatre.

Broderick Crawford's voice came over the wireless at that moment. "And the winner is . . ."

After a theatrical pause while they could hear the envelope rustling as he opened it, he announced that Jose

Ferrer had won Best Actor. Mrs Olsen gave a little cheer, to be immediately shushed up by Gracie. Jose Ferrer, like many of the other Oscar nominees, was in New York, appearing on Broadway with Gloria Swanson.

The ABC radio network in Hollywood picked up his emotional acceptance speech from the New York theatre and relayed it all around the country.

"You know why he's so emotional, don't you?" Mrs Olsen said, always keeping up to date with the gossip columns concerning the movie stars.

"No. Why?" Rose said.

"He's recently been subpoenaed by the House of UnAmerican Activities Committee, and they don't take kindly to any suspicion of subversive goings-on—"

"Hush up, will you?" Gracie said irritably.

Jose Ferrer was still speaking, and when he called his Oscar a vote of confidence and vowed that he wouldn't let anybody down, it seemed to confirm what Mrs Olsen had said. Rose knew nothing of American politics, nor any other kind, but she knew by now that emotions could be very explosive whenever politics or unAmerican activities were mentioned. She only had to remember the way Theo Klinkski's Russian ancestry had been brought out of the closet after his modelling agency burned down.

When all the excitement had died down the nomination for Best Actress followed the same procedure, building up the suspense and the usual tributes to the nominees.

"My money's on Gloria Swanson," Mrs Olsen muttered.

"*Shush!*" Gracie snapped.

They were like a comic act, Rose thought, hiding a smile. The one bursting to talk, and the other one trying to shut her up. She'd never expected Gracie to be so interested, but here in LA it seemed everyone was touched by movie magic, to a greater or lesser degree.

"And the winner is . . . Judy Holliday for *Born Yes-terday*."

Rose gave a small cheer, but to her fury whatever acceptance speech Judy Holliday made from New York was cut off by a bad radio connection. Gracie turned off the crackling noise in disgust.

"That's that, then. It's all over for another year, and we might as well have some coffee."

She looked at Rose without attempting to make a move out of her chair.

"I'll make it," Rose said good-humouredly. Her favour-ite had won, and Gracie's hadn't, but as she said, it was all over for another year now. It would be the talk of the town for a couple of weeks, and the entertainment and movie magazines would be full of interviews and pictures. And then everything would revert to normal, and they'd be looking for new gossip and new scandals to report.

And she was becoming very cynical, she thought, if such things could no longer shock her the way they had when she first came here. But she was intelligent enough to know it wasn't just LA. There might be a fierce concentration of opportunities here, but what Merv would call wheeler-dealers existed everywhere, ready to exploit all ambitious hopefuls trying to make it in the movie business. Thank God she had never been one of them, Rose thought fervently.

She made the coffee and took it into the living-room for the three of them. Mrs Olsen had brought down some of her home-baked cookies, and they dunked amicably.

"Will your other folks be listening in to the Oscar ceremony, Rose?" Mrs Olsen said.

"I shouldn't think so. Mam always laughed at me for borrowing the movie magazines from the older girls in the village, and the boys weren't interested."

"They're a bit different from the boys around here then," Gracie said. "Every young good-looking guy thinks he can make it big in the movies, just as much as the girls."

"That's right, Gracie," Mrs Olsen said. "They imagine all this big money and they hear about the fabulous life-styles of the stars, and they think it happens to everybody, instead of just the few."

"Well, I think Evan and Dai would have their feet too firmly on the ground to be dazzled like that," Rose grinned.

"What are they like then? To look at, I mean? Not dogs, are they?"

Gracie chuckled. "You'll get our Rose going if you call her boyos dogs, Mrs O. She always thought the sun shone out of their backsides – the older one's, anyway."

Rose ignored her. "They're good-looking boys, Mrs Olsen, and Evan's quite tall and broad. Dai's shorter, and more like a typical Welshman, very muscly and wiry. He needs to be strong, working down the mine."

"And what does the other one do?"

"Evan's the brainy one," Rose said, her voice uncon-sciously softening. "He works in a solicitor's office in the village, but I think he has ambitions to go further afield. Maybe down to Cardiff."

She paused, because although Evan had spoken of it in the past, she'd never really listened all that much. And compared with the rich movie deals those Oscar winners were going to make now, it sounded a pathetically small ambition to move from Pontyrowan to go just twenty-five miles or so to Cardiff.

"You miss them all, don't you, Rose?" Mrs Olsen said, and she gave a small shrug.

"You can't live for all those years with a family without growing attached to them. But we're still in touch. We exchange letters, and Evan gives me a monthly progress report on Mam's health."

For a second, it was as if she was looking into a distant

273

future, and one that she didn't want to see. If and when anything happened to Mam, what would she do? And where would she be? Still here, under Gracie's thumb, or living as the successful LA business girl in her own apartment? Rose didn't really care for either image. The one was oppressive, and the other seemed impersonal and lonely.

"Well, you wanted to come here badly enough, didn't you?" Gracie said, and Rose didn't miss the little barb of resentment in her voice.

As if to say that Rose wasn't showing nearly enough gratitude for her sister funding her college fees and paying her fare over here and housing her all these months. Rose ignored the fact that she'd been paying Gracie back handsomely ever since Gracie's appendix operation, because it probably didn't compare financially after all. She said quickly that of course she'd wanted to come, and it had been a dream she'd had for years.

"Anyway, there's nothing like your own folks, when all's said and done," Mrs Olsen said comfortably, and Rose did her best to keep her expression totally bland.

Cindy and Gloria weren't quite so friendly after the way they considered Rose had run out on them after the Academy Awards.

She had a hard time convincing them that while she was more than happy to go out with them, she had no intention of getting involved with the kind of guy who wanted her to stay with him all night, and risk landing herself with a heap of trouble.

"I suppose your Welsh guy would never ask you to do such a thing," Gloria said with a sneer.

"No, he wouldn't. He respects me too much for that."

Cindy put her spoke in then. "You were rooting for Judy Holliday to win Best Actress, weren't you, Rose? That film might have been made especially for you."

"Oh?"

"Yeah. *Born Yesterday*, wasn't it?"

They both saw Lacey bearing down on them, and concentrated on work, and Rose thumped her typewriter keys with tears stinging her eyes. She was out of her depth all over again, feeling as gauche and vulnerable as on the day she'd arrived in this office and faced all these smart California girls. She was never going to be one of them, not in a million years. You had to be born and bred here to understand the way they were.

So just why she thought she could identify so easily with her Welsh family, was another of life's ironies, she thought bitterly. Because she hadn't been born and bred there either. She was a Londoner, and everything she had loved so dearly there had been blown to bits by one of Hitler's bombs. She didn't belong anywhere.

It was the beginning of April, and every new month was always a hectic time, with phones ringing every minute, and no time for anything except Jefferson's business. At lunchtime, Cindy and Gloria went off chattering together, effectively leaving Rose out in the cold. Mam always told her to take the bull by the horns and face any situation, and she couldn't stand this feeling of isolation one minute longer. She followed Cindy and Gloria to the canteen and took her tray to sit beside them.

"Look, I'm sorry if I spoiled things for you, I really am. But your friendship means a lot to me, and I don't want to lose it. Can't we start again?"

For a minute she thought they weren't going to respond, and then Cindy began to smile.

"I may just forgive you, hon," she said, and then she could keep her news to herself no longer, and the smile became wider. "You know who I got a phone call from this morning?"

"Who?" Rose said, just so thankful to be on sociable

terms again she wouldn't have been envious if it had been from the King of England.

"Tom. You remember Tom? The guy you could have had on the night of the Oscars?"

"I remember Tom," Rose murmured. And what she remembered most was that he had the arms of an octopus, given the chance to use them.

"Tom's asked me out on a date on Saturday night," Cindy said triumphantly. "He sounds really keen, and I think we could be going steady."

"Well, that's great for you, Cindy," Rose said, injecting as much warmth in her voice as she could. "So maybe I did you a good turn after all."

God, she hoped that didn't sound as if Tom was taking Cindy as second-best because Rose had turned him down . . . but clearly, she didn't see it that way. She just laughed and squeezed Rose's hand.

"So you did, hon, and it's probably for the best, anyway. You were never really Tom's sort."

Not if it meant staying at a beach house all night and getting into the tortuous arms of the octopus . . . for some reason, Rose couldn't get the image out of her mind, and she turned quickly to Gloria before her face betrayed her.

"Have you forgiven me too?"

Gloria shrugged. "Sure. Life's too short to hold grudges for ever."

Rose didn't comment, but she was perfectly sure Gloria would have held out for ever if Cindy hadn't backed down. Gloria was the louder of the two, but she was still a follower, not a leader. And what am I? Rose asked herself, and couldn't give herself an answer.

But nights out as a threesome were confined to mid-week now, and then dwindled even further as Cindy and Tom spent more and more time together. Rose didn't envy Cindy her man, but she envied the close-ness that had evidently grown between them, and the glow that surrounded Cindy whenever she spoke about him.

May came in with a hint of an early summer, and Rose began to think about looking for a shared apartment again. The medical bills were finally paid off, and she was able to put part of her salary aside each week. She had no properly formed idea about moving out. It was just a distant goal, but she'd learned long ago that life without a goal was an aimless existence.

The duty letters from Pontyrowan came regularly, and Rose wished she didn't think of them in that way. They were usually bulky packets, containing a letter from Evan in his neat, businesslike script; maybe a few scrawled lines from Dai, who'd never been interested in letter-writing, anyway, and always a page or two written in Mam's shaky handwriting.

It was getting worse, Rose thought. Mam must be barely seventy, but life in the mining valleys was harsh, and the women had always seemed old to Rose. But there was a sense of weariness in Mam's letters now, that alarmed her. And Evan's monthly phone call did nothing to reassure her.

"She's no better and no worse," he said cautiously, and she guessed that Mam was hovering near in the little front room near the telephone. "The doctor nags her to take her pills, but I'm not sure that she always does as she's told—"

"You must see that she does, then! It's up to you, Evan. Don't leave her to do it on her own."

"All right, Miss Bossy-boots," he said, the smile in his voice taking the sting out of his words. "I can see you've grown up since you've been in America, *cariad*. You never used to be so pushy."

She tried to smile back into the phone. Grown up? Oh yes, she had done that all right, but not in the way he meant.

"Just you look after her, that's all," she said tightly. "And let me talk to her."

But when he told her she was resting on the sofa and almost asleep, Rose was even more alarmed. If she couldn't even speak into the telephone, what kind of shape was she really in? But he wouldn't say any more, just that she was short of breath at times, and it was best that she didn't exert herself.

There was definitely something wrong, Rose thought, when the call was over. She may not have the kind of mystical sixth sense some of the Welsh people themselves were supposed to have, but she knew well enough when someone she'd known as long as she'd known Evan, was trying to fob her off.

And if he wouldn't, or couldn't, tell her anything over the telephone, then he could surely explain it all in a letter that was for her eyes only. She wrote to him at once, demanding that he told her exactly what the situation was. Not that she could do anything about it. She was thousands of miles away, but her heart was still there, in a dank little valley house with that stoical and unemotional woman. Despite Mam's natural reserve, there had still been love and kindness for the bewildered child who had been foisted on her family.

But Rose herself was anything but unemotional. After she'd sealed the letter and put it in the mailbox, she shut herself in her bedroom and cried her heart out.

A couple of weeks later Merv came home in the early hours from a valeting job, in time to hear the phone ringing.

"Goddamn people, calling at this hour," he snarled, fully expecting it to be some guy complaining that he'd scratched his precious car when he parked it at the hotel, and trying to get compensation. Didn't the buggers know they got valet service at their own risk?

"Yeah?" he barked into the phone without bothering to put on the light in the hallway.

"Let me speak to Rose, please."

For a minute Merv's brain didn't connect with the voice. He'd had plenty to drink that night, and he badly needed a pee.

"Who the hell is this?" he shouted.

"It's Evan Pritchard, and I need to speak to Rose. Is she there?"

"Of course she's bloody here. Where the hell else would she be in the middle of the night, you bum—"

Before he knew what was happening, the phone was snatched out of his hand. He hadn't even heard Rose's door open, but he was still sober enough to register that she hadn't stopped to throw on a dressing-gown over her nightie, and that her hair was tousled from sleep. She'd woken with a start from an uneasy dream, and she didn't need to be psychic to tell her who would be calling at this hour, or why. She gripped the telephone cord tightly, her voice hoarse.

"Evan, what's happened?"

Chapter Eighteen

Merv was comforting her, and taking every advantage of the fact that she was soft and pliant in his arms, and that there was only a thin bit of fabric separating her body from his embrace. She was shivering with shock and distress, and he could feel her nipples pressing into him, and smell the musky scent of her body, fresh from sleep. It stimulated all his juices in a way that Gracie used to do.

"Don't take on so, kid," he muttered into the tangled hair, while he gently moved against her in the dark hallway. "There ain't nothing you can do if the old girl's snuffed it, 'cepting let your old Uncle Merv take good care of you."

He was building up towards letting one of his hands slide down her back to squeeze those delectable buns, when he felt himself wrenched away from her. It wasn't even the kid herself who did the wrenching, either, since she didn't seem to know what day it was any more. It was Gracie, wide awake and livid, and snapping on the light. And crashing her hand against the side of his head so hard he howled with rage.

"Take your hands off her, you bastard," she screamed. "Or I swear I'll break your pecker next."

"What the bloody hell did you do that for!" he yelled, rubbing his stinging head. "I ain't doin' nothing. The kid's had a shock. Look at her, if you don't believe me."

Gracie looked, and saw Rose cringing back against the wall, appalled at yet another unprovoked scene between them, when all her emotions were at breaking point at Evan's news. As Gracie saw the whiteness of Rose's face, her expression changed at once, and she spoke sharply.

"What's going on, Rose? I heard the phone—"

Before she could even answer, Merv tried to rectify the situation as best he could. "The old Welsh woman's snuffed it, that's what, and if I can't give a bit of brotherly comfort at such a time. . . ."

Rose took a deep, choking breath, feeling as if she'd been holding it in check ever since the conversation with Evan. Her eyes were emerald-bright in the pallor of her face. And then as the release of her breath released all the tension inside her, she heard herself screaming at this pig of a man.

"She's not dead, and don't you dare say that she is. And you're not my brother, either. I'd as soon have a rattlesnake for a brother as you, Merv Hackett!"

"Good God, Rose, calm down, or you'll have the whole apartment building thinking we've had a murder here," Gracie said, her cheeks scarlet with rage now. "Come into the parlour and tell me what's going on. And if Merv really was trying it on with you—"

"Do you think I care about him? I've got more important things on my mind."

"What things? For God's sake, put us all out of our misery. Merv, go make some coffee, hot and strong with plenty of sugar. Come on, Rose, let's have it."

One of her old cardigans lay over the arm of the sofa, and she wrapped it around Rose's shoulders. Finally the tears spilled out. At this rate, she'd be flooding the whole bloody apartment, Rose thought. But she couldn't stop, and it took quite a while, and plenty of hot, strong, sweet coffee, before she could finally repeat the words she'd dreaded hearing.

"The phone call was from Evan," she stuttered. "Mam's not dead, but she's very ill, and the doctor's told them she's not expected to last more than a month at most. They should have let me know before. Evan should have warned me, not kept letting me think she was all right, and that once the summer came, she'd improve. Mam didn't want to worry me, but it wasn't fair of them to keep it from me."

She stopped, catching her breath, but by now her voice was full of anger. She was bitterly hurt and upset that Evan hadn't told her all this before, regardless of what Mam might have said. She'd had a right to know. But even as she thought it, she knew she really had no rights at all. She wasn't Mam's daughter.

And even in the midst of her distress, she couldn't rid herself of the shameful, treacherous thought that swept into her mind. That maybe that nice Rhiannon Williams from up the valley, was helping to care for Mam, and acting more like her daughter now.

"Well, it's sad, and I can see you're upset," Gracie said, awkward as ever in trying to say the right things. "But we all have to go in the end, Rose. You couldn't expect her to live for ever. We all know what those damp mining valleys do to folks' chests. Her husband went the same way, didn't he? And now there's Dai always bringing coal dust into the house—"

"I don't want to talk about that," Rose said, knowing it was true. It was the dust that had killed Mam's husband, working its insidious way into his coal-miner's lungs, and leaving her with two young boys to bring up alone.

"Well, there's nothing you can do about it, Rose," Gracie went on. "Except maybe send home a bit of money for a few things now the bills have all been paid. It won't be the first time food parcels have gone from here to there."

She was trying her best, but everything she said only wounded Rose more. And the last thing Mam or Evan

282

would want was charity. There was only one thing she could do.

"I have to go back," she stated.

Gracie stared at her. "What?"

"I'm going back. I'll ask Jefferson for unpaid leave, and I'll stay as long as they need me. Until – well, *until*," she finished.

"They won't expect this of you, Rose."

"But *I* would expect it of me."

She had already said as much to Evan, and been told there was no need. The situation wasn't imminent, and he would keep her informed on a weekly basis now. But she couldn't tell Gracie that. It had seemed too much like a slap in the face when Evan had as good as said he didn't need her, and he didn't want her.

Next day at the office, everyone could see there was something wrong. She was as pale as death, and she kept making mistakes. Lacey snapped at her that she'd be out on her ear if she didn't soon buck up her ideas.

"Maybe that will solve all my problems then," Rose said sharply. "But now you're here, I want to ask for some indefinite leave, and I'd be glad if you'd put in my request to Mr Jefferson right away, please."

It was the accepted procedure, and far preferable than having to approach Jefferson herself. And if she hadn't felt so tightly strung, she would have laughed at the disbelieving expression on Lacey's face.

"Well, you've got some nerve, I must say. You've hardly been here five minutes, and you think you can ask for indefinite leave just like that. I hope you know your job will be on the line if I put in such a memo."

"I'll have to take that risk. My . . . my . . . it's important that I go back to Wales for a few weeks, and maybe longer."

She had confided in Cindy and Gloria, and sworn them to secrecy, but she couldn't bear the sympathy of the rest of the office staff. And she certainly didn't want Lacey Venables trying to probe the details out of her.

Lacey's eyes narrowed, and Rose could almost see the brain cells working. She knew without being told that when her memo finally reached Jefferson, it would be couched in the most vicious terms, but she was beyond caring now. And Lacey had no option but to do as she was asked.

Mary-Lou Templar's voice came over the intercom in the middle of the afternoon.

"Would Rose Forster please come to Mr Jefferson's office immediately?"

Rose closed her eyes for a minute. Whatever Lacey had put on the memo, it had to be bad for Jefferson to send for her without notice, and she fully expected to be given instant dismissal. She took the elevator up to the vast office, remembering the first time she had come here for her interview, all fingers and thumbs inside her cotton gloves, practising her rounded English vowels, and totally unaware that Jefferson was seated in his red leather chair, listening to every word she said.

He was standing by the huge plate glass window now, looking out at his city, while Mary-Lou told Rose to sit down by the desk, not on one of the leather sofas. Mary-Lou sat nearby, her silk-clad legs crossed and showing plenty of leg. Rose thought fleetingly that she must study the pictures in the movie magazines all day long to get just that effect.

Jefferson spoke without turning round, and she jumped at the sound of his voice.

"So you want indefinite unpaid leave, do you, Rose?"

"That was what I requested," she muttered, wondering if this was going to be some cat and mouse game until he'd done with her, and then tell her to get out.

He turned around and came slowly back to the desk. Despite all she had learned about him in the past months, he was just as she remembered him on that first day, darkly handsome and charismatic. Nobody could deny that. He sat down, and seemed fractionally more human.

"Perhaps you'd care to look at Lacey's memo, and then tell me the reason for the request."

Rose read the printed form quickly. It was brief and to the point. At the bottom there was a space for Lacey's personal comments, and among other things it said that these English girls were all the same, and couldn't be trusted to give reliable service when their thoughts were always somewhere across the Atlantic. Her face burned at such spitefulness. She screwed up the memo in her hand and gave Jefferson an unblinking stare.

"I have to go back to Wales because the woman who cared for me during the war is dying, and she needs me," she said brutally.

Jefferson's expression altered.

"Did Lacey know about this?"

Rose shook her head, praying that she wasn't going to burst into tears again. He didn't speak for some minutes. She saw him glance at Mary-Lou and then glance away, and Rose felt a *frisson* of hope.

"And how are you proposing to get back there?"

"I haven't thought that far ahead."

"Well now, Miss Forster," Jefferson said, suddenly seeming more relaxed as he leaned back in his chair with his hands locked behind his head. "I can see that this is important to you. And it just so happens that Miss Templar and I have business meetings in London in a week from now. We're leaving in the corporation plane on Friday. You're welcome to hitch a ride with us."

Rose heard Mary-Lou gasp, and guessed that this arrangement wouldn't suit her at all. Rose wasn't sure that it suited her, either.

"I wouldn't want to be such a nuisance to you, Mr Jefferson," she said quickly.

"It's no problem. Unless I'm paying you too much, and you've got money to splash about on commercial air-fares," he said mockingly, knowing too much about her, and knowing very well that she didn't have that kind of money. When she didn't answer, he nodded.

"Then that's settled. Mary-Lou will see to all the paperwork, and I'll inform Lacey Venables to that effect. All you have to do is be at the airport on time."

Mary-Lou didn't like it one bit. That much was obvious in the way her eyes flashed when she showed Rose out of Jefferson's office. She went back to the typing pool in a daze, wondering if she was doing the right thing in accepting. But he'd been right, of course. The commercial air-fare would probably be out of her reach. It was no more than kindness on his part, and she should be grateful.

She wasn't so grateful when she discovered that Mary-Lou had relayed it to one of her cronies in the office, and that before the end of the afternoon it had spread around the office like wildfire that Jefferson was taking two women to England in the corporation plane.

"I hope you know what you're doing, Rose," Gloria said, echoing her own concern.

"I don't have any choice. I need to get there quickly, and this solves my problem."

She didn't understand, then, why Lacey made no attempt to add her own bitchy remarks to the news.

Rose called Evan as soon as possible to tell him she was coming home at the weekend and would stay as long as she was needed. She prayed that he wouldn't protest, and he didn't, which gave her a crumb of comfort.

"I'll call you again when I arrive in England on Saturday, Evan," she said, a little daunted by the journey ahead of her now. "Lord knows how long the train will take to get from London to South Wales."

"I'll meet you in London," he said at once. "You just

let me know approximately when you're likely to get to Paddington Station, and we'll travel back here on the next available train."

"Oh, but you don't have to do that."

"Yes, I do," he said. "I'll see you on Saturday, *cariad*. Under the clock on Paddington Station."

Saturday. This very Saturday. . . .

Rose hung up the phone slowly, her heart beginning to feel as if it was bursting in her chest. On Saturday she would be with Evan again. And just for one wonderful moment, the reason and the circumstances faded away, and all she could think about was the glorious fact that on Saturday they would be together again.

"How long do you expect to be gone, Rose?" Gracie asked, bringing her back to the present.

"I don't know. Maybe a month. Maybe less. It all depends on Mam's condition."

"It'll be a sad visit," Gracie said. "Providing it is just a visit."

"What do you mean?"

"Nothing. Except that if you decide you want to stay, we won't think badly of you, Rose. It's your life."

"Are you trying to get rid of me?" she said huskily.

"No. Just being realistic, that's all. I don't think anything here has quite come up to your expectations, has it?"

"Not entirely," Rose said carefully.

"Well then. Say it like it is, kid."

Nothing was anything like she expected when she saw the gossip column in one of the smuttier newspapers next day. Somebody had put a copy on her desk, left open at the right page.

'Jefferson boss to escort two glamour-girls to England in private corporation plane. And what will his fiancée have to say about that little playtime? It's well known that Bradley Piers Jefferson the third has a roving eye, but surely this is going too far? All those hours alone in the air with these two beauties may tax a normal man's strength, but Jefferson is reputed to be quite a stud when it comes to the ladies.'

There was more of the same, and Rose was trembling with fury by the time she had read through it. She tore the page into shreds and dumped it in her trash bin, praying that nobody else had seen it. Through the glass door of Lacey's office, she could see the woman grinning at her now, and she knew at once who had tipped off the newspaper reporters.

But until that moment she hadn't realized how this trip might appear to scandal-hungry gossip writers, nor to the other girls in the office. A cosy little threesome, no less, and nothing could be farther from the truth.

Whenever she'd been unmercifully taunted over her London accent at the Pontyrowan village school, Mam used to tell her to keep her dignity and say nothing, and the taunts would soon stop. If she once retaliated, they would know they had riled her . . . she remembered that advice now, and said nothing to anyone about the article, and nobody mentioned it to her.

But she had overlooked Gracie's reaction. She should have known it was the kind of newspaper Merv would bring home, and although the gossip column didn't name names, Gracie was furious at the insult.

"Aw, come on, it'll do the kid no harm," Merv said lazily, as if Rose wasn't there at all. "Especially if she ever wants to get into the movies. Most of the big names have got some kind of scandal attached to 'em. It adds to the glamour, see?"

"Well, I don't want to get into the movies, and I never did," Rose snapped. "And I'll thank you not to go around telling people that I'm involved in this gossip, either."

She was thankful when Friday came. She and Cindy and Gloria had had a farewell night out, and Merv and Gracie were going to take her to the airport. She hadn't expected Gracie to stir herself to come, nor to hug her close as if she was saying goodbye for ever.

"I'll turn up again, Gracie, just like a bad penny," Rose said in embarrassment.

"Somehow I don't think you will, our Rose," Gracie said. "But just remember that we did our best for you."

"I'll remember," she said, wriggling away as Merv tried to hug her too. "You take care of yourselves, and I'll call you as soon as I'm settled."

None of them was comfortable at saying goodbye, and Rose was thankful to see Mary-Lou tripping out to the executive aircraft with 'THE JEFFERSON PRINTING CORPORATION' emblazoned on each side of it. It was time to go. She got her suitcase out of Merv's Chevy and walked out across the tarmac on shaking legs. Jefferson stood in the doorway speaking with the pilot, and he gave her a brief smile as she climbed up the steps.

Once inside, she got a shock. The interior of a luxury private aircraft was nothing like that of a regular passenger plane. Without the usual cramped rows of seats, it was far more spacious for one thing, more like a comfortable sitting-room, with easy chairs and sofas arranged around a table. There was a more official-looking filing cabinet as well, which was presumably there for business purposes.

"The sleeping quarters are in back," Mary-Lou told her. "Yours is one of the single cabins, and I'll show you where to put your stuff."

She made it sound as if they were on board ship, but Rose saw that each cabin was well separated from its neighbour, so there was absolute privacy. And from the smirk on Mary-Lou's face, she didn't need to know whose cabin she would be sharing.

By the time they had been in the air for some hours, she wished she was somewhere else. It was obvious that Jefferson and Mary-Lou were seeing this trip as a love-jaunt, and she was an unwanted third party. Mary-Lou was openly resentful, while the glint in Jefferson's eyes seemed to be saying that all this could have been Rose Forster's, if she hadn't been such a small-town girl.

They were obliged to land for refuelling several times on the long flight, and each time Rose was glad to get out of the plane to stretch her legs and take a meal in whatever airport eating-place they happened to be in. Not that she could eat much. She felt airsick and retched most of the time, and was thankful to have the excuse to crawl into bed in her cabin, and leave them to it.

It was a relief to land for the last time, and to know that she was actually in England again, although by now she felt completely numb. Jefferson had a car available to whisk them up to London, and to deposit her at Paddington Station.

"Will you be all right?" he said, as she looked about her uncertainly.

"I'll be fine, thank you. Evan knows roughly what time I expected to be here, and I'll just wait for him under the clock like we arranged."

"All right. And Rose . . ." she recognized the hardness in his voice. "I'm leaving for LA in ten days' time. You can reach me at my hotel any time, but if you're not ready to fly back with us then, you'll have to make your own way back. Is that clear?"

"Perfectly."

"Good. Then I wish you well."

Then he was gone, walking swiftly back to the black Daimler car where Mary-Lou waited to be taken to their posh London hotel. While Rose sat on a bench on

Paddington Station and couldn't rid her thoughts of that other time, when she waited for a train with a battered suitcase at her feet, her gas-mask in a cardboard box slung around her shoulders, and a label around her neck as if she was an unwanted parcel. She had so wanted to stay with her mother and father and sister, and her eyes blurred at the memory of that seven-year-old child, and a way of life that had never come again.

"Hello, Rose."

Swamped with futile misery, she hadn't seen how the space in front of her had filled with a large and familiar figure. Her head jerked up at the sound of his voice, and her heart raced. He was taller and broader in the ten months she had been away, but so dear and unmistakable, and for a moment she could hardly breathe with the joy of seeing him.

"Evan – oh Evan . . ." she threw herself into his arms, and at such an unexpected reaction, his arms folded tightly around her. She heard him give a smothered oath, and his kiss was as unlike a brotherly kiss as it was possible to be. For long minutes, they remained locked in one another's arms, and then he reluctantly let her go.

"I didn't mean to half-strangle you, but it's so good to see you, Rose. I never thought this day would come."

"Didn't you?" *How foolish you were then, because I always knew we'd be together again, somehow, some-where. . . .*

He held her away from him for a minute, looking her over from head to foot, and he gave a small shake of his head.

"Well?" she said, smiling. "Am I still the same?"

"No," he said slowly. "No, you're not the same Rose who went away. I just hope they haven't changed you too much."

"Of course they haven't, whoever *they* are," she said, thinking how quickly the joy could go out of the day.

One minute he had been smiling, and there was love in his eyes, and now . . . now he'd got that unfathomable morose Welshness in him that she'd never been able to understand.

"How's Mam?" she said quickly. "That's the reason I'm here, after all, and it doesn't matter about whether you think I've changed or not."

"She's about the same," he said, and Rose gave an irritated exclamation.

"Don't fob me off any more, Evan. I haven't come all this way to hear platitudes. Anyway, I'll soon see for myself. So how is she really?"

She wanted him to say it was all a mistake, and that Mam was nothing like as bad as the doctor had said. The weather had turned very warm this past week, and Rose knew the sunshine had always been good for her chest.

"All right, then. She's dying, just like I told you, and nothing's going to change that," he said, as brutally as she had said it to Jefferson.

She drew in her breath. "Then thank God I came home," she said, hoping he wouldn't think it an imposition for her to refer to it in that way, and wondering how they had grown so far apart that she could even think such a thing.

On the interminable train journey to Wales, she tried to get more out of him, but he seemed tongue-tied by her smart American clothes and her cropped hair-style and the nylons and high-heeled shoes. She had wanted to look so good for him, and he was treating her as if she was a stranger.

"Why don't you talk to me, Evan?" she said, when the other people in the compartment had left, and only the two of them remained. "I still feel as if you're shutting me out."

"Don't be daft."

"It's not daft!" she said angrily. She had come all this way to be with him – and Mam – and she needed his strength for the days to come. "Didn't you want me here?"

"Of course I did. And Mam wanted you, even though she'd never have asked you to come back in so many words. But as far as I was concerned, she didn't have to. It was always your face she wanted to see, Rose. You were always Mam's girl."

He'd used those words before, and Rose had to look away to stare through the grimy windows of the rocking train.

"Dai would have put it into words," she mumbled in a sudden fit of petulance that would have done credit to the child she'd once been.

"Well, Dai can say everything and mean nothing, and I'm just the opposite," he retorted.

Rose tried to see if there was anything significant in the remark, but in the end she gave up. She was exhausted from travelling, and after they left the train, they still had a long bus-ride before they reached Pontyrowan.

They hardly spoke again, and Rose became more tense as the bus rattled its way through the narrow roads of the old Welsh towns and villages. She began to recognize familiar landmarks. The coal mines stood out in relief against the skyline with the gleaming slag heaps and the hazy mountains behind. There were the winding rows of narrow houses with no front gardens to speak of, and the no-nonsense chapels and village meeting-rooms. It all looked so beautiful, bathed in early evening sunlight, as if to welcome Rose Forster home.

She pushed such fanciful thoughts out of her mind as the bus stopped within a stone's throw of the house in Pontyrowan, and Evan helped her down from the step and carried her suitcase. And nerves suddenly got the better of her.

"I'm scared," she said in a husky voice. "I haven't faced anything like this before."

She felt her arm being tucked inside his. "She'll be all the easier for having you to face it with her, *cariad*."

293

It was about the warmest thing he had said to her on the entire journey.

Just before they reached the house, they both turned as they heard a welcoming shout. Rose's heart leapt with pleasure as she saw Dai Pritchard racing down the hill towards them, his boots ringing on the cobbles. It wasn't a working day, so he didn't have his dirty mining clobber on. But even if he had, she'd still have wanted to be hugged and kissed and held as tightly.

"*Dieu*, but there's grand you are, *bach*," he said, still as exuberant as a puppy. "I hardly recognized you for a minute. I thought Evan must have brought a film star home with him by mistake."

He grinned his nice, cheerful grin, and Rose laughed, flattered. But she didn't see Evan laughing beside her, and she straightened her face at once, remembering why she was here. Inside this house, a sick woman lay dying, and it seemed less than tactful to be laughing and joking on the pavement.

"It's no film star, only me, Dai," she said with a brief smile. "I couldn't even compete, and I wouldn't want to, neither."

"Well, you look the part to me all right," he said admiringly. "America obviously suits you, Rose."

"Shall we go inside?" Evan said. "If Mam hears us talking out here, she'll be getting impatient to see Rose."

"Oh aye," Dai said easily. "By the way, you remember Rhiannon Williams, don't you, Rose? I saw her in town this afternoon, Evan, and she wanted to know if it was all right to come over to see Mam tomorrow. I said I was sure it was. Did I do right?"

So there it was. That name Rose had tried so hard to keep out of her consciousness all this time. . . .

"Of course," Evan said. "Rhiannon knows she's welcome here any time."

He opened the front door, and they went inside. It was

quite dim after the brightness outside, and Rose was glad for a minute that the shadows hid her face. Otherwise she was quite sure she would have betrayed the surge of jealousy she felt at hearing the other girl's name. Both on Evan's account, and on Mam's. *Rose* was Mam's girl, not Rhiannon Williams. . . .

"She stays in bed most of the time now," Evan said quietly. "She usually has a sleep before we take her supper upstairs, but I bet she tried to stay awake today."

"Why didn't you tell me it was this bad?" she said, appalled. "You should have warned me."

It sounded like an awful existence if Mam didn't even have enough energy to stay awake before she could eat her supper. And who was preparing it . . .? As if to answer her question, Evan spoke abruptly.

"We both muck in with the cooking, Rose. It'll be stew tonight, if you can call a dish of vegetables with a bit of beef and stock thrown into it a proper stew."

Rose had completely forgotten that rationing was still in operation, but she remembered reading recently that the meagre meat ration had been cut even further. So, even as she resolved to help out all she could, she knew her presence was going to put a strain on everybody. But the uneasy thought flew out of her mind as she heard the querulous voice calling her name from upstairs, and she dropped her bag at once and ran up the familiar old staircase and into Mam's bedroom.

It struck her that she'd never been invited in here before. In fact, she'd never known Mam to be sick before, and she was shocked at the way she seemed to have shrunk as she lay, white-faced, against the pillows.

"Oh – Mam . . ." she croaked, and crossed the distance between them to hold her in her arms.

"Now then," Mam whispered. "You're not to be sad, Rose, *bach*. I waited for you, see? I knew my own girl would come home in time."

Rose felt her blood freeze at the resignation in the once-strong voice.

"Well, now I'm here to take care of you, and you're going to get well again. . . ."

Mam shook her head feebly, and Rose was immediately aware of the strange smell in the room, bittersweet and rancid at the same time. Hadn't Mrs Olsen once mentioned a death-smell, and how it helped to put some eucalyptus drops under your nose to ward off any nausea you felt . . .? Rose shuddered, wanting so much to be here, and at the same time wishing she could be anywhere else in the world.

Later, she fed Mam her supper, seeing the pathetically small amount she ate, and how quickly she drifted off to sleep again. Rose left her, trying to hide her tears, and after an hour talking with Evan and Dai she needed to be by herself.

Her room was exactly the same as if she had never gone away. The ornaments were in the same place and all the little knick-knacks were still on their lace doilies in Mam's finicky Welsh fashion. It was almost creepy, and yet it was also reassuringly safe. She belonged again, even though she already knew she could never live here again. It was too small, too cramped, and too full of memories. She hated LA for making her feel the claustrophobia of it all, but she couldn't help it.

She heard the boys come to bed, and she was very aware of every small night-sound that Evan made in the room next door to hers. He was so close, and yet so far away. . . . And when she dreamed, it was to dream of herself and Evan in a love-making fantasy that was shamelessly erotic and beautiful. And whatever happened in the future, she now knew for certain she could never again think of him as a brother.

Chapter Nineteen

In the middle of Sunday morning the doctor's car arrived, and later the district nurse came to wash Mam and make her comfortable. As Evan saw the question brimming on Rose's lips, he told her quickly that this was a daily procedure now.

"It's only been like this for the past few days, when things have begun to move more rapidly. When I first phoned you, we thought she might have a month." He paused, while the words sank in.

"And now?" she asked, dry-mouthed.

"Dr Millard says it'll not be above another forty-eight hours. I think she was waiting for you, Rose."

She felt herself mentally back away. Because if that was so, and if she hadn't come, then maybe Mam wouldn't be ready to die yet. She knew it was senseless and illogical to think that way, and she had to say something ordinary, to stop such wild thoughts.

"Mam always said how she wanted a girl in this house of men, but I'm not the only one, Evan. Your Rhiannon will be here this afternoon, won't she?"

"You're the one she needs," Evan said. "And she's not *my* Rhiannon. She's Dai's girl."

"What?" Rose said stupidly. "But I thought—"

"Whatever you thought, you got it all wrong. Dai and Rhiannon Williams have been going together for weeks now."

She couldn't think of anything to say that wouldn't give

her feelings away, and this wasn't the time. There might never be a time, but it certainly wasn't now, with what lay ahead of them. When she didn't reply, Evan spoke more briskly.

"Do you want to help me get the dinner ready? We still try to have a Sunday roast, even though the meat shrinks away to almost nothing by the time it's done. You can chop up the cabbage, if you like."

It felt endearingly intimate to be doing these domestic chores together, and seeing how deft Evan was at the tasks didn't diminish him at all in Rose's eyes. Nothing could. She wore a cool summer dress now that the wearisome travelling was over, and she had tied one of Mam's old aprons around her waist. And she didn't miss the way Evan looked at her.

"You look more like the girl I remember now," he said suddenly.

"I'm still the same inside, Evan. I haven't changed."

"Yes, you have. Everybody changes. We all move on, *cariad*, and it's the normal way of things. I'll be doing the same after it's all over."

For a minute she didn't know what he meant, and then she realized he was talking about what was to happen after Mam's death. She didn't want to hear such talk, but Evan obviously wanted to bring it out in the open.

"I've got the chance of being transferred to London, see, to a larger branch of my firm, where there'll be far more chance of advancement."

"*London!*" Rose echoed.

"You needn't look so sceptical. Don't you think a hay-seed from the Welsh valleys will fit in there?" he said.

"I think you'd fit in anywhere," she said quickly. "But London – I never thought you'd want to go there – and hearing you talk about it makes me feel a bit homesick too."

The feeling took her completely by surprise, but all

the sights and sounds and smells of her early years were suddenly as sharp and vivid as if it was yesterday.

"You? Homesick for London? I thought Hollywood was your stamping-ground now."

"Then maybe you don't know me as well as you think you do. Maybe you don't know me at all any more!"

Without knowing how it had happened, Rose knew that the atmosphere between them had subtly cooled. They were poles apart again, and she was stunned at the way everything had changed so abruptly. She knew that Evan was aware of it too. He put his hand on her shoulder.

"Rose, don't let's fight," he said quietly. "I wouldn't have told you if I thought it would upset you."

"It hasn't, not really. But what about Dai if you move to London? He'll never leave Pontyrowan, will he?"

"I dare say Dai will be asking Rhiannon to marry him and keep on the house here," he said. "It looks as though it's heading that way. And by the way, I told you about London in confidence. Nobody else knows about it but you, and I haven't made up my mind yet."

Rose nodded and carried on with her vegetable chopping, keeping her eyes down low. It sounded so simple for Dai and his girl. While nothing had ever gone simply for Rose, and all her wonderful dreams seemed to have turned to ashes.

"That's it, then," Evan said, when the aroma of the meat in the oven was beginning to fill the tiny kitchen, and they had finished their preparations. "I'll take Mam up a cup of cocoa and then we'll have something too. Coffee, I suppose. That's what Americans drink, isn't it?"

She was good and mad at him then.

"Why are you doing this, Evan?" she said baldly.

"Doing what?"

"Trying to goad me all the time. I'm not American and I never will be. I love this place and all the people in it, but ever since I came home you've seemed determined to make me feel like an outsider."

He looked at her without speaking, and even though she was mad with him, she loved him so much . . . but she was damned if she was ever going to tell him so, when it was obvious that he didn't love her after all. And that kiss on Paddington Station . . . that wonderful, sensual, unbrotherly kiss that she had thought might mean something special to him, had clearly meant nothing at all.

The kettle sang out, and he turned quickly to make Mam's cocoa, leaving her to make two cups of coffee for when he came downstairs again. Her hands were shaking, and she thought how lucky Rhiannon was to have a cheeky, uncomplicated man like Dai to love her.

She tried to picture Evan in London, and knew he would succeed in whatever he wanted to do. He was that kind of man. And Dai would be content to continue working at the coal-face, like his father before him. And then she realized she was doing what Evan had done, making plans for the future while Mam lay dying. Planning for everybody except herself, she thought. She was the one who was rootless. . . .

Evan was upstairs for a long time, and she began to feel uneasy. But if anything was wrong, he would surely have called her. She was relieved when he finally came down again with Mam's empty cup and saucer.

"Sorry it took so long. She wanted to sip it slowly, and then she wanted to talk. Now she's having a sleep."

Rose knew by now that it was partly the doctor's pills that were making her sleep all the time, releasing her from the gnawing pain in her chest and the difficulty in breathing.

"She wanted to talk about you, Rose. She's insistent about leaving you something, and she wouldn't give me any peace until I heard about it. It's all in her will, but she wanted me to tell you now that it's for Mam's girl."

Rose swallowed, shaking her head, and not wanting to

hear any of this. But Evan went on relentlessly.

"She wants you to have her best china tea service and her bits of jade. And her wedding ring."

Rose couldn't speak, thinking that all the precious things Mam wanted her to have should be going to Evan's wife, or Dai's. Not to a little waif who'd been sent down here under protest because of old Hitler's bombs. Her shoulders began to shake, and then she was in Evan's arms, and crying on his shoulder. And he was comforting her and calling her his darling, and saying that they mustn't be sad, because it wasn't what Mam wanted.

She had composed herself by the time Dai came home, and it was Rose's idea for them all to have their dinner with Mam. If she couldn't come downstairs, they would all go up. It took a bit of juggling with a small card table, and it wasn't the easiest of things to arrange in the small bedroom, but she could see Mam was pleased as she pecked at her food.

And in the afternoon Rhiannon Williams came to see her, bright and young, and making Rose feel oddly old. Rose wasn't yet nineteen, but in terms of living, she felt she was years older than the fresh-faced valley girl. But it was easy to see that she and Dai were in love, and that was enough to fill her with a sense of envy too.

"We'll sit with Mam this evening," Dai told her. "She likes to see Rhiannon—"

"That's if you don't mind, Rose," the girl said anxiously in her lilting voice. "I know you've come all this way to see her—"

"Of course I don't mind. In fact, I thought I might go to Chapel tonight. It's the best place for meeting up with old friends, as I remember," she said with a forced smile.

"I'll come with you," Evan said. "Folk will be glad to see you, Rose, and to hear how Mam is."

And they would all know why she had come home.

*   *   *

301

She and Evan sat together in the chapel in Pontyrowan's main street, as they had done so many times before, in the row that had always been occupied by Mam Pritchard and her boys. Rose knew these people, and they knew her, and were clearly pleased to see her again. But she found it a very poignant experience, and was thankful to get out of there, despite the inspiring singing of the strong Welsh voices.

They walked home in companionable silence. It wasn't quite like being an engaged couple, Rose thought, but she could make-believe that it was, as Evan tucked her arm in his and walked her home.

"I suspect the next time we're there, it will be for a very different reason, Rose."

His words jerked her out of the dream, and she knew exactly what he meant.

"You needn't come to the funeral, of course. Most of the women stay away, but one or two are always at the house to provide sandwiches and Welsh cakes and tea. I dare say Dai will ask Rhiannon to help out as well."

Rose stood stock still on the pavement, her eyes flashing. If it upset her to discuss Mam's dying and afterwards, this upset her even more.

"If you think I've come all this way not to follow Mam safely into the cemetery, you've got another think coming, Evan Pritchard," she snapped.

It was hardly the thing to be arguing about in the street, but she heard him chuckle, and he squeezed her arm tightly to his side.

"I should have known. Right then you sounded exactly as you did on the first day you came here, Rose. Do you remember? You told me if I thought you were going to follow behind me and Dai all the way to some village school where you wouldn't know anybody, then we had another think coming. You were such a bossy, defensive little kid."

"I was not," she said immediately, and then grinned at her own words. "Anyway, I don't remember any of that, and I think you just made it up."

"No, I didn't. I remember lots of things about those days, Rose. How you were so unhappy when you came, and how you gradually blossomed just like your name."

"Good Lord, that was almost poetic," she said, too touched to be anything but cynical.

"Oh, even Welshmen have their poetic moments," he said.

The end for Mam Pritchard came quickly. On Tuesday morning when Evan took in her breakfast tray, he found that she had slipped away in her sleep. From then on, the house was filled with grief, followed by all the necessary and businesslike trappings of death.

"We've decided it's best if she's taken to the funeral parlour where folk can go and make their private goodbyes until the funeral on Saturday," Evan said, to Rose's wild relief. She couldn't bear to think of Mam lying there, cold and alone in that little bedroom for the rest of the week. And Rose wasn't that brave, anyway, to know she was just a few doors away. . . .

She telephoned Gracie as soon as she could, and heard her sister make the expected responses.

"Well, she'd had her time, and I'm sure it was a kindness for her to go, Rose. And she'd have been glad you were there."

"Oh yes, she was," Rose said woodenly.

"Have you decided when you're coming back?"

"I can't think about that yet," Rose said. "There are things to do here and I have to help the boys."

"Oh yeah, of course. Well, you just look after yourself, and let us know if we can do anything, hon."

Rose hung up, thinking it was one of Gracie's dafter remarks. What the heck could she do, all those miles away? She hadn't thought much of Mam to begin with, and had always rather looked down on Rose's little Welsh family. At the thought, Rose felt fiercely defensive of them all.

She phoned Jefferson at his London hotel. He wasn't there, so she left a message with the receptionist, asking him to call her at the Pritchards' number. He could afford these calls more than she could, she thought recklessly. And when the phone rang that evening and Evan handed the receiver to her, she heard his sharp American twang.

"Rose. I got your message from the desk clerk. Is this bad news?"

"Mam – my foster mother is dead," she said. "The funeral is on Saturday."

"Ah." He wasn't falsely comforting, to Rose's relief. "So does this mean you'll be coming back to London afterwards? We leave on the following Tuesday afternoon, as I told you."

Rose stared at the telephone. He wasn't being callous, merely practical, the way everyone was trying to be. Everyone had their own lives to lead, and couldn't spare too much time for grieving, especially for someone they didn't even know.

"I'll call you again on Sunday evening with my decision. We have people in the house, and I can't talk now."

She hung up. She didn't want to discuss it, nor even to think about it. She was in limbo right now, and all her energies were concentrated on the days ahead. She couldn't think beyond them.

On Saturday the cars called at the house, one of them carrying Mam's flower-strewn coffin, and the other one for the family. Rhiannon remained at the house with a woman neighbour, as Evan had suggested. They would see to the food and teas for however many mourners chose to return for a bite, and to exchange memories of the woman who had lived among them all her life.

Rose remembered very little of the service. What she remembered most was the way it seemed that most of the village had turned out to follow the coffin to the cemetery in a long walking procession. There had been few women in the chapel, but many more were at the back of the line to pay their respects. As for her, she walked at the head of them all, her arms linked between Evan and Dai, uncaring what people thought of her being seen as a close family member.

When it was over, she was pale and heavy-eyed, and it was a relief to get back to the house and pull back the curtains now to let in light and warmth once more. Several dozen mourners crammed inside the little rooms, but it wasn't a sad occasion. In any case, most of them had done their crying by now, and it was a time for talking over old times and unashamedly making new plans.

"You'll be needing to look after yourselves now then, boys?" an old family friend from up the valley asked Dai.

Dai shrugged. "We've been doing that for quite a while, Mr Roberts."

"Aye, and the place is a credit to both of you," his wife said approvingly. "There's spruce and clean it is."

"It's not all down to us," Evan put in. "Mam was unable to do anything these past few months, and me and Dai did what we could. But it's been great to have Rose back, and she's the one responsible for making it seem like a home again."

"Aye, there's nothing like a woman's touch for home-making," the man agreed.

Rose turned away, but not before she caught Dai whispering something in Rhiannon's ear. She saw the girl shake her head, and Rose sensed that he might have wanted to say something about their future. If he had,

Rhiannon obviously had more tact than he did, and the moment passed.

The mourners lingered for several hours, until finally the four of them were alone in the house. Rose helped Dai's girl with washing the dishes, and insisted that the boys went out for a breather before they opened Mam's will.

It also gave Rose a chance to talk to Rhiannon alone.

"Have you and Dai any definite plans for the future?" she said. "Tell me to mind my own business if you like. . . ."

"No, I don't mind you knowing. I'm glad to talk to you. I know the boys always think of you as their sister, anyway, so you're as good as family."

Rose flinched, but Rhiannon was continuing in her sing-song voice, and it became more breathless by the minute.

"Dai wanted to tell them all just now, but I said it wasn't right at such a time," she said, confirming what Rose suspected before she even said it. "But me and Dai want to be married as soon as possible, and we'll live in this house and I'll take care of both of them."

"Both of them?"

For a minute, Rose stared at her, completely forgetting that Evan had spoken to her in confidence about his tentative plans for going to London. She saw the other girl blush furiously.

"I mean Dai and Evan, of course, Rose. I'm not – we haven't done anything wrong – and there's no cause for a hasty wedding, except for loving each other and wanting to be together all the time."

"I never even thought it," Rose said swiftly, seeing the way the girl's thoughts were going by the indignity in her eyes. Impulsively, she gave her a hug. "And I think it will be the best thing for you both."

To her surprise, Rhiannon turned away, her shoulders drooping a little.

"But will folk think it's bad taste if we want to be married soon after Mam Pritchard's death?" she said miserably.

"I'm sure they won't. I'm sure they'll think it the right and proper thing to do for two people who love one another the way you do."

She was glad Rhiannon was so caught up with thoughts of her future that she couldn't see the bleakness that she was sure came over her own face then. They all had plans, and Evan's would surely come to fruition too. He'd go away to London and become successful in whatever he chose to do. And she would go back to Los Angeles and take whatever advancement came her way at the Jefferson Printing Corporation.

The will was predictable, with no surprises. Mam didn't have any money to speak of, just a few meagre savings that were to be shared between her boys, along with the house and its contents. Rose's bequests were just as Evan had told her, and she felt acutely embarrassed when the wedding ring was mentioned.

"I'm not sure I should have it," she murmured.

"Yes you should," Dai said, to her surprise. "Normally, it would go to a daughter, and you're the nearest thing to a daughter Mam ever had. She really loved you Rose, even though she found it hard to show it."

"I still think it should have been given to Evan's wife, or yours," she said diffidently.

Evan gave a short laugh. "Well, since I don't have any prospects of a wife on the horizon at present, and Dai isn't too bothered about it, you have our blessing, Rose. Take it, and keep it for when some lucky man proposes."

Her throat was too full for her to answer, and she felt that he was as good as telling her he wouldn't be the one. She meant nothing to him, other than a sister.

"You know me and Rhiannon mean to marry as soon as it's decent, Evan," Dai told his brother a while later, when the four of them were finishing up the remains of the funeral tea. "Do you have any objections to that, or to Rhiannon moving in here with us afterwards?"

"Why should I have any objections? I can't see any point in waiting for a mourning period. Nobody paid attention to such things during the war when bereavements were ten a penny, and I don't think folk would blame you now for wanting to settle down. As for living here, well, this is your house as much as mine, but you'll probably be having it to yourselves, anyway."

"Why? Where will you be?" Dai said, startled. "Rose hasn't persuaded you to go back to America with her, has she?"

The sweet innocence of the remark took Rose by surprise, and she had to say something tart to cover the heartache at the thought that such a thing would never happen.

"That'll be the day when I can persuade Evan to do anything he doesn't want to do!"

Evan spoke directly to his brother. "I haven't said anything about it before, and I'd never have left while Mam was so ill, but I've got the chance to go to London to a larger branch of my firm. It's a big step up, and I'm seriously considering it."

"It would be a big change for you, Evan," Rhiannon said when Dai didn't answer.

"*Dieu*, man, what the hell do you want to go to London for?" Dai said explosively at last. "There's all that rubble still there from the bombing, all those people crammed into a space too small to breathe—"

"It's not like that at all!" Rose said. "You don't know what you're talking about, Dai. London's always been beautiful. There's lovely parks and the palace, and elegant churches, and Big Ben and the Tower, and not even old

Hitler's bombs could take away the heart and soul of it, and Evan's always had an eye for beautiful things far more than you ever did, and he'll love it."

She stopped for breath as they all stared at her, and she realized how the remnants of her old accent had slipped into her impassioned speech. Dai grinned.

"Well, I've got an eye for one beautiful thing, and that's my Rhiannon," he said. "But good luck to you if that's what you intend doing, Evan."

"I haven't totally made up my mind yet," Evan said. "Nothing against you, Dai, but I feel as if I'm stagnating here, and I feel the need to stretch my wings a bit."

"Just like Rose did," Rhiannon said softly.

During the week they sorted out all Mam's belongings and sent them off to various good homes. Dai had plans for repainting and wallpapering the entire house for when he and Rhiannon were married, and Rose could tell that for once he was tentative at saying too much about it to Evan. As if it was already his house, and he was dictating what was to be done in it. But Evan was the one who spoke his mind.

"Do what you like, Dai. You and Rhiannon will be living in it, whether I'm here or not. It will be your first married home, if not your last, so you must both make all the choices, and don't worry about me."

It struck Rose that he was almost as much in limbo as she was herself, needing to make a decision, and uncertain which way to go. Whether to stay in Pontyrowan, or to take a chance and go to London . . . to Rose, the very thought of it was like letting a shaft of fresh air into her lungs.

She had been born a city girl, familiar with London's backstreets and the cheerful, raucous way of life. She knew the markets and their colourful stallholders, bellowing out the merits of their wares in Cockney slang to catch the tourists. She knew the river, winding, mysterious, always

309

busy with small craft and larger ones, and the majestic bridges, spanning it. . . . It was home, in a way that this coal-blackened, crowded village had never been, however much it had welcomed her and taken her in . . . she knew that too.

Gracie actually phoned her on Sunday afternoon, to ask how things were going, wanting to know if they could expect her home on Jefferson's private plane. Incredibly, over all those miles, Rose could swear she could hear Merv belching in the background, and pictured him, sprawled out in an armchair in his habitual vest and trousers.

"Gracie, I'm going to stay for a while," she said, before she could change her mind. "I don't know what I'm going to do yet, but I shan't come back with Jefferson. It's too soon, and I'm – I'm still needed here."

"Well, whatever you say, kid," Gracie said comfortably. "Just keep in touch."

"I will, of course I will—" but Gracie was gone, keeping the international call down to a minimum.

Evan came into the room as she put down the phone, and she spoke quickly, knowing he must have heard everything.

"That was Gracie. I've told her I'm staying a while longer, and I hope that's all right with you. I'm not ready for LA yet. Do you mind if I call Mr Jefferson to tell him, while I've still got the nerve?" she asked.

"You can do whatever you like in this house, Rose. You know that."

It was such a non-committal answer that she wondered if she'd done the right thing after all. Maybe he really didn't care what she did or where she went. But for once she had said exactly what was in her heart. She wasn't ready for LA yet.

It took a while for Jefferson to answer after the call had been put through to his hotel room, and he was curt when he heard her voice.

"I thought I should let you know right away that I've decided to stay on for the present," she said abruptly. "I know I can't go on having unpaid leave indefinitely, so please take this as my resignation. I'm sorry."

He was silent for a moment, and for the life of her, Rose couldn't help wondering what she had interrupted between him and Mary-Lou Templar. Maybe they had been in the middle of a Sunday afternoon torrid love-making session, and even though she didn't envy Mary-Lou's involvement with him one little bit, she could still be envious of two lovers who were oblivious to everything else.

"It's probably for the best, Rose," she heard Jefferson say coolly. "I'll arrange to have your salary to date sent on to you. And I wish you good luck."

The phone went dead, and that was that. He hadn't cared one iota, she thought, enraged. He was too busy with his little slut . . . the word caught her up short, and she smothered a sob. Nobody seemed to care for her at all. Gracie was easy whether or not she came back to LA; she was out of a job; Dai had his girl, and Evan . . .

She couldn't think about Evan. She felt suddenly stifled by this house and its piquant mixture of sad and happy associations. She had to be outside where she could breathe, and she called out that she was going for a walk, without even waiting to find out if anyone had heard her.

She walked quickly through the quiet, Sunday afternoon village, through the rows of identical narrow houses and past the chapel and meeting-house and the public house on the corner, and the little schoolroom where she had learned so painfully to cope with being 'different'. She walked up the hillside, where the grass was short and green, leaving the village far behind.

Half-way up the hill she passed the gleaming coal tips that could look so beautiful glinting in the sunlight, and be so treacherous when a persistent rainstorm made the coal slip and go sliding down the heaps of slack to threaten the valley. The pit was silent now, as befitted the day, but tomorrow it would be alive with activity, and Dai Pritchard would be one of the miners reporting for his shift, now that the week's mourning for his Mam was over.

Rose felt as if her feet had minds of their own, leading her on to where the green landmark of the mountain beyond looked down benevolently on the village of Pontyrowan that it guarded. The summer breezes blew through the grasses and heathers, scenting the air with their sweetness, and where Rose had come so often to gaze down in awe at the Lilliputian village below. It was where she had once been kissed by Dai Pritchard and rubbed angrily at her mouth, and had the kiss replaced by his brother Evan. . . .

"Rose! Hold on a minute!"

She turned slowly, and yet with no real surprise, as if she had always known that Evan would follow. As if Mam's sixth sense had told her to come here, to this special, most romantic place on top of the world.

He stopped a few feet from her, his face almost accusing, and any thought she might have had of falling into his arms vanished at once.

"How long have you known?" he said.

"Known what?"

"That you weren't going back to America. Like you told Gracie, and that Jefferson bloke."

She stared at him, while the breeze ruffled her hair and whispered through the grass. And he was so *stupid* if he couldn't see that if she once came home, she would never go back . . . even if the illogical truth of it only just hit her like a thunderbolt . . . but she saw nothing but aggression in his face, and her anger spilled over.

"Does it matter in the least to you what I do, or where I go?" she cried out. "We've all got our own lives to lead, so don't try to interfere in mine."

312

"Is that what you want? What you really want? Or have you forgotten what you said to your sister?"

All Rose could remember was that she'd told Gracie she was staying on here for a while. Evan moved closer and held out his hands to her, and after no more than a second's hesitation, Rose put her hands in his.

"You told Gracie you were needed here, Rose. And do I really have to spell it out to you just how much you're needed, and by whom, *cariad*?"

He drew her closer, and all the love she had ever wanted was in his eyes. And before she could even speak she was in his arms, and he was kissing her with all the passion of a lover, and she knew at last that all the pretence of being her brother was over.

"God knows I've loved you for so long, Rose," he said, his voice thick. "But I could never be sure how you felt. It was only when I heard you say you weren't going back to America that I dared to hope. Was I wrong?"

"No, oh *no*. I love you so much, Evan."

They sank down together onto the soft green turf, holding each other as if they could never bear to be apart again. And, with his mouth never more than a breath away from hers, he was telling her everything she wanted to hear.

"Then we'll go to London together, and you'll show me all those places that are dear to your heart. And you'll be my wife, and we'll live in a flat overlooking the river and watch the boats go by every evening, and make love all night long."

He looked down at her then, so soft and pliant beneath him, and Rose knew that he was hers for ever, and that he wanted her now, as much as she wanted him.

And if the gods had smiled on them this far, bringing her back to him from half-way across the world, she didn't think they would disapprove now. For wasn't this what Mam had always wanted, when she had bequeathed Rose her wedding ring? Hadn't she, in effect, left her Evan as well?

"Love me now," she whispered. "Oh, love me now, Evan."